D0883697

MEPHISTO WALTZ

Glenrock Branch Library
Box 1000
Glenrock, WY 82637

39092 09667085 8

Center Point
Large Print

**This Large Print Book carries the
Seal of Approval of N.A.V.H.**

MEPHISTO WALTZ

A Max Liebermann Mystery

FRANK TALLIS

CENTER POINT LARGE PRINT
THORNDIKE, MAINE

This Center Point Large Print edition
is published in the year 2018 by arrangement with
Pegasus Books.

Copyright © 2017 by Frank Tallis.

All rights reserved.

The text of this Large Print edition is unabridged.
In other aspects, this book may vary
from the original edition.
Printed in the United States of America
on permanent paper.
Set in 16-point Times New Roman type.

ISBN: 978-1-68324-779-1

Library of Congress Cataloging-in-Publication Data

Names: Tallis, Frank, author.
Title: Mephisto Waltz / Frank Tallis.
Description: Center Point Large Print edition. | Thorndike, Maine :
    Center Point Large Print, 2018. | Series: A Max Liebermann mystery
Identifiers: LCCN 2018003606 | ISBN 9781683247791
    (hardcover : alk. paper)
Subjects: LCSH: Liebermann, Max (Fictitious character) — Fiction. |
    Large type books. | GSAFD: Mystery fiction.
Classification: LCC PR6120.A44 M47 2018 | DDC 823/.92—dc23
LC record available at https://lccn.loc.gov/2018003606

MEPHISTO WALTZ

PRELUDE

GENEVA, 1898

Luigi was sitting at a corner table inside a small, dilapidated café, sipping a black, bitter liquid, the color and taste of which described his mood with uncanny accuracy. There would be no "great deed." Prince Henri of Orleans, claimant to the French throne, had changed his plans and would not be coming to Geneva, and life would carry on in much the same way, one disappointment following another, just as it always had. Why had he thought that it would be any different this time? He had been a fool to think otherwise. This was his fate, his destiny, to be frustrated at every turn. Abandoned by his mother, shunted between foundling homes and charitable institutions, laboring, vagrancy; only once in his life had he experienced contentment and that was while serving with the cavalry in North Africa. Apart from this single exception, his existence had been unremittingly wretched. It occurred to him that he might remedy the situation by returning to Italy. King Umberto would be easy enough to find. Unfortunately, Luigi had no money to pay for carriages or trains and the distance was too great to walk.

7

One day he would die, and thereafter, it would be as though he had never lived. The thought filled him with cold horror.

It was still very early and the other tables were empty. The proprietor, whose physique was oddly angular, lit an oil lamp and hung it over the open pages of a ledger. He licked the end of a pencil and began making entries. A mangy cat jumped up onto the counter and mewed for attention.

Luigi heard the sound of footsteps and the accompanying tap of a cane on cobbles. A bell rang and a man entered. He was wearing a long coat and had the appearance of a gentleman. With unhurried movements he removed his hat and gloves and caught the proprietor's eye. The cat arched its back, hissed, leapt off the counter, and skittered into darkness, its claws unable to find adequate purchase on the floorboards. A mysterious communication seemed to take place between the stranger and the proprietor, because the proprietor nodded—as if agreeing to a request—and immediately followed his pet into the kitchen.

The stranger looked directly at Luigi. He was in his fifties or early sixties and his pointed beard and aquiline nose created a devilish impression: Lucifer, in the guise of an aging libertine. He sauntered over to the corner table and, without asking permission, sat down in a vacant chair. "Well, my friend, I suppose you've been considering your options." His Italian was slightly accented.

Luigi raised his eyebrows. He didn't believe in magic but the stranger seemed to have read his mind. "I don't remember having been introduced. You are . . . ?"

The stranger smiled and the slow retraction of his lips made him look even more diabolical. "There's nothing wrong with your memory."

"Then who are you? What do you want?"

"A few minutes of your time—that's all."

Luigi shook his head. "I'm sorry, I don't know you." As he began to rise, the stranger grabbed his arm and pulled him down again.

"But I know a great deal about you. We have mutual friends." The stranger reached into his coat pocket and produced some coins, which he pushed across the table. "I understand that you are presently in need of financial assistance. Go on. Take them. Buy yourself a decent breakfast." Luigi cautiously picked up the money.

"I don't understand . . ."

A cart rolled by, rattling loudly.

The stranger removed a newspaper from under his arm and indicated an article. "When I was a child, on old serf who I adored used to say to me: 'Every seed knows its time.' Read this. You'll find it very interesting, I promise you." Then, the stranger stood, put on his gloves with some ostentation—tugging the hems to ensure that the

9

fit was snug—before making his leisurely way back to the door.

"Wait a minute," Luigi called out.

The man didn't turn. He inspected his reflection, adjusted the angle of his hat, and exited the café. When the bell had stopped tinkling the silence was unnerving. Luigi checked the coins, fearing that he had fallen asleep and dreamed the whole episode. The touch of metal was reassuring. He bowed his head over the newspaper and began to read. The item appeared to be about a female aristocrat who was staying at one of the big hotels overlooking the lake.

The proprietor emerged from the kitchen. "Who was that man?" Luigi asked.

"What man?" the proprietor replied.

The Countess von Hohenembs was standing in the foyer of the Beau-Rivage Hotel. She was aware of the manager and his assistant staring at her, even though she was facing away from them. It was like a sixth sense.

Becoming the world's most beautiful woman was an accomplishment that had necessitated a will of iron, grit, steely resolve, and fixity of purpose. She ate mostly oranges and very occasionally ice, flavored with violet. When she was feeling strong, she would stop eating altogether. Society gossips maintained that she drank blood, but in reality she only ever drank milk or clear soup. She had converted her dressing room in the palace, with its thick red carpet, brocade wallpaper, and gilt furniture, into a gymnasium. Below the enormous chandelier were parallel bars and monkey bars. She had even suspended rings from her doorframe. Sometimes she would hang from them, fully dressed, and raise her legs to strengthen her stomach muscles.

Then there was the matter of her complexion, the preservation of which required face masks of crushed strawberries or raw veal. Her hair had to be combed for three hours a day, and every fortnight washed with cognac and egg yolks—a ritual that took from morning till night. Keeping her figure, which was impossibly slender, particularly for a woman who had given birth to four children, had necessitated determination on a truly heroic scale: asphyxiating corsetry and going to bed with her hips wrapped in vinegar-soaked bindings. Such measures, although extreme, had proved very effective. Her waist could fit into the circle made by the connected forefingers and thumbs of an average-size man.

Maintaining her pre-eminence had damaged her health. She suffered from fatigue, shortness of breath, fainting spells, and "greensickness"; pain from sciatica, neuritis, and rheumatism. Specialists whispered about a murmuring heart. Consequently, she frequented all the best spas, the Hungarian Baths of Hercules in the

Carpathian Mountains, Bad Kissingen in Lower Franconia. . . . None of them did her much good, and, over the years, she came to realize that she didn't have quite as many problems as the doctors had suggested. Really, she had only one problem, and that was the passage of time. She was getting old.

What was she to do?

Her answer was to travel.

Tall, dressed in black, and always equipped with a white umbrella to hide behind, she dispensed with her entourage and wandered the world like a glamorous ghost. She developed a particular fondness for being at sea, because time seemed to stop when she was out on the water and she could pretend she was like the Flying Dutchman, restless and immortal. So deep was her affection for the sea, that she had an anchor tattooed on her shoulder, like a common sailor.

After all the fame and adulation, the portraits and the photographs, the fawning and the flattery, she yearned for anonymity. But even at sixty, the Countess von Hohenembs was still a very striking woman, which was why the manager and his assistant were still staring.

The previous day she had visited Baroness Rothschild, not because she had wanted to, but as a favor for her sister. Unfortunately, the former Queen Marie of Naples had become somewhat dependent on the Rothschild family. It was a questionable arrangement. Funds made available in exchange for the company of a royal. Quite tasteless. Although the countess had enjoyed talking to the Baroness, they could never be true friends.

"Has the luggage been taken?" the countess asked her lady-in-waiting.

"Yes," Irma replied. "Some time ago."

They were leaving a little later than intended. The countess stepped out of the hotel foyer into bright sunlight.

"What a lovely day."

She set off at a brisk pace with Irma following a few steps behind.

From the promenade, she could see across the glittering lake, which was surrounded by low mountains. The funnel of the steamship came into view and the prospect of crossing a large body of water raised her spirits. A lyric from an operetta came into her mind: "Happy is he who can forget what can no more be changed."

A man ducked beneath her umbrella. He was wearing a cheap, tatty hat and shabby clothes. His complexion was dark—an Italian, perhaps? She froze and was shocked when his arm flew out. The strength of the blow made her teeter, she lost her balance, and then she was lying on her back, looking at high white clouds in the blue of the sky. Her fall had been broken by her skirts, and her head had been protected by her thick cushion of pinned-back hair. How embarrassing. Faces began to appear, all of them speaking in different languages, all offering assistance. She jumped to her feet and thanked the people who had gathered, first in German, then in French and English. Irma was brushing the dust from her clothes. "Don't fuss," said the countess. The porter from the Beau-Rivage was there: "Countess," he said. "Perhaps you should return to the hotel?"

"No," she replied. "That won't be necessary." She didn't want to miss the steamship.

Acting as if nothing had happened, she took her umbrella from Irma and continued walking. "What did that man actually want?"

Irma was shaken and confused. "The porter?"

"No," the countess replied, slightly irritated. "The other one. That dreadful person."

"I don't know. But surely he must be a vicious criminal . . . a lunatic!"

"Perhaps he wanted to take my watch."

They crossed the gangway and almost immediately the steamer departed. The countess was relieved. Looking over the water, she suddenly felt very weak. Her legs lost all of their strength and she collapsed.

"Help!" Irma cried. "Is there a doctor on board?" Several people came to her assistance but none of them were medically qualified. One of them, however, was a retired nurse. "Let's get her comfortable and massage her chest."

Three men carried the countess to the top deck and laid her on a bench. Irma unbuttoned the countess's bodice. Was it delayed shock? Or was her corset too tight?

"What's that?" said the retired nurse.

A tiny brown spot had appeared on the countess's batiste camisole, and when Irma looked closer she saw a hole. The countess's eyelids flickered and she stirred.

"Are you in pain?" Irma asked.

"No," the countess replied. "I'm not in pain. What happened?"

Before Irma could reply the countess had lost consciousness again.

The captain decided to turn the boat around. He smiled benignly at Irma and said, "Don't worry. We'll get the countess back to the Beau-Rivage in no time."

"She's not a countess," Irma whispered.

"What?" The captain leaned closer.

"She not a countess," Irma continued. "She's an empress. She only uses the name Hohenembs to disguise her true identity."

The Captain swallowed. "An empress . . ."

"Yes. Empress Elizabeth of Austria."

The captain studied Irma with renewed interest. He searched her face for signs of eccentricity, but she was perfectly respectable and her expression

15

was quite serious. "Ah," said the captain. He paused, emptied his lungs of air, and when he opened his mouth to speak again, he was disappointed to hear only a second, this time slightly tremulous, "Ah . . ."

The steamer chugged into its vacant berth and the gangway was extended. A makeshift stretcher was constructed from oars and velvet chairs and the "countess" was carried back to the hotel. When the doctors arrived, they could do nothing to save her, and at ten past two, Empress Elizabeth of Austria, Queen of Hungary, Queen Consort of Croatia and Bohemia, was pronounced dead.

On the promenade, a man with an aquiline nose and pointed beard was leaning against the railings. He raised the brim of his hat with the handle of his cane, lit a cigar, and walked off toward the town center.

PART ONE

A Man Without Qualities

ONE

VIENNA, 1904

Liebermann was sitting opposite his father in The Imperial. The pianist had just finished playing a wistful ländler and before the applause had finished he was already several bars into the "Trish-Trash Polka."

Mendel raised his menu and one of the waiters—noting the gesture—swerved toward their table. "Thank you, Bruno. A topfenstrudel for me and apfelschmarrn for my son."

The waiter glanced at the empty cups. "More coffee?"

"Yes, please."

"A melange for Herr Liebermann and a schwarzer for Herr Doctor Liebermann?"

"Precisely."

Bruno bowed and departed, weaving between the tables and dodging his colleagues. The Imperial was full of patrons, all of whom seemed to be talking very loudly.

"So," said Mendel. "How are you?"

"Very well, father." Liebermann replied, "And you?"

"My back, my knees . . . what can you do? A man of my age has to expect aches and pains."

"Perhaps you should lose some weight."

"What?"

"That's what Pintsch told you to do." He paused and added, "Over a year ago, I think."

"Life has too few pleasures as it is," Mendel grumbled. "I'm not giving up eating. You'll appreciate what I'm saying when you're older."

"I didn't tell you to stop eating, Father—and nor did Professor Pintsch."

"Maxim: the empress ate only oranges. Look what good it did her."

"She was assassinated."

"There you are."

"I'm not sure I follow, Father."

"I want to enjoy the time I have left. It might not be very long." Their brief exchange had already begun to sound peevish and argumentative. Liebermann changed the subject. They discussed the newspapers and Mendel mentioned a banker whose name had appeared in the obituaries. "I went to school with him—he used to live on our street. Ended up mixing with royalty, who'd have thought it?"

Bruno returned and deftly unloaded his tray before withdrawing discreetly.

"How is Hannah?" Liebermann asked. He pitied the younger of his two sisters, still stuck at home with aging parents.

"Happy enough," said Mendel. He paused before adding, "Almost eighteen." It was not an innocent observation and he was frowning.

"She's still very young," said Liebermann.

"Not so young that I don't have to think about her future," Mendel snapped. A group of immaculately groomed men and women at an adjacent table roared with laughter. "I know that you have—" Mendel rotated his hand in the air "—opinions: opinions concerning how your mother and I go about such things, but how else is Hannah going to meet an eligible young man? Herr Lenkiewicz has a son—Baruch—a bright boy with a good head for figures. He's already keeping his father's books and their business is expanding. We arranged for them to meet—Hannah and Baruch." Mendel shook his head. "It wasn't a great success."

"I'd be happy to make some introductions."

"What?" Mendel was unable to conceal his disapproval. "One of your psychiatrist friends?"

"Not necessarily. But really, Father, would that be so bad?" Mendel glared at his son. "Hannah is interested in people, not figures, and she likes reading, art—"

"Then she needs a husband who can afford books and paintings—a husband with good prospects."

Liebermann picked up his fork and tasted his apfelschmarrn—apple pancake sprinkled with sugar and cinnamon. He was mildly surprised by the complexity of its flavor. The sweetness

21

of the fruit was augmented by hints of caramel and vanilla. An uncomfortable silence was eventually relieved by some fitful talk about politics. Liebermann noticed that, on several occasions, his father was about to say something, but then appeared to decide against it. Mendel was also showing signs of agitation, his fingers were restless. Mendel cleared his throat and said: "Leah came to see your mother the other day."

Leah—the older of Liebermann's two sisters—was always visiting their mother. Clearly, there was something particular about this visit that had distinguished it from the others.

"Oh?" said Liebermann, chewing and swallowing.

"Yes," Mendel continued. "Last week, she was on her way home from the theatre and she saw you walking down Alserstrasse." Mendel looked up from his topfenstrudel. "She said you were walking, arm in arm, with a woman; a very attractive woman."

Liebermann put his cup down and dabbed his mouth with a serviette. "Ahh, that would have been Amelia."

"Amelia." Mendel repeated the name and maintained eye contact.

"She's English."

"I don't recall you having mentioned her."

"Actually—"

"Not the sort of thing I'd forget, Maxim."

"She lives with Mimi Rubenstein."

Mendel's expression showed sudden recognition. With increasing confidence he said, "The governess who moved in after Herr Rubenstein died? The one who needed somewhere to live?"

"Yes. That was Amelia."

"Wasn't she ill?"

"She had just completed a course of treatment at the hospital."

"With you—wasn't it?"

Liebermann hadn't expected his father to have such a good memory. His reluctance to answer extended the syllable: "Yes."

Mendel dug his fork into his topfenstrudel. "Am I to understand, then, that you have formed an attachment to one of your patients?"

"One of my *former* patients," Liebermann corrected. Once again, Mendel stopped himself from saying something. "Father," Liebermann continued. "I thought very carefully about the propriety of our friendship."

"And she is fully recovered?"

"Completely."

Mendel was evidently unconvinced.

The pianist was now playing a piece that Liebermann didn't recognize, a mazurka in a minor key.

"I take it that your association is more than just a dalliance."

"Considerably more."

"So when, exactly, did you intend to tell your mother about this development?"

"The opportunity never seemed to present itself."

Mendel stroked his beard. "English, you say?"

"Well, not exactly," said Liebermann, toying with a crescent of apple. "Her father is English and her mother is German."

"Is she from a good family?"

"Her grandfather was a court physician."

Mendel evaluated this response and nodded. "I'm sure your mother would be very keen to meet this . . . Amelia."

"Yes, I'm sure she would," Liebermann agreed, his voice brittle.

"Why don't you bring her to dinner?" Mendel leaned back in his chair. "One Friday night, perhaps?"

"Another night would be preferable."

Mendel tilted his head. "She's not. . . ?"

"Jewish? No."

Mendel's face became inscrutable, a mask behind which he could hide his disappointment. "A governess . . ."

"No. Not anymore," Liebermann explained. "She's is now enrolled at the university and occasionally works with Landsteiner—the blood specialist. He has given her special permission to undertake research in his laboratory."

"Does she intend to practice medicine too?"

"Either that or pursue a scientific career. She hasn't decided yet."

Liebermann wondered how many times he might get away with postponing the proposed dinner engagement. Twice—perhaps—three times if he were lucky? Now that his mother knew about Amelia, her life would have but a single purpose. She would be indefatigable.

"What's wrong with your apfelschmarrn?" Mendel asked. "You've hardly touched it."

TWO

Detective Inspector Oskar Rheinhardt was standing in the middle of a long, functional workshop. He couldn't remember the precise date when Gallus and Sons had been declared bankrupt, but their demise was relatively recent. No more than a year was his considered estimate. Against the exposed brickwork of the opposite wall were the empty carcasses of several unfinished pianos: two uprights and a concert grand. Another two uprights were standing back to back between two pillars. None of these cases had been polished and the wood was mottled with green mold. Every object and surface was subdued by a patina of dull, wintry light that refracted through high, latticed windows. In the far corner he saw a tangled mass of metal strings, hammers, keys, and tuning pins. Water had dripped through the ceiling and collected on the floor in shallow puddles, amplifying the cheerless atmosphere of dereliction and decay.

The dead man was seated on a wooden chair. His legs were extended and the soles and heels of his shoes were exposed. They showed signs of considerable wear. His collarless shirt was woven from a coarse, gray material, the kind often worn by workmen or farm hands. Rheinhardt stood behind the chair and studied the hole in the back of the man's head. It was roughly circular. Several yards in front of the dead man were three evenly spaced empty chairs. The central chair was directly ahead and it seemed unlikely that this alignment was accidental.

Resolve was required to overcome the revulsion that—at least initially—prevented Rheinhardt from returning his attention to the front of the dead man's head. The cartilage of the nose had dissolved, exposing the nasal cavity, and the orbits of the eyes were filled with a clear, gelatinous substance. Singed hair hung over melted, blistered flesh and there were no lips to hide a maniacal grin. The smell was overpowering.

Rheinhardt's assistant, Haussmann, entered the factory and marched over to his superior. "Nothing outside, sir. No footprints, nothing." The inspector nodded and crouched in front of the chair. He made his right hand resemble a gun and held it under the dead man's chin. "The bullet must be embedded in that oak beam. Would you be so kind as to dig it out for me?"

"It's quite high up, sir."

"Indeed."

"And we don't have a ladder, sir."

"Haussmann, I was hoping that you would show some initiative."

The young man looked around and his eyes

expanded when he noticed the upright piano cases. Pointing, he said: "Do you think one of those would support my weight, sir?"

"There is, I would suggest, only one way to find out."

"Very good, sir." Haussmann clicked his heels, bowed, and crossed the factory floor.

A few minutes later the police photographer and his apprentice appeared. The photographer acknowledged Rheinhardt and silently set up his tripod and camera in front of the body. When he had finished his preparations he caught the detective's eye and his expression soured.

"I know," Rheinhardt nodded. "It's not very pleasant." Then he added, "I would be most grateful if—in addition to routine photography— you would also include some wider perspectives. Those three chairs . . . I would like some images that include those three chairs *and* the body."

"Of course, inspector."

The photographer burrowed under a black cloth and the apprentice struck a match. There was a brilliant flash and the dead man's fixed grin and appalling disfigurement became garish and monstrous.

Rheinhardt turned away. He had not gone very far when he came across a volume of music on the floor. Picking it up, he let the torn pages fall open and he hummed the notes on the treble stave: the opening of Mozart's Piano Sonata number

16 in C Major. Respectfully, he laid the volume on an empty crate, and continued walking, but the innocent melody haunted his inner ear, a bizarrely inappropriate accompaniment to the vivid horror that inhabited each of the repeated magnesium flashes. Smoke wafted through the air, its arrival presaged by the odor of invisible fumes. Through a curtain of haze, Rheinhardt could see Haussmann standing on an upright piano case, inspecting the beam behind the dead man.

At the back of the factory was a green door. Rheinhardt pushed it open and stepped outside. There wasn't much to see, a cluster of small buildings in the middle distance, and beyond these, the land rising slowly, bringing the horizon forward and concealing Vienna. It was a bleak prospect. The Mozart melody was still flowing through Rheinhardt's mind: grace notes, trills, effortless invention. As he turned to re-enter the building he noticed a mark on the door—a small dark oval—and when he leaned forward to examine it more closely, he saw that it was composed of a pattern of minute concentric rings. The blackness of the impression suggested that it had been made with ink—or blood.

Rheinhardt called his assistant, who jumped off the piano case and came running over.

"Sir?"

"Look at this, Haussmann. Can I assume that

you have been keeping up with the latest forensic developments as reported in the *Police Gazette*?"

"Yes, sir. The new method. Not everyone agrees . . ."

"There is some debate, that's true. But—if I'm not mistaken—this is a thumbprint, and a very good one. See how clear the ridge pattern is. It would be remiss of us to overlook evidence of this quality. Get me some tape, a piece of cardboard, and a saw."

"We didn't bring a saw, sir."

"In which case, get me a screwdriver instead. We'll take the door off its hinges."

"You're going to take the door back to Schottenring, sir?"

"Well, what else would you suggest, Haussmann?"

"Sir," Haussmann reached into his pocket and extended his hand. In the middle of his palm was a misshapen bullet.

"Good man," said Rheinhardt, taking it from his assistant. "I was expecting it to be more compressed."

"The beam was rotten, sir."

"Just the one?"

"Yes, sir. Just the one."

THREE

Professor Mathias was positioning and re-positioning his tools on a metal trolley, unable to find a satisfactory arrangement. He cursed, muttered something unintelligible, and finally chanced upon a layout that dispelled his agitation. Rolling up his shirt sleeves, he put on his apron and turned to face Rheinhardt: "A lady friend of mine—don't look so surprised, inspector—yes, a *lady friend* of mine, who possessed an exquisite contralto singing voice, owned a Gallus and Sons piano. I'm not very musical, but even I could tell the tone was poor. She sold it to an impecunious music teacher."

The door opened and Liebermann appeared.

"Max!" Rheinhardt cried, "Thank you so much for coming."

"My apologies," said Liebermann. "I was delayed by a late admission—a middle-aged woman whose principal symptom was continuous, compulsive laughter."

"Ha!" Mathias scoffed. "Perhaps she's simply more perceptive than the rest of us."

Liebermann bowed, clicked his heels, and spoke with reserved courtesy: "Good evening, Professor Mathias. I trust you are well?"

31

Mathias nodded and continued: "Laughter. Ultimately, the only rational response to the human condition." It was impossible to tell whether he was being serious or joking. Liebermann assumed a neutral expression and remained silent.

An electric light with a wide conical shade hung over the peaks and troughs of the mortuary sheets. The old man shuffled closer to the dissection table and uncovered the body. Beneath the sustained, unremitting brightness of the electric light, the melted face glistened.

Liebermann did not flinch. "Who is he?"

"We have no idea," Rheinhardt replied. "He was found in the derelict Gallus and Sons piano factory, propped up on a chair and shot through the head."

"Who found him?"

"Two businessmen who have an interest in buying the land. The factory is in Favoriten—on the edge of the city."

Mathias felt the coarse cloth of the dead man's shirt sleeve. "He's dressed like a laborer."

"Yes," said Liebermann. "But he obviously isn't a laborer. Look at his hands."

"Well observed," said Mathias. His voice acquired the condescending cadences of a pedagogue. "A laborer would, of course, have abrasions and callouses. You will also have noticed, no doubt, the absence of chafing or abrasions on the man's wrists. He was never tied up . . ."

"What are his teeth like?" Liebermann asked. "Perhaps they could be matched with the records of a local dentist?"

Mathias put on some very tight gloves and proudly displayed his covered hands to his companions. "Rubber gloves: invented a few years ago by an American surgeon. I've just started using them. They provide protection but you hardly know you're wearing them. They're like a second epidermis."

"Ingenious," said Rheinhardt, throwing a weary glance at Liebermann.

"Yes," Liebermann agreed. "Quite ingenious."

Mathias prised the dead man's jaws apart. The opened mouth immediately made the dead man look as if he were screaming. "Several extractions," said Mathias. "Wisdom teeth too— *that* must have been painful, poor fellow. But really, Herr Doctor, how many dentists are there in Vienna, or Austria for that matter? And are they all conscientious record keepers? Your suggestion is entirely impractical."

Liebermann walked around the table and studied the hole in the man's skull. The cavity was deep and shadowed. Catching Mathias's eye, Liebermann asked, "Did *you* remove his coat, Professor?"

"No." Mathias replied.

"He wasn't wearing a coat," said Rheinhardt. "It must have had a shop label sewn on the inside, or something else that would have helped us to identify him."

"I wonder if he's famous?" said Mathias. "Perhaps that's the reason for the disfigurement?"

"If he's famous," Rheinhardt responded, "then his absence will soon be noticed. But look at those shoes."

"I suppose we can assume," said Liebermann, "that he was shot and then disfigured, rather than disfigured and then shot?"

"That was certainly my assumption," said Rheinhardt. "It makes sense, doesn't it? With respect to motive? And if he wasn't tied up . . ."

"Gentleman," said Mathias "May I proceed?"

"By all means," Rheinhardt replied.

Professor Mathias picked up a large pair of scissors and started to make cuts in the dead man's clothes. When he had completed this task he was able to undress the man by pulling away strips of material.

"Well," Mathias said, lifting one of the dead man's arms, "What have we here?" Mathias's breath condensed in the cold air as his rigid forefinger traced three dark stripes that disappeared beneath the dead man's body. "Gentlemen, some assistance, please?"

Liebermann and Rheinhardt helped Mathias turn the corpse over. It was an awkward maneuver and the slap of flesh on the table was uncomfortably reminiscent of meat on a butcher's chopping board. The dark stripes were now entirely visible. They were scabby and formed a V shape that converged at the base of the spine.

Mathias produced a magnifying glass. "He's been flogged—and very recently. With a riding crop."

"Dear God," said Rheinhardt, shaking his head. "Torture too?"

"No," said Liebermann. "Quite the contrary. These injuries were inflicted in the bedroom. If he'd been flogged by the same person or persons who killed him then I suspect these injuries would have been far worse."

"You see, that's the trouble with you psychiatrists," said Mathias. "Always something sexual."

"Do you disagree?" Liebermann asked.

Mathias studied the stripes again. "The bleeding *was* superficial. And I have to admit, I've seen a great deal worse."

"A small woman," said Liebermann.

"I beg your pardon?" said Rheinhardt.

"She was positioned directly behind him—bringing her arm down with moderate force. And he was probably standing up against a bedpost. His upper back is untouched."

"A prostitute?"

"That is very likely. But one should not assume

that violence performed for the purpose of sexual gratification is confined to Vienna's brothels. It is my impression that the practice is more widespread than many psychiatrists are willing to acknowledge."

"You see," said Mathias. "That patient of yours, Herr Doctor, the one who can't stop laughing—she has a point."

"With respect, Herr Professor, sexual deviation is—in most cases—perfectly comprehensible. Those who insist on being beaten in the bedroom usually think, albeit unconsciously, that they deserve it."

Mathias shook his head. "The dead are so much more straightforward than the living."

Rheinhardt was growing impatient. "Is there nothing here that might help us to identify him?"

Mathias used his magnifying glass again. "His skin is uncommonly clear, the odd blemish, but nothing particularly memorable." He raised his head, noticed that the dead man was still wearing shoes and socks and addressed the corpse. "Oh, I beg your pardon." He walked to the end of the table and, grasping the heel of each shoe, removed both simultaneously. After putting them aside, he peeled off the socks, hesitating slightly before dropping them onto the trolley. He studied the dead man's bare feet and began to smile.

"What is it, professor?" Rheinhardt asked.

"Come here."

Mathias separated a big toe from its neighbor, revealing a translucent membrane. "The next two toes are fused, but the last three are similarly connected." The effect was like opening a lace fan. "He has webbed feet, inspector."

"Well, well," said Rheinhardt, suddenly more cheerful. "That *is* distinctive."

FOUR

Peter Nikolayevich Razumovsky was seated at a table next to a stove, sipping Becherovka and peering through thick smoke. Paraffin lamps provided a weak, fitful light.

The beer cellar was situated halfway along a blind alley in a ramshackle corner of Leopoldstadt populated by Hasidic Jews. Most of the patrons who drank there called it The Golden Bears, but there hadn't been a sign on the door for years and even the local residents were barely conscious of its existence. Admission necessitated a perilous descent down steep stone stairs that plummeted into shadow and the shutters were never open. Given that The Golden Bears was some distance from the Innere Stadt, it was surprisingly busy. All the tables were occupied and many patrons were standing in small, animated groups.

Razumovsky could easily identify the various parties: artists, occultists, radicals. All had their own way of dressing. The nihilists were the easiest to identify—shoulder-length hair, bushy beards, red shirts, and knee boots. Their female companions styled their hair in a neat bob and concealed their shapeliness with loose, baggy dresses. Some of their number had taken to wearing blue-tinted spectacles and all of them smoked without pause, the glowing remnant of one Egyptian cigarette being used to light the next.

A lean youth took a flute from its case and an artist with a wide-brimmed hat and tasseled scarf encouraged his neighbors to clap. After some preparatory fussing, the musician raised the instrument to his lips and began a demanding moto perpetuo that immediately won yet more applause. A solitary man, with the melancholy visage of a jilted lover, had become too drunk to stand and fell to the floor. The proprietor—a burly Czech called Pepik Skalicky—emerged from a trap door, kicked the supine customer, shrugged, and joined his perspiring, fleshy wife who was serving bowls of liver dumpling soup and rye bread from behind a simple counter made from trestles and planks.

The surface of Razumovsky's table was covered in newspapers. Perhaps the body hadn't been found yet? Or perhaps the police were wary of releasing the details? The Viennese were so highly strung, so nervous, even symphonies got them agitated. Either way, it didn't really matter. The purpose of his perusal of the press reports was simply to satisfy his curiosity. He had always been something of a showman, and, like any vainglorious actor, he wanted to read his reviews.

A woman was shamelessly flirting with a group of young men from the university, one of whom had a very conspicuous dueling scar. She was in her early thirties, but still slim and vivacious. For a few moments, Razumovsky paused to observe the way she raised her chin to reveal the whiteness of her long neck; the way she laughed and never failed to display her décolletage to best advantage. Razumovsky knew who she was, where she lived, and the key facts relating to her history. Her name was Della Autenburg. She was the wife of Eduard Autenburg, who Razumovsky now imagined sitting at home, comfortably ensconced in an armchair, also surrounded by newspapers.

Razumovsky took another sip of his bittersweet liqueur and picked up a copy of the *Wiener Zeitung*. He scanned the pages, registering headlines, until his attention was captured by an announcement. A very senior member of the judiciary was retiring and his distinguished career was to be celebrated at several state functions, including a formal dinner at the Palais Khevenhüller. An as yet unnamed royal personage was expected to attend. Razumovsky had not thought about Georg Weeber for decades—an arrogant lickspittle monarchist puppet, a pettifogging bureaucrat, elevated by a rotten, corrupt system, who had spent a lifetime dispensing punishments in lieu of justice on behalf of the very same inbred emperor who had appointed him.

Weeber had been instrumental in crushing the movement in Austria. He had sentenced many of Razumovsky's comrades to hard labor and all of them were now dead. One of their cell had been a woman with whom Razumovsky had had an affair: a brave, spirited soul, with curly auburn hair and a supple, almost muscular body. She had hanged herself in a washroom after only two days of incarceration.

It had all happened so long ago . . .

Razumovsky had only one more thing to accomplish in Vienna—and then it would be wise to move on. Yet, he found himself reading and re-reading the announcement and considering possibilities. He had earned a reputation for seizing opportunities—inspired, spontaneous action. Indeed, there were many in the movement who said that this was not only his métier, but his genius. Georg Weeber. In Razumovsky's mind, the name had a certain synaesthetic ripeness, like an apple, ready to fall from a tree.

FIVE

Liebermann was escorting Amelia Lydgate home. They had been to the Court Opera to see "Der Corregidor," a comedy composed by Hugo Wolf.

"A sad irony," said Liebermann. "The poor man died last year—in a private asylum."

"Why was he admitted?"

"Melancholy, delusions—he'd been suffering for many years." A carriage rolled by and the driver cracked his whip. "I love his songs," Liebermann continued. "Wolf pays such close attention to the poetry and his accompaniments are so intelligent."

When they reached the university, Amelia said: "I attended a cardiograph demonstration yesterday."

"Who was the demonstrator?"

"Professor de Cyon. Have you heard of him?"

"Vaguely."

"He works in Paris and was invited to Vienna by Professor Föhrenholz—they are old friends. De Cyon also brought one of his new machines for the department." A soldier in blue uniform advanced toward the couple and inclined his head as he passed. "There was a great deal of gossip before the demonstration," Amelia continued. "Herr Schenkolowski said that de Cyon had had to leave St. Petersburg following protests from his students. He was a harsh marker of examination papers and used to make provocative remarks during his lectures. Consequently, he was pelted with eggs and gherkins."

"What was he like?"

"Disappointingly ordinary: we required no ammunition." Liebermann smiled, supposing that Amelia was joking, but when he looked at her he found that her expression was neutral. She had simply been stating a fact. Her eyes flashed as they passed beneath a streetlight. "De Cyon said something rather interesting."

"Oh?"

"He said that the cardiograph can be used to detect lies."

"The unconscious is always betraying truths. Slips of the tongue, dreams, fidgeting. Involuntary changes of heart rate would be yet another measure of its independence."

"Perhaps cardiographs could be used to aid psychoanalysis. They might hasten the process?"

"Most patients wouldn't like being connected to a machine. And then there is the issue of propriety. I'm not sure many female patients would be happy loosening their corsets and revealing their feet and legs to a gentleman."

"When there are more lady doctors one must suppose that disrobing will be altogether less problematic."

"Indeed," Liebermann replied, feeling that he had received a subtle reprimand.

They walked past the Votivkirche and entered Alsergrund. Liebermann had been waiting for an opportune moment to broach the subject of his parents.

"I saw my father the other day." Amelia said nothing and waited patiently for more. Liebermann swallowed. "He—and my mother—would like to meet you. They've invited us to dinner at their apartment."

Amelia nodded. "Well, I'm sure that will be delightful."

"It might be delightful," said Liebermann. "But I feel obliged to warn you that there's a good chance that it won't be."

SIX

Eduard Autenburg was sitting in his library composing a pamphlet on sexual equality; unfortunately, he had written only half a page in over two hours. The carriage clock struck one. He was agitated and couldn't concentrate. For the umpteenth time he read the last line he had written: *The New Woman of today is the woman of the future.* He was satisfied with its direct brevity and he imagined his words painted across a banner held aloft by two viragos, marching at the head of a crowd of their militant sisters. But nothing else followed. No more words came into his mind and the empty, lower half of the page made him feel slightly ill. He rose from his chair and circled the table, biting his fingernails. Eventually he stopped and looked behind the curtains.

The gas lamps had become ill-defined yellow orbs floating in a sea of mist. The effect was like leaning over the bulwark of a boat in order to observe phosphorescent jellyfish. Obere Weissgärberstrasse was often misty because of the closeness of the Danube Canal.

Autenburg heard a shriek, laughter, and footsteps on the cobbles outside. He returned to the table, picked up his pen, and attempted to look like a man absorbed by a great and noble undertaking. A few seconds later there was some noise on the landing and the jingle of keys. Autenburg retained his heroic attitude.

"No—he's not here. He must be writing . . ." It was Della in the hallway.

The door opened and she stepped into the library. Strands of loose hair hung over her face and her complexion was flushed. "Ah, there you are."

"I've been working on the pamphlet," he replied, stroking his Van Dyke beard.

"Good. When will it be ready?"

"Soon." He was aware of Axl Diamant standing behind his wife. The young man's fingers curled around her waist. "Where have you been?"

"Oh, only The Golden Bears. The nihilists were there again. They're becoming regulars. You should come."

"When I've finished the pamphlet . . ."

"Of course." Della blew Eduard a kiss and said, "We're awfully tired. We're going to bed." She retreated into the hallway and closed the door. Diamant whispered something and Della responded with a low-pitched, lascivious chuckle.

Eduard read his last line again: *The New Woman of today is the woman of the future.* He picked up the sheet of paper, balled it up, and threw it across the room.

SEVEN

Well, Oskar?" said Liebermann. "What shall we finish with?"

Rheinhardt turned the pages of the Schubert volume on the music stand. "An den Mond"—To the Moon. It was one of their favorite songs.

Liebermann began playing an introduction that slyly referenced Beethoven's celebrated "Moonlight Sonata." The bass register of the Bösendorfer was darkly sonorous, almost sinister, beneath the creeping, stealthy progress of the right hand triplets, and when Rheinhardt sang the opening phrase of Ludwig Hölty's poetry, his warm, fluid baritone conjured a landscape of silvered beech trees and meadows, in the dead of night, populated by fleeting phantoms.

They were both pleased with the performance and when Liebermann's hands descended on the final chord, he looked up at his friend and nodded approvingly before the notes had faded. "Wonderful, Oskar—I think your voice is improving with age."

The detective sighed. "I *am* getting older, but would prefer it if you didn't remind me quite so often."

"I was paying you a compliment, Oskar."

"Next time, perhaps you could think of a way

47

Glenrock Branch Library
Box 1000
Glenrock, WY 82637

of praising my voice without referring to my age?"

Liebermann closed the piano lid, placed the Schubert volume on top of a tower of music books, and folded the music stand. "Perhaps your occupation, which necessitates so much contact with the dead, is making you excessively aware of your own mortality?"

"Max." The inspector's expression was even more world weary than usual. "This evening, I do not wish to be analyzed."

They walked across a sparsely patterned rug and entered, through open double doors, a paneled smoking room, where they sat in leather chairs that faced a crackling fire. As was their custom, Rheinhardt took the right chair and Liebermann the left. Between the chairs was a small table designed by Kolomon Moser on which Liebermann's servant had placed a decanter of brandy, crystal glasses, and a box of cigars. The two men stared into the fire for several minutes before Liebermann poured.

"So, Oskar—any progress?"

"None at all; however, I've released some information to the press. We've told them that the body of a man with webbed feet was discovered in the old Gallus and Sons factory and that we are willing to reward anyone who comes forward with information that leads to his identification." Rheinhardt produced an envelope and handed it to Liebermann. "Take a look at these." Liebermann opened the envelope and took out a set of postcard-size photographs. "They show the dead man, exactly as we found him."

Liebermann looked at each image in turn and when he had examined the entire series, he started again from the beginning. Halfway through, he stopped, and selected a photograph which he handed back to Rheinhardt.

"Those three chairs . . ."

"What about them?"

"They appear to be lined up."

"The middle chair was positioned directly in front of the body." Liebermann offered Rheinhardt a cigar. "Thank you, Max."

"I doubt such a precise arrangement is attributable to chance."

"That's what I thought."

"Then . . . were three people present when the man was murdered?" Liebermann took a cigar out of the box and lit it. "If so, was the man subject to some form of interrogation? Did he have information that was of great value to them?"

"They troubled to conceal the identity of the man by pouring acid over his face—but didn't bother to move the chairs . . ."

Liebermann shrugged, opened his mouth, and released a cloud of smoke. "Interrogation is one possibility."

"And the other?"

"Perhaps the chairs were occupied by individuals who sat in judgement. The dead man was the defendant in some sort of sham trial, and after his guilt was determined, he was executed."

"A jury of honor?"

"Professor Mathias found no chaffing or abrasions on his wrists. Perhaps he came to the factory of his own volition, to prove his innocence, but failed to convince his judges."

"A jury of honor," Rheinhardt repeated. "So what are you suggesting? A secret society?"

"Well, at least a group of individuals who subscribe to a collectively upheld code of conduct."

"There are many secret societies in Vienna. But none of the secret societies that have been exposed to date have ever executed errant members."

"Then perhaps," said Liebermann. "The people you're looking for aren't Viennese."

Rheinhardt picked up his brandy glass, swirled the contents, and took a sip. "A poor man, with sexual predilections that are most probably satisfied in brothels. He is summoned to the abandoned factory in Favoriten, where he is judged by three of his associates. He submits to their will—or is simply taken unawares—and shot through the head. His associates wish to

50

conceal the man's identity, so disfigure him with acid and remove his coat."

"One more thing."

"What's that? "

"They are disturbed: a noise outside, a dog—something—and they leave quickly, forgetting their conspicuous seating arrangement, and run for the most discreet exit."

"A green door at the back of the factory: I found a bloody thumbprint on it."

"Did you?"

"Yes."

"The new method," said Liebermann, pensively. "I wonder if it will have much effect on how you—in the security office—go about your business?"

Rheinhardt exhaled a cloud of smoke. "We'll see. I'm quite hopeful."

EIGHT

The day after the Favoriten murder was reported in the newspapers, two women presented themselves at the Schottenring station. They were both married to web-footed men who had recently vanished; however, neither had the right physique—a fact confirmed when the contents of their wardrobes were examined. The missing husbands were tall with wide shoulders, whereas the dead man was of average build and slim. Then followed two uneventful days during which Rheinhardt received no further visitors. On the third day, however, there was a knock on the door, and Haussmann entered with an unkempt man in a tattered frock coat. He wore circular glasses, the lenses of which were rather greasy, and he sniffed continuously, as though he had a cold.

"Sir: Herr Globocnik," said Haussmann. "He says he has information."

"Please," said Rheinhardt, "do take a seat, Herr Globocnik."

The man sat down and Haussman stood by the door.

Rheinhardt flicked open a notebook and picked up his pen. "Your full name?"

"Lutz Vilmos Globocnik."

"Address?"

"Hickelgasse 27."

"Occupation?"

"Office clerk."

When Rheinhardt had finished taking down the preliminary details he raised his head. Globocnik continued to sniff, although not once did he search his pockets for a handkerchief.

"You want information?" said Globocnik. "You want to know who he was—the man you found in the piano factory?"

"Indeed."

"His name was Helmut Bok."

"And how do you know this, Herr Globocnik?"

"It was me who killed him."

NINE

You're a clever one." It was something that Jov often said to the young prince. After which the old serf would stroke his brindled beard and qualify his praise: "But don't think too much, Master Peter. Too much thinking will get you into trouble." Jov had been right on both counts. The young prince was indeed clever, and, in the fullness of time, thinking had got him into trouble.

When Razumovsky graduated from the Academy of the Corps of Pages, his record of achievements was unprecedented. The most prestigious military commissions were his for the asking. So when, after considerable and characteristic deliberation, he chose to join a regiment of Cossacks billeted in Siberia, there was much whispering behind closed doors at the imperial court. *I've always thought him odd— haven't you?* Razumovsky knew what they were saying. He'd always known what they were saying, because closed doors had *never* prevented him from discovering what he wanted to find out.

The journey to Irkutsk was long and arduous. He passed starving peasants with skeletal children; he passed through the Eastern labor camps, where convicts mined gold in freezing water; he passed through quarries where men and women dug salt out of the earth with their bare hands. Peasants collapsed in front of his horse, convicts lost consciousness and sank beneath the water. He saw transports arriving from occupied Poland, prisoners, shuffling along the road, linked together with heavy chains.

He had had so many experiences during the course of his long life, yet it was always these memories that surfaced when he was bored; recollections of the years in which his thoughts had clarified. Up until that point, it was as if he had been looking at the world through unfocused binoculars, and then all of a sudden, the thumb-screw had been turned and everything had become sharp and perfectly clear. After a brief and indifferent military career he had decided that science might be the answer. He studied biology and traveled continents, but he soon realized that science would never be enough. It would take more than science to relieve suffering in the world.

Razumovsky was standing behind the Palais Khevenhüller, a large, gray, eighteenth-century building in Josefstadt. The back of the palace was rather plain and dreary. Occasionally, a cart would roll up and a steward would come out to accept delivery of foodstuffs for the kitchen. Razumovsky looked at his pocket watch, counted the seconds, and at exactly six o'clock a petite young woman stepped out and trotted nimbly down the stairs. Razumovsky followed her as she made her way across the eighth district and into the seventeenth. She stopped briefly to buy some chestnuts from a man standing next to a brazier. The young woman continued walking and eventually entered a shabby apartment block. Razumovsky followed her in and listened as she crossed the first floor landing. He heard her trip on a loose tile. A door was opened and she called: "Mother—I've bought you some chestnuts."

Later, Razumovsky stood outside the young woman's apartment and listened. He heard her talking to an old woman—and a small child coughing.

The next morning, Razumovsky was waiting for the young woman in the foyer. He heard her walking along the landing and when she reached the bottom of the stairs he smiled, raised his hat and bowed. "Fräulein . . ." She was startled by his presence. It was still dark outside. "I'm so sorry, I didn't mean to frighten you—I swear, I mean you no harm."

"Who are you?" she asked.

"A friend—I give you my word."

"What do you want?"

The young woman was still not reassured.

"Please, allow me to explain. I won't keep you long and what I have to say will be of considerable interest. I would like to offer you a chance to improve your circumstances, not only you, of course, but also your mother and child." A dry bark broke the silence. "That cough: it sounds rather bad to me," Razumovsky continued. "I hope you've been able to afford good medical advice."

TEN

"May I introduce my colleague," said Rheinhardt, addressing Globocnik. "Herr Doctor Liebermann."

The clerk stood up, clicked his heels and bowed. His upper body remained bent over for longer than was necessary and when he finally raised his head, his eyes narrowed. "A doctor?"

"Yes."

"But there's nothing wrong with me."

Rheinhardt ignored Globocnik's objection. It was one that he had heard many times before. "Please sit, Herr Globocnik." Rheinhardt offered Liebermann a chair and soon all of them were seated.

Liebermann crossed his legs and leaned forward. "Herr Globocnik, who is Herr Bok?"

Globocknik looked quizzically at Rheinhardt. The inspector treated the look as a question and replied, "Please answer Doctor Liebermann."

The clerk sniffed. "Bok was a bad man."

"And what did he do that was bad?"

"I think he must have always been bad—from birth. It was, for him, quite natural, to do bad things. Do you believe that this is possible, Herr Doctor? For a man to be born bad?"

"Herr Globocnik, my opinion concerning philosophical niceties is really rather secondary to our purpose. You say that Herr Bok was a bad man. Why? What did he do that was bad?"

The clerk sniffed again, this time managing to invest his sharp inhalation with a certain amount of disdain. "Even the church acknowledges the doctrine of original sin. Which means that no one is truly pure. One must suppose all of us have the potential to do wrong. But even casual observation of the way humans behave suggests that this potential is more likely to find expression in some more than others."

Liebermann nodded. "All right. Herr Bok was a bad man; a man who was born bad. So what did he do to you? How were you wronged?"

Globocnik answered elliptically. "It's a question of morality . . . personal morality." Then he fell silent.

"What was the nature of your relationship with Herr Bok?" Liebermann asked.

"We were acquaintances."

"Where did you meet?"

"Here—in Vienna. It was a long time ago."

"How long?"

"My memory for dates has never been very good, but recently it has become considerably worse."

Liebermann glanced at Rheinhardt who returned a sly, knowing smile. It was particularly expressive, so much so, he might have said aloud, *I told you so.*

The young doctor continued his interview. "What were you and Herr Bok doing in the abandoned piano factory?"

"We had to go somewhere," Globocnik answered.

"Did you lure him there? Did you get him to accompany you under false pretenses?"

"Lure? No . . . I didn't lure him there."

"You were carrying a gun?"

"Yes. I was carrying a gun."

"Then you planned to shoot Herr Bok. That was your intention?"

"I wanted him dead, certainly."

"What kind of gun do you have?"

"A pistol."

"Manufactured by?"

Globocnik's brow furrowed. "Borchardt?" Then he added with more confidence, "Yes, Borchardt."

"And where did you get it from?"

"Does that matter, Herr Doctor? How is that relevant?"

Globocnik took off his spectacles and cleaned them with a handkerchief. The handkerchief was torn, and when he put the spectacles on again it was apparent that his efforts hadn't met with success.

Liebermann tried again: "Herr Globocnik? Why did you murder Herr Bok?"

The clerk considered the question as though it had never been put to him before. "He was a bad man. I think he must always have been a bad man. From birth I imagine."

The interview continued, proceeding in a circular manner, and during which Liebermann's questions repeatedly failed to elicit clear answers. The clerk's manner of speech was always vague. Intermittently, his mind wandered and he stared vacantly at a stain on the floor. Liebermann signaled to Rheinhardt that he had heard enough. The inspector straightened his back and said: "Thank you, Herr Globocnik."

Rheinhardt showed Liebermann out of the room, where a constable was standing guard. The two men walked along the corridor to the bottom of a staircase.

"Well," said Rheinhardt, "what do you think?"

Liebermann paused for a moment then declared: "He didn't shoot the man you found in Favoriten. He wasn't even there."

"And why do you say that?"

"You had already noted the oddness of his speech. The way he provides approximate answers to straightforward questions."

"Indeed, that's why I wanted you to see him."

"What we have here is a case of pseudologia fantastica."

"What?"

"Pathological lying: it's a rare condition,

61

and only recently described in the literature. Naturally, I haven't seen many patients who would merit this diagnosis, but I would judge Herr Globocnik to be very severely affected."

"Does he know that he is lying?"

"I suspect that he has very little insight."

"Why would someone confess to a murder they didn't really commit? Does he want to be hanged?"

"There may be an unconscious, suicidal wish—yes. Although, the main reason he is lying is probably in order to feel more powerful or dangerous. Something happened to him, something traumatic, and he has constructed an elaborate fantasy as a kind of defense—a bastion against a reality that he cannot accept because it threatens his sanity."

"You think he's sane?"

"I think he is saner than he would be if his psychological defenses had not been deployed. Have you sought to discover if a man called Bok really exists?"

"No. I wanted to hear your opinion first. But, yes, that is what I intend to do next." Rheinhardt removed a packet of small cigars from his pocket and the two men smoked in silence for a minute or so. Their cloudy exhalations twisted up the stairwell. Rheinhardt ventured one more piece of information: "The bloody thumbprint I found on the factory door doesn't belong to Globocnik . . ."

Liebermann nodded, but he was clearly absorbed by his own thoughts. He tapped his cigar and some ash drifted to the floor. "What are you going to do with him?" Rheinhardt shrugged and Liebermann continued. "I'd be more than happy to admit him to the hospital. Pseudologia fantastica . . . it's a fascinating condition."

ELEVEN

Rheinhardt had been sitting at his desk for over an hour, staring at the wall and toying with a pencil, while considering the meager facts of the Favoriten case. The exercise had not resulted in any fresh insights. Eventually, he shook his head, opened a drawer, and removed a tin of biscuits that his wife, Else, had baked the previous evening. He worked the lid off with his thumbs and studied the contents: shortbread stars of various sizes, some sprinkled with icing sugar, others crusted with a pale, zesty rime. His hand was poised over the tin and he had already begun to salivate when there was a knock on the door.

"Enter."

Haussmann appeared.

"A woman's just arrived, sir. She's come about the reward."

"Well, I suppose you'd better send her in."

Haussmann disappeared and returned with a petite young woman whose décolletage, cheap jewelery, and bright red lips betrayed her profession.

"Fräulein Lurline Król," said Haussmann. Rheinhardt indicated that the woman should sit. "That will be all, Haussmann. Thank you." Haussmann left the office.

Rheinhardt wrote the name down and then studied the woman. Her restless hands suggested unease. She reminded him a little of his eldest daughter, who sometimes put on her mother's hat and stole when pretending to be an adult in a game.

"So, Fräulein Król," Rheinhardt smiled. "You have some information."

"In the newspapers it said you'd pay?"

"Indeed."

"How much?"

"Well, that rather depends on the information. If it's useful then you will be remunerated accordingly."

Fräulein Król looked over her shoulder as if she suspected a trap. There was something about her nervy, feral agitation that reminded Rheinhardt of a fox. "I work as . . . ," she hesitated, unsure of how to proceed.

Rheinhardt spared her unnecessary embarrassment. "You work in Spittelberg?" The area was full of brothels.

"Yes." Fräulein Król looked relieved. "Yes, that's right. There was a man. He used to see me once a week. What you might call a regular. A foreign gentleman."

"Where was he from?"

"Italy—I think."

"You think?"

"We never talked about where he came from,

but he had an accent—and his skin was quite dark."

"What was his name?"

"Tab."

"That doesn't sound very Italian."

"It's what he called himself. And that's what the people around Spittelberg called him." Rheinhardt made some notes and when he looked up again his informant continued. "For two months he'd been coming—every week. Then, all of a sudden, he stopped."

"When was that, exactly?"

"Last week. He had a regular time. He didn't come last Tuesday and he didn't come this Tuesday either. I went and knocked on his door—because he owes me some money—but he wasn't in."

"Where does he live?"

"Just around the corner from me."

Rheinhardt picked up the biscuit tin and held it in front of Fräulein Król. Her face lit up with childlike excitement.

"My wife made them."

Król selected a large star and bit off one of its five points. "She's a good cook."

"An excellent cook." Rheinhardt helped himself to a smaller star and sat back in his chair. "Fräulein Król, you will recall that the man we seek to identify had a distinctive anatomical feature."

"Webbed feet," Król replied. "Yes. Tab had webbed feet. He used to joke about it—said he was half lizard." She pressed the last piece of the biscuit she had been eating into her mouth and stared at the tin. Rheinhardt supposed that she might actually be hungry. "Please, take another if you wish."

"Thank you." Król looked for a second large star and her eyes widened when she found one.

"Forgive me, Fräulein Król, but I must ask you a rather delicate question. Did this man—Tab—have any unusual predilections? Did he ever ask you to—"

Fräulein Król spoke with her mouth full and a few crumbs tumbled onto her bosom. "He liked being beaten."

"What with?"

"A riding crop: he used to bring one with him."

"I see."

The innocent pleasure that this young woman derived from eating biscuits was difficult to reconcile with her professional activities. Rheinhardt felt a strong urge to offer her some fatherly advice, but he said nothing. He had long since learned that the ladies of Spittelberg were immune to any form of moral guidance.

"Well," said Fräulein Król, "have I been helpful?"

"Yes," Rheinhardt replied, "you've been very helpful." He took out his wallet and laid a banknote on the table. It was more than the usual amount paid to informants, but the fact that Fräulein Król reminded him of his daughter had affected his objectivity.

"For me?"

"Yes, for you."

Fräulein Król pawed the note off the table and her hand disappeared among the folds of her dress.

"Do you think it's *him* then—the man you found?"

"Perhaps."

"Do I have to visit the morgue?"

"No, that won't be necessary. But I'd be grateful if you would provide me with Herr Tab's address." When Rheinhardt had finished writing he said, "Would you like some more biscuits—for later, perhaps?"

Fräulein Król nodded. "Yes . . . please."

TWELVE

Professor Waldemar Seeliger and Frau Professor Seeliger were enjoying a short break in a spa town that had been recommended by the dean of the university. They had left their daughters in the care of Frau Professor Seeliger's sister. Although Danuta and Gabriela were very loveable, they were also very demanding.

Frau Seeliger had retired early and the professor, in a somewhat agitated state, informed his wife that he was going for a walk. His wife, who was sitting up in bed, surrounded by large pillows, replied, "Very well, but take care when you return. I don't want to be woken up."

"Of course, my dear," said the obliging professor. He put on his frock coat and made his way down to the hotel foyer where he paused to light a cigar before stepping outside. From the porch of the hotel he could look up and down the length of a pleasant valley; the town tumbled away beneath his feet, illuminated by strings of decorative light bulbs and a gloriously refulgent full moon. He set off and walked along a road that resembled a seaside esplanade. He was at liberty to enjoy the view to his right, but occasionally, he would turn his head to the left to look at the white stucco villas, fountains, and bandstands. Some of the shops—particularly the coffeehouses—were still open. Through the windows he observed well-heeled ladies and gentlemen eating assorted pastries and chocolate cake.

Another gentleman, a rather grand fellow wearing a homburg and fur-collared coat, was coming toward Professor Seeliger. They said "good evening" to each other and raised their hats a fraction. As he proceeded, Seeliger encountered other similarly overdressed individuals. They were mostly from the sanatoria—although none of them looked particularly ill. Legitimate convalescence was being replaced by a form of hypochondriacal tourism. His wife was no different, really. She loved coming to spa towns and usually drank large quantities of foul-tasting water which she swore "calmed her nerves." She also made every effort to make the acquiantances of any dowager from Vienna who might prove useful on their return. The ink in her address book was rarely dry.

This time, Professor Seeliger had needed to get away from Vienna too. Life was getting far too complicated.

What did they say? There was a phrase that people often used to describe the problem of modern living: *hurry and haste*—that was it. Hurry and haste. There was already too much speedy travel in trains and carriages, and some people were predicting an increasing number of motorcars. So much noise, so much pollution—and things were getting worse. Paradoxically, the desire for more speed was causing everything to slow down. Sometimes the roads in Vienna were so full of carriages and trams that traffic came to a standstill. A gentleman might be delayed in a side street for some considerable period of time when he was on his way to an important appointment. That *couldn't* be good for the heart. Professor Seeliger recognized that he was much like everybody else. He was in a hurry too. Indeed, spurred on by his wife, his hurry and haste might have become reckless in recent months.

The attraction of spa towns was that they were supposed to be the opposite of the city. They represented purity and a return to nature. But as Professor Seeliger walked along the carefully constructed walkway, he saw nothing but artifice. He had hoped that the waters might help him too. But his nerves were just as bad and the mountebanks who masqueraded as doctors were unable to give him any helpful advice. His indigestion had been particularly troublesome and sleep was becoming ever more elusive.

Eventually, Professor Seeliger arrived at the Grande Hotel, where the porter recognized him. "Better luck this evening, sir."

"I hope so," Seeliger replied. He descended the stairs to the basement where he stationed himself close to the roulette wheel. The air was perfumed and smoky and the table was surrounded by languid and vaguely reptilian men and women.

Professor Seeliger was not a casual observer. This much was obvious from his tense posture and the sudden expressive movement of his eyes. He watched, remembered outcomes, and calculated probabilities.

Ah, he almost cried aloud. *Now I see it. Now I understand where I went wrong last night.*

He performed more calculations and managed to convince himself that he had the answer. Everything would be fine after all. He prepared to place his first bet. . . .

Professor Seeliger spent over an hour at the roulette table, and when he left the Grande Hotel he did so a much poorer man. He'd have to find a bank tomorrow.

"How did it go, sir?" asked the porter.

"It could have gone better."

"Well, everyone says that."

"No—it really could have gone better."

"Maybe tomorrow, sir? Maybe tomorrow will be your lucky night."

"I'm going home tomorrow."

"Vienna?"

"Yes. Vienna."

"Beautiful city—I've only been once. Yes, the tables can be disappointing, but it can't be that bad? Eh, sir?"

"Actually—" Seeliger stopped himself from saying any more. What on earth was he doing talking to this idiot? The porter was only being sociable because he wanted a tip—and Seeliger didn't have a single heller in his pocket. The professor made a dismissive gesture and said brusquely, "Goodnight."

"Oh." The porter sounded a little surprised. "Good night, sir. See you again soon."

"I very much doubt that," said Seeliger as he walked away.

Seeliger retraced his steps along the promenade but stopped when he reached a bandstand. He climbed the steps and stood beneath the canopy, looking across the valley at the beautiful fir-covered incline, silvered by moonlit snow. He took a few more steps and grabbed the railing in order to steady himself. He felt quite faint.

THIRTEEN

Rheinhardt and Haussmann were proceeding down a wide, cobbled street, their strides coinciding to produce an insistent, regular beat. A young man wearing a hat with a low brim—hands in his pockets—was loitering in a doorway and looking distinctly untrustworthy. He turned his back to them as they passed. The facades of the houses on either side were pocked where circles of plaster had fallen away and the air smelled of sewage. Ahead, an ordinary whitewashed building had been aggrandized by a turret surmounted by an onion-shaped dome—it introduced a hint of exoticism into an otherwise bleak purview. Turning onto a narrow side street the two men arrived outside a small eighteenth-century house that was streaked with grime. Above the lintel a weatherworn relief of a female figure, possibly a saint, was surrounded by a wreath of flowers. Rheinhardt struck the door with his fist. When no one answered he produced a bunch of skeleton keys and by a process of trial and error eventually found one that engaged the bolt.

The two men entered. On the ground floor they found a single room. There were no rugs covering the floorboards and the wallpaper was peeling in several places; a scratched table and two rustic chairs were positioned by the window. Muted light filtered through net curtains and fell on a moldy half-loaf of bread and cheese.

"How long do you think they've been there?" Haussmann asked.

"Long enough," Rheinhardt replied. "Let's take a look upstairs."

As soon as they entered the bedroom the inspector and his assistant wrinkled their noses. A chamber pot—which could be seen under the bed—was full of stale urine and the smell it produced was sharp and caustic. Some clothes had been draped over a rack and an oil lamp hung from a hook that had been screwed into the ceiling. Leaning up against the wall, behind the stove, was a short riding crop.

Rheinhardt lifted a pair of trousers off the rack and started to search the pockets. After removing a grubby handkerchief, he found a folded menu from a beer cellar called The Golden Bears. A list of mostly Czech beverages was followed by descriptions of three simple dishes: liver dumplings, pork with red cabbage, sausages and sauerkraut. Only one meal was available on particular days of the week—and no food was available on Mondays.

"The Golden Bears," said Rheinhardt, raising the menu. "Do you know it?"

"No," said Haussmann. On the back of the

menu someone had written a name and address: Clement, Tempelgasse 14—Leopoldstadt. "This is interesting . . ."

Rheinhardt looked across the room toward his assistant, who was kneeling by the bed. "What's interesting?"

Haussmann raised his hand, showing his superior a roll of banknotes. "A lot of money . . ."

"Yes," Rheinhardt agreed, "especially for someone with only two pairs of trousers."

FOURTEEN

Razumovsky had supplied the maid who worked at the Palais Khevenhüller with a rather feeble pretext for wanting to know the pianist's name; however, the poor girl wasn't very intelligent and she was far too deferential to question the motives of a gentleman. When he paid her for her trouble she was overwhelmed with gratitude—he suspected that after his departure she might even have shed a few tears.

Twenty-four hours later, Razumovsky knew everything he needed to know about Frimunt Curtius and it was all extraordinarily auspicious. Razumovsky didn't believe in fate, but if there was such a thing then the presiding Personifications had apparently decided to work decisively in his favor. Curtius was perfect. A talented interpreter of Galant keyboard works, but one who had never been championed by an influential critic; an unattractive man—quite portly—with a double chin, receding hair, and a swollen, varicose nose; a bitter man, acutely conscious of the fact that his musical accomplishments had never been formally recognized. He still performed regularly, even so, his recitals were poorly attended and his main source of income was teaching. Every day, he was obliged to spend several hours seated beside the languid, perfumed daughters of court officials, listening to poorly executed scales and arpeggios. The invitation to play at the Palais Khevenhüller had been issued by the father of one of these fragrant, juvenile graces. Curtius was also a lonely man, an aging bachelor who—because of awkwardness in the company of women—had become a habitué of a shabby-genteel brothel close to the Nordbahnhof.

Razumovsky had been waiting outside this brothel for just over three hours and it was past two o'clock in the morning when Curtius finally emerged. The pianist had been drinking heavily and was unsteady on his feet.

"Is it you?" said Razumovsky, pointing his cane and stepping forward. "Yes, it is you. Good evening, Herr Curtius."

The pianist moved his head backward and forward because his eyes alone were unable to establish a satisfactory focal length.

"Who are you?" Curtius squinted.

"An admirer," Razumovsky replied. "I simply adore your C.P.E. Bach. Your sonatas are the gold standard, the pinnacle—such elegance, such lightness, such delicacy."

Curtius straightened his back. "Are you a critic?"

"No," Razumovsky shook his head. "Philistines—every one of them—what do they know, eh?"

"Not very much," Curtius agreed.

"Are you walking this way—toward the canal?"

"Yes, as a matter of fact I am."

"Please, permit me to accompany you."

The two men strolled down the street and Razumovsky was delighted to discover how easy it was to engage and manipulate his companion. Curtius was soon railing against the Viennese musical establishment and enumerating petty slights and discourtesies on his fingers. Spittle flew from his mouth as he articulated splenetic insults.

As they crossed the Franzensbrücke, Razumovsky began to slow his pace, and when he reached the middle of the bridge he stopped and leaned over the railing. Curtius—as if under the control of some strange, sympathetic power—did exactly the same. They contemplated the shimmering, reflected disc of the moon, which broke up and reassembled when a breeze momentarily agitated the surface of the black water. On either side of the canal, the buildings were high, with large sloping roofs. The sound of a night cargo train rattled into silence.

"You know," said Razumovsky, "your life . . . it doesn't have to be this way."

"What?" Curtius asked.

"You could make a new start—among like-minded people who would welcome you into their society. Like a brother."

"I'm not sure I understand what you're suggesting."

"Introductions could be made—very easily, in fact. You would soon become acquainted with a wide circle of charming women—cultured, intelligent—with modern attitudes; women who do not share the Viennese obsession with superficial appearances, who value inner beauty, nobility, and truth. Berne. That's the place for a man like you."

"Are you Swiss?"

Razumovsky laughed. "No, I'm not Swiss."

Curtius turned to look at his companion properly for the first time and registered his diabolical aspect: the intensity of his gaze, the sharp, groomed point of his beard. A sudden chill reminded Curtius of his childhood and Živka, his old nanny, who came from Visěgrad and who used to tell him stories, one of which was about a man who had met the devil on a bridge and wagered his soul during a game of cards.

"Are you about to make me some sort of proposal?" asked Curtius.

Razumovsky's head rotated slowly and he smiled. "What a perceptive fellow you are."

FIFTEEN

Rheinhardt handed Clement Kruckel the menu he had found in the murdered man's bedroom. Herr Kruckel—an elderly journalist—turned the card over and grunted his assent. "This is my handwriting. I wrote my name and address down for a gentleman called Tab—an Italian. I'd just met him."

Kruckel was in his late sixties. His forehead was abnormally high and there was something peculiarly distinct about the lines and planes of his face that created an effect similar to lithographic portraiture.

"Do you know his full name?"

"Yes. Angelo. Angelo Callari, but he preferred to be called Tab." Kruckel passed the menu back to Rheinhardt. "He's been in Vienna for about a month or so, I believe."

The tabletop between the two men was covered with books, pens, and sheets of paper. Kruckel was sitting behind the keyboard of a large Adler typewriter, the shiny black casing of which was gilded with a symbolic eagle.

"Why did you give him your address?"

"So he could contact me—of course."

"You formed a friendship?"

"He was interested in joining my educational

81

society. We print pamphlets, organize lectures, disseminate information; he came to a discussion group, held here, in this very room—just after Christmas."

"Does your society have a name?"

"Yes. Fraternitas. We encourage friendship between nations and encourage politicians to ensure that better provision is made for the poor. Tab hasn't got into trouble, has he?"

"When was the last time you saw him?"

"A couple of weeks ago, in The Golden Bears."

Rheinhardt made some notes. "What did Signor Callari do for a living?"

"I think he mentioned having been employed as a servant—but that was back in Italy."

"Did he intend to stay in Vienna?"

"I have no idea."

"Was he looking for work?"

"I don't know. Look, what did he do? If he's in trouble then I'd like to help him—if I can."

A moment of silence preceded Rheinhardt's response: "On Monday the eleventh of January, the body of a man was discovered in the abandoned Gallus and Sons piano factory in Favoriten."

"Yes," said the journalist, nodding. "I read about it in the newspapers."

"I think there's a very good chance that the dead man was Signor Callari."

Kruckel's fingers spread over the typewriter

keys. He tapped one of them a few times and said, "I see . . . you want me to identify the body?"

Rheinhardt shook his head. "The man's face was badly disfigured with acid." Kruckel nodded—very slowly—and appeared to sink into a state of thoughtful self-absorption. "Did Signor Callari ever give you any reason to suspect that he might be evading enemies?"

"No."

"He was never nervous, jittery—prone to looking over his shoulder?"

"Quite the contrary, he was always very composed and collected."

"We found a large sum of money under his mattress."

For the first time the journalist looked surprised. "Do you think he stole it?"

"Possibly."

Rheinhardt continued asking Kruckel questions; however, the old journalist's answers weren't very illuminating. Eventually, Kruckel started showing small signs of impatience and irritation. Rheinhardt made a final entry in his notebook and rose to leave. At that point, instead of voicing the usual perfunctory courtesies, Kruckel rifled through the clutter on the tabletop—lifting books and pushing papers aside—until he found a pamphlet which he handed to Rheinhardt.

A crude illustration showed a laborer with rolled up shirtsleeves climbing toward a beacon on a hill. Below this there was a caption: "Nothing to lose—everything to gain—Fraternitas."

"Read it," said Kruckel. "We haven't admitted any policemen into our circle. Well, not yet, anyway. You might see some merit in our cause." Rheinhardt felt a little awkward. He was familiar with the fanaticism of pamphleteers and supposed that he wouldn't have much in common with the members of Fraternitas. Instinctively, he wanted to hand the pamphlet back to Kruckel but resisted the urge—not wishing to offend the old man. "How much do *they* pay you?" Kruckel continued. "I daresay it's nowhere near enough—not when one considers what's expected of a man like you. How many times have you risked your life in the line of duty, eh? Quite a few, I imagine."

Rheinhardt slipped the pamphlet into the inside pocket of his coat. "Thank you."

Kruckel stood up. "Who benefits most from law and order? Your family, your friends? Or *them?*" The old journalist's eyes were suddenly bright with iconoclastic fire. "Comfortable and secure in their palaces—the people on top, the people who have *always* been on top."

Rheinhardt sighed. "You know, Herr Kruckel, that sort of talk could very easily get you into trouble."

SIXTEEN

As Vala Feist walked through the long dark tunnel, she reflected on some of the academic performance grades she had entered in the little red class book. She had written "insufficient" beside at least ten names. Had she been too strict? A mental picture formed in her mind: gas jets flickering, children, sitting on benches, looking up at her, expectant, some even fearful. She demanded a great deal from her pupils, not because she was a martinet, but rather, because she feared that they would miss an opportunity for betterment. The acquisition of good reading and writing skills—combined with a sound grasp of basic mathematical principles—was probably the only means by which any of them would be able to escape lifelong poverty.

A man without shoes was sitting with his back against the wall. He opened his eyes and stared at her. Even in his drunken state, he was sufficiently aware to appreciate the peculiarity of what he was seeing: a somewhat prim, spinsterish woman wearing a high-necked blouse and a bonnet decorated with artificial flowers, holding a paraffin lamp high above her head. In her other hand she clutched the straps of a bulging hemp shopping bag.

"Good evening," Vala said as she passed.

The man was too shocked to reply.

Vala reached the end of the tunnel and turned onto a gravel path that followed the course of one of the broader sewage channels. It was wide enough to accommodate a canal boat. The stench didn't bother her. She had been exploring the sewers beneath Vienna for many years and had become quite inured to the smell. Some of the waterways were said to date back to Roman times.

She had witnessed many strange things on her forays into this vast, benighted labyrinth: a caravan of men and women splashing across an underground stream, each carrying a paper lantern; a small, dying alligator—its jaws snapping feebly in a culvert; a blind hurdy-gurdy player being led on a leash by a gypsy dwarf. On St. Erminold's feast day she had encountered two well-dressed gentlemen, a journalist, Herr Kläger, and a photographer, Herr Draw, on a balcony above a cataract of reeking effluent. These explorers were accompanied by a shifty individual—armed with brass knuckles—who they had employed as a guide. Their intention, so they said, was to document the wretched lives of the thousands of unfortunates who colonized the sewers every winter. Herr Kläger had offered to escort Vala back to the surface and she had had enormous trouble getting him to accept that she didn't require his or his henchman's assistance.

Turning right again, Vala entered a vaulted passage. The walls were damp and puddles had collected on the ground. She arrived at a rusty iron door which she struck with a balled fist. When it creaked open she stepped into a crowded, smoky chamber in which fifteen or so people huddled around a makeshift brazier. They were like a tribe of troglodytes and greeted her in an unintelligible Slav dialect that suggested some remote, rural provenance—possibly Carpathian Ruthenia. All of the women were wearing head scarfs and baggy brown coats. One of them was surrounded by a circle of small children and had a baby attached to an exposed breast.

A man resembling a shepherd in an operetta stood up and approached Vala. He only spoke a few words of German: "Lady—good lady— thank you, thank you." She handed the man her bag and he distributed the contents: pickled fish, black bread, and some vanillekipferl biscuits. The starving men and women ate like animals, fast and furtive, as if their ration might be snatched away by a stealthy scavenger. Vala was invited to sit on an overturned crate and the "shepherd" produced a bottle. He dribbled a small amount of brown liquid into a cracked cup. Vala didn't want to injure the man's pride so she accepted his hospitality and took a sip. It was a strong, herbal liquor, not unpleasant, but sufficiently alien to confuse the palate. The aftertaste was peppery and hot. An old woman began to sing in a low, coarse voice. It was an exotic melody that occasionally incorporated the augmented interval of a harmonic scale. Was it a lament or a lullaby for the children? The old woman's hard, fixed expression gave no indication.

When the song was finished, Vala recovered her bag and mimed her readiness to leave. The "shepherd" opened the door for her, bowed his head, and repeated, "Good lady—thank you—thank you." When he looked up the lower rims of his eyes had become glimmering crescents: tears of gratitude were imminent.

"I'll come again. Tomorrow, if I can." She said this knowing that he wouldn't understand.

Some of the others raised their arms and uttered what must have been good wishes in their mother tongue. The old woman sketched a benediction in the air.

Vala hurried back along the tunnel. Behind her, the squealing of hinges preceded a sonorous clang.

She reached the broad sewage channel. Her footsteps produced an echo, but after a minute or so, the regularity of the double beat was complicated by a cross rhythm. Vala stopped abruptly and heard the unmistakable crunch of gravel beneath the sole of a shoe—an echo—

then nothing but water droplets landing in a puddle. Someone was following her. She turned and called out: "Who's there?" The acoustic properties of the vault encouraged several iterations of the question.

A man stepped out of the darkness and into the pool of light. He looked like a down-at-heel impresario: long coat, broad-brimmed hat, and baggy, ripped trousers. Vala couldn't see his face very clearly, but his nose was abnormally large, so much so, that she was reminded of Pulcinella.

"Can I help you?" Vala asked.

He sniffed—as if he were trying to detect her scent.

"Do you need light?" Vala tried again. "I can give you a candle if you wish?"

He came forward quickly, arms outstretched, fingers spread. Vala lowered her paraffin lamp and lifted her chin so as to make it easier for him to grab her neck, which he did. She wanted to keep his hands occupied and she was confident that the metal ribs she had sewn into her high collar would prevent him, at least initially, from crushing her windpipe. She felt some constriction, but not enough to induce panic. The man's breath was foul and his eyes were burning with deviant pleasure. Vala reached into her skirt pocket, removed a small pistol, and pressed the barrel against her attacker's chest. She saw him register the sensation and made sure that her smile was broad when she pulled the trigger. A loud report was reproduced several times, becoming less distinct with each repetition. The man's fingers weakened and his legs gave way. His sudden collapse was almost comic, like an ill-judged theatrical stunt.

Vala put the pistol back in her pocket and hung the lamp on a conveniently placed metal hook. She rolled the body to the edge of the water and then found some loose bricks which she stuffed down the man's trousers. Finally, she rolled him into the stagnant canal. The dead man sank quickly and after his disappearance, air bubbles disturbed the slick, oily surface. A large rat swam by, changing direction to avoid the suction from below.

PART TWO

The Course of History

SEVENTEEN

Liebermann was standing in the doorway of his bedroom gazing at Amelia Lydgate. Her hair was bright and fiery against the whiteness of the pillow. She was positioned on her side and her exposed back was faintly luminous, reflecting light like an alabaster nude in a museum. Although Amelia was perfectly still, Liebermann could hear her breathing, which made him think of surf on sand, the mesmeric regularity of the sea. A carriage rattled along the cobbled street and Amelia began to stir; however, the noise wasn't loud enough to wake her. Liebermann derived an inordinate amount of pleasure from observing Amelia asleep. He enjoyed the stillness and the intimacy.

But was it right, what he was doing?

Of course, marriage was a ludicrous institution and completely redundant in the modern world. The idea that sexual relations should be postponed until the completion of a religious ceremony was absurd in the extreme. Even so, it was considerably easier for a man to adopt a modern outlook than a woman, because there were no costs for men. Women, on the other hand, paid dearly. If—for whatever reason—their relationship ended and they separated, Amelia would have immense difficulty finding another suitor. She would be judged harshly for her "libertinage." It was abhorrent, but this was the social reality.

They had discussed the matter again and again, but Amelia had always been adamant. "If our goal is to create a truly civilized society, then there must be absolute equality between the sexes. The human animal is a biological organism. It isn't shameful to eat or sleep, and likewise, neither is it shameful to satisfy the erotic instinct. We must be rational. We have a duty to live in a way that is consistent with our values." It was peculiar how comfortable Amelia was with the dismissal of bourgeois prohibitions. She was less confused, less troubled by outmoded moral strictures, whereas Liebermann's thinking was still being affected by gentlemanly scruples, the result of which was a pervasive sense of guilt. And his parents would be horrified . . .

Amelia changed position and the gentle rhythm of her breathing faded to silence. Her eyes opened and she sat up. A crease appeared in the middle of her forehead and she said, "Why on earth do people still take Hegel seriously?"

"I beg your pardon?" Liebermann asked.

"He lacks clarity."

"Do you really wake up thinking about philosophy?"

"Yes," Amelia replied. "Often . . ."

Liebermann began to laugh but the vertical crease that divided Amelia's forehead simply deepened.

EIGHTEEN

Herr Bok's factory was in Favoriten and not far from Gallus and Sons. As Rheinhardt approached the entrance, he saw a large, red-faced man waiting outside. He was wearing a suit and sported a shaggy walrus moustache that drooped over his mouth. When the man saw Rheinhardt approaching, he threw his cigar aside and stepped forward. "Inspector Rheinhardt?" It was impossible to see his lips moving when he spoke.

"Indeed," Rheinhardt responded. "Herr Bok?"

The man nodded and bowed. "Good morning, inspector."

Rheinhardt followed Bok into the building and through a large, open space where twenty or more women were at work. The clatter of sewing machines was occasionally drowned out by a loud hissing noise which predicted the appearance of a cloud of steam.

"What do you make, Herr Bok?"

"Quality shirts for sale at competitive prices. We supply a large number of gentlemen's outfitters in Vienna but we also have a thriving export business—all of the major cities of the empire—as well as London and Paris." Bok bounced a finger in the air. "Each of these women has one small job to do—which makes the process of manufacture fast and efficient. We can finish making a shirt every two minutes this way. The collars are made separately—just over there." At the end of the production line Bok picked up a shirt and held it up for the inspector's approval.

"Very good," said Rheinhardt. He was not a connoisseur and judged it unwise to be more specific.

They entered an office in which two desks were positioned to form an L shape. Behind the smaller desk, a young woman was turning the crank handle of a bulky Brunsviga calculating machine.

"This is Fräulein Mugoša," said Bok. The young woman stood and Bok addressed her less formally. "Milica, please make Inspector Rheinhardt a cup of tea." She made a note in her ledger and then left the room, her shoes clicking on the floorboards like a metronome. "Please sit, inspector." The two men lowered themselves into chairs and Bok slid his hands together over his substantial stomach. "So," he continued, "you want to talk to me about Globocnik? Where is he?"

"In the General Hospital."

"That doesn't surprise me in the least."

"When was the last time you saw him?"

"Just over a week ago: he had some sort of fit and then ran off. I haven't seen him since."

"Fit? What kind of fit?"

"He became horribly agitated." Bok pointed to the smaller desk. "That's where he used to sit. He was working quietly when all of a sudden he got up and started ranting and raving. He picked up the letter opener—threatened to stab me—and called me all sorts of names. Some of his language was extremely intemperate."

"Why would he do a thing like that?"

"I have no idea. It was completely out of character. As I said: a fit."

"What did you do?"

"I ordered him to leave."

"And he complied?"

"Yes, although it took a while."

Fräulein Mugoša returned with a tray. As she prepared the tea Rheinhardt noticed that she was rather well-dressed for a secretary. Moreover, the ring on her finger appeared to be a large garnet.

"Was anyone else present?" Rheinhardt asked.

"Yes, Fräulein Mugoša." Bok shifted to face his secretary. "Milica, tell the inspector what happened last week—tell him about Herr Globocnik."

"He went mad," said Fräulein Mugoša. Her German was accented. "Shouting—swearing—waving the letter opener."

Rheinhardt scooped four sugars into his tea. "Were you frightened?"

"Yes," the secretary replied. "It was like he was

possessed by the devil." She made the sign of the cross.

"How long had he worked here?"

"Just over a year," Bok replied. "He could be a little irritating at times and he sniffed a lot—he always seemed to have a cold—but he was very reliable and hard-working."

Fräulein Mugoša was about to add something else but Bok frowned at her and she retreated.

"Do any of his relatives live in Vienna?"

"He didn't mention any."

"What about friends?"

"It was my impression that he was something of a loner. He kept himself to himself."

"Do you know if anything happened to him recently that might explain his sudden loss of reason? Bad news—a shock of some kind?"

Bok shook his head. "Do drink your tea, inspector, or it'll get cold."

NINETEEN

The Golden Bears was thick with smoke. Every oil lamp was surrounded by a trembling aureole and separated from its neighbor by a belt of shadow. Most of the patrons were inebriated and the floor was awash with spilt beer. Two occultists were arguing loudly about the classification of demons in an arcane work called the *Liber Octo Quaestionum*; an artist in a paint-spattered kaftan was giving an incoherent, slurred lecture on symbolism; and a gaggle of women—dressed in men's clothes—were burning a copy of Krafft-Ebing's *Psychopathia Sexualis* in the stove.

Razumovsky was seated at his usual table, listening and observing. The object of his interest was Della Autenburg, who was, as usual, flirting outrageously with a group of male students. One of her admirers, a lean young man with a dueling scar, was showing signs of possessiveness. He frequently shifted position in order to interpose himself between Della and his competitors and, at one point, Razumovsky saw him remove an insolent hand from Della's buttocks. Della laughed, quaffed one stein after another, and seemed completely oblivious of the small dramas that were developing around her—the vying for attention, the hostile glaring, the pushing and shoving. Razumovsky, however, wasn't fooled. Everything she did was clearly calculated to excite desire.

The young men had started to brag in order to impress her. There was much swaggering and showing off. At first, they boasted about minor, inconsequential acts of sedition—small provocations and protests. Then, one-upmanship emboldened them, and their braggadocio escalated. They spoke over each other, disclosing their plots and plans—sabotage, arson, blackmail. As the bluster and rodomontade continued, the stakes were getting higher and higher.

"You're all lily-livered cowards!" the young man with the dueling scar cried, waving his stein above his head and showering the company with beer. "Cowards! The lot of you."

"Axl," Della whined while retaining a mischievous smile. "You mustn't be rude to your friends."

"Yes, Diamant, calm down," said a youth with a goatee beard. "Why do you always have to be so uncivil?"

Diamant ignored their counsel. "Talk, talk, talk!" He simulated a chattering mouth with his free hand. "That's all you lot do. But it's time for direct action now."

Della straightened her back and the sudden trespass of her cleavage into Diamant's line of vision made him stop and blink before he was able to continue. "I'm going to change everything. One morning, you'll all wake up and discover that you are living in a different world."

A student wearing pince-nez sneered. "What *are* you talking about?"

"From the Tyrol to Silesia, Galicia to Dalmatia . . . you'll see. No more tinkering at the edges, no more empty gestures; someone has to be prepared to do what has to be done, someone has to be man enough." Diamant beat his own chest with a clenched fist like an ape in the zoo.

"And what would that be?" asked the student with the goatee.

"The old fool," roared Diamant. "We've got to get rid of him—and it would be so easy— he's such a creature of habit. Every morning he goes to have breakfast with that ghastly actress. The coachman waits just around the corner from Gloriettegasse. People often gather there— hoping to catch a glimpse of him."

Razumovsky leaned closer. Was this young hothead talking about the emperor?

"Don't be ridiculous," scoffed the student wearing the pince-nez.

Diamant responded angrily. "Lucheni managed it!"

"And he's rotting away in prison."

"Why wasn't he hanged?" someone inquired in a higher register.

"He was tried in the Canton of Geneva," the student with the goatee replied. "They've abolished the death penalty there."

One of the occultists raised his voice: "The Jagiellonian Princess Zymburgis is reputed to have been so strong she could straighten horseshoes with her bare hands. How could this be? I suspect that this was achieved with supernatural assistance . . ."

Razumovsky wanted to silence the occultist with his cane, but resisted the urge. Instead, he was obliged to wait patiently for the man to complete a lengthy account of the defeat of the Teutonic knights by the Polish and Lithuanian armies at the battle of Tannenberg.

"It would never work," said the student with the goatee.

"You'll see," Diamant responded. "I've thought it through. It's possible, believe me."

Della pressed up against Diamant and allowed him to wrap his arm around her waist. He drew her closer and she kissed his dueling scar. "You wouldn't, would you? You wouldn't dare!"

The others laughed. The student wearing pince-nez called out to the landlord's wife. "Kamilla—over here—two more jugs of the usual."

Razumovsky sipped his cognac and waited for the burn. Skalicky and his wife only stocked cheap bottles. The burn came.

If this imbecile made an attempt on the emperor's life then it could ruin everything. The intelligence agencies would be alerted and there would be increased security everywhere. Razumovsky put his glass down on the table and hummed. The low note could be felt but not heard.

It might prove necessary to do something about Axl Diamant.

TWENTY

The lord marshal—whose office was responsible for the house of Habsburg's legal business—had met Georg Weeber many times over the years, and it was only right that the Palace should acknowledge the judge's retirement from public service. Be that as it may, the function at the Palais Khevenhüller was not high on the lord marshal's list of priorities and he hoped that his meeting with Kuhlbert von Behring would be relatively brief. Von Behring was a colleague of Weeber and one of the principal organizers of the Palais Khevenhüller event.

"We have engaged a choir," said von Behring.

The lord marshal's pen hovered over his notebook. "Which one?"

"The St. Valentin's parish choir for indigent children. It's one of Georg Weeber's charities." Von Behring waited for the lord marshal to stop writing before he continued. "Father Johann, the choirmaster, will make the necessary arrangements, and needless to say, he will be conducting the boys. We thought they might sing while dinner is being served."

"An excellent idea." The lord marshal's nib scratched on the paper. He raised his head and asked: "Who will choose the programme?"

"Father Johann."

The lord marshal sat back in his chair. He was in his late fifties but age hadn't softened his features—quite the reverse, in fact. His expression was often described as "hawkish." His beard was closely trimmed and his stiff moustache projected horizontally. He stared at von Behring for such a long time without speaking that the judge became uncomfortable, and said, "Lord marshal?"

"I am sure," said the lord marshal, "that Father Johann will do his utmost, and that he will select pieces appropriate to the musical ability of the children; however, as you know, His Majesty has expressed a desire for the Palace to be represented at this celebration, in which case . . ." The sentence remained incomplete.

"Lord marshal?"

"Might I make a suggestion?"

"By all means, lord marshal."

"Perhaps Father Johann could be urged to rehearse a few pieces that reflect the empire as a whole and the diversity of its people? Something Hungarian or Czech? A Galician folk song?"

"Why, of course."

The lord marshal noticed that one of his many medals was slightly skewed. He paused for a moment to untangle a ribbon and then made another note. While he was still writing he said, "The pianist . . ."

"Yes. Herr Curtius."

"I haven't heard of him." The lord marshall sat back in his chair again.

"Actually," von Behring continued, "he was recommended by someone in your office."

"Oh. Who might that be?"

"Brinkerhoff. Curtius teaches his daughter." A further uncomfortable pause ensued. Von Behring cleared his throat and added, "Curtius is Vienna's finest exponent of Galant keyboard works."

"Forgive me. Is that . . . relevant?"

"Judge Weeber is a great lover of the Galant style. C.P.E Bach and so forth."

"Another suggestion if I may?"

"By all means, lord marshal."

"Perhaps Herr Curtius should be invited to consider performing one or two *accessible* pieces."

"Accessible?"

"Popular."

The lord marshal interpreted von Behring's momentary hesitation as resistance and frowned. Von Behring knew better than to challenge the lord marshal. "What, specifically, did you have in mind?"

"My dear fellow," said the lord marshal disingenuously. "I wouldn't dream of interfering. It's up to you. That said, you really don't want to see any bored expressions." The lord marshal tapped the side of his nose.

"Do we have any indication, as yet, as to who will be representing the Palace?"

"The matter is in hand. You will forgive me if I am not more forthcoming."

"As you see fit, lord marshal."

The discussion continued for another ten minutes, during which the lord marshal offered further "advice" on the seating plan and the menu. Then, rising from his chair he bowed and said simply, "Your honor."

Von Behring understood that his audience had come to an end. "I am most grateful for your guidance, sir." He stood, returned the lord marshal's bow, turned, and walked toward the gilded double doors, both of which miraculously opened before his arrival. A palace official was standing next to a Louis XIV sofa on the landing. "This way, please," he said, directing von Behring toward a staircase with a sweeping gesture. Von Behring was glad to be on his way.

TWENTY-ONE

Herr Globocnik was lying on a gurney in one of the examination rooms of the General Hospital. His eyes were closed and his hands were crossed over his chest. A small, high window admitted a pastel light that made everything appear soft-hued. At the head of the gurney sat Liebermann, observing his supine patient closely.

"You say that you killed Herr Bok in the Gallus and Sons piano factory . . ."

"I did."

"The body has now been identified. The dead man was actually an Italian. His name was Angelo Callari."

"You have been misinformed, Herr Doctor."

"I have spoken to Inspector Rheinhardt on the telephone. He was categorical."

Globocnik's head rolled from side to side on the pillow. "No, Herr Doctor. Inspector Rheinhardt has made a terrible mistake." Liebermann remained silent. A marching band and horses' hooves could be heard in the distance. Globocnik sniffed and added, "There is another possibility—a simple explanation for the inspector's confidence. Herr Bok's body might have been removed and replaced by Signor Callari's."

"Why would anybody want to do that?"

"I have no idea. But stranger things have happened in this world and there are some very odd people living in Vienna."

Liebermann crossed his legs, rested his elbow on the chair arm, and lowered his chin onto the palm of his hand. The marching band passed. "Herr Bok is still alive. Inspector Rheinhardt has spoken to him."

The silence deepened until it became a paradoxical roar.

"Why are you doing this, Herr Doctor?" Globocnik asked. "Your purpose is beyond my understanding. Are we engaged in some sort of psychological game? Are you trying to trick me? I have confessed to a serious crime—the most serious of all crimes—and I accept that I must be punished. Please return me to my police cell and allow the legal process to run its course. I am not frightened of dying."

"Herr Bok is alive," asserted Liebermann with flat certainty.

"No, Bok is dead." After a pause of several seconds Globocnik added, "He is dead . . . to me."

The qualification made Liebermann sit up. Was this the first chink in Globocnik's defensive armor—indicative of residual insight—evidence of a surviving connection (albeit attenuated) with reality? "He's dead to you . . . ," Liebermann repeated softly, offering the qualification back to Globocnik, hoping that it would encourage him to open up a little more. But Globocnik simply bit his lower lip and sniffed. "What do you do for a living?" asked Liebermann.

"I am . . . I am . . ."

Liebermann was concerned that Globocnik's hesitancy was meaningful, that his febrile brain was about to supply another fantastical answer, so the young doctor quickly interjected. "You work in an office."

"Yes, that's right." Globocnik spoke grudgingly.

"As a clerk?"

"No business can succeed without good bookkeeping."

"Indeed." Liebermann responded. "And you are an excellent bookkeeper. You were employed, I believe, by Herr Bok, who owns a shirt factory in Favoriten."

"It is true that Herr Bok and I had business interests in common."

Liebermann was amused by Globocnik's grandiosity. "Herr Bok has alleged that you threatened him. Why did you do that?"

"I didn't threaten him, Herr Doctor. I killed him."

"There was a witness. Herr Bok's secretary: Fräulein Mugoša." Globocnik's expression suddenly changed and for a fleeting moment anguish distorted his features. "Do you remember her?"

Liebermann continued, "This woman—Fräulein Mugoša?"

Globocnik took a deep breath: "Bok was a bad man. I think he must always have been a bad man. From birth I imagine. You see, it's a question of morality . . . personal morality."

TWENTY-TWO

Rheinhardt and Liebermann were seated at the back of a coffeehouse near the university. Most of the other patrons were students, many of them reading textbooks or writing essays. It was getting dark outside and the head waiter, a haggard, careworn Hungarian, was lighting the gas lamps. The blue, naked flames shimmered through the cigar and cigarette smoke. Rheinhardt lifted a copper pot and poured himself a Türkische coffee. "Callari met Kruckel at a beer cellar in Leopoldstadt called The Golden Bears. Have you heard of it?"

"Can't say that I have," Liebermann replied. "There's a Renaissance building in Prague called The House of the Two Golden Bears. I walked past it a few years ago. Perhaps there is some connection?"

Rheinhardt shrugged. "Kruckel is a journalist, a political agitator, and the senior representative of a socialist society called Fraternitas. Callari attended a Fraternitas meeting at Kruckel's apartment."

Liebermann raised his cup and took a sip of his schwarzer. "Physical deformity engenders a sense of difference; oddity, exclusion from the mainstream. Callari would have been drawn toward an organization offering fraternity."

"He only arrived in Vienna shortly before Christmas."

"Not enough time to make mortal enemies, surely?"

"Then perhaps he was pursued," Rheinhardt speculated.

"By men who wanted their money returned?"

"I have heard that there are criminal families in southern Italy who adhere to a strict code of honor. Any violation of that code cannot be countenanced, and it is their practice to mete out punishments of the most extreme kind."

Liebermann shook his head. "If Callari were tortured, he would have told his tormentors where he had hidden the money and you would never have found it."

The young doctor looked up at an old print that was hanging on the paneled wall next to their table. It showed a horseman leading an army across a bridge, his sabre raised, galloping furiously toward a horde of turbaned warriors.

"Zrínyi's last charge," said Rheinhardt.

"I beg your pardon?"

"It shows the Hungarian-Croat commander, Zrínyi, attacking the Ottomans at the siege of Szigetvár. All the Hungarians perished, but not without causing Suleiman the Magnificent so much grief that he had a seizure. It killed him I believe."

"Curious."

"What is?"

"I'd never noticed it before."

Rheinhardt was mildly irritated by his friend's preoccupation with the print. "How are you getting on with Globocnik?"

Liebermann picked a cuticle off his finger and dropped it into the ashtray. "I have made some progress, but not as much as I'd hoped for."

"Would you care to explain?"

"As you already know, I believe that Herr Globocnik experienced a trauma that could only be accommodated, psychologically, by the creation of complex delusional defenses. Although he is a man of modest achievement and plain appearance, I suspect that he is both proud and intelligent. Consequently, I am inclined to suppose that the trauma was injurious to his dignity and reputation. His homicidal fantasy serves two purposes: the restoration of self-respect and the promise of eternal release."

"What do you mean 'eternal release'?"

"Murderers are hanged. Globocnik is suicidal. He wants to die."

"Why?"

"There are many reasons why a man might yearn to leave this world." Liebermann smiled and added, "Did you see Fräulein Mugoša when you visited Herr Bok?"

"Yes, I did."

"A young woman?"

"Yes."

"Quite attractive—but not conventionally so?"

"Well, yes . . ."

"Was she, by any chance, wearing an eye-catching item of jewelery?"

"As a matter of fact she was: a garnet ring. The stone was uncommonly large."

"Yes"—Liebermann nodded—"I thought as much." Then looking back at the print he added, "I wonder why I didn't notice this before. It is—after all—quite a striking image."

Rheinhardt's expression darkened. "Max. Will you please stop being obtuse and just tell me what you've discovered!"

TWENTY-THREE

Eduard Autenberg had been talking for some time. He knocked the dottle from his pipe and continued: "The way forward, as I see it, is the complete and total abolition of government bodies. Indeed, the whole concept of government is inimical to our ultimate goal. The existing institutions must be replaced by a free collective of producers and consumers. There is a broad consensus concerning the struggle for better pay and working conditions. But what I am proposing is far more radical. Low wages are not the problem. It is wages *per se* that are the problem. We should seek to abolish the wage system altogether."

Della, who was stretched out on a chaise longue and obscured by a cocoon of Egyptian cigarette smoke, said, "And what would you replace wages with?"

"Nothing," Autenburg replied. "A perfect society has no need of money." Axl Diamant was standing by the fireplace. He was about to say something but stopped when Della raised the hem of her skirt and examined the pointed toe of her shoe. She rotated her ankle and tapped the floor with her heel. Her stockings were bright red and only a eunuch would have overlooked the

117

pleasing shapeliness of her calf. Eduard coughed, filled the bowl of his pipe with tobacco, and added, "I'm going to include this suggestion in my next pamphlet. I imagine it will cause quite a stir."

Diamant tore his eyes away from Della's stocking and said, "Words. Really, what's the good of words? It's going to take more than words to make things better."

"Actually," Autenburg huffed. "Words are very powerful things." He relit his pipe and adopted a self-satisfied expression.

Diamant pushed himself away from the fireplace, strode over to the window, and pulled the curtains aside. Staring down at the street below, he saw two Hasidic Jews, both dressed in long coats and large, circular fur hats. One of them was gesticulating while the other nodded. "What are we waiting for?" Diamant's breath condensed on the glass. "Nothing changes. We talk and talk and talk and nothing *ever* changes. They use force to protect *their* interests: capital punishment, the police, the army—all at their disposal. So why shouldn't we?" The Jews began walking and were followed by a mangy dog.

"I am not troubled, Axl, by the moral question," said Autenburg, drawing from his pipe. "I am as committed—in theory—as you are to propaganda by deed. But one mustn't be rash."

"Nor must one be complacent . . ."

Autenburg undid the top button of his waistcoat and shifted in his chair. "There would be little likelihood of escaping capture."

"No battle was ever won without sacrifice." Diamant turned away from the window. Beyond Autenburg's balding head he could see Della, lazily turning the tip of her pointed toe into the floorboard. "We must reestablish the standing of the movement in Vienna. We must stand proud—as equals—with Berne and Paris."

"Remember Hartmann," said Autenburg.

"Who?"

"Lev Hartmann—of the People's Will—who blew up the tzar's train. After the explosion everything went red. As far the eye could see—red—red—a nightmare landscape, a bloodbath! But the air didn't smell of iron, it smelled of sugar. It wasn't blood or the remains of the tzar and his entourage that drenched the earth, it was fruit conserve. The train had been transporting jam to the imperial residences in the Crimea." Autenburg chuckled softly. "The tzar had got off earlier and at the time of the explosion he was safe in Moscow."

"What's that got to do with anything?"

"My point is this," said Autenburg, raising his pipe. "Hartmann's fiasco did little for the international standing of the People's Will. If you want to better our reputation, then you must be absolutely confident of success. Ineffectual exploits, however bold, will earn us only the contempt of our peers and charges of hubris. Incompetence does not inspire terror and we must always be mindful of the effect our actions might have on the movement as a whole."

"Let me do what I think is right!" said Axl, angrily.

"No," said Autenburg with uncharacteristic firmness. "You do not have my permission. I have never denied you anything," he added, glancing at his wife, "because belief in total equality demands that we transcend the limitations imposed upon us by convention. In this instance, however, there is a conflict of interest. I have responsibilities. I must answer to the executive and consider consequences."

Della shifted along the chaise longue and patted the seat. "Come—sit, Axl. Don't be angry." She closed her lips around the cigarette and the extremity burned. Then she pouted and released a thin stream of cigarette smoke.

The young man studied her for a few moments and the cast of his expression changed. One kind of fire had been replaced by another.

TWENTY-FOUR

Professor Seeliger crossed the Danube Canal, passing as he did so through the wide metal cage of the Sophie Bridge, and entered the wide-open green space of the Prater. He was clutching a sheet of blue notepaper on which someone—someone as yet unknown to him—had drawn a map and marked a meeting place. Professor Seeliger continued walking, glancing this way, then that, to a cultivated area divided by several pathways until he reached a particular lamppost. He checked the map again, in order to confirm that he had found the right location and consulted his pocket watch. Ten minutes early. He removed his top hat, tucked it under his arm, and dabbed his forehead with a handkerchief. It was cold, but he was perspiring and he unbuttoned his coat to cool down. Apart from some people he could see in the distance, there was no one else in his immediate vicinity.

The light was just beginning to fade and mountains of gray cloud had collected at every cardinal compass point. Professor Seeliger had an unobstructed view of the massive lantern and sloping, circular roof of the Rotunda. The building had been constructed for the 1873 Vienna World's Fair, and even though it was thirty-one years old, it was still the largest cupola construction in the world, superseding in size even the marvels of antiquity. However, there was nothing aesthetically appealing about the Rotunda; it looked completely alien, like a steel marquee erected by giant invaders from another planet. Professor Seeliger was reminded of *The War of the Worlds*, a terrifying new novel by the English author H. G. Wells: the German translation had only just arrived in Vienna. The thought of tentacled martians inhabiting the interior of the Rotunda made him feel even more uneasy. A gust of wind carried with it screams and an incongruous scrap of barrel organ music from the amusement park.

Professor Seeliger tensed when he saw the figure of a man appear from behind a row of trees. He was carrying an umbrella and his gait was unhurried. The man approached, assuming a smile as he got closer. He was in his late thirties and well-groomed, not quite the scoundrel Seeliger had been expecting.

"Good afternoon, Professor Seeliger." The man bowed.

Seeliger put his hat back on and said: "You are . . . ?"

"Gerd Kelbling."

Removing the blue sheet of notepaper from his pocket, Seeliger shook the folds out and held it up: "What is the meaning of this?"

"I think it's clear enough—don't you? Cooperate or go to prison." Kelbling's German was perfect, but his stresses fell in slightly irregular places.

Professor Seeliger was not accustomed to impertinence. He expanded his chest and said, "I hope you have considered the likely consequences—for you, I mean—of issuing such a threat to a man of influence."

"Indeed." Kelbling's smile broadened. "You have friends in high places, which is why I am quite certain that you will cooperate. You have worked very hard to win the trust of palace officials, judges, and generals, and you wouldn't want all that effort—years of obsequious flattery and fawning, bootlicking and sycophancy—to go to waste, would you? And how would your wife react now, if your plans unraveled—at this point—just when your name is about to be submitted for the emperor's approval? She would be inconsolable."

Seeliger spluttered, "Are you—are you acquainted?"

Kelbling ignored the interruption. "Sometimes, I wonder which of you is the more ambitious?"

The professor took a step backward. Another gust of wind delivered distant screams and further intimations of eternal torment. Seeliger opened his mouth to speak but no words were forthcoming. He simply stood there, gaping, like an idiot.

"I know everything," said Kelbling. He traced a circle in the air with the tip of his umbrella, creating an airy suggestion of the globe to emphasize his omniscience.

Seeliger swallowed and said, "Speak plainly, please."

Kelbling feigned disappointment. "You know, Herr Professor, I was secretly hoping that we could dispense with specifics. Details always require bluntness, indelicacy. But . . . if that's what you want." Kelbling stabbed his finger against Seeliger's chest. "You sir, are a thief. No different, in actuality, to the cutpurses who operate in the market squares. You have been embezzling university funds for well over a year now. Picking pockets—a little here—a little there—a small fortune. I understand that it's not your fault really. It's that wife of yours again: always wanting you to go back for more—a woman with expensive habits. We've all made that mistake. And so ambitious for Danuta and Gabriela!" Kelbling paused to watch a hot-air balloon rising above the amusement park then continued: "What would happen, I wonder, if the provost were to be informed? Can you imagine the brouhaha that would follow? The press would have a field day. Your wife would be beside herself, hysterical. Frankly, I think it would all be too much for her—she'd end up in one of the asylums. Am Steinhoff, most probably."

"What do you want?" said Seeliger, his voice was without emotion, like a mechanical device grinding out the parts of language.

"Isn't it obvious?" said Kelbling. "You are reputed to be one of the most intelligent men in Vienna. Surely I don't need to spell it out."

TWENTY-FIVE

Gloriettegasse was an elegant, respectable street, dignified by its proximity to the Schönbrunn gardens. Like many other buildings in the locality, number 9 was painted a shade of yellow in respectful imitation of the adjacent palace. Sulphur and primrose, lemon and dandelion, the front elevations of Gloriettegasse were almost monochromatic. The occupant of number 9—Katharina Schratt—being a woman of the theatre, retired late most nights, nevertheless, she was expected to be ready to receive His Royal Highness for breakfast at seven thirty, precisely. Franz Josef's daily schedule was prescribed—minute by minute—although he was also punctual by nature.

Katharina was obliged to rise when it was still dark, attend to her toilet, apply makeup, and then oversee the laying out of the breakfast things—the smooth white napery, the kipferls, and the extra fine coffee for which she was renowned—and when Franz Josef appeared, her obligation extended to the assumption of a fixed, friendly smile. After breakfast, Katharina and Franz Josef would leave the villa, cross Maxingasse, and enter the Schönbrunn gardens through an inconspicuous doorway. It was rumored among society gossips that entertaining the emperor was beginning to put a strain on the actress's nerves.

Throughout the duration of Franz Josef's visit, his conveyance would be parked around the corner from number 9. This was an entirely empty piece of etiquette, a mere show of discretion, because the royal coach and coachman were easily recognized and usually people stopped and waited to see if they could catch a glimpse of the returning emperor. On this particular morning, standing near the front of the small gathering, was a young man whose good looks were mitigated by a dueling scar.

Diamant was thinking about Della, the intensity of her kisses and the ease with which she could make him mad with desire. He was not supposed to want her like this, not in a possessive, jealous way—it was contrary to the principles of the movement—but he could not master his emotions; he wanted her all to himself, he wanted to *own* her, like property, like chattels.

What did she see in Autenburg? She claimed that he was a great intellect. Well, that might have been true once, perhaps—but not anymore. Autenburg could be ridiculous. That nonsense about Hartmann and the jam—what on earth was he talking about? The People's Will had triumphed in the end. They had assassinated Alexander II.

"Not long now," said a woman to her younger female companion. "God bless him."

Diamant recreated the regicide in his imagination with eidetic clarity: the first blinding detonation, the imperial sleigh swishing to a halt and throwing up plumes of ice; the tzar, jumping down and surveying the carnage, soldiers clutching shrapnel wounds, some already dead; Grinevitsky, throwing the bomb, another bright flash, and then the tzar, crawling on his hands and knees, leaving a bright red trail in the snow, his innards dropping out of the gaping hole in his abdomen. Diamant's heart had started to beat faster and he was feeling excited.

A collective gasp returned Diamant to the present.

Franz Josef—Emperor of Austria, Apostolic King of Hungary, King of Bohemia, Dalmatia, Croatia, Slavonia, Galicia, Lodemeria, Ilyria, *et cetera, et cetera*—was walking down the street. He was wearing a peaked cap and a plain blue military uniform and he looked more like a retired private on his way to a regimental reunion than a demi-god.

Margrave of Upper and Lower Lusatia, in Istria, Count of Hohenems, Feldkirch, Bregenz, Sonneberg, *et cetera, et cetera.*

Everything was held together by this unimpressive man, the product of a thousand years of in-breeding. And he was so obviously mortal. Without his sashes and medals and symbols of power, he was just an old fool besotted with an actress, without his "inalienable heirlooms"—the Habsburg unicorn horn and the agate bowl believed to be the Holy Grail—he was nothing. Diamant had once read that the emperor wrote his telegrams on old scraps of paper to save money. What a miser, what a miserable old skinflint!

Grand Prince of Transylvania, Lord of Trieste, Kotor, and the Wendish March. Grand Voivode of the Voivodship of Serbia, *et cetera, et cetera.*

A policeman came forward, holding up his hand—indicating that the people who had assembled near the coach should not come forward. "Disperse," he called out. "Disperse at once." Franz Josef was suddenly standing next to the officer and Diamant could actually hear the emperor's stern reprimand. "There is no reason why these good people should not greet their sovereign." The policeman seemed to shrink and he stuttered an apology before bowing so low he was in danger of toppling over.

It would be so easy—a bomb, like Grinevitsky—that would do it! No, not even a bomb—a dagger—the emperor could be reached with a single lunge! Franz Josef smiled at his subjects and waved like a clockwork automaton before climbing into the carriage.

Leaning against a tree, looking on, was a

gentleman with a pointed beard. His broad-brimmed hat was tilted low over his eyes and he was holding a cane against his chest. By the time the coach had rolled away and the people had finished cheering, the gentleman had melted away. Even if he had chosen to remain by the tree, Diamant wouldn't have noticed him. The young man was far too busy making plans.

TWENTY-SIX

Commissioner Brügel's adjutant handed Rheinhardt a sealed envelope and barked, "Read it now, inspector." Rheinhardt reached for his paper knife and slit the flap. Inside was a summons, written in a distinctive Gothic hand, the ornateness of which contradicted the blunt simplicity of the message: *Favoriten. My office—to discuss report. Half past two. Brügel.* Rheinhardt addressed the self-important adjutant: "I would be most grateful if you would inform the commissioner that I will be present at the specified time." The adjutant sneered, jerked his head in lieu of a bow, and made a hasty departure—slamming the door.

Haussmann stopped writing and looked up. "Sir, why do you always treat him with such civility?"

"Because," Rheinhardt replied in the tone of a weary sage, "it costs me nothing to be civil and those who are quick to anger often find themselves in an early grave."

"The commissioner appears to be in excellent health—"

"There are always exceptions, Haussmann."

The detective ate some zimtsterne biscuits—cinnamon stars—instead of going out for lunch and he found himself glancing at his watch with increasing frequency as the hour and minute hands approached half past two.

Commissioner Manfred Brügel sat behind his desk beneath a portrait of Franz Josef dressed in full regalia. The commissioner and the emperor were not dissimilar in appearance on account of a common preference for muttonchop whiskers, and, if Rheinhardt squinted, he could reproduce an effect that resembled double vision. Much of Brügel's desktop was covered in photographs of the Favoriten murder scene: the three chairs, the disfigured body, a long view of the piano factory floor. Brügel consulted Rheinhardt's report and said, "Angelo Callari?"

"Yes, sir."

Brügel picked up an image of the dead man's melted face. "How can you be sure?"

"We can't be sure—not absolutely—he didn't have any papers. Nevertheless, I'm confident that the man we found in the factory was the same one who arrived in Vienna a few months ago and called himself Tab."

The commissioner grimaced as if he'd suddenly developed a painful zygomatic tic. "Webbed feet—the word of a prostitute . . ."

"The crop marks on his body, the crop itself, and Herr Kruckel's interview . . ."

Brügel nodded, grudgingly. "What about the landlord?"

"The landlord is represented by an agent—a Slovenian gentleman who is proving difficult to trace."

"Have you contacted our colleagues in Rome?"

"I have sent three telegrams to the Italian security office."

"And?"

"We are still awaiting an acknowledgment. The Italians are never in danger of appearing overzealous."

Brügel's overcast expression was interrupted by a brief show of complicit recognition. The storm clouds quickly gathered again behind his eyes and he grumbled, "This Kruckel character . . ."

"I believe he was once an influential political columnist."

"The name *is* familiar." Brügel picked up the Fraternitas pamphlet and studied the image of the laborer climbing toward the beacon. He read the caption: "Nothing to lose—everything to gain." Then he flicked through the pages. "Seditious drivel. Yes, Kruckel. I remember reading articles by Clement Kruckel. He was a young firebrand when I was still a police cadet. I haven't come across any of his provocative denunciations in a long time now."

"Indeed, sir. None of the mainstream newspapers publish him anymore. His views are considered to be too extreme—even by those who share his socialist sympathies."

The commissioner tossed the pamphlet aside with disdain and craned forward to take a closer look at the photograph of the three empty chairs. "You have indicated in your report that a jury of honor may have convened at the Gallus and Sons factory."

"Actually, sir—it was Herr Doctor Liebermann who made that suggestion."

Brügel produced a low growling sound. "You still feel the need to consult him?"

"He is remarkably perceptive and—"

"Has provided the security office with invaluable assistance on many occasions, I know, I know—so you keep telling me." The commissioner fell silent and his index finger tapped out a solid, heavy rhythm. He was clearly ruminating. His pendant, dissatisfied expression was becoming increasingly baleful. Eventually, he muttered, "This won't do, Rheinhardt."

"I'm sorry, sir?"

"This really won't do." The commissioner's finger stopped tapping. "Three weeks. You've been working on this case for three weeks and—as far as I can see—you've achieved nothing."

"We've identified the body, sir."

"No, you haven't, detective inspector." Brügel slapped his palm down on Rheinhardt's report. "You know what the dead man called himself—Angelo Callari—but you still don't know who he was, or what he was doing in Vienna. Where are your suspects? Why was there so much money under Callari's mattress? Who gave it to him? If Callari was a political agitator, then we cannot afford to be complacent!" Brügel's cheeks had become mottled and his breathing was clearly audible. He slapped the report again for good measure, pushed his chair back, and gestured toward Franz Josef. "Rheinhardt! Consider the terrible fate of our beloved empress!" The commissioner picked up the photograph of Callari's ruined face and held it out. "What kind of person might have a large quantity of acid conveniently at hand?"

"A scientist?" Rheinhardt spoke tentatively. "Someone who works in a laboratory?"

"Think again, man!"

"A chemist of some description?"

"What do you need to make explosives?"

Rheinhardt whispered his reply. "Acids . . ."

The commissioner exchanged Callari's photograph for Rheinhardt's report. "I'm going to have to pass this on to the intelligence services."

Rheinhardt felt profoundly uncomfortable. The commissioner was intemperate, cantankerous, and critical, but in this instance, his harsh words were excusable.

Yes, thought Rheinhardt. *He's right. I've been complacent.*

TWENTY-SEVEN

The cab jounced along an uneven stretch of road. Liebermann sighed and said, "I really didn't want to put you through this."

"I'm being introduced to your family," Amelia replied. "Not having a tooth extracted." She smiled and Liebermann was relieved to see that she'd intended the quip to be amusing.

"Yes, I suppose so." Liebermann pulled the curtain aside and looked out of the window. The streetlamps flashed past—then doorways, caryatids, pediments; a man carrying a double bass on his back. "We're almost there."

"Actually," said Amelia. "I've been looking forward to this evening."

"Have you?"

"Yes. I'm rather curious. It will be interesting to meet your parents—to see which of your traits has been transmitted by their germ plasm."

Liebermann turned and rested a hand on Amelia's sleeve. "Perhaps you should try to avoid saying things like that at the dinner table."

They arrived at their destination, a large apartment building on Concordiaplatz with tall, oblong windows. Liebermann and Amelia stepped down onto the cobbles and Liebermann paid the driver, adding a very generous tip. He felt like a condemned man; the value of money had become an irrelevance. Doffing his cap, the driver wished Liebermann luck and shook the reins. The horse trotted away and its clopping hooves produced a loud, ringing echo.

Liebermann and Amelia entered the building and climbed a wide stone staircase that glittered with silica crystals. The first floor landing was tiled like a chessboard and they advanced toward a pair of carved oak doors. Liebermann pressed an ivory button, a bell sounded, and they were admitted into a long hallway by a Czech servant who greeted "Herr Doctor Maxim" warmly and took their coats and Amelia's hat. Another servant was opening a door to their right. Voices could be heard—but they fell silent almost immediately. Liebermann whispered, "Are you all right?"

"Yes, of course." Amelia replied. For the first time he saw apprehension in her eyes.

"Come . . ."

Liebermann squeezed Amelia's hand and led her into a spacious reception room. All of Liebermann's family—with the exception of Daniel, his little nephew—had gathered for the occasion. A circle of expectant faces: Mendel, his father; Rebecca, his mother; his older sister, Leah; her husband, Josef; and Liebermann's younger sister, Hannah. Liebermann couldn't help noticing that his family looked somewhat frozen, arrested, speechless, perhaps even shocked, and when he turned to introduce Amelia he understood why. He had been so distracted and so full of dread that he hadn't registered her appearance. Her clothes were, as usual, very simple, but she was standing beneath a glittering chandelier and her hair, which she had not pinned up, was a blazing cascade, flame red and coruscating with glints of copper and gold. The illusion of movement commanded attention and everything in the room seemed to dim by contrast. Hannah's mouth had dropped open. Liebermann was obliged to break the spell: "Good evening." He rotated his hand in the air, an absurd, nervous flourish that he instantly regretted. "This is Amelia. Amelia Lydgate." Josef raised an eyebrow.

"Miss Lydgate," said Mendel, stepping forward. "I am Maxim's father, you are most welcome." He bowed, kissed Amelia's hand and continued. "Allow me to introduce my wife, Rebecca, our two daughters—Leah and Hannah—and my son-in-law, Josef." Although he was smiling, Mendel appeared rather awkward and Liebermann's mother and sisters bobbed up and down, improvising a genteel greeting the likes of which Liebermann had never seen before. He supposed that this was on account of Amelia being English.

When everyone was seated, Mendel addressed his guest: "Maxim tells me you're from London."

"Yes," Amelia replied. "One of the villages just north of the capital."

"London," Mendel repeated. "A very fine city. I've been to London many times on business. I used to bring Maxim along, when he was younger, when I thought I could interest him in textiles. But it wasn't to be. What is the name of your village?"

"Highgate," Amelia replied.

"I'm afraid the name is unfamiliar."

"It is situated on an eminence and on a clear day the views over London are very pleasing. One can see as far as the Thames. There are many inns and the air is considered good for the constitution. Our great poet, Coleridge, is buried in the local church. My father is of the opinion that his philosophical works are much underestimated."

Mendel wasn't sure how to respond. The only poetry he'd ever read for pleasure was Goethe. "Your father—he is your English parent?"

"Indeed—Samuel Lydgate—a science master at a school of some distinction."

"And your mother?"

"Greta—is German."

"Which explains your fluency."

"An accent is still detectable, I believe."

"Hardly."

That went well, thought Liebermann. The small talk continued and Liebermann was distracted by an enormous, antique menorah—the Jewish ceremonial candle holder—standing proudly on the sideboard. He hadn't seen this particular menorah before and guessed that Mendel must have purchased it only recently. Whether his father's prominent positioning of the menorah had been consciously or unconsciously motivated didn't really matter. The old man was prepared to be civil, but he didn't like making compromises—and the marriage of his son to a gentile would be the most painful and difficult of all compromises.

Leah was asking Amelia a question. "You are studying medicine?"

"It is something of a family tradition."

"Ah yes," said Mendel. "Maxim told me about your grandfather. He attended royalty, didn't he?"

"He was invited to Great Britain by the prince consort and he was subsequently appointed physician-in-ordinary to Queen Victoria." The members of the Liebermann family looked across the room at each other and nodded their approval. "I have his diaries in my possession. They are extremely interesting, particularly his speculative writings on diseases of the blood."

Liebermann was about to interrupt in order to prevent Amelia from expounding at length upon an unsuitable subject, but he was beaten to it by his prescient younger sister. "Miss Lydgate," Hannah cried. "Where did you buy those pearl earrings? I've been wanting a pair like that for ages!"

The conversation that followed, with a little judicious steering, flowed more naturally, and the atmosphere became less intense. An aperitif was served, people changed places, and thankfully, Amelia ceased to be the sole focus of attention.

Liebermann leaned toward Hannah and spoke confidentially: "I'm sorry—I've been neglecting you."

"Oh, that's all right, Maxim. I know you're always busy."

"I'll take you out somewhere soon, I promise. Where shall we go? Julius Epstein is performing at the Bösendorfer-Saal."

"Really?"

"Yes. Liszt and Chopin."

"That would be lovely."

"I'll get tickets."

Hannah gave her brother a quick kiss on the cheek and then flicked her eyes at Amelia. "She's very beautiful."

"Thank you."

"And that hair—my God—it's like her head's on fire."

"You know, as a compliment, that doesn't quite succeed."

Hannah laughed. "She seems to be getting on rather well with Father."

It was true. Mendel and Amelia were sitting

together and they seemed to be engaged in a very animated discussion. Liebermann and Hannah listened.

"Are the bolts of a different circumference?" Amelia asked.

"Yes." Mendel replied. "Some this big"—he drew a small circle in the air—"others this big." He then drew a much larger circle.

"Might I make a suggestion?"

"By all means."

"If you placed the smaller bolts of cloth within the larger bolts," she slotted her right hand through an arch made with her left, "you would immediately halve your transportation costs."

"Good God," said Mendel. "Why didn't I think of that?" He clapped his hands together. "Ha!"

Everyone stopped talking.

"What is it, Father?" Leah asked.

"Miss Lydgate has an excellent head for figures and has indicated how a number of efficiency savings might be made. These would lead to a significant increase in profit margins—especially with respect to transport."

At that moment the head servant appeared: "Dinner is served."

Mendel offered Amelia his hand. "Perhaps we could continue this interesting discussion over the chicken soup?"

"If you wish," Amelia consented. "I'm happy to do so."

It was then that Liebermann looked over at his mother. She had hardly said a word all evening and she was staring at Amelia with narrowed, suspicious eyes.

TWENTY-EIGHT

The statue of Lady Justice showed no interest in the waltzing couples. A grand staircase spilled down from her throne like a waterfall; the final step—a great semicircle of stone—was like a pool or basin in which the tumbling spate had collected. On either side of the hall was a double layer of arches that emphasized the great height of the glass ceiling. Positioned along parallel balconies were the members of an orchestra who were playing the "Verdicte Waltz" by Eduard Strauss; their elevated concealment created an eerie impression of music delivered from heaven, melodies made in a paradise modeled on Vienna and where celestial coffeehouses lined the principal approaches to the pearly gates. The lawyers' ball was one of the most important dates in the social calendar and the great and the good were always represented there in large numbers. In addition to the judiciary and allied professions—various legal functionaries and secretaries—there were politicians, chamberlains, senior security office personnel, wealthy philanthropists, and even a few members of the lower aristocracy. The men were attired in black tails and white gloves, the women in exquisite gowns. As the couples rotated, the facets of diamonds, rubies, and emeralds reflected the light from hundreds of decorative lanterns. It was as if the dancers were waltzing through a miniature galaxy of exploding stars.

Standing beneath the lower colonnade, close to the staircase, was the lord marshal. He was speaking to a similarly hawkish gentleman who was wearing a sash, and, like the lord marshal himself, was festooned with crosses and medallions.

"I trust that you are looking forward to your retirement?" said the lord marshal.

"Yes," Judge Weeber replied. "Very much so, lord marshal, although there are always mixed feelings—a sense of loss, perhaps? The realization that one is no longer relevant . . . I'll miss the drama, the cut and thrust, the company of my esteemed colleagues. My wife says I won't know what to do with myself."

"Any plans?"

"Some travel, I think. I've always wanted to visit some of the old battlefields in the southeast. They say that you can still find the skeletons of Ottoman camels—as well as the bones of the men who fought and died there. And then there's the piano of course. I used to be quite accomplished when I was a young man. I'm looking forward to renewing my acquaintance with C.P.E. Bach." The judge raised both arms and wiggled his fingers over an invisible keyboard. "Do you play, lord marshall?"

"Sadly not."

"Pity."

"Indeed."

The lord marshal leaned closer to his companion and said, "An aide from the intelligence services visited the Palace yesterday. They've received a report from the security office." He nodded toward Commissioner Brügel who was standing with two generals underneath the arch opposite. "Did you hear about the Favoriten murder?"

"Yes, I did."

"They suspect that the victim may have been executed by a jury of honor."

The judge pressed his lips together and harrumphed. "We haven't had one of those in a long time."

"Thanks to you," said the lord marshal, raising his champagne flute.

"Come now." Weeber's apparent embarrassment wasn't very convincing. "You are too kind, lord marshal. I was only doing my job."

The lord marshal leaned closer. "They—the intelligence bureau—have advised caution."

Weeber nodded. "I'm always vigilant. Always have been—old habits die hard."

As the "Verdicte Waltz" came to an end the two men moved apart and the dance floor erupted with cheers and applause.

"Georg, my dear!" A woman was approaching. Her stick-thin body was encased in black brocade and her neck was obscured by a lace ruff. There was something semi-supernatural about her appearance—a hint of witchy charisma. Although her face was wrinkled, her eyes were bright and youthful. "The next dance is ours." She turned to face the lord marshal, managing to smile and glare at the same time. Here was a woman who would not tolerate contradiction. The lord marshal capitulated with a low bow as the introductory bars of the next waltz floated down from above.

TWENTY-NINE

Well, what shall we finish with?" Liebermann played a trill to strengthen the little finger of his left hand.

Rheinhardt searched through the scores and picked up Schubert's "Schwanengesang" which he opened roughly at the halfway point. He placed the music on the stand and Liebermann said, " 'Atlas' . . . very well."

The young doctor produced a raging storm in the lower octaves of the Bösendorfer and Rheinhardt began to sing, sinking slightly as his knees buckled. He seemed possessed by the songs sentiment, every bone and sinew responding to Heinrich Heine's poetry. It was Atlas who led the Titans against Zeus, and, when defeated, was condemned to carry the sky on his shoulders. The hammer blows of fate rained down: crushing, devastating, without mercy. Rheinhardt fell back into the curve of the piano and gripped the case with both hands, like a dazed pugilist beaten onto the ropes. The notion of solitary anguish had acquired symphonic grandeur. Schubert's insistent tonality was like a prison from which no singer could escape and Rheinhardt writhed hopelessly, trying to shake off invisible shackles. The central section of the song offered only brief respite, before the torment and terror returned. When Liebermann reached the final valedictory bars, Rheinhardt looked exhausted and emotionally wrung out.

The two men retired to the smoking room and assumed their customary places, facing the fire. Liebermann poured cognac from a decanter and offered Rheinhardt a cigar. It was some time before Liebermann spoke.

"Atlas is a challenging work for any singer, even the seasoned concert artist. It requires a voice of extraordinary power and range. I've heard you sing it many times before, Oskar, but never quite so well."

Rheinhardt patted his stomach. "I've been eating more than usual—I'm sure my body becomes more resonant when I'm heavier."

"Really, Oskar, you don't expect me to accept that sort of nonsense!"

"No, I don't. I just wanted to see how long it would take for you to become impatient. Not long at all it seems."

Liebermann turned to look at his companion and made a small hand gesture—an oscillation that might have found equal utility as a deterrent for mosquitoes. "You chose Atlas because you feel that you are bearing a great burden. Of course, as a detective inspector, you are always bearing a burden—the burden of keeping us all safe, the burden of fighting crime. But tonight, that burden is weighing particularly heavily on your shoulders." Liebermann drew on his cigar. "What, I wonder, weighs most heavily on the soul of a detective inspector? For a man whose whole existence is bound up with issues of right and wrong, it must be something that weighs on his conscience. Yes, I see it now. You feel guilty about something."

"Max, you are absolutely right!"

"Atlas was punished by Zeus and the security office has its own Zeus in the person of Commissioner Brügel. So, might I be correct in supposing that you have done something wrong, a professional oversight, perhaps, and that Commissioner Brügel has threatened to remove you from the Favoriten case? He hasn't given it to another detective, has he?"

Rheinhardt sighed. "No, it's worse than that."

"There's something worse?"

"Oh yes. He's sent my report to the intelligence bureau. If they get involved it will be intolerable."

"Why?"

"I'll have to cooperate with them and I really don't like their methods. They are always of the opinion that ends justify means."

"What was your professional oversight?"

"Acid." A shower of sparks erupted onto the hearth. "Not only can it be used to disfigure faces, but it can also be used to make explosives."

"I see."

"Commissioner Brügel said I was being complacent and for once I'm inclined to agree."

Liebermann tapped the ash from his cigar. "Have the intelligence bureau contacted you yet?"

"No—but they will." Rhinehardt stubbed out his cigar and lit another. Then, speaking in a less troubled tone of voice, he added, "Haussmann's been keeping an eye on The Golden Bears. He's compiling a list of patrons. They're an odd lot—political types, women who dress in men's clothes, mystics, eccentrics. I suppose we should interview the lot of them, but it will take up so much time—more time than I have. This city is a madhouse."

Liebermann smiled. "You don't need to tell me that."

THIRTY

Vala Feist's parlor was tainted with a smell reminiscent of rotten eggs. This was because her humble abode was located between the gasworks, a chemical plant, and the Danube Canal. It had taken her many years to secure such an ideal situation, and unless her circumstances changed dramatically, she would never move out of the third district. Although the local miasma had once bothered her, she hardly noticed it anymore. In fact, she had become inured to unpleasant smells, which was just as well, given how much time she spent traipsing around the sewers.

Razumovsky had made valiant efforts to disguise his discomfort. Even so, Vala had noted the intermittent flaring of his nostrils. Although the unwholesome vapors had very likely diminished his interest in the tea and walnut cake she had prepared for him, they had had no effect on his libido. He casually suggested that they might go to bed together "for old time's sake" and Vala agreed. She led him up to her bedroom and closed the heavy curtains, leaving a narrow gap that admitted a thin partition of dusty light. After removing her outer garments she sat on a chair, and, kneeling in front of her, Razumovsky removed her coarse woollen stockings and kissed her toes. When she removed the pins from her bun and shook out her gray hair, he arranged it around her face and gazed at her as if, once again, she were young and beautiful. He made love to her as he had always made love, slowly and silently. She allowed herself to believe in his legend and her head filled with images of naked Sabbath witches cavorting with sovereign evil. It brought her to a shuddering culmination and made her whimper with pleasure.

The winter sun descended behind flecked, chainmail clouds. They lay on the bed together for over an hour, smoking cheroots and talking in a desultory fashion. Presently, they dressed and made their way down to the cellar.

Vala lit a paraffin lamp. Its bright, dancing flame illuminated a surprisingly deep and wide underground space. Lined up along one of the walls were several mattresses and a clothes rack on which outfits were hanging—suits, dresses, and military uniforms. Beneath these a selection of shoes and boots of different sizes for both sexes. A tap at the end of a pipe was dripping into a large chamber pot.

"Have you had any guests this year?" Razumovsky asked.

"No," Vala replied. "It's been very quiet."

"Well, it won't be quiet for much longer."

These words made Vala's stomach flutter.

Razumovsky strolled over to a bank of sagging shelves. Each one was crammed with big glass jars and containers. Leaning closer, he studied the handwritten labels: Sulphuric Acid, Nitric Acid, Glycerine, Mercury, Potash, Methylated Spirit. He opened a rusty metal box that appeared to contain gray string.

"The finest quality," said Vala.

"Of course," said Razumovsky. "You wouldn't accept anything less!" He closed the lid and inspected a tower made of zinc sphere halves, a row of empty tin cans, and some short lengths of iron piping. Beyond these were several washtubs and a pile of concrete blocks. "I doubt that our Swiss friend will find any cause for complaint here—even accepting his pedantry."

"It was the right decision—wasn't it?"

"I'm sorry?"

"Callari."

"Yes, without question. The Okhrana have already contacted Professor Seeliger."

"How do you know that?"

"Kruckel had him followed."

Vala nodded. "When should I expect a visit from our Swiss friend?"

"Very soon," said Razumovsky. "I've already written to him." He reached for a length of iron piping, picked it up, and pretended to throw it. They exchanged smiles and Razumovsky laughed. "I miss the good old days."

THIRTY-ONE

Bok stroked his walrus moustache.
"So, Herr Doctor, how can I be of assistance?"

Liebermann was studying the calculating machine: "Is that a Brunsviga?"

"Yes, it is."

"And the latest model if I'm not mistaken."

"Indeed, Herr Doctor—you are not mistaken."

"Extraordinary—that a mechanical device, an assembly of cogs and gears, can do the work of a human mind?"

"Yes, when you put it like that—I suppose it is."

"Perhaps, in the distant future, much of our labor will be undertaken by automata."

"That isn't something I've thought about."

"Imagine—a world without employment. Good for some, but bad for others I suspect."

"Herr Doctor?" Bok made a flamboyant show of extracting his watch from the fob pocket of his waistcoat. "Shouldn't we be discussing Herr Globocnik?"

"I thought we were."

"I'm sorry?"

"The machine is his replacement, isn't it?"

Bok's expression soured. He pressed his watch back into its pocket and answered. "Yes.

155

I purchased the Brunsviga for my secretary and I don't regret the expenditure. It seems that Fräulein Mugoša can do everything Globocnik could do—and a great deal more besides."

"I'm sure she's very capable." Liebermann brushed a hair from his trousers. "Actually, I was hoping to speak with Fräulein Mugoša."

"I'm sorry, but that isn't possible. She's at home."

"At home?"

Bok coughed nervously. "*Her* home—her apartment."

"When will she be returning to work?"

"This afternoon . . ."

"Is she ill?"

"I beg your pardon?"

"She isn't at her desk—so I assumed she must be unwell."

"Fräulein Mugoša has a robust constitution."

"Have you given her the morning off?"

"No, not exactly."

"Then why isn't she here?"

"Herr Doctor, you will appreciate—I hope— that I am a busy man. If you want to discuss Globocnik, then—"

"Yes, of course," Liebermann cut in. "My apologies."

Bok grumbled to himself and challenged his inquisitor. "Have you worked out what's wrong with him?"

"The brain is very complex, Herr Bok—even more complex than a Brunsviga." Liebermann threw a glance at the calculating machine. "And when the mind goes wrong, you can't just open the skull—like that machine's case—and put things right with a few drops of oil. If only psychiatric treatment were that easy! Are you married, Herr Bok?"

"What?"

"Are you married?"

"Yes . . . but my wife and I recently separated."

"A difficult time . . ."

"Thank you for your sympathy, Herr Doctor, but it would be better to save your solicitations for your patients. Their need is surely much greater than mine. Now, what was it you wanted to know about Globocnik?"

Liebermann made a steeple with his index fingers and tapped them together. "A lonely man, wouldn't you say?"

"Yes."

"Good at his job?"

"Good enough."

"And always sniffing . . ."

"Yes. He sniffed a great deal."

"Nerves, perhaps?"

"I couldn't say."

Liebermann leaned forward. "Have you lost weight by any chance, Herr Bok?"

"What?"

"Your waistcoat," Liebermann pointed over the desktop. "It's creased. Horizontal lines—evidence of former straining. Yet you experienced no difficulty extracting your pocket watch."

Bok pinched his waistcoat and tugged it away from his stomach. "I have lost a little weight, yes."

"Why do you think that is?"

"I . . . I don't know."

"Have you been exerting yourself more than usual?"

Bok's ruddy complexion intensified. "I am in the habit of taking a short walk every day. That hasn't changed. Herr Doctor, with respect—"

"Herr Globocnik—of course." Liebermann removed his spectacles, cleaned the lenses with a handkerchief, and put them back on again. "Ah, that's better."

"Well?"

Liebermann squeezed his lips and appeared to be in a state of deep contemplation. After a few seconds his hand dropped to his lap and he smiled. "Thank you, Herr Bok."

"I'm sorry?"

The young doctor stood up and bowed. "You have been most helpful."

Bok made various huffing noises. "What about Globocnik?"

"What about him?"

"Weren't we supposed to be discussing his fit?"

"Whatever gave you that idea?"

"You're his doctor!"

Liebermann lifted his astrakhan coat from the stand and draped it over his shoulders like a cape. "Good morning, Herr Bok. And thank you once again for being so generous with your time." Bok remained seated but continued emitting plosive sounds. Liebermann left the office quickly before indignation and bewilderment became anger.

The young doctor crossed the factory floor, aware that his progress was being closely observed by Bok's employees. They were all women and most of them looked tired and undernourished. He noticed that one of them had a black eye. The clatter of the sewing machines was relentless and the air was opaque with steam. Before stepping outside, he paused and looked back. He was struck by the efficiency of the production line; however, he couldn't help feeling that such repetitive work was bad for the soul. These women exercised no skill (other than the single action that they had overlearned) and consequently would experience no emotional connection with the result of their industry; no pride or satisfaction, no sense of mastery. He remembered his earlier flippant remark about machines taking over the work of humans in the future. Perhaps such a development would prove unnecessary, if humans were reduced to the condition of machines first. And all in pursuit of profit! He hoped that his father's textile factories weren't like this.

Liebermann exited the building and blinked at the bright sun. Apart from a few wispy clouds the sky was clear and blue. He lit a cigarette and began to march across a yard littered with empty crates and toward metal gates that had been left wide open.

"Excuse me." He turned and saw that he had been followed out of the factory by the woman with the black eye. She was wearing a blouse with the sleeves rolled up and a brown skirt that was made of a coarse material that had the appearance of hemp. Her hair hadn't been brushed in a while and the individual strands had clumped together to form a peruke of rat tails. "You're Lutz's doctor?"

"Yes, that's right."

"Please, Herr Doctor, could you give him this?" She produced a handful of change that amounted to about ten kronen.

"If you wish."

"It's money I owe him. He was kind to me, Lutz—a good friend."

She tilted her palm and the coins changed hands. Liebermann counted the amount and tipped the money into his trouser pocket. "And your name is?"

"Dagna."

"I'll give it to him this afternoon."

"Thank you." The woman looked over her shoulder before addressing Liebermann again. "I saw him come out of Herr Bok's office—that day—the day he had the fit. He was in such a terrible state."

"He must have been very . . . distressed."

Dagna lowered her voice. "Did he really try to kill Herr Bok?"

"I'm not sure."

"He wasn't like that—not Lutz. He wasn't like that at all. But if he had a fit, well, I suppose anything's possible." Liebermann offered the woman a cigarette which she took and placed behind her right ear. "I'll save it for later. Poor Lutz—it was so embarrassing . . ."

"Embarrassing?"

"You know . . . like a baby."

"I'm sorry?"

"You know . . . the wetting." She made a gesture with both hands, up and down her own body. "He was wearing a gray suit and the dark patches were everywhere—all over him."

"Even on his jacket?"

"Jacket, trousers . . . terrible; how is he, poor Lutz? I had an uncle who got put away when I was a girl. Never saw the light of day again."

The factory door opened and a woman's head craned around the vertical edge. "Dagna! Quick! Get back in here now!"

Dagna nodded. "Pardon me, sir—I've got to

go—more than my job's worth if I get caught out here chatting." She lifted her skirt to prevent it from dragging on the gravel and ran toward the door. Liebermann drew on his cigarette and when he exhaled the smoke gave substance to the sunlight.

THIRTY-TWO

Eduard Autenburg and Axl Diamant were striding down the middle of an empty street, side by side, yet separated by a noticeable gap. It was as if some fundamental physical power, like magnetic repulsion, was keeping them apart. The two men cast sharp shadows that extended and contracted as they passed between stunted, rusty gas lamps. Already, the air was beginning to smell of fish and effluent. They had not spoken to each other for several minutes when Diamant exclaimed: "I can't wait any longer!"

Autenburg continued looking straight ahead. "You must not act alone—do you understand? It is forbidden."

"Why must I always do what *you* say?" Diamant sounded like a peevish, whining schoolboy.

"Because we are a collective."

"I'm sick of your prevarication."

"Your feelings are irrelevant—as are mine. The only thing that matters is the cause." Autenburg asked himself how it was that their relationship had arrived at this sorry impasse. Diamant had been Autenburg's protégé. Only a year earlier, they had been boon companions, kindred spirits. Now, they just bickered between awkward silences. Autenburg sensed the young man's frustration. "We are at war," he continued with firm determination. "An army cannot function without generals and foot soldiers, without a chain of command and discipline."

"Did I hear you correctly?" Diamant scoffed. "You imagine us to be like an army? Please allow me to remind you that an army attacks its enemies."

"We *are* attacking our enemies."

"What with? Pamphlets?"

"Words are powerful things."

"But no match for a gun."

"I can assure you that the movement is always active, always performing great deeds."

"Though never in Vienna. Perhaps the moment has come for you to step aside."

Autenburg produced a humorless, gravelly laugh. "And leave the way clear for a younger man?"

"Yes. Why not?"

"Don't be absurd."

"Why is that absurd?"

Autenburg didn't distinguish the question with a direct answer: "If the decision is made to initiate a campaign of propaganda by deed in Vienna, then I will submit your name with an appropriate recommendation; however, until I receive such notice, you must be patient."

"Have you ever wondered why such notice never comes?" The inquiry was purely rhetorical.

"It's because they don't think we're good enough." As the two men turned into Obere Weissgärberstrasse a startled cat ran through a pool of gaslight and disappeared into a shadowed alley. Diamant muttered, "I'm wasted here."

"If that's what you think, go to Berne."

"I want to speak to Mephistopheles."

Autenburg threw Diamant an angry glance. "Not so loud."

"I want to speak to him."

"You don't call Mephistopheles! He calls you!"

"I don't believe that."

"Believe what you like!"

They had arrived at Autenburg's building.

"Who is he?" Diamant's eyes had widened and he sounded desperate.

"Not here!" Autenburg beat the air downward.

"Did you see him?"

"Yes, of course I did."

"At the factory?" Autenburg nodded. "And where is he now?"

"I don't know. No one knows."

"You're keeping me away from him, aren't you? Just so you can carry on being in control."

"That is a ridiculous accusation. Go home and I'll accept your apology in the morning."

Autenburg tried to step forward but Diamant barred his way. "I want to see him! I insist!"

"Do you really think that you—a philosophy student—are in a position to make such a demand? Do you really think that you can ring a bell and he'll come running?"

"He doesn't even know of my existence—does he?"

"We had no reason to discuss you."

"You could have told him about me, you could have explained how dedicated I am, how eager I am to participate. But you chose not to."

"The circumstance was not conducive to such a conversation. Now let me pass."

"I'll find a way."

"You'll do nothing of the sort."

"You can't stop me. I'll make my own enquiries."

"That would be very ill-advised."

"Well, you would say that, wouldn't you? It serves your interests."

"Enough!"

"Or what?"

"Axl . . ."

"Or what? What are you going to do?" Flecks of spit accompanied Diamant's invective. "What *can* you do? How are you going to stop me?" The younger man lowered his arm and straightened his back to emphasize his height. "Accept the truth, Eduard. Face the reality of your situation. You're getting old. You're not the man you used to be. You've gone soft—and in more ways than one I gather!"

Suddenly, Autenburg's fingers were around

Diamant's neck. Although he was squeezing hard, his efforts had little effect: he met unexpected resistance, muscle and bone, rather than soft tissue. The younger man grinned, gripped Autenburg's wrists, and wrenched them away. Autenburg retreated a few steps and said, "Either accept my authority, or go. You cannot act alone. And if you threaten to do so again—"

"What?"

"I will have to report you."

"Yes, you do that. Report me to Mephistopheles."

"Have a care, Axl. Have a care . . ." Autenburg tugged at his coat and straightened his tie. Then, he whispered, "Not a word about this to Della, you understand? She hates it when we argue."

Diamant shook his head. "You don't understand her at all, do you?"

THIRTY-THREE

The women's society at the university did not have many members and they met in a room on the top floor, overlooking the courtyard. Officially, they gathered in order to provide each other with mutual support and exchange ideas concerning methods of study, but in reality, they had far more important matters to discuss, namely, the rights of women, gender equality, and the delicate subject of reproductive anatomy.

Amelia Lydgate enjoyed the company of her fellow female students, all of whom shared a similar outlook and commitment to a life of the mind. Most of them planned to marry and have children, although none envisaged a future in which their intellectual ambitions would be endangered by running a household.

Only a few months earlier, the convener of the women's society had invited Raissa Adler to give them a talk. Adler—who had studied biology in Zurich—was the mother of two children and still managed to be a significant voice in the women's movement. When Amelia had told Max about Adler's visit, she had been surprised to learn that he was acquainted with Adler's husband— Alfred—another acolyte of Freud. Max had said, "Yes, I know Alfred. He's got a very good voice.

I once accompanied him at a party." Vienna was a great city, but a curiously small world.

Clarimonda—a chemistry student—had been reading aloud from a pamphlet that she had been given by a woman on the street. It concerned the "new woman" and should have been interesting, but the anonymous author was somewhat preoccupied with equality of sexual license between men and women—rather than the general principle of equality. Much was made of the dissident communities in Switzerland, who practiced free love. Indeed, it was suggested that the politically enlightened male should encourage his spouse to take as many lovers as she desired. When Clarimonda had finished reading, she looked around the circle of faces, tacitly inviting comment.

"I can't help feeling," said Lorne, a student of classical literature, "that this pamphlet is the work of a gentleman."

"That was my impression also," said Amelia.

"His approach is rather narrow," Lorne interjected.

"Almost obsessive," Amelia added with healthy disdain.

"The sexual question is important," said Clarimonda, "but not *that* important. Moreover, the majority of women do not equate emancipation with the indiscriminate pursuit of sensual gratification."

"One might even argue," said Lorne, looking over her spectacles, "that his conception of the female character is rather demeaning, a creature driven primarily by base instincts—consumed by wanton appetites."

"Immoderate," said Amelia

"Lacking in self-control," Clarimonda agreed.

"He writes about the woman of the future," said Lorne, "yet his understanding of women is rooted in the past. He mounts an attack on the conventions and traditions that have led to our subjugation, but at the same time reinforces the most unflattering and backward-looking prejudices."

The hum of collective consent was quite loud. Like a swarm of bees.

Hedy—who had only recently joined the society—raised a finger and reddened a little before speaking. "The issue is not so much the woman of the future. I think we know what she'll be like. She'll be like us. No. It is rather, the man of the future. What will he be like?"

After a long pause Clarimonda said: "Quite confused."

THIRTY-FOUR

Axl Diamant had decided to eschew the pleasure of drinking and eating at The Golden Bears. He didn't want to be distracted from his purpose. Instead, he settled at a table in a beer cellar near St. Leopold's. The landlord was a Ruthenian who wore a peasant tunic, a shaggy waistcoat, and a hat with a floppy brim. He had also grown an extraordinarily long beard, the pointed tip of which was tucked beneath a wide leather belt. Diamant ordered a bowl of kapusniak—a pork and cabbage soup served with sour cream. It was very filling. By the time he'd drunk half a bottle of horilka, his lips had gone numb.

The clientele smoked pipes and played arcane card games. Voices were only raised when someone had won a bet. At half past ten, an ill-kempt musician carrying a balalaika entered. It was an odd-looking instrument, possessing a triangular body, a flimsy, thin arm, and only three strings. The musician perched himself on a high stool, pressed his knees together, and placed his feet on an overturned crate. Then, after a brief pause, he began to play. Some of the gamblers voiced their approval. It sounded like a folksong. The first section was melancholic, but the second section modulated to the relative major and became faster and faster with each repetition of the melody. The musician adopted a hunched position, occasionally looking up at the ceiling and contracting his features so that he looked like a shrivelled gnome. His rapid right hand was so limber it became a fleshy blur as he executed a superhuman accelerando. When he strummed the final chords, he received—perhaps unfairly—only a smattering of applause. A man sitting nearby flicked a coin that spun through the air. The musician caught it and said "thank you" in several languages. After performing two more pieces—another folksong and Brahms's "Wiegenlied"—he jumped off the stool and snatched a few more spinning coins out of the air. When he opened the door to leave, he admitted a chill gust of wind that made the flames of the paraffin lamps shake and flare.

One by one, the card games came to an end and over the next hour the tables emptied. Eventually, the landlord called out, "Drink up—time to go home." Diamant discovered that his legs were a little unsteady. This didn't cause him any great concern. It was a long walk to Schönbrunn.

Outside, the night was fresh and clear. Stars sparkled with cheerful brilliance. Diamant crossed the canal, marched down Rotenturm-strasse and passed the cathedral. On Kärntner Strasse he came across a group of revellers, one of whom—a loud, stout man—was shaking a bottle of champagne. After popping the cork, the man held the neck of the bottle in front of his crotch and allowed a jet of frothy liquid to arc into the gutter. The joker's companions roared with laughter. Diamant was overcome by a wayward impulse to stop the revellers and give them advanced warning of the coming cataclysm.

When you wake up tomorrow morning, everything will have changed—everything will be different.

The urge was so strong he had to hurry forward.

I am going to alter the course of history!

Diamant encountered fewer people on the streets of Mariahilf, and, very soon, he found himself walking alone. He stepped into a doorway and removed a dagger from his coat pocket. After unsheathing the blade, he tested its sharpness with his forefinger. The reflection of his face moved across the narrow mirror: a young man with a dueling scar, an ordinary face, really, but a face that would soon be reproduced in newspapers on every continent. The thought of achieving global notoriety was accompanied by a quasi-erotic thrill. Diamant chose not to consider the significance of this sporadic and mildly perplexing phenomenon. He slid the dagger back into its sheath and continued his journey westward.

Was he ready to die for the cause? He fully

accepted that this was the most likely eventuality. Nevertheless, he still harbored hopes of escape. After stabbing the empress, Luchini had managed to flee from the scene of his triumph, and if he hadn't been apprehended by two cab drivers and a sailor, he might still be alive and safely ensconced in an Alpine hideaway. Diamant supposed that if none of the people who gathered by the royal carriage chased after him, he could—with a little luck—evade capture and make his way to the woods.

Diamant arrived outside number 9 Gloriettegasse in the early hours of the morning. He imagined Katharina Schratt, tucked up in her bed—fast asleep—inhabiting some dream of greasepaint and limelight. Then he imagined her receiving the news of the emperor's assassination, her operatic anguish, her collapse, her hand clutching a white tablecloth—the breakfast things tumbling to the floor, the crash of the silverware, the china coffee cups shattering on the parquet. She would act her part as if she were performing in front of a full house at the Court Theatre. In reality, she'd be quietly grateful that she was at last free of her onerous obligation to amuse the old man.

Consulting his pocket watch, Diamant wondered why he had set off for Gloriettegasse the instant he'd been asked to leave the beer cellar. He suspected that his decision had been influenced by the bottle of horilka. It would be many hours before the royal carriage appeared, so he decided to walk into Meidling. He wandered around backstreets, smoking and occasionally stopping to look in a shop window. A dishevelled prostitute, who seemed quite lost, offered to lift her skirts for him behind a tannery for "just one krone." Naturally, he declined. A little while later, as he strolled down a shadowy street illuminated by a single gas lamp, he thought he could hear footsteps following. He turned, ready to berate the stubborn whore for her tenacity, but all he could see were paving slabs and cobbles. The same thing happened again shortly after, but when he turned a second time he was surprised to discover a gentleman standing only a few paces behind him: a well-dressed man carrying a cane. Where had he come from? There was something familiar about him.

"Do I know you?" Diamant asked.

"No," the gentleman shook his head. "We've never been introduced; however, perhaps you recognize me? You've seen me before—quite a few times."

"Yes . . ."

"It'll come, I'm sure." The gentleman stepped closer and removed his hat. "Does that help?"

"Yes . . . I've seen you at The Golden Bears."

The stranger smiled. "There, I told you it would come." He was much faster than the balalaika player. His hand sliced beneath Diamant's chin and the would-be assassin was choking on his own blood before a single thought formed in his mind: *I won't be altering the course of history after all.*

PART THREE
The Beatrix

THIRTY-FIVE

She's a bit odd if you ask me," said the constable. His body didn't fill his uniform and his spiked helmet was also perhaps a size too large. "There might even be something wrong with her." He pointed at the woman standing beneath the solitary gas lamp. Her blank expression, shabby clothes, and general limpness made her look like an oversize rag doll.

"Wrong?"

"When she talks she doesn't always make sense."

"Do you think she has an infirmity of the mind?"

"I wouldn't know, sir. Her name's Uhe. Geralyn Uhe."

"Thank you, constable. That will be all."

The young man bowed and clicked his heels.

Rheinhardt walked over to the prostitute. Her coat was unbuttoned and the hem of her skirt fell short of her boots. A wide gap revealed torn yellow stockings. Her face had been plastered with a cosmetic paste in order to conceal the spots around her mouth and a small oval scab hovered above her right eyebrow. She wore no hat and her tawny hair was piled so high it resembled the crown of a pineapple.

"Good morning, Fräulein Uhe," said Rhein-hardt, producing a notebook and pencil. "Thank you for waiting. I am Detective Inspector Oskar Rheinhardt of the security office, and, if I may, I would like to ask you a few questions." The woman nodded. "Where do you live?"

"Wilhelminen Strasse 119."

"Ottakring?"

"Yes, a little boardinghouse." Her delivery was slow and effortful, as if pronouncing each syllable was intolerably tiresome. "I'll be staying there for the next week or so . . . or longer. I'm not sure yet."

Although it was cold the woman was perspiring and drops of sweat had striped her makeup. She scratched the back of her left hand with long fingernails: a short burst of activity, like a dog attacking a flea. When she had finished scratching, the skin was inflamed.

"What business did you have in Meidling?"

The woman shrugged. "The usual business. But I didn't make any money."

"That doesn't surprise me, all things con-sidered. Why did you choose to spend the night here, of all places?"

"I'm not sure . . . it wasn't something I'd planned." She made a languid gesture and blinked. "I walked for a while and just found myself in the streets behind the tannery."

"And at what time did you discover the body?"

"I don't know. I had to sell my watch." She scratched the back of her hand again. "Of course—I didn't know he was dead. I thought he'd fallen over and banged his head. But when I got close and saw the blood. So much of it . . ."

"That must have been very frightening."

Fräulein Uhe looked a little embarrassed. "Not really."

The constable was right, she was distinctly odd.

Rheinhardt scribbled a few notes. "You didn't touch the body, did you?"

"Why would I do that?"

"Forgive me," Rheinhardt smiled. "But would you be so kind as to show me the contents of your pockets?" The woman pulled out the grubby linings and left them hanging, before opening her coat wide to demonstrate that there were no other places of concealment. A scent came off her clothes, a sickly sweet smell that wasn't perfume. "So," Rheinhardt continued, "what was the next thing you did?"

The woman stuffed the linings back. "I went around to the police station on Hufelandgasse. They didn't believe me at first." She paused, coughed, and added, "I'd seen him earlier."

"I'm sorry?"

"The dead man, I'd seen him by the tannery."

"Did you speak to him?"

"He wasn't interested. He didn't want to talk."

"What did he say, exactly?"

" 'Go away' . . . and he used some very bad language."

"I see. And did you encounter anyone else by the tannery?" Fräulein Uhe sucked her lower lip and her brow creased. She was obviously engaged in some form of inward deliberation. "What is it?"

"Well, I thought I saw . . ." The sentence remained incomplete.

"Yes?" Rheinhardt prompted.

"No—it was nothing—a shadow—sometimes I see things that aren't really there. It's an eye problem. Can I go now? I'm very tired."

"Are you sure it was just a shadow?"

Fräulein Uhe's answer bore no relation to the question. "They didn't thank me, the Hufelandgasse constables. I did my best to help."

Rheinhardt found some coins in his pocket and showed them to Fräulein Uhe. Her eyes widened. "Now," he said, "if I were to offer you this small token of appreciation, would you consider spending it on a hearty breakfast—rather than opium?"

She looked from side to side, like a naughty child avoiding the censorious gaze of a parent. "I *am* hungry . . ."

"I guessed you might be." Rheinhardt wrote down the name and address of a women's hostel, tore the page from his notebook, and handed it to

Fräulein Uhe. "After breakfast, might I suggest you repair immediately to this establishment, where you will be given a bed, medical attention, and good counsel."

Fräulein Uhe scraped the coins from Rheinhardt's palm and hurried away, worried, perhaps, that he might suddenly change his mind. Rheinhardt signaled to one of the constables that Fräulein Uhe should be allowed to pass and he watched her until she disappeared around a corner. Would she find a coffeehouse and enjoy a hearty breakfast—as he had suggested? Eggs and käsekrainer sausages, a kaffee crème, warm bread, croissants, and plum conserve? Rheinhardt's stomach rumbled at the thought. Or would she go straight back to a life so sordid and chaotic that not even a brothel could make use of her? Sadly, the latter was far more likely than the former.

Rheinhardt walked toward the police photographer who was already at work with his assistant. Magnesium flashes illuminated the body and smoke hung in the air. A carriage overtook Rheinhardt and when it stopped the door flew open and Haussmann jumped out with considerable athleticism. He landed perfectly and stood to attention. "Good morning, sir." Rheinhardt took out his watch and tapped the glass. "Problem with the first cab, sir—broken wheel—could have been nasty."

"Are you familiar with the word 'hyperbole,' Haussmann?"

"Yes, sir. Exaggeration used for effect."

"Quite. I hope that isn't a smile, Haussmann."

"No, sir—perish the thought."

They both looked down at the body. A wide gash showed where a razor or some other sharp instrument had been drawn across the man's throat at the level of the laryngeal prominence. It was deep enough to reveal the open pipe of the trachea. He had lost an enormous amount of blood, most of which had congealed on the pavement.

"Finished," said the photographer, coming out from under his cover. "Poor chap . . . and so very young." After collecting their things together, the photographer and his assistant climbed into a waiting carriage. The driver cracked his whip and the photographer waved out of the window. When the rattling had diminished and it was possible to speak again, Rheinhardt said, "Well, Haussmann?"

"Young—dueling scar—a student, most probably."

"That's what I was thinking."

Rheinhardt squatted and tugged at the man's scarf. It was caked with dried blood and did not come away easily. Turning the material over revealed a label. Although stained, it was just about legible. "Ha! Boegal! The outfitters near the university." Rheinhardt felt inside the man's coat and found a book. *"Das Wesen des Christentums."* The Essence of Christianity.

"A theology student?"

Rheinhardt read: " 'God is man—man is God.' Perhaps not." He turned the book over and examined the spine. "Ludwig Feuerbach. I think it may be a critique of Christianity." He read out another sentence: " 'Religion is the dream of the human mind.' I strongly suspect that our friend Dr. Liebermann would agree with that. 'Christ was no miracle worker, nor, in general, that which he is represented to be in the Bible.' " Rheinhardt handed the book to Haussmann who placed it in an envelope. "What have we here . . ." Rheinhardt withdrew a dagger and held it up.

"Looks like he was expecting trouble, sir."

"I'm inclined to agree."

"Sir." Haussmann crouched down next to Rheinhardt and looked very closely at the victim's face.

"What on earth are you doing, Haussmann?"

"Sir, I think I've seen him before."

"Where?"

"He was one of the people who I followed— you know—one of the people who drank at The Golden Bears."

"What was his name?"

"I can't remember, there were so many of them. But I can remember where he lived. Obere

Weissgärberstrasse—the third district, near the canal. His name will be in the records."

The sound of horses' hooves made them look up. The mortuary van had arrived.

THIRTY-SIX

Herr Düsterbehn's eyebrows sprouted owlish curlicues and his beard was in dire need of barbering. He was a small, crabbed man, whose manner was gruff and discourteous. It was possible that he was simply having a bad day, but it seemed far more likely to Rheinhardt that Herr Düsterbehn was habitually out of humor.

Rheinhardt showed Herr Düsterbehn the photograph.

"Yes, that's him."

"How long has Herr Diamant been lodging with you?"

"Since October."

"A student."

"Yes."

"A philosophy student?"

"How should I know?" Düsterbehn snapped. Rheinhardt noticed that Haussmann was smirking. As Rheinhardt slipped the photograph back into its cardboard sleeve, he took the opportunity to glare at his assistant.

"Herr Diamant had a duelling scar . . . ," Rheinhardt ventured.

"He was always getting into scrapes." Düsterbehn thumped his chest and snarled, "Now what am I going to do?"

"I beg your pardon?"

"It's inconvenient. I'll have to find another lodger—and then there's all his things to get rid of, his books and his clothes." A new thought diluted the landlord's rancor: "Might be worth a couple of kronen."

"With respect, Herr Düsterbehn, you must not touch Herr Diamant's property."

"It's my house—I'll do whatever I like."

"Disturb his belongings and you'll be charged with obstructing the course of justice."

Düsterbehn treated Rheinhardt's threat with disdain. "You won't find what you're looking for under Diamant's bed or in his laundry basket, inspector!"

"And what do you suppose we're looking for?"

The splenetic landlord muttered a profanity and pointed out of the window. "You've come to the wrong address."

"I'm sorry?"

"Talk to Autenburg and his wife."

"Who?"

"Autenburg."

Düsterbehn's mouth twisted and it looked for a moment as if he were suffering from toothache. After a few seconds he produced a sound and Rheinhardt realized that actually, the landlord was chuckling. "And why should we do that?" Rheinhardt asked. Düsterbehn got up from his armchair and poured himself a glass of schnapps. "Well?"

"People are very stupid, inspector. Genius has its limitations but stupidity is boundless." Düsterbehn threw his head back and downed his liquor. "My doctor says it's good for the constitution. The air's not good here—near the canal . . ." He shuffled back to his armchair.

A cuckoo clock chimed and each strike was accompanied by the compression of miniature bellows and the appearance of a crudely carved bird through an aperture with flapping doors. Unexpectedly, Düsterbehn looked up and his face showed something approximating innocent pleasure. When the clock fell silent, Rheinhardt was direct and firm. "Tell us about Autenburg."

"The boy was always running across the road. And sometimes he didn't come back."

"He stayed there all night?"

"Yes, all night. You wouldn't believe what they got up to."

"Who?"

"The boy and Autenburg's wife. The curtains were never drawn. They didn't care."

Rheinhardt twisted one of the upturned horns of his moustache. "Was Herr Autenburg aware of what was going on?"

"Of course he was. They all slept under the same roof."

"And Herr Autenburg didn't object?"

"Perhaps that was the problem. Perhaps it all built up."

"What built up?"

"Resentment, anger—there's only so much provocation a man can take. The night before last, I saw them outside, arguing."

"Autenburg and his wife?"

"No. Autenburg and Diamant. Autenburg ended up trying to throttle the boy. He didn't get very far, he's not strong enough—but he tried all the same."

"They didn't see you?"

"No. I didn't have the lamp lit and they were too busy arguing."

"Could you hear what was being said?"

Düsterbehn shook his head. Rheinhardt removed a form from his inside pocket. "You are absolutely sure that the altercation you observed was between Autenburg and Diamant?"

"Yes."

"Then I must ask you to make an official statement."

"What, now?"

"Yes, now!"

Düsterbehn mumbled execrations into his chest and said, "I'll need some more schnapps."

THIRTY-SEVEN

Liebermann was confident that Herr Globocnik would be easily hypnotized. The man was highly suggestible—he *had* to be. After all, what was his illness, if it wasn't an extreme case of auto-suggestion, a self-induced distortion of reality? Globocnik was lying on the gurney and Liebermann was sitting behind him, just out of view.

"Are you ready?" Liebermann asked.

"Yes, I'm ready," Globocnik sniffed. "But I'm not sure what you hope to achieve."

"Just relax."

"I am relaxed."

Liebermann leaned back and looked up. "Do you see that small circular stain on the ceiling?"

"Yes."

"Well, I want you to empty your mind and concentrate on it."

"As you wish . . ." Globocnik's eyebrows drew closer together.

"Focus on the stain," Liebermann continued. "Keep focusing and very soon you will find that your eyelids are feeling heavier." Liebermann modulated his voice, slowing down his rate of delivery and allowing the pitch to drop. "Heavier and heavier . . ." Globocnik began to blink with

191

increasing frequency. "Feel the weight of your limbs—your arms feel heavy, your legs feel heavy—every time you breath out, you get a little closer to sleep." Liebermann continued in this manner, repeating sedative phrases, observing the small signs that presaged success. Globocnik was going to make an excellent hypnotic subject. The clerk's eyelids were fluttering and he seemed to be engaged in a struggle to stay awake. "Let go," Liebermann whispered. "Let go. When I count to three you will sink into a deep, dreamless sleep. But you will be able to hear my voice and answer my questions. One, two . . ." Globocnick's eyes were glimmering slits. "Three."

Liebermann allowed a few seconds to pass before he spoke again. "When did you see Fräulein Mugoša for the first time?"

Parallel lines appeared on the clerk's forehead. "November."

"At the factory?"

"She was working on the production line—collars."

"And did you find her attractive?"

"I thought she was . . ." Globocnik closed his mouth tightly and Liebermann could see the raised muscles.

"Relax," said Liebermann. "You are perfectly safe and can speak freely."

"I thought she was very beautiful," said Globocnik. Liebermann sensed that the clerk was about to say more and waited. "Her hair . . . I was always fascinated by its lustrous waves—and her mouth, its shape and color—and her eyes—their darkness and mystery." The rhythm of Globocnik's language was like a prayer. "No one else noticed these qualities. It was as if she was invisible."

"Did you speak to her?"

"No. It could never be. I had never known a woman and she was so very shapely and graceful. All I could do was admire her from afar. I was constantly finding excuses to tarry on the factory floor, just so that I could look at her. How wretched I became. The yearning that I experienced was a sweet and terrible agony, a torment that I recognized from the works of Goethe and other great poets. I was afflicted, stricken—and there was no hope of happiness, because I would never feel the warmth of her embrace. Then, one day, a miracle happened. I was in the yard, smoking, when she came out of the factory and asked me for a cigarette. She smiled and we talked. She said that I must be a very clever man to do the bookkeeping—and she said that she liked the cut of my suit. I felt like a giant. She suggested that we meet in Café Schwarzenberg the following Sunday. I could not believe that the gods had favored me with such good fortune. It was the first of many assignations."

"Did you make love?"

"Yes, we made love, on the tenth of December 1903, between the hours of nine and ten o'clock. During that hour, I was transformed. I became a man."

"Tell me . . . did Fräulein Mugoša ever ask you for money?"

"I helped her with some debts," said the clerk grandly. "And her wardrobe was rather small. I bought her a new dress from Taubenrach und Cie—and a hat in Habig's. She was like a bud that had suddenly burst into flower." Globocnik's expression became troubled. "But flowers are conspicuous in a dull, colorless world. People want to pick them and possess them."

"Herr Bok started to take an interest in her?"

At the mention of Bok's name Globocnik became agitated and Liebermann had to offer him more assurances of safety. When the clerk was still again, Liebermann repeated his question. No answer was forthcoming.

"What happened?" Liebermann asked, "After Herr Bok took an interest in Fräulein Mugoša? You must answer *all* my questions—honestly, truthfully."

"Herr Bok was a bad man," Globocnik replied, as his customary defenses reassembled. "I think he must always have been a bad man. From birth I imagine. You see, it's a question of morality . . . personal morality."

"Answer my question, Herr Globocnik. Do not be afraid. No harm will come to you." Liebermann placed his fingers on Globocnik's temples and pressed gently. "As the pressure increases, your memories rise out of darkness and clarify." Globocnik twisted his neck to free himself but Liebermann did not let his hands slip and he pressed harder.

"She grew cold," Globocnik whispered. "A garnet ring appeared on her finger. 'Where did you get that from?' I asked. 'I bought it,' she replied. But I knew she was lying. It was an expensive stone. We were sitting on a bench in the Stadtpark . . ."

"Yes?"

". . . and she said," Globocnik sniffed and groaned. "She said that we could not continue—that it had been a mistake—a regrettable misunderstanding. I begged her, I fell on my knees and kissed her hand, 'Milica, Milica, Milica, please, you are my life, you are my sun and stars, please, don't leave me.' But she was impervious to my entreaties. He had warped her mind, polluted her thoughts—hardened her heart. She was a simple country girl, easy prey for a man like Bok. He had corrupted her, made her impure—his plaything. I think he must always have been a bad man. From birth I imagine. You see . . ."

Liebermann pressed Globocnik's temples

195

again. "No. Go back. What happened next—after the Stadtpark?"

"I was sick with despair. I didn't sleep—I stayed up all night, smoking—pacing—beating my mattress and weeping into my pillow. In the morning I went to work. What else was there to do? I hoped that I might change her mind. She wasn't on the production line and when I went into the office, I found her sitting at my desk. Herr Bok told me to sit down. He told me that he had decided to invest in a calculating machine and that he no longer required my services." The clerk reproduced Bok's resonant braying as he relived the moment: " 'I know that I'm giving short notice, but be assured, Globocnik, you will be compensated.' I was dumbstruck. 'Come now, Globocnik, be reasonable. All is fair in love and war.' I looked over at Milica but she turned away. 'What have you done to her?' I demanded. I was convinced that he had exercised some malign influence, a clever manipulation, or even worse— blackmail, perhaps? It was up to me to save her. Who else, if not me? 'Don't be ridiculous, Globocnik.' Our exchanges became heated. 'Get out!' he shouted. 'Get out of my office before I throw you out.' He stood, grabbed my shirt, and lifted me off the ground. 'You sniveling piece of vermin.' His face had gone bright red and he was spitting. He pulled back his fist, ready to punch me on the nose, but I snatched the letter opener off his desk and held it up. I wanted to kill him, I wanted to thrust it into his heart . . . but I couldn't. I let my arm drop and Bok hurled me across the room. I stumbled and fell. An instant later he had kicked me in the stomach and all the air went from my lungs, I couldn't breathe, I couldn't move. And then, he was unbuttoning the flap of his trousers. He was a bad man . . ."

"No," Liebermann said, "you must remember. Be strong, Herr Globocnik, be strong!"

"He emptied his bladder." Globocnik sighed. "He pissed on me. And when I caught sight of Milica . . ."

"Go on."

"She . . . she was smiling. I scrambled to my feet and ran from the office, across the factory floor and out into the yard. I ran and ran, trying to distance myself from my humiliation. But you cannot run away from yourself—and wherever I ran—I burned with shame."

Liebermann released Globocnik's head. He folded his hands on his lap and said, with gentle emphasis, "Listen to me, Herr Globocnik. You do not need to escape from your shame—because you have nothing to be ashamed of. It is Herr Bok and Fräulein Mugoša who have disgraced themselves."

The clerk sighed and said in a distant, uncertain voice: "I have nothing to be ashamed of . . ."

"No, nothing at all."

"Nothing at all," Globocnik echoed.

"When you wake, you will recall everything we have discussed today. These memories will still cause you pain, but it is a pain that you will be able to withstand."

". . . a pain that I will be able to withstand."

A gentle knocking captured Liebermann's attention. He tip-toed to the door and opened it a fraction. The face of a young nurse could be seen through the narrow gap.

"What is it?"

"Telephone—a policeman called Rheinhardt. He says it's a matter of some urgency."

"Take his number and tell him I'll call him back shortly."

The nurse nodded and withdrew. Liebermann closed the door and returned to his seat, where he remained for a few moments, gazing down at his patient, reflecting on the easy, commonplace dispensation of human cruelty. Where would it end?

THIRTY-EIGHT

Liebermann and Rheinhardt were seated opposite Eduard and Della Autenburg. Between them, the surface of the table was cluttered with pens, ink pots, and papers. There were also several academic publications and an old, yellowing copy of the *Neue Freie Presse*. The room in which they were seated was a well-stocked library. Haussmann had chosen not to sit and was standing with his hands behind his back, adjacent to an aspidistra on a high wooden stand.

Rheinhardt opened his notebook. "What is your occupation, Herr Autenburg?"

"I am a publisher," Autenburg replied. "History and philosophy, mostly."

"That must be a very rewarding profession."

"Certainly, although, it is becoming increasingly precarious."

"Oh?"

"I can't help feeling with so many distractions—cheap seats at the opera house, exciting new rides on the Prater, and free reading matter readily available in the coffeehouses—people are buying fewer books these days."

"Well, I'm sorry to hear that. As far as I am concerned, there is nothing quite so improving or enjoyable than an evening spent at home, seated in a comfortable chair, with a book on one's lap. You know, I was talking to a writer only the other day. Clement Kruckel?"

"The journalist."

"Do you know him?"

"We've met many times. I've always wanted to publish a collection of some of his early writings. They are incisive and often very amusing; a sharper wit than Kraus, in my humble opinion." He laughed and then said more soberly: "But I'm sure you're not here to discuss our coffeehouse wits. Forgive me, inspector, but why are you here?"

Rheinhardt smiled politely. "I understand that Herr Kruckel has become very active in the field of education."

"He has always considered it of great importance that the working man should be politically well-informed."

"Does the name 'Fraternitas' mean anything to you?"

"Yes. It's the name of Kruckel's society."

"Have you ever attended one of his meetings?"

"No," Autenburg shook his head. "We're only acquaintances."

Della caught her husband's eye and asked, without the necessity of language: *What's going on?* Autenburg shrugged and pursed his lips. Rheinhardt made some notes and said, "The Golden Bears . . ."

"Yes." Autenburg's perplexity intensified.

"Do you know it?"

"I know it very well. It's a beer cellar in Leopoldstadt, not to everyone's taste, but it attracts an interesting clientele and the atmosphere is convivial."

Rheinhardt turned to address Della. "Do you go there too?"

"Eduard works hard," Della replied. "We don't get the chance to go there together very often."

She was younger than Autenburg. A slim woman endowed with a disproportionately inflated bust, a long neck, and thick chestnut hair. Her eyes were constantly slipping away to the side, almost with intent, as if she were trying to surreptitiously communicate that she wished to talk in private.

Rheinhardt tapped his pencil on the open page of his notebook. "Did either of you ever meet an Italian gentleman called Tab?"

Husband and wife looked at each other, shook their heads, and then looked back at their inquisitor with blank expressions.

"Tab wasn't his real name," Rheinhardt continued. "His real name was Angelo Callari." Autenburg's head continued to shake. "He met Herr Kruckel in The Golden Bears and attended a Fraternitas meeting in Kruckel's apartment."

"I'm sorry," said Autenburg. "The name means nothing to me."

Liebermann felt a shoe knock against his foot

under the table. Opposite, Della Autenburg was giving him a smoldering look, and, as was her habit, apparently suggesting the direction of some imaginary assignation with her restless eyes. Liebermann coughed and crossed his legs, removing his foot out of harm's way. He had already made his diagnosis.

"What about Axl Diamant?" said Rheinhardt.

Autenburg replied, "Ah—yes—we know Axl Diamant very well. He lives across the road in the house opposite."

"And what is the nature of your relationship?"

"I often meet young men of promise and have made it a kind of avocation to offer them guidance and, where it is in my gift, opportunities for advancement. I assisted Axl with his essays, allowed him to use my library." Autenberg raised his hands and made horizontal circles in the air. "And once, I paid for the production and distribution of a polemical pamphlet he wished to write."

"What was it about?"

Autenburg made an appeasing gesture and appeared a little uncomfortable. "You will appreciate, I hope, inspector, that we—that is, my wife and I—inhabit a social milieu where no topic is considered unsuitable for debate. We have few, if any, sacred cows."

"What was it about?" Rheinhardt repeated frostily.

"The pamphlet," Autenburg continued, "was a critique of the church; well, not so much the church, but rather the church's vested interest in the preservation of traditional family values. Axl proposed some interesting alternatives to the accepted social order, a more *communal* approach to the raising of children, for example."

"Do you have a copy?"

"No—I'm afraid not. Do you, Della?"

"No," Della replied. "I gave the last one away some time ago."

Rheinhardt was about to ask another question when he was interrupted by Liebermann. "Herr Autenburg," said the young doctor, leaning some way forward. "I notice that you bite your nails."

"Yes," said Autenburg, glancing at his fingertips. "I suppose I do."

"How long have you been doing that?"

"I couldn't say. A long time—I might even have done so as a child."

"No, I think not."

"I beg your pardon?"

"There is no deformity, no scarring. Years of nail biting can destroy the nail bed and cause repeated infection. Moreover, you exhibit no malocclusion of the anterior teeth."

"I'm sorry?"

"There is no misalignment. Your teeth are straight. No, this is a much more recent development."

Everyone present was expecting Liebermann to continue, but instead, he looked at Rheinhardt and said respectfully, "My apologies for interrupting, inspector. Please continue."

Rheinhardt did not react, except for a barely perceptible pinching at the corner of his mouth. He twirled his moustache and continued as if Liebermann hadn't spoken. "When was the last time you saw Axl Diamant, Herr Autenburg?"

"The night before last," Autenburg replied.

"Where?"

"Right outside this building, we had been to a fascinating talk on Sombart's two volume history: *Der moderne Kapitalismus*."

"Who?"

"Werner Sombart. He's an economist."

"Do you know where Herr Diamant went, after you parted?"

"He went home. Well, that's where I assumed he was going. He might have changed his mind, but I was already inside before he'd reached the other side of the road. Why are you asking these questions?"

Liebermann coughed and raised a finger. "I'm sorry, Herr Autenburg, but have you been suffering from more stomach complaints than usual?"

Autenburg was momentarilly confused. "I—well—yes. Yes, I have actually. But what has that—"

Liebermann cut in: "They tend to go together, you see. Nail biting and stomach complaints. If you stopped biting your nails the stomach complaints would very probably improve."

The publisher eyed Liebermann with suspicion and said with brittle courtesy, "Thank you for your advice, Herr Doctor. I am sure that it will prove very useful."

Liebermann struck a haughty attitude. It was as if he had transcended the quotidian plane and existed in some refined Hippocratic realm where expressions of gratitude from patients were unnecessary and, if anything, slightly annoying.

"Have you finished, Herr Doctor?" asked Rheinhardt, who in actuality was now also eyeing Liebermann with a degree of suspicion.

"Yes," Liebermann replied. "I've finished."

Rheinhardt made a note and while he was still writing said, "Frau Autenburg, what was the precise nature of your relationship with Herr Diamant?"

"We were friends," Della replied.

Rheinhardt's expression showed obvious dissatisfaction with the answer. "With respect, Frau Autenburg, would it be perhaps more accurate to—"

"That's enough, inspector!" Autenburg slapped the table top. "Have you been spying on us?"

Rheinhardt sighed. "I really do not wish to embarrass Frau Autenburg; but unfortunately

I am obliged to clarify the nature of her relationship with Herr Diamant for reasons that will soon become apparent."

"I'm afraid that you are confirming all my existing prejudices with respect to the police," said Autenburg angrily. "Am I wrong to suppose that we live in a free country, where citizens are at liberty to do as they please in their own homes, providing they cause no harm to others?"

"Believe me, Herr Autenburg, your domestic arrangements, however unorthodox, are of no particular interest to the security office."

"Indeed!"

"However . . ."

Autenburg took a deep breath, but his attempt at self-control failed miserably. "The world is changing, inspector. Women are no longer willing to accept the inequalities of the past. A human being should not be treated as a possession and ownership has no legitimacy in a civilized and enlightened society. What you call our unorthodox domestic arrangements represent a step forward—the future."

"I meant no offense," said Rheinhardt.

Liebermann was drumming his fingers. When the drumming stopped, he said, "Those nails of yours . . ."

"What?" Autenburg growled.

"Do you really believe that we are free to live any in any way we choose? That we can simply ignore our primitive instincts? We are animals—after all—sophisticated apes. And in the animal kingdom, the male of the species jealously guards his mate and fights off competitors. To repress the primitive requires the expenditure of enormous amounts of psychic energy—the individual becomes excessively fraught, anxious."

"That is utter nonsense, Herr Doctor. Every time we postpone sleep or a meal, we are denying our biological imperatives—and with no ill effect."

"I don't think that's quite the same thing. One's wife isn't really comparable to a beef stew."

Haussmann let out a laugh and Rheinhardt rounded on him. "Haussmann!"

"Sorry, sir." The assistant detective bowed his head in shame.

"The night before last, Herr Autenburg," Rheinhardt resumed. "When you and Diamant parted . . . did you do so amicably?"

Autenburg touched the apex of his Van Dyke beard. "We had been discussing a point of political philosophy. There may have been a difference of opinion—what of it? We are always debating issues."

"Debating—or arguing?"

"Yes, we argued—because we are men of conviction. How can one establish what is true without argument?"

"Did you disagree often?"

"Yes, of course."

"These ideological debates," said Liebermann. "Has it occurred to you, Herr Autenburg, that all along, you were really arguing about something else entirely?"

"I'm afraid, once again, I am finding your interjections rather opaque, Herr Doctor."

"Then might I draw your attention, *once again,* to the condition of your nails. They are not the nails of a man who is entirely comfortable with his domestic arrangements."

Autenburg ignored Liebermann and addressed Rheinhardt. "What is your business here?"

Slowly, Rheinhardt took a photograph from his pocket and slid it across the table, negotiating a path between the clutter. "The body of Axl Diamant was found early this morning. His throat had been cut."

Della gasped and looked away.

"He was always getting into trouble," Autenburg shook his head. "I knew something like this would happen in the end."

Rheinhardt closed his notebook. "The night before last—before you parted—you tried to strangle him."

"I—" Autenburg's mouth opened but no words followed.

"We have a witness," Rheinhardt continued. "Herr Düsterbehn from across the road. He's already made a statement."

Finally Autenburg recovered his voice. "Are you accusing me of murdering Axl Diamant?"

Rheinhardt picked up his notebook with an air of finality. "I am afraid you'll have to accompany us to the Schottenring station."

Della stood up and distanced herself from her husband. "Eduard. You didn't. Tell me you didn't."

"Of course I didn't!" Autenburg cried.

Della placed the back of her right hand against her forehead and her body shaped itself into a collapsing spiral. She did not so much hit the floor, as artfully unfurl into a supine position with her legs and arms projecting at equidistant angles. Her ample bosom was rising and falling, the flesh threatening to escape containment as her lungs filled with air.

"Shouldn't you attend to her?" Rheinhardt prompted his friend.

"Oh, I suppose so," Liebermann replied, with some reluctance.

Liebermann, Rheinhardt, Autenburg, and Haussmann stepped out onto Obere Weissgärberstrasse. A constable in a long coat was hurrying toward them, his hand raised.

"Detective Inspector Rheinhardt?"

"Yes."

"Constable Plücker—Rudolfsgasse, sir." The constable clicked his heels and waited a few moments to catch his breath. "Urgent message— Schottenring." Rheinhardt nodded and the two men stepped aside. "You are to proceed without delay to the Beatrix Hotel." The constable handed Rheinhardt a scrap of paper with a barely legible address scribbled on it. "Thurngasse: 9th district."

Rheinhardt dropped the scrap into his pocket. "Why?"

"Oh yes, sorry, sir—forgot to say, went right out of my head, what with the rush—I didn't think I'd get here in time to catch you." The constable looked over his shoulder before whispering, "A gentleman, sir. Shot dead, sir."

Rheinhardt beckoned Liebermann. "I don't suppose you're free for the rest of the afternoon?"

"No, Oskar," Liebermann replied. "I really must get back the hospital. Is there a problem?"

THIRTY-NINE

As Rheinhardt emerged from the cab he glanced up at a high facade decorated with balconets, pilasters, and raised rococo pendants. The overall effect, however, was rather moribund; the cracked, faded stucco somehow suggested the lined face of an old duchess. This impression of sad disintegration was reinforced by the foyer, a yawning, dusty chamber which was dominated by a feebly glowing crystal chandelier. An imitation Roman amphora, positioned in the middle of a round wooden table, had been filled with artificial flowers, but even these had started to droop. The stems could not support the weight of the silk petals. Beyond the table and standing in front of the reception desk were two men, a dapper fellow with wavy hair and a thin moustache and a constable from the Schottenring station.

"Constable . . ." Rheinhardt recognized the stout policeman but had forgotten his name.

"Schwacke, sir." The constable turned toward his well-dressed companion, who exuded a sweet and overpowering fragrance that resembled a combination of lilac and marzipan. "May I introduce the manager of the hotel, Herr Okolski."

The dapper man's low bow was foppish and complex. "Feliks Okolski. At your service, Herr Inspector." He also had a slight lisp.

"My name is Rheinhardt and this is my assistant, Haussmann."

The manager repeated his impressive bow, adding further flourishes and cried, "What a fearful tragedy!" He pulled a red folded handkerchief from the breast pocket of his jacket and shook it open, releasing another heady scent. He then dabbed his forehead, somewhat unnecessarily, because he wasn't perspiring. "I can't believe that this atrocity was perpetrated in *my* hotel."

"Murders can happen anywhere, Herr Okolski."

"But *my* hotel! Really . . ."

Rheinhardt glanced at Haussmann who was, once again, attempting unsuccessfully to disguise a smirk.

"Was the murdered man one of your guests?"

"Yes," Okolski replied. "His name is—perhaps it would be more fitting to use the past tense? His name *was* Herr Kelbling. Gerd Kelbling."

"What do you know about him?"

"Very little, I'm sorry to say. He made his reservation some time ago and as I recall he was very particular about his requirements. He wanted the fourth suite on the second floor and wouldn't accept any other, even though they're all identical. He took the suite for three months and paid the full remittance two weeks in advance of his arrival. He never spoke to anyone or ordered food. In fact, I'd never laid eyes on him before today."

"Three months?"

"Our rates are very competitive, our accommodation is spacious, and though I say so myself, our restaurant serves a truly delicious bryndzové halušky. We have a new Slovak chef. I poached him from the Imperial and you wouldn't believe what he can do with a little sheep's cheese and bacon."

Rheinhardt spoke through a forced smile. "I'm sure that your chef is very gifted, but returning to the principal issue . . ."

"Of course, inspector." Okolski's consent was accompanied by a decorous flap of his handkerchief.

"How long has Herr Kelbling been residing at the Beatrix?"

"Nine weeks."

A maid appeared, balancing a mop on her shoulder. Rheinhardt waited for her to pass before asking his next question: "And when was the body discovered?"

"About two hours ago. There was a loud bang." Okolski clapped his hands together, concerned that Rheinhardt might be in danger of underestimating the volume of the report. "And I decided that I would investigate myself, with the assistance of Herr Bajramovic."

"Who?"

"Herr Bajramovic, our porter."

"Where is he now?"

"Oh, he's in the kitchen, having a drink. A little early, perhaps, but he's very fond of cognac and I thought his willingness to assist should be rewarded. To be perfectly honest, I might not have ventured up the stairs without his encouragement." He refolded the red handkerchief and pushed it back into his breast pocket, allowing a neat triangle to show. "Some of the guests had, rather foolishly, come out onto the landings and I had to be quite firm with them. I told them to return to their rooms and to await further notice. On the second floor we found a door wide open—suite number four. Herr Bajramovic and I entered and . . ." Okolski shuddered.

"You didn't see anyone rushing away from the scene, trying to leave the building in a hurry?"

"No?"

"What about the guests? Did they see anyone?"

"I don't know. You'll have to ask them, inspector."

"I'm assuming that you went up that staircase over there," Rheinhardt gestured across the foyer.

"Yes."

"Are there others?"

"Yes. There is a second staircase on the other side of the building and a service staircase that is not for public use. Once the gunman was on the ground floor he could have made his way to the back of the building and made his escape through one of two exits. I suspect that he used the exit that is reached through the store rooms."

"All right," said Rheinhardt. "I suppose we'd better go up."

Okolski led the way, assuming an air of great importance. When they arrived outside suite number four, Okolski unlocked the door and ushered his party in. Reinhardt paused and instructed Schwacke: "Don't let anyone pass unless they're from Schottenring." The constable clicked his heels and stood to attention.

A body was stretched out between an armchair and a sofa—arms angled on either side of the head.

"It's getting dark," said Okolski, "I'll attend to the lighting."

Rheinhardt and Haussmann stood over the dead man: early forties, brown, slightly brindled hair, and a tidy beard. There were no rings on his fingers. Okolski returned and said, "All the lamps have been lit. Before I go, can I get you anything? A pastry from the kitchen, perhaps?"

It was only Haussmann's cautionary, raised eyebrows that gave Rheinhardt the strength to resist. "That is a most generous offer, Herr Okolski, but regretfully, we must decline."

"Of course, of course." Okolski bowed and

reversed out of the room with his head still bent forward.

The dead man was wearing a white shirt, the entire front of which was stained with blood. Rheinhardt knelt on the floor and held a small hand mirror under the dead man's nose, but no condensation formed on the glass.

"Unlikely, sir," said Haussmann.

"Yes, I know," Rheinhardt replied.

Rheinhardt withdrew the mirror and searched the man's pockets. He found a tram ticket which he handed to his assistant. "A floor plan, please?"

"Yes, sir."

Rheinhardt stood up, with some difficulty, and walked over to an attractive writing bureau with carved feet. He lowered the hinged flap and found some stationary, supplied by the hotel, and an envelope stuffed with 100 kronen banknotes. Behind an adjacent door was a large bedroom. The wardrobe smelt strongly of napthalene because a whole box of moth balls had been carelessly emptied beneath the hanging clothes. A drawer at the bottom of the wardrobe contained underwear, a few ties, collar studs, and cuff links. An umbrella was hooked over the clothes rod. On entering a second, smaller bedroom, Rheinhardt was surprised by the pomposity of the décor: velvet curtains, gold tasseled ropes, and a four-poster bed, behind which was a floor-to-ceiling tapestry populated by knights, ladies in wimples, and rampant unicorns. The coverlet was a little wrinkled and there was a slight depression in the pillow. On the wall opposite the tapestry was a crudely executed portrait in oils of a kingly man with curly hair and mad eyes. An engraved metal plate set into the lower horizontal of the picture frame read: "Bolko the Small, ruler of Schweidnitz, Piast Dynasty." A chest of drawers was completely empty, except for a half-sphere of black rubber, about the size of a coffee cup, attached to a short length of flexible tubing.

Haussmann appeared, notebook raised. He leaned against the doorjamb and said, laconically, "Two bedrooms."

"Indeed," Rheinhardt replied. "Why would a single man, with hardly any possessions, pay for a whole suite for three months?"

"Maybe he was waiting for someone?"

"And why did he want this suite—specifically?"

Haussmann walked over to the window and peered through the nets. "Perhaps you can see something from here that you can't see from anywhere else?"

Rheinhardt wasn't convinced. "What do you think this is?" As Haussmann turned, Rheinhardt held up the rubber half-sphere and pulled the length of tubing so it was taut.

"Looks like a piece of medical equipment. Something you might use to deliver gas to a patient."

Rheinhardt placed the rubber dome over his nose, took a few breaths, and then removed it. "No, I don't think so. It doesn't cover my nose and mouth. A gas mask would have to be larger and a different shape."

"Then something a chemist might use?"

"Perhaps."

There were voices outside and Rheinhardt left the bedroom to see who had arrived. He found the photographer and his overburdened young assistant gazing at the dead man.

"Two in one day, inspector. I'm glad that it's you who reports directly to the commissioner and not me."

"Thank you," said Rheinhardt, rolling back on his heels. "That is *just* what I wanted to hear."

FORTY

Razumovsky was standing on a corner opposite the opera house. He studied his pocket watch and then turned to admire the westward prospect: high buildings on either side of the wide boulevard receded into a milky distance. The fine domes and lanterns of the art and natural history museums were like an exquisite mirage, a magical kingdom materializing at the end of a long canyon. He put his watch away and looked up at the white sky. There were two statues of winged horses on the opera house, preparing to leap into space and ascend into the heavens. A great deal of traffic, mostly trams, rattled by, and the sidewalks were bustling with people: men in bowler hats, boys pulling carts, ladies trailing capes, and porters pushing trolleys heavily laden with boxes. Three street cleaners, wearing baggy coats and peaked caps, were unwinding a hose. The majority of the hose was wrapped around a drum suspended between two massive wooden wheels. When a sufficient length of the hose had been freed, the senior cleaner—who looked surprisingly regal—aimed the nozzle and released a jet of water onto the cobbles. A pile of horse excrement was pushed toward a drain and some of the spray spotted the hem of

Razumovsky's trousers. He stepped back a few paces, tugged his gloves, and repositioned his ornate Turkish scarf. It was important that the scarf should remain visible.

One of the many bowler-hatted men stepped out of the fast flowing stream of passersby and said, "What have you got for me?"

Razumovsky handed the man a piece of paper. "Go to this address. You'll find the larder very well stocked."

The man slipped the paper into his coat pocket and looked across the road to the opera house. "I might catch a performance while I'm here."

"Yes. Why not?"

The man tapped the brim of his hat. "Good day."

Razumovsky nodded and the man walked off at a brisk pace. Two musicians carrying violin cases jumped over the water jet and the street cleaner shook his fist at them with evident good humor. When Razumovsky looked for the bomb-maker he was already gone.

FORTY-ONE

Straight through the sternum," said Professor Mathias. He picked up a small fret saw and laid its sharp metal teeth on the plate of exposed bone. He then began to move his arm backward and forward. The grating sound made Rheinhardt look away.

"You know," said Mathias, casually. "I have a great fondness for the first Joseph. He was a truly splendid emperor."

"Really?" Rheinhardt responded. "I thought he was a heavy drinker with a weakness for improper sexual conduct and firearms."

"Exactly!" Mathias laid his fret saw aside and pulled the dead man's rib cage open. "He was only on the throne for a few years."

"Yes," said Rheinhardt. "We'll never know what a man with his qualities would have achieved if he'd lived longer. Presumably he was syphilitic?"

"Oh, inspector, please, don't be such a prig! The great pleasure of history is its parade of colorful characters."

"I wasn't being sanctimonious, professor, I was being sarcastic."

"A form of wit best avoided, I feel—especially where there is no evidence of natural aptitude."

The old man seemed to be rummaging around in Kelbling's chest in much the same way as he might if he were at home searching through a sock drawer. His forearms were spattered with blood and a few drops had dried on the lenses of his spectacles. "Have you heard the story about Joseph and the Jesuit, inspector?"

"No."

Mathias removed Kelbling's torn heart, pointed out the damage, and slapped it down on the table. "As you might imagine, Joseph was never overly vexed by matters of the spirit and he became increasingly intolerant of religious divisions and fundamentalists. Thus, it didn't matter to him one jot that a particular man he chose to favor with an elevated station was of the protestant persuasion. A Jesuit, shocked by Joseph's profanity, decided on a scheme that would renew the emperor's commitment to the one, true congregation. After disguising himself as a ghost, the Jesuit gained entry into the emperor's bedroom, where he applied himself to the considerable challenge of terrifying his monarch; however, Joseph was not a credulous man. He immediately rang for his servants and promptly ordered them to throw the Jesuit out of the window."

"Did the Jesuit die?"

"I don't know," Mathias shrugged. "Presumably." The old man turned to pick up what looked like a pair of pliers from his cart.

"Have you found it?" Rheinhardt asked.

Mathias ignored the question and said, "*Amore et timore.*"

"I beg your pardon?"

" 'Through love and fear' . . . that was Joseph's motto. And not a bad motto, if a motto is supposed to be instructive as well as representative. I'm sure your friend Dr. Liebermann would agree that much of the human comedy is shaped by either love or fear." Mathias craned over the corpse, his elbow moving backward and forward. "This is a little like extracting a tooth. Ah, success. Hold out your hand, inspector." Rheinhardt did as he was instructed and Mathias dropped the bullet onto the policeman's palm. "It was lodged in the fifth thoracic vertebra," Mathias added, with unusual gaiety.

Rheinhardt wiped the bullet clean and held it beneath the electric light.

"What?" Asked Mathias.

"How strange."

"What's strange?"

"I think it's the same."

"You're not making much sense, inspector."

"My apologies, professor. I think it's identical to the bullet we found in the abandoned piano factory."

"Projectiles are fairly standard, aren't they?"

"This one isn't."

FORTY-TWO

Rheinhardt was sitting in his favorite armchair, smoking a mild, faintly sweet cigar that baited the palate with hints of toffee and burnt almond. Exhaling a cloud of smoke, he turned the pages of the *Police Gazette*. In the international section he read that the United States Bureau of Identification was about to establish a fingerprint collection. *Interesting,* he thought. They were clearly convinced of the new method's utility. He attempted to carry on reading but Therese, the elder of his two daughters, was playing Suk's D minor "Elegy" for the piano, a sad tune that floated over an insistent, dotted quaver monotone. The result defied categorization and fell somewhere between a funeral march and a lullaby. Mitzi, his younger daughter, was perched on a stool, sketching her piano-playing sister with a piece of charcoal. He returned his attention back to the article and carried on reading until his wife, Else, touched his shoulder. With a minute movement of her head, she communicated that she wished to speak to him in private. Rheinhardt stubbed out his cigar and followed Else out of the room. As they walked down the hallway he admired her figure. The passage of time and the accumulation of avoirdupois had not altered her essential, hourglass shape and he experienced a quick, fiery lick of desire.

They entered their bedroom and when Else turned to face him, she was frowning.

"What is it?" He asked.

"There's something wrong with Mitzi," Else replied.

"She's unwell?"

"No. She's perfectly healthy, she just isn't herself. She's out of sorts."

"What do you mean?"

"She's been very quiet lately—withdrawn— I've caught her crying a few times."

"Did you ask her what was wrong?"

"Yes, of course . . . but she just shakes her head and says it's nothing."

"Perhaps it's her age."

"No. I don't think so."

"All right—I'll talk to her."

Else leaned forward and kissed him on the cheek. "Thank you."

"I'm sorry," Rheinhardt sighed. "I hadn't noticed."

"You're busy, I know. It doesn't matter." She smiled and combed his hair back with her fingers.

When they returned to the parlor Rheinhardt yawned and stretched his arms. "I need some fresh air. Come along, Mitzi, you can keep me company."

Therese stopped playing and objected. "What about me?"

"Finish your practice," Rheinhardt replied. "Another time, perhaps."

Mitzi placed her charcoal and sketchbook on the table and slid off the stool. "Where are we going?"

"Nowhere in particular," Rheinhardt replied.

Outside, the evening was fresh and clear. They wandered around side streets talking intermittently about subjects of little consequence: a new ride at the Prater, the possibility of snow, a long postposed ascent of the Kahlenberg. Eventually they found themselves on Josefstädter Strasse, where they stopped to look at the vast number of volumes displayed in the window of Steckler's bookshop.

"I wonder how long it would take to read all those?" Mitzi asked.

"A lifetime," Rheinhardt replied. "But a lifetime well spent." His knees cracked as he lowered himself into a crouch that permitted him to meet his daughter's gaze. For a few seconds, he was speechless, overthrown by the miniature perfection of her features. Parental pride made Rheinhardt's chest swell and his eyes prickled with emotion. "You're mother tells me that you haven't been happy lately."

A long silence followed and Rheinhardt had to change position to relieve the pain in his lower back.

"You mustn't do anything," said Mitzi anxiously. "You mustn't arrest anyone."

"I'm sure that won't be necessary."

"There's this girl at school. She's bigger than the rest of us. Her name's Tibelda."

"And what does Tibelda do that is making you unhappy?"

"Whenever we're alone she pinches me and pulls my hair and says horrible things."

"Why don't you tell your teacher?"

"You get called names for doing that."

"Yes," Rheinhardt nodded, sagely. "That's true. A difficult situation . . ."

A soldier marched past. He was carrying sealed documents under his arm and he was clearly in a hurry. Everything about him suggested that his errand was a matter of importance and urgency.

"Were you ever bullied at school?" Mitzi asked.

"Yes," Rheinhardt replied, "when I was small. I know it's hard to believe, but I was smaller than you once. The thing to remember, my dear, is this: bullies are, fundamentally, cowards. They only intimidate those who don't retaliate. As soon as I realized this, the solution to my predicament seemed relatively straightforward." Her lower lip was trembling. He could feel her pain and confusion. "Look," Rheinhardt continued. "Let me show you something. I want you to copy me." He stood up and presented his left side to his daughter. "Never make it easy for your opponent.

227

The less of you they see, the less they can hit." He drew his right fist back and pressed it against his hip, the clenched fingers facing skyward. Mitzi imitated the stance. "Good. I'm going to do this slowly." He extended his right arm and rotated his body counterclockwise at the same time. "You can make a punch so much more powerful if you put the weight of your body behind it. And at the point of impact, give your fist a quick turn. Do you see?" Mitzi reproduced her father's sequence of movements. "Excellent, now do it as fast you can." Her mimicry was perfect. "Do you know, my dear, that was rather good."

Rheinhardt stood squarely in front of his daughter. He opened his coat and said, "Right—now—I want you to imagine that I am Tibelda and I want you to punch me in the stomach as hard as you can."

"Are you sure?"

"Yes."

"But what if it hurts?"

"I'm hoping it will."

Mitzi reversed her fist. Rheinhardt hadn't bothered tensing his abdominal muscles because he wasn't expecting the punch to be very hard. Subsequently, he was surprised when Mitzi's knuckles twisted into his gut. He threw his head back and laughed at the stars. "Mitzi, you're a natural! That was quite exceptional! Particularly the twist at the end—I'll have a bruise tomorrow, almost certainly." Mitzi laughed along with her father, giddy with empowerment. "Not very ladylike of course," Rheinhardt continued, "but there you are . . ." He lowered his voice. "Better not tell your mother, eh? I suspect she won't approve. Do it again, only harder. See if you can knock me through Herr Steckler's window."

Mitzi threw another punch and Rheinhardt pretended to stumble. "Almost!"

A steady, neutral voice said: "Good evening, sir."

Rheinhardt turned his head and discovered that the voice belonged to Constable Schwacke.

"Ahh . . ." Rheinhardt cleared his throat. "You again."

"Yes, sir. Me again." Schwacke repeated.

"Out on your beat?

"Yes, sir."

"This is my daughter—Mitzi."

The constable bowed, revealing the sharpness of the spike on his helmet. Mitzi responded with a curtsy. When his upper body was vertical again, Schwacke said, "Might I ask, sir: what are you doing?"

"What does it look like?"

"You appear to be encouraging your daughter to deliver punches to your stomach."

"Do you have any children, Schwacke?"

"No, sir. But I am courting."

"Well, that's a start. You see, if you had

children, constable, I'd be more inclined to explain myself. As things stands, I'm not at all sure that it would be worth the effort. Anything to report?"

"No, sir. It's been a very quiet evening."

"Good, good. Let's hope it stays that way."

Schwacke, bowed, clicked his heels, and walked off, his sabre clicking against his boots.

"Can I hit you again?" Mitzi asked.

FORTY-THREE

Rheinhardt arrived at Liebermann's apartment much later than usual. He was welcomed cordially by the young doctor and they went directly to the piano where they played and sang until eleven o'clock, the hour at which all domestic music makers in Vienna were officially obliged to stop. Their last choice of song was Schubert's setting of Heine's "Ihr bild"—Her Likeness—a bitter poem about a man weeping over the image of his former lover. Such genius, thought Liebermann as he played the bare, exposed B flats at the beginning. They were the tonal equivalent of a numb, grief-stricken stare. Rheinhardt adopted a frozen pose and his expressive baritone described the grim reality of lost happiness:

Ich stand in dunkeln Träumen . . .

I stood in dark dreams . . .

Apart from a brief modulation into the key of G flat Major, the music was relentlessly bleak and remarkably explicit. It was obvious to Liebermann that the purpose of the echoing phrases was to contrast the poet's miserable present with the fading recollections of his happier days.

Rheinhardt invested the last line with terrible, almost unbearable sorrow:

Und ach, ich kann es nicht glauben.

And ah, I cannot believe I have lost you.

Liebermann pounded the last dread chords and the two men waited, motionless, for the notes to fade. A faint reverberation, a residue of the song's essence, seemed to hang on the air.

The two men entered the smoking room. They lit cigars and Liebermann poured brandy into crystal glasses. After a few minutes Rheinhardt shifted in his seat, cleared his throat, and said, "So. Why did you keep on mentioning Autenburg's finger nails? What was all that about?"

Liebermann swirled the liquid in his glass and took a sip before speaking. "I suspect that Frau Autenburg would have been of great interest to Krafft-Ebing. I'm sure that if he had had the opportunity to assess her, he would have found room for Frau Autenburg in the *Psychopathia Sexualis*—between cases 189 and 190."

"Why those?"

"They were celebrated nymphomaniacs."

Rheinhardt tutted. "Max, I asked you about Autenburg's nails."

"Indeed." Liebermann continued. "But Autenburg's onychophagia was clearly caused by his wife's sexual delinquency. One can imagine the poor man, sitting in his library, tormented by the sound of creaking bed springs and his wife's groans of pleasure; tortured by imaginings of her pale, naked body writhing on a rumpled sheet, her hair in disarray."

"Yes, yes, Max." Rhenhardt made an impatient gesture. "You don't have to be quite so graphic. I'm perfectly capable of picturing the scene."

"This is the problem with socialists and anarchists," Liebermann said with disdain. "They espouse sexual equality, but then go too far, they overcompensate. It isn't possible to live beyond natural tolerances without having to pay a high emotional price. Autenburg bit his nails because, in reality, however much he pretended otherwise, he could not repress his true feelings. He couldn't bear the thought of another man enjoying his wife. He only allowed his wife to sleep with Diamant to demonstrate his commitment to a political ideal." Liebermann hammered his temple with a bent finger. "It was all up here—in his head—an intellectual pipe dream. The *real* Autenburg—the flesh and blood human being, with a beating heart and emotions—hated himself for yielding his connubial privileges to a younger man, a former protégé no less. Subsequently, he expressed his self-loathing by means of an unseemly act of oral aggression."

"Nail-biting?" Rheinhardt protested. "Not that unseemly, surely?"

"A finger resembles the male reproductive organ."

"Oh, come now, Max."

"His onychophagia was symbolic."

Rheinhardt sighed. "So he was enacting the punishment that he thought he deserved?"

Liebermann shrugged. "That's one way of putting it."

"I've heard you use much the same words—and on many occasions." Liebermann shrugged again and looked away. Rheinhardt crossed his legs, leaned back, and examined the ceiling. "Isn't it possible that Autenburg bit his nails simply because he was anxious?"

"Yes," said Liebermann. "And that would be true. But it isn't a very penetrating or meaningful observation. It doesn't tell us very much about Autenburg."

A tongue of flame flickered in the fireplace and seemed to detach itself from a glowing log. It floated for a few moments, like a marsh light, then vanished.

"If your thoughts on Autenburg's state of mind are accurate," said Rheinhardt, "what are we to conclude? That ultimately, his aggression found a more natural outlet? That he stopped biting his finger nails and instead, followed Diamant into the night with the intention of killing him?"

"You said that Diamant was carrying a dagger. It appears he was expecting trouble. And then there is the matter of the attempted strangulation."

"Which was unsuccessful. Do you *really*

believe that a man like Autenburg could overcome a young, athletic duelist?"

"If he managed to creep up on Diamant from behind."

"Soundlessly? Autenburg?"

"A stealthy approach wouldn't have been quite so essential if Diamant was inebriated. We know he was fond of beer cellars."

Rheinhardt considered the possibility and blew a smoke ring that slowly expanded and broke into transparent ribbons. He rested his cigar on the ashtray and reached down to pick up a leather case. Releasing the clasps he opened it and removed a wad of photographs which he handed to Liebermann.

"Ah, the new murder." The young doctor studied the images.

"His name is Gerd Kelbling," said Rheinhardt, retrieving his cigar. "He had reserved a spacious suite at the Beatrix for a period of three months. He was traveling with few possessions; however, we found a considerable sum of money, an envelope full of 100 kronen banknotes, in the bureau."

"Who was he?"

"We don't know yet. The hotel manager couldn't tell me anything. Apparently, he was never seen."

"Another man without qualities . . ."

"Now, it's interesting that you should say that.

The bullet that Professor Mathias dug out of Kelbling's spine was of a distinctive weight and size—identical to the bullet that killed Callari."

"Are you sure? I thought the stresses of detonation and impact resulted in significant deformation."

"Yes, and in many instances it is impossible conclude very much. But these bullets are quite distinctive—so much so that I suspect, after perusal of the relevant military almanacs, we will be able to determine their provenance."

"So, the same perpetrator."

"That is what I believe."

"What connects our itinerant Italian with this gentleman?" Liebermann held up one of the photographs, a close-up of Kelbling's face.

"Both of them had a lot of money."

"A commonality that isn't *very* illuminating."

"I agree. We need to know more about Kelbling."

"If Callari was condemned by a jury of honor, then it would be reasonable to suspect that the motive for Kelbling's murder might also have been political."

Rheinhardt turned toward his friend. "Odd, isn't it? Callari and Kelbling—Autenburg and Kruckel—Della and Diamant—The Golden Bears. Like links in a chain."

"Yes, but they don't quite fit together, do they?"

Rheinhardt was distracted by something on

his chair. He pinched his thumb and forefinger together and pulled an adhesive thread off the arm. He held it up and Liebermann realized that his friend was studying a long, red hair. The policeman's eyes expanded.

"I almost forgot," Liebermann blurted out. "I have some important news for you." Rheinhardt released the hair and it fell to the floor. "I managed to get to the bottom of Herr Globocnik's pseudologia fantastica. It was quite straightforward in the end. As soon as Herr Globocnik had settled and felt more relaxed in my company I was able to use hypnosis. There were some resistances, of course, but these were quickly overcome by employment of the pressure technique—you've seen me use it— do you remember?" Rheinhardt nodded. "My original formulation was correct," Liebermann continued. "The root of the problem was a traumatic memory—an unconscious memory of humiliation."

Liebermann recounted the story of Globocnik's ill-fated romance with Fräulein Mugoša, and when he reached the point where Bok emptied his bladder over the lovelorn clerk, Rheinhardt said angrily, "Dear God! One wonders what the future holds for mankind. What a creature! Capable of such petty, frivolous malice. Animals do not sink as low."

"My sentiments exactly, Oskar—it was an act

of such senseless cruelty—made worse by its ease. And worse of all, when Globocnik looked up at that dreadful Mugoša woman, she was smiling—delighting in his degradation."

"Is he cured now? Globocnik?"

"Needless to say, it will take time for him to fully adjust. He has been rudely awakened to a new and brutal reality. But yes, he has recovered, insofar as he no longer escapes his pain by inhabiting a homicidal fantasy. There is, however, a minor problem."

"Oh yes?" Liebermann hesitated and appeared somewhat embarrassed. Rheinhardt frowned. "Max?" The syllable was extended and articulated on a rising glissando.

"When I got back to the hospital today." Liebermann's delivery was hesitant. "I was told that he'd absconded."

"Should we be concerned?"

Liebermann offered his friend an uncertain smile. "No. Not yet, anyway."

"That doesn't sound very reassuring."

The young doctor drew on his cigar, released a tumid cloud of smoke, and said, "What do you think of the brandy?"

FORTY-FOUR

Rheinhardt was awakened by an early telephone call from Schottenring.

"What did they want?" asked Else.

"I'm not sure. Something about Haussmann and a tapestry. The duty sergeant isn't very good with messages. I've got to go straight to the Beatrix."

A short distance from his apartment, Rheinhardt bought a pork sausage from a street vendor. The steaming meat exuded a spicy fragrance that made him salivate. He covered the sausage in mustard and consumed it in a matter of seconds. The street vendor smiled, "Good?"

"Very good," said Rheinhardt.

"The salt comes from Sečovlje—the pans. You wouldn't find a better sausage in Ljubljana."

Rheinhardt licked his fingers and etched an informal salute. "I'm inclined to agree."

Josefstadt and Alsergrund were adjacent districts and the walk to Thurngasse was relatively short. Rheinhardt stepped into the foyer of the Beatrix where he was informed by Herr Okolski that Haussmann had already arrived and was waiting for him in suite four.

"I hope this is important, Haussmann." Rheinhardt grumbled as they entered the second bedroom. "I had to rush breakfast."

"I think it is, sir," Haussmann replied.

Rheinhardt registered the tapestry and remembered the duty sergeant's garbled message. "Well, what have you found?"

Haussmann climbed onto the bed and raised the wall hanging, behind which was a hole in the wall. The aperture resembled the mouth of a letter box, although much wider.

Rheinhardt removed his hat and scratched his head. "Couldn't you have just told me?"

"There's more, sir." Haussmann reached into the hole and pulled out a rubber hose, which dropped as far as the pillows.

"I see. You've found a hole—*and* a pipe. Would you care to explain why you think these discoveries merit my immediate attention?"

Haussmann's response was unexpected. He sat down, legs outstretched, with his back against the wall. Then, he produced the half-sphere of black rubber—with its short length of tubing—that Rheinhardt had found in the otherwise empty chest of drawers. Haussmann inserted the short length of tubing into the hose. "Exact fit, sir." He then covered his right ear with the half-sphere. "It's a means of eavesdropping, sir. You can listen to the people talking upstairs."

Rheinhardt's mouth fell open. It took some time for it to close again. "Who are they?"

"I don't know. I didn't ask the manager for the

register. I thought it best not to say anything until you got here."

"And when did you discover this apparatus?"

"Late last night, sir."

"Have you been making use of it?"

Haussmann nodded. "A man and a woman, sir. Quite well to do, although they didn't say very much this morning—something about a concert—the 'Academic Festival Overture'?"

"Brahms, Haussmann."

"And something else about a dean—that's all. The other end of this pipe comes out in their bedroom. When I listened yesterday I just heard snoring."

Haussmann got off the mattress and waited for instruction. Rheinhardt postioned himself in front of his slender junior and let his hands fall heavily on the young man's shoulders. He then gave him an affectionate shake. "Well done, Haussmann, excellent detection. Whatever made you look behind that tapestry?"

"It was moving, sir—when by rights it should have been still. A draft, I expect—coming through the hole in the wall. Are we going upstairs, sir?"

"Yes, Haussmann," Rheinhardt replied. "We are most certainly going upstairs."

FORTY-FIVE

The door was opened by a Hungarian maid. Her manner was somewhat guarded until she discovered that they were police officers and it was only then that she became more courteous and deferential. "Please, gentlemen—come in. If you don't mind . . . please sit. I'll let the férfi know you are here." Two minutes later a tall, distinguished man entered the room. He was in his fifties and his receding hairline exposed a high, freckled forehead. He wore steel-rimmed spectacles and a vertical strip of hair below his lower lip descended to meet a pointed, tawny beard. The effect resembled an anchor. His shirt sleeves were puffy, he was wearing a blue silk tie, and his waistcoat was fastened with small silver buttons.

Rheinhardt and Haussmann stood and bowed.

"Good morning," said Rheinhardt. "Herr . . ."

"Seeliger." The man dipped his head. "Professor Waldemar Seeliger."

"My apologies," Rheinhardt made a penitent gesture. "I am Detective Inspector Rheinhardt of the security office and this is my assistant, Haussmann."

"Is this about the murder?" asked Seeliger.

"Well, yes." Rheinhardt responded. "I suppose it is."

"I'm sorry to disappoint you, inspector," said Seeliger. "But I really can't help. I was teaching all day yesterday, my wife was visiting her sister, and my children were at school. I returned late and went straight to bed."

"Is your wife here now?"

"No, I'm afraid you've just missed her. She's organizing a fundraising event at the university—a concert. It takes place this evening and she won't be back until this afternoon."

Rheinhardt looked around the parlor and noticed two packing cases near the window. "Do you live here?"

"A temporary inconvenience," Seeliger replied. "Our house in Wieden has structural problems— rotted beams, an insecure wall. We'll be lodging at the Beatrix until the masons and carpenters have finished their repairs. Annoying, but there it is. I miss having all of my books on hand but the children actually like living in a hotel. They see it as an adventure. Okolski—the manager—is a splendid fellow; always eager to please, so one shouldn't complain." Seeliger linked his hands behind his back and raised his chin. "If that is all, inspector, I have a busy day ahead." Seeliger extended his arm to indicate the direction of the exit, but Rheinhardt and Haussmann didn't budge. Their blank expressions communicated nothing. "Inspector?" Still, there was no response. Seeliger tugged at his cuffs with fidgety irritation.

"Where is your bedroom, Herr Professor?"

"What?"

"Your bedroom. We would like to see your bedroom."

"Why?

"If you would be so kind . . ."

Seeliger shook his head and tutted before replying. "I will oblige, inspector; however, I trust that you will not be looking for a murder weapon! If that is your intention, I can assure you in advance that your search will be unsuccessful and that you will consequently owe me an apology."

The sagging flesh beneath Rheinhardt's eyes seemed to descend a fraction. "Professor, the bedroom please."

Suite number eight was identical to suite number four. Seeliger guided the policemen to the second bedroom, which was exactly the same size as its twin on the floor below, although it appeared smaller on account of a few extra items of furniture. In addition to a four-poster bed and a chest there was a large wardrobe and a dressing table, the surface of which was crowded with womanly paraphernalia: a hairbrush, pins, kohl, perfume bottles, pots of rouge, and jars of unguents. Seeliger's wife was evidently a woman who liked to look her best. There were many books on the floor and a French horn case.

"Do you play?" asked Rheinhardt.

"I used to," Seeliger replied. "I don't really have the time now. And my technique has suffered through lack of practice."

"There is always time for music, professor."

"Well, that rather depends."

Rheinhardt addressed his assistant. "Haussmann—please clear this area."

Haussmann knelt down and rolled the Persian rug into a tight cylinder.

"What on earth are you doing?" asked Seeliger

"We are making it easier to move the bed."

"Now look here—"

"Patience, professor. Patience!"

Rheinhardt and Haussmann pulled the bed away from the wall and then stood a short distance apart, gazing with rapt interest at an aperture in the skirting board that looked very much like a mouse hole—a low arch with rough, scalloped edges. Rheinhardt went down on all fours and peered into the dark opening. "Yes," he said, looking up as his assistant. "I can see it."

"What can you see?" asked Seeliger, hovering behind Rheinhardt, his head bobbing up and down as he tried to get a better view.

Rheinhardt took out his penknife, pried a nail out of the floorboard, and pulled a length of hose out of the hole. He then stood up, before waving the end of the hose at Professor Seeliger and looping it around one of the bed posts. The professor's face blanched; he stumbled a few steps backward and walked over to the dressing table, where he sat down and stared at his own reflection.

"So," said Rheinhardt. "You understand the significance of our discovery?"

The professor stirred. "No. What is it?"

"Really, professor."

Seeliger recovered his composure and his eyes met Rheinhardt's in the mirror. "I don't know what you're talking about."

"All right, feign ignorance if you wish, professor." Rheinhardt moved closer to the dressing table. "It's a listening device, a means of eavesdropping on your conversations. The other end of that hose comes out downstairs, in suite number four, where the body was discovered yesterday."

"I think you are being fanciful, inspector."

Rheinhardt stepped forward again, halting directly behind Seeliger. "Why would anyone be interested in your private conversations, the secrets and confidences that you might share with your wife before sleep?" Seeliger remained silent. "The only reason, as far as I can see," Rheinhardt continued, "would be to use such information for nefarious purposes. Namely, blackmail. What do you think Haussmann?"

"Yes, sir," Haussmann replied. "Nefarious purposes."

"And now." Rheinhardt twisted one of the

horns of his moustache. "The individual who was in all probability blackmailing the good professor is dead."

"Indeed, sir," said Haussmann. "A fact of evidence that is very troubling."

"Very troubling." Rheinhardt spoke again to Seeliger's reflection. "What did he want, professor?"

"Are you are *really* accusing me of murder?" Seeliger stiffened. "This interview cannot proceed. I wish to seek legal advice."

"That would be most unwise."

"Most unwise," Haussmann echoed.

"Think about appearances, professor." Rheinhardt picked up one of Frau Seeliger's pots and studied the written label. "Why do you need legal advice?" Rheinhardt put the pot back on the dressing table and continued: "Naturally, we will be making extensive enquiries into your affairs—occupational, financial, social. I daresay a picture will emerge. Of course, you could save us a great deal of bother by being more cooperative. And I would urge you to remember that our judges are always well disposed toward those who have shown a willingness to expedite investigations. In my experience, those who obfuscate, delay, or obstruct elicit little sympathy."

"I never met the man downstairs." Seeliger's voice had become thin and weak. "I never saw him—ever."

"His name was Kelbling," said Rheinhardt. "Gerd Kelbling."

Seeliger swallowed. He placed his elbows on his thighs and lowered his forehead onto the heels of his palms.

"Dear God," Seeliger groaned. "I'm not a murderer. I didn't kill him—I didn't even know that he was here."

Rheinhardt took no pleasure in his triumph. He felt sorry for the broken professor and reached out to grip his shoulder. "Perhaps you should tell us what happened."

Seeliger turned his chair around and Rheinhardt sat on the edge of the bed.

"I don't know where to begin," said the professor. He loosened his tie and undid the top button of his waistcoat. His high forehead was glazed with perspiration. "I have debts. There's an irony for you. I'm a physicist—good with numbers. I developed a system for winning roulette and there *were* some early successes. But in the end, I lost a great deal. My wife is very ambitious. She wants our daughters to marry well. But it all has to be paid for—the balls, the dresses, the spas." Seeliger unfastened another silver button. "I am responsible for the management of a large number of bursaries that are awarded through the science department at the university. It was my wife who suggested that I borrow a small amount from these funds, in order to facilitate a little speculation. But my investments were not very profitable and I foolishly continued to abuse my position of trust. One day, I received an anonymous note, a kind of thinly veiled threat—and instructions to meet the correspondent at a location on the Prater. The man who appeared introduced himself as Gerd Kelbling. He knew everything. I thought my wife had been indiscrete. You see, she's very close to her sister. They talk—as sisters do. But my wife was adamant. She hadn't breathed a word of our financial predicament—not to her sister nor to anyone." Seeliger looked over at the hose and grimaced.

"Who was Gerd Kelbling?" Rheinhardt asked.

"A total stranger."

"And what did he want?"

"Some documents."

"What documents?"

"I am not at liberty to say. Please, inspector, understand. I am not being evasive or uncooperative. But I cannot be very specific. I have been working on a project for the war ministry—a special project—and I have been sworn to secrecy."

"And you can prove this?"

"Yes, very easily. There is a particular civil servant I answer to. He will vouch for me I can assure you. And if his word isn't sufficient you can speak to more senior figures at the ministry—

if you can get the appropriate authorization, of course."

"Did you give Gelbling the documents he wanted?"

"We met on the Prater again yesterday morning. I gave him adulterated copies."

"Weren't you worried that Gelbling would see through your ruse and pursue his threat of exposure?"

"He would have to be a very gifted mathematician. He would also have to be an expert on ballistics, chemistry, and certain technical aspects of engineering."

"Gelbling—or whoever sent him—would eventually discover your deception."

"Perhaps. But I reasoned by that time, I might have returned the monies I had embezzled."

"Are you expecting an inheritance?"

"No." Seeliger paused for a moment and massaged his forehead. "I'm working on another system . . . for card games, this time. It's loosely based on d'Alembert's observations."

"Who?"

"Jean-Baptiste le Rond d'Alembert. An eighteenth-century French mathematician. He developed the fundamental theorem of algebra and the ratio test."

Rheinhardt was unable to resist rolling his eyes.

"Who do you think Gelbling was working for?"

"I don't know. He spoke perfect German

although there was something about his speech that wasn't quite right. One must suppose he was spying for a hostile power." Rheinhardt offered Seeliger a cigar. "Thank you," said the professor. They smoked in silence for a while and then Seeliger added, "You know, my wife is fond of saying that, one day, our daughters will mix with archdukes and princes. I doubt that's very likely now."

Rheinhardt leaned forward. "If you tell us the truth, the whole truth, and manage to return the funds you have embezzled—then you might, if all goes well, escape incarceration. But no, your daughters will not be dancing with archdukes."

"A new start perhaps?"

"Yes, a long way from Vienna. Provincial schools are always in need of excellent mathematics masters."

The professor looked away and wiped his cheek, but his attempt to dispose of the tear was gauche and his eyes were filmed with a thickening layer of shining transparency.

FORTY-SIX

Shafts of light slanted through high, leaded windows, illuminating metals sinks, benches, and glass-fronted cabinets filled with scientific apparatus: measuring cylinders, conical flasks, beakers, and burners. A rabbit in a cage was eating cabbage leaves. Rheinhardt—who was seated at a laboratory bench next to the cage—reached through the bars and scratched the rabbit's head. "I'm feeling a little hungry too."

In front of Rheinhardt was a small square of wood cut from the door he had removed from the Gallus and Sons piano factory. The bloody thumbprint—black against the green paint—was protected beneath a thin microscope slide. Beside the square of wood was a white card on which there was an impression of Eduard Autenburg's right thumb.

Autenburg had been angry—and probably with good reason. He had been abandoned in a cell, and then Rheinhardt, without explanation, had arrived, only to roll the man's thumb on an inky plate. "I thought I was being detained for further questioning? Look, my hands are filthy now—I demand a bar of soap!"

Surrounding the two thumbprints were open editions of the *Police Gazette*. Many pages were covered in diagrams that looked like a bird's eye view of river formations. A heading identified these as "Ridge Characteristics." There were also numerous enlarged ovals filled with swirling patterns of parallel lines, labeled "Arch," "Loop," and "Whorl." An oversize magnifying glass had been laid aside on the cloth cover of an English book titled *Fingerprint Directories* by Francis Galton.

The rabbit's nose twitched and it hopped to the back of the cage. "Well, my little friend," said Rheinhardt, "the plot thickens."

"Are you talking to me, sir?"

Startled, Rheinhardt turned to see his assistant standing behind him. "God in heaven, Haussmann! Don't creep up on me like that! What ever happened to the common courtesy of knocking before entering?"

"The door was wide open, sir."

"That's no excuse. And I wasn't talking to you, I was talking . . ." His sentence trailed off.

"To the rabbit, sir." Haussman's expression was deadpan. "Herr Autenburg is becoming very agitated again. He called me a misguided instrument of oppression, sir."

"Well, he could be right about the misguided part. Come here, Haussmann. I want you to study these two thumbprints closely, using this magnifying glass." Haussmann picked up the heavy, mounted lens, and moved it backward and forward. "Now," Rheinhardt continued, "can you identify the general shape? These examples in the *Police Gazette* should be helpful."

"I would say that they are both whorls, sir."

"Very good. Now, count the ridges outward from the central point. Superimpose a clock face and ascend an imaginary hour hand at ten o'clock. Stop when you reach the fifth ridge and note how it breaks into two—note how it forks. The technical term for this division is a 'bifurcation.' Compare the two."

"They appear to be the same, sir."

"Count three ridges out from the center— ascending the hour hand at eleven o'clock. Note that the third ridge is connected to the fourth by a small bridge. This is called a 'crossover.' "

Haussmann's head oscillated between the samples. "Again, the same, sir."

"At six o'clock—the very last ridge—see how it divides and then joins up again?"

"Ah yes, sir."

"The technical name for this is an 'island.' "

Haussmann raised his head and grinned. "Identical."

"I could go on, Haussmann. But you will no doubt have already reached the obvious and inevitable conclusion."

"Autenburg was at the Gallus and Sons piano factory."

"Without a doubt."

"Really, sir? Without *any* doubt?"

Rheinhardt swept his hand over the diagrams and illustrations. "The evidence is overwhelming. Every set of fingerprints is unique to the individual." There was a loud rap and both men turned. A constable was standing in the doorway. "See, Haussmann?" said Rheinhardt. "Knocking. A custom universally practiced among civilized people."

The constable came forward. He was new and very nervous. "Detective Inspector Rheinhardt?"

"Yes."

"Some people are waiting in your office—a man and woman—something about a maniac. They're very upset."

"Who are they?"

"I don't know. The duty officer didn't say."

"Who let them into my office?"

"Not me, sir." The young constable bowed—a movement so fast it resembled the peck of a chicken—and reversed out of the laboratory. His disappearance was followed by the sound of reverberating footsteps that accelerated to running speed.

"He's gone, sir," said Haussmann.

Rheinhardt looked up at his assistant and released a sigh of titanic proportions.

FORTY-SEVEN

Rheinhardt entered his office and discovered that it was occupied by Herr Bok and Fräulein Mugoša. They were sitting at his desk but as soon as they had heard the door open they sprang up from their seats. Herr Bok was wearing a long coat with velvet lapels and he was gripping a cane. He looked prosperous, but his general air of salubrious respectability was compromised by the bluish-purple florescence that surrounded his right eye. His companion's lips were pressed together tightly and her eyebrows were slanted inward.

"Inspector Rheinhardt," Bok roared, "you led me to understand that Globocnik was in the hospital."

"Well," Rheinhardt responded, "that was certainly true at the time."

"It is not true now."

"Would you care to sit down, Herr Bok?" Rheinhardt made circles in the air, which he hoped would encourage the couple to return to their chairs.

"The man is insane. Dangerous! Look what he did to my eye!"

"It has been blackened rather badly."

"He took me by surprise, otherwise I would

256

have . . ." In lieu of finishing his sentence Bok snatched the air.

"If you would kindly sit, I will take a statement."

"What good will that do, inspector? You're wasting valuable time. You need to get out there"—he jabbed his cane at the window—"and catch him."

Fräulein Mugoša took out a handkerchief and dabbed her cheek. "He said horrible things. He called me a—" A sob made her final word incomprehensible.

"Don't fret, my dear," said Bok. "It won't happen again." He rounded on Rheinhardt. "Will it, inspector?"

"Globocnik attacked you?"

Bok stamped his foot and Fräulein Mugoša did exactly the same thing. "Haven't you been listening? Last night, Fräulein Mugoša and I were finalizing the accounts. We didn't leave the building until nine o'clock. We were crossing the yard and Globocnik jumped out from behind some crates. He punched me in the eye and insulted Fräulein Mugoša. Then, before I could lay my hands on him, he ran off, skipping and howling with laughter. He is mad, quite mad."

"I was told that Herr Globocnik's treatment had been successful."

"You were misinformed, inspector. And frankly, that doesn't surprise me. I met his doctor.

A young fool called Liebermann. He made an appointment to see me in my office and asked the most idiotic questions. Now, what are you going to do about Globocnik, inspector? Something must be done and it must be done soon! We want assurances."

"I regret to say that I can't give you any."

"What?" Bok raised his cane and brought it down in frustration. The tip clipped Rheinhardt's knuckles. "This is the security office? It is your duty to ensure our safety. And if you fail to do so, then you leave me no choice but to register a formal complaint at the highest level." Bok looked at Fräulein Mugoša and she returned a satisfied smile. "Well, inspector?"

"I can't assign you a special constable. We don't have the resources."

"Then you really must catch this scoundrel."

"We'll keep an eye out for him."

"That simply isn't good enough."

"It's the best we can do." Rheinhardt extended his hand. "Thank you for reporting the incident. I will make a note of it in our records."

The two men shook hands. "That's all you're going to do?"

"For the moment, yes."

When Bok tried to break away, Rheinhardt increased the tightness of his grip.

"Inspector?" Bok looked uncomfortable. Fräulein Mugoša heard the note of alarm in her companion's voice and turned to face him. The big man grimaced and then let out a cry of pain. "Inspector! Let me go! What are you doing?"

Rheinhardt released Bok's hand. "I was merely bidding you adieu."

Bok raised a finger. "I'm not a fool, inspector. You did that on purpose."

"I'm afraid I don't know what you're talking about," Rheinhardt replied. "Herr Bok, Fräulein Mugoša." He bowed and clicked his heels. "Good morning." When Bok reached the door he hesitated. He looked back at Rheinhardt, with suspicion and uncertainty. "Good morning," Rheinhardt repeated.

"What is it?" Fräulein Mugoša asked.

"Nothing," said Bok. "Let's go." He looked confused and a little shaken.

The door closed and Rheinhardt sat behind his desk. He opened a drawer and helped himself to a marzipan mouse that Mitzi had made with some help from her mother. He addressed the small pointed face. "I am no psychiatrist, but it would appear to me that Herr Doctor Liebermann's treatment has been highly effective." He bit the creature's head off and his mouth was suffused with flavor: vanilla essence, almonds, apricot conserve, and a hint of lemon. The sweetness of the marzipan was equal to the sweetness of his satisfaction, as he remembered Bok's yelp of pain and nervous exit.

FORTY-EIGHT

The windowless room in the basement of the Schottenring station was illuminated by a bare glass bulb that emitted a sallow, meager light; an insufficient hazy luminosity that strained the eyes and cast stunted shadows beneath a triangle of chairs. On the wall opposite the door was the usual portrait of the emperor. This particular likeness was photographic and featured a much younger incarnation: plentiful hair, a strong nose, and dark—as opposed to white—muttonchop whiskers. He was wearing a pale military jacket with a high, embroidered collar. The young emperor was looking into the distance, with bright, piercing eyes. Once, while visiting the lord marshal's office at the palace, a chance encounter with Franz Josef had given Rheinhardt an opportunity to study those eyes at close quarters. They were clear and very blue. The experience had been quite unnerving.

"I want to speak with the commissioner." On hearing the sound of Autenburg's voice, Rheinhardt was returned to the present. "You will not subject me to further indignities. My treatment in your custody has been disgraceful."

"Please sit down, Herr Autenburg."

"I intend to write a detailed account of your

lamentable conduct. This will not reflect well on the security office."

"It is regrettable that your detention has for the most part been solitary. But I can assure you that this was not my intention. Unfortunately, I have been rather busy since your arrest—the nature of police work. Needless to say, I have been most anxious to continue our interview."

"I want to see my wife. Why aren't you allowing her to visit me?"

"I'm afraid your wife hasn't asked to see you, Herr Autenburg."

"Is she . . . well?"

"I really wouldn't know. Should you wish to dispatch a message, then that can be arranged."

"She hasn't asked?"

"No. I'm sorry. Now, if you would please sit down, Herr Autenburg, we can proceed."

Autenburg sat on his chair, muttering in a low, incomprehensible register and huffing loudly. Rheinhardt and Haussmann also sat, but with less fuss and expulsion of air. A buzzing sound accompanied a brief intermittency of light. They all looked up at the flashing bulb for a few moments then lowered their heads when the light became continuous once more.

Rheinhardt leaned forward. "Herr Autenburg, the repetition of questions you have already answered will no doubt test your patience still further, but I must ask you again: did you ever meet Angelo Callari—the man I mentioned before—the man who called himself Tab and frequented The Golden Bears?"

"No, I never met this . . . Callari."

"The name isn't even vaguely familiar to you?"

"No."

"Callari's body was found in an abandoned piano factory in Favoriten. He had been shot through the head and his face was horribly disfigured with acid." Autenburg's expression showed no emotion. "You've never been to the Gallus and Sons piano factory?"

"No. Never."

"You're quite sure?"

"Of course I'm quite sure. Why would I visit an abandoned piano factory?"

"You know nothing about Angelo Callari?"

"Nothing."

Rheinhardt looked at his assistant. "Did you hear that, Haussmann?"

"Yes, sir." Haussmann replied. "He says he knows nothing."

"And he is *quite* sure."

"Indeed, sir. Categorical."

Rheinhardt shifted in his chair and studied Autenburg. The bulb flashed but neither of the two men allowed the fault to distract them. When Rheinhardt spoke he enunciated each word with careful precision. "Herr Autenburg, I would urge you to think very carefully about your situation."

A fulvous veneer of perspiration appeared on the publisher's forehead. He removed a handkerchief from his pocket, cleaned his spectacles, and pretended to reposition a tuft of hair while slyly wiping away the excessive moisture. Within seconds his forehead was gleaming again.

"Herr Autenburg," said Rheinhardt, in a friendly, confiding tone. "We know you were present at the Gallus and Sons piano factory when Callari was shot."

"Don't be ridiculous! Where is your proof? Where is your witness?"

Rheinhardt hummed and leaned back in his chair. "As things stand, it looks very likely that you will be tried for the murder of Angelo Callari and the murder of Axl Diamant. On the balance of probabilities I would estimate your chances of escaping a death sentence to be vanishingly small."

"I didn't kill anyone!"

Rheinhardt finally raised his voice. "In which case you really had better start telling us the truth." The injunction rang out, generating harmonics that found sustenance in the enclosed space.

"I did not kill Diamant!" Autenburg's rebuff was equally loud. "Yes, it's true, we argued and I was stupid enough to put my hands around his neck. But he was never in any danger. He was a strong fellow and a skilled swordsman. I am not a fighting man. I could never have bettered him. It is absurd to suggest that I could have cut his throat—even if I'd wanted to. His reactions were quick—very quick. I've watched him take on a gang of nationalists and knock out every one of them. They didn't know what had hit them."

"And what about Callari?"

"I never met Callari."

"Herr Autenburg, I would be most grateful if you would refrain from further deceit. It is becoming tedious."

Autenburg struck the arm of his chair. "I never had the pleasure of meeting Signor Callari and I have never been to the Gallus and Sons piano factory. You cannot extract confessions by means of bluff and bluster, inspector. Where is your witness?"

"He is sitting in front of me."

"What?"

"You are my witness. You have unwittingly incriminated yourself." Rheinhardt watched Autenburg's hand slowly rising. The publisher's teeth closed on either side of a fingernail and he produced two loud clicking noises as he bit into the keratin. "I suspect it was you who removed Callari's jacket," Rheinhardt continued. "That is when you got blood on your hands. There was a disturbance of some kind—a dog barking, men talking, a carriage stopping outside? You and your accomplices hurried to the rear of the factory and made your way out. At some point, you must have touched the door, and, in doing so, you left a very good impression of your right thumb on the paintwork."

Autenburg's hand dropped and his lips curled slowly into a smile. "Ah, I see. That's what you were up to earlier this morning—with the ink and paper." He laughed, almost hysterically. "I see. You have discovered that the print you took this morning and the print you found at the factory share similar characteristics."

"They are identical, Herr Autenburg."

"Well, what does that prove?" Autenburg peered at his own thumb. "There must be hundreds, no, thousands of people who share the same markings. Purchase any occult encyclopedia, turn to the chapter on palmistry and examine the diagrams closely. You will quickly see that all human hands have common, universal features: the major lines of the head, the heart, life, and destiny—the mounts and valleys—crosses, grilles, stars, and tridents."

"With respect, Herr Autenburg, occult encyclopedias will not help us to resolve this particular argument. We are better advised, in this instance, to consult the articles of biometric scientists; men such as Galton or Henry. The case for fingerprints has been proven. Every print is unique. You were at the Gallus and Sons piano factory the night

Callari was shot. This is an irrefutable fact. And the more you pretend otherwise the more you will prejudice the justice system against you. Come now, Herr Autenburg, be reasonable. Your evasions are serving no purpose."

Autenburg's head lowered until his chin was touching his chest. "I didn't kill Callari."

"Then tell us who did."

A long silence was punctuated by more electrical buzzing. Eventually, Autenburg whispered. "To what extent are you willing to . . ." He hesitated before adding, "Negotiate?"

"That rather depends on how helpful you are."

"I will need false papers, a new identity—and somewhere safe to go."

"You are not the first to request special provision, Herr Autenburg."

"And are such accommodations ever made?"

"If the information we are given merits leniency, yes."

Autenburg was clearly deliberating. He wrapped his handkerchief tightly around his fist and then let it loosen. This action seemed to be linked with some inner increase and release of tension. "I didn't kill anyone," he said on a forceful outbreath. "However, if I tell you the truth, I am a dead man. I will go to prison, serve my term, and when I am released I will be executed. Without false papers and somewhere to hide, I am a dead man."

Rheinhardt glanced at the photograph of Franz Josef. "The empire is very, very large. Marianské Lazne, Przemyśl, Split, Trento. Pécs, Braşov, Ivano-Frankivsk. Endless marshes, remote salt pans, and an infinite number of mountain passes. Perhaps we could come to some arrangement with the army. The garrison stationed in the Sanjak of Novi Pazar must generate quite a lot of paper work. That's well off the beaten track and even the most enthusiastic assassin would have trouble getting there."

"The Sanjak of Novi Pazar?" Haussmann queried.

"Not now, Haussmann." Rheinhardt shook his head and leaned forward again. "Who killed Angelo Callari?"

"Callari was a traitor."

"And who did he betray?"

"The movement."

"What movement?"

"We are an international collective, committed to the eradication of poverty and the provision of equal rights for all."

"Activists . . ."

"Is it wrong to pursue a noble ideal, inspector? To feel compassion for those ill-favored by fortune?"

"Callari, Herr Autenburg, you were telling us about Callari."

"He was selling information to the Okhrana, the Russian secret police."

"What information?"

"Names, addresses, anything he overheard of interest. The Russians are generous sponsors and they pandered to his needs, his predilection for orgies and the sting of a whip. A pattern emerged. Wherever Callari went, trouble was sure to follow. Some of our people lost their lives. He was a fool, complacent and careless. He believed that he could persuade a jury of honor of his innocence and carry on enjoying the Okhrana's largesse; however, he was gravely mistaken."

"There were three chairs facing Callari at the piano factory. You had been sitting on one of them. Who occupied the other two?"

Autenburg pulled at his Van Dyke beard. His hand was shaking. "Inspector, you haven't given me any assurances that appropriate measures will be taken to ensure my safety."

"Your willingness to assist will be taken into account," said Rheinhardt.

"That isn't much of an assurance."

"It would be sheer folly to stop aiding our inquiry at this juncture, Herr Autenburg. I would urge you to proceed."

Autenburg's body seemed to deflate. He nodded and continued: "The other two were very senior. The first was my immediate superior."

"What is his name?"

"No. Not his name, *her* name. My immediate

superior is a woman." Autenburg hesitated, grimacing as he struggled to overcome his scruples. "Vala Feist. She lives near the gas works. But it wasn't her, she didn't execute Callari. It was the third member of our jury. I can't give you his name, because it isn't known to me. He is a veteran of our movement. I can only give you his code name." Autenburg hesitated again before saying: "Mephistopheles."

Haussmann's expression communicated skepticism and mild amusement. He was unimpressed by the excessive theatricality of the code name, which carried with it suggestions of melodrama and burlesque. It erected a proscenium in the brain, beneath which a man wearing a cape and top hat was stepping out of shadow into the glare of a stage light. When Rheinhardt returned his attention to Autenburg, he was surprised to see that the publisher's face had become a rictus of terror, as if he had just uttered a magical incantation that might summon a diabolical manifestation from hell.

"Can you give us a description of this . . . Mephistopheles?" Rheinhardt asked, feeling self-conscious as he did so.

"No. I can't." Autenburg did not look well.

"Why not?"

"Because he was wearing a hood. Only senior figures in our movement know what he looks like."

Rheinhardt frowned. "Why did Mephistopheles shoot Gerd Kelbling?"

"Who?"

"Gerd Kelbling. The projectiles that killed both Callari and Kelbling were of the same caliber, weight, and general appearance. Quite unusual, in fact."

Autenburg shook his head rapidly from side to side. "I've never heard of Gerd Kelbling."

"You might have known him by some other name, perhaps? He was staying at the Beatrix Hotel where he was spying on Professor Seeliger, a physicist who lectures at the university."

"Kelbling? Seeliger? No, I've never heard of them."

"What about the Beatrix? Do you know anybody connected with that hotel?"

Autenburg continued shaking his head. Twisting the horns of his moustache, Rheinhardt's eyes narrowed and became two doubting slits.

"Inspector." Autenburg pleaded. "Surely you do not mean to implicate me in a third murder!"

FORTY-NINE

Professor Freud had been listening very carefully to Liebermann's account of Herr Globocnik's treatment. He had raised a finger to indicate when he had a question. These interruptions had been few in number and always considered. Mostly, he had remained silent, smoking cigars and toying with the ancient statuettes that populated the top of his desk. By the time Liebermann had reached his conclusion, Freud was peering through a taupe fog.

"Pseudologia fantastica," Freud enunciated the term as if each syllable was moist and succulent. "Perhaps, when you have ordered your case notes, you would be willing to present this patient at our Wednesday evening Psychological Society?"

"I would be delighted," said Liebermann.

Freud offered Liebermann a cigar. "These are very good: woody with hints of aniseed."

"Thank you," said Liebermann, removing a cigar from a box and lighting it with a match.

"One wonders," Freud continued, "to what extent the dynamics of the love triangle you have described represent another recapitulation of what is now becoming a familiar Sophoclean theme. Was this drama rooted in an unresolved

271

conflict that can be traced back to the nursery? Did the little clerk wish to kill the factory owner because the factory owner had become associated with paternal authority? Did the coquette resemble the clerk's mother? And was there some connection between the clerk's choice of weapon—a letter opener, a blade—and fear of castration? Regrettably, we will never know. Your recourse to the suggestive method of Charcot and Janet, although expedient, provides us with few insights into ultimate causation. Even so, the material you bring us will—I am sure—provide a stimulus for much profitable debate."

Liebermann couldn't determine whether he had just been praised or admonished and he thought it judicious to change the subject as quickly as possible. A book had been laid next to the ink stand, the pages open and facing down. On the spine, Liebermann read: *Psychologie des foules*—the psychology of crowds.

"You are reading Le Bon," Liebermann observed, affecting a nonchalant air.

"Yes," Freud nodded. His brow became smooth and a vague sense of unease dissipated. "I am a great admirer of this work." He tapped the cloth cover. "We can only know the unconscious by indirect means, for example, through the interpretation of dreams, slips of the tongue, and memory failures. At present, these means are somewhat limited in scope and number.

Consequently, I have been exploring other possibilities, other phenomena that might give us further insights into unconscious mental life, and among these phenomena, I have—of late—been giving particular consideration to the behavior of crowds." Freud paused and picked up one of his statuettes which he placed on the book cover. It was a falcon-headed figure made of wood.

"Le Bon," Freud went on, "suggests that the particularities of the individual become obliterated in groups. Distinctiveness vanishes. We might say that the superstructure of personality is removed, and the unconscious foundations—which are similar in everyone—stand exposed to view." He placed a blue brachycephalic dwarf next to the falcon-headed figure and continued moving other statuettes along similar trajectories to the same destination. "Once absorbed by the group, the individual feels invincible. He yields to instincts which he would perforce have kept under restraint. He becomes anonymous and his sense of personal responsibility disappears entirely. He becomes impulsive, less thoughtful. By the mere fact that he is now part of a group, a man descends several rungs down the ladder of civilization. Isolated, he may be a cultivated individual; in a crowd, he is a barbarian—a creature animated by primitive drives. A crowd is vengeful, fickle, and prone to extremities of purpose; a crowd is quick to persecute and bay for blood; a crowd is always close to becoming a mob."

"Do you think," Liebermann inquired, "that Le Bon's psychology is also applicable to political groups and movements?"

"Of course," the professor answered. "Politicians are always oversimplifying, always engaging the public by making emotional appeals that owe more to prejudice than rationality. They are buoyed up by the people who stand behind them, carried forward on waves of feeling. Yes, a political party is just another form of crowd."

Liebermann noticed that a large number of statuettes were now standing on the splayed cover of Le Bon's opus. While talking, the Professor had inadvertently constructed his own diminutive assembly. Freud realized at once that he had created a scene to accompany his thoughts and he acknowledged his embarrassing transparency with a wave of his hand.

Liebermann reflected: "It is often men who desire most strongly to improve the lot of their fellows that do the greatest harm."

The professor picked up a bronze vulture and held it up to the light to see it better. "The nationalist declares his vile calumnies while thinking that he is in fact making the world a better, purer place. When the anarchist throws his bomb, he is convinced that he is ridding the world of oppression and poverty. But really, they are both in the thrall of the unconscious." Freud made some room for the vulture on the book and then smiled at his young friend. "So . . . Mandelbaum goes to see his doctor, Zingel, in order to get his test results. Zingel has the papers from the laboratory in his hand. He looks over his spectacles and says, 'I have some good news and some bad news.' Mandelbaum says, 'Tell me the good news first.' Zingel nods and says, 'All right. The good news is that you're not a hypochondriac.' "

Liebermann laughed, but he was still thinking about politics and the statuettes that Freud had collected together on the book cover.

FIFTY

Rheinhardt rubbed condensation from the carriage window and peered through a porthole of transparency at the four large gas towers. They were impressive redbrick constructions with meniscus roofs, each surmounted by the industrial equivalent of an architectural lantern. There was something grand and ominous about these buildings that demanded musical accompaniment, something dark and Wagnerian. "Siegfried's Funeral March," perhaps? Rheinhardt grumbled a bar or two and imagined the orchestration, restless flurries in the lower strings, stabs of brass and timpani.

A little farther on Rheinhardt instructed the driver to stop.

"Wait here," he called up as he stepped down onto the cobbles. The air smelled unpleasant. He walked along the canal, observing a plume of black smoke rising from a tall chimney and eventually spied his assistant, standing discretely behind a derelict street-vendor's cabin.

"Good morning, sir."

"Good morning, Haussmann."

"She left early, was gone for about an hour, and came back about ten minutes ago carrying a full shopping basket."

"Is there anyone else in the house?"

"I don't think so, sir."

Rheinhardt studied the ramshackle group of small dwellings on the other side of the road. They had been positioned in a haphazard way, none of them sharing the same orientation. Many had been enlarged by the addition of lean-to structures abutting windowless walls. It wasn't a pleasing prospect.

"Right," said Rheinhardt. "Let us proceed."

They came out from behind the stall and walked over to a squat house, the exterior of which was badly in need of repair. Damp stains striped rendering that retained only mottled remnants of paint. Rheinhardt knocked on the door and presently it was opened by woman in a high-necked blouse and a brown skirt. A bun of gray hair was neatly pinned on her crown. Her leanness created an initial flattering impression of a woman in the early middle years of life, but on closer inspection, the lines that spread out from the corners of her eyes and the vertical creases above her thin, colorless lips suggested that she was, in fact, much older.

"Fräulein Feist?" said Rheinhardt.

"Yes," the woman replied.

"I am Detective Inspector Oskar Rheinhardt and this is my assistant, Haussmann."

"Security office?"

"Yes. We would like to ask you some questions."

"Me?" Her voice was incredulous and she touched her flat chest.

"Yes," Rheinhardt confirmed.

"Well," the woman responded. "You had better come in." She turned and started walking. "This way please. Would the young officer be good enough to close the door behind him? Thank you." She led them into a musty parlor where she offered them seats at a table. "I'll make some tea and get some walnut cake."

"That won't be necessary," said Rheinhardt.

"No, I must."

"With respect, we have no—"

"You are my guests," Feist interrupted. She disappeared into an adjoining kitchen and preparatory sounds followed—the clatter of plates and cutlery, the boiling of a kettle. When Feist reemerged she was carrying a tray, crowded with tea things, which she set out on the table. "Excuse me," she said, and returned to the kitchen.

Haussmann leaned closer to his superior and whispered, "Have we been tricked, sir?"

Rheinhardt emitted a low, pensive growl. "Why would Autenburg lie?"

"I don't know, sir." Haussmann shrugged. "But this . . . situation." He circled his hand above his head. "It doesn't look very promising."

Feist returned carrying a walnut cake which she placed beside the teapot and began to cut and serve. "It's a very old recipe—possibly Greek."

Rheinhardt was momentarily distracted by the fragrance of the flecked yellow slice that landed beneath his flaring nostrils. Haussmann coughed—a sharp, impatient bark.

"May I ask." Rheinhardt captured Feist's attention. "How long have you lived in this house?"

"Oh, two or three years, perhaps. I moved in just after they'd finished building the gas towers."

"And where were you living before?"

"The sixteenth district," Feist replied, pouring the tea. "I've always lived on my own. Rather bookish you see—an odd term, bookish—and sometimes employed as a pejorative. I can't think why. Please . . . your walnut cake."

"Thank you," said Rheinhardt, picking up his fork. The sponge was dense and full of large pieces of crushed walnut. "Do you have an occupation, Fräulein Feist?"

"I was fortunate enough to inherit a sum of money from my father. Not a great deal, but enough. I've always been a conscientious house-keeper, you see. Prudence: a much underrated virtue." She sampled her cake and her expression suggested satisfaction. She nodded reflectively then continued. "I teach a little—kindergarten, mostly. And I have also found occasional employment with charitable institutions undertaking administrative and secretarial work."

"Tell me, Fräulein Feist. Does the name Autenburg mean anything to you?"

She stopped chewing. "Yes, it does. Herr Autenburg the publisher?"

"You know him?"

"Well, I wouldn't say I *know* him. That would imply we are better acquainted than we actually are. I met Herr Autenburg last November. He gave a public lecture which was held under the auspices of the Socialist Education Alliance and the General Austrian Women's Association. I believe the subject of Herr Autenburg's talk was the inevitability of political reform. A rather dry talk, as I recall, but the event was relatively well attended, all things considered. The hall is usually only full when our guest speaker is a famous actress or singer. Herr Autenburg was kind enough to donate some of his recent publications to the Alliance's lending library."

"Did you ever meet Herr Autenburg's wife?"

"Yes, I did, and she—" Feist checked herself. "One shouldn't gossip."

"What were you going to say, Fräulein Feist?"

"She is a very colorful character, that's all." Feist smiled. "Do you like the cake, inspector? Not too sweet?"

"No," Rheinhardt replied. "It's very good—and certainly not too sweet."

Feist addressed Haussmann. "What about you, young man? Is the cake satisfactory?"

Haussmann inclined his head. "Yes, very satisfactory. Thank you."

"The Socialist Education Alliance . . . ," Rheinhardt continued.

"Yes?" Feist tilted her head. "What of it, inspector?"

"I wonder if you ever met an Italian gentleman at one of these public lectures? A gentleman called Callari. Angelo Callari."

Feist raised her tea cup and sipped. "Callari. The name is familiar." Sudden recognition widened her eyes. "I read about him in a newspaper. Yes. Callari. Wasn't he—" She hesitated and her voice descended to a lower register. "Wasn't he murdered?"

"Indeed," said Rheinhardt.

"A ne'er-do-well," Feist continued. "That's how he was described. I do not associate with ne'er-do-wells, Herr Inspector. And whatever makes you think a man like that would attend a public lecture?"

"He was actually very interested in socialism. We know that he attended educational evenings organized by Clement Kruckel."

"Really? Clement Kruckel? I used to read his column—many years ago. Amusing but always rather spiteful, I thought. Too spiteful, his malice undermined his arguments, which were otherwise well-constructed and persuasive." Feist drained her tea cup. "Herr Inspector, I am not at all clear why you are asking me these questions. I cannot help but feel that you under some misapprehension."

Rheinhardt swallowed his final mouthful of cake and dabbed his mouth with a serviette. "Very good—the texture especially—substantial but not heavy." He then checked the points of his moustache and said, "And what of Mephistopheles?"

Feist glared at him as though he were mad. "Is this some kind of prank, inspector?"

"Mephistopheles," he repeated. "Have you ever encountered a gentleman who uses this moniker as an alias?"

Feist laughed. It was a surprisingly pleasant and unexpected sound to be issuing from the mouth of such a desiccated person. "Really, inspector, Mephistopheles! The only Mephistopheles I know is the one who appears in fairy tales and Faust. I do not associate with ne'er-do-wells and I most certainly do not consort with the devil. Can I interest you in a second slice of walnut cake?"

"No thank you, one slice is quite enough." He patted his stomach before rising. "I am afraid I must trespass further upon your hospitality, Fräulein Feist. I must search your house."

"Really?" Feist appeared amazed. "Whatever are you looking for? If you told me, I could perhaps offer you some assistance. My bedroom is upstairs and I also have a little room where I write and keep my books. There's not much to see as I have very few possessions. Go up, by all means. I'll tidy these things away." She began to load the tray. "The stairs are by the door."

Rheinhardt indicated that Haussmann should remain in his chair. He then crossed the floor and climbed a single flight of bare wooden steps to the top floor. Feist's bedroom contained a single bed—beneath which he discovered a chamber pot decorated with a floral glaze—a wardrobe, and a sink. He opened the wardrobe door and studied the clothes: a coat, a few old-fashioned blouses, and several brown and gray skirts made from practical and hard-wearing fabrics. Since his arrival, he had become accustomed to the tainted air of the locality. In fact, the smell hardly registered, but on opening the wardrobe door he became aware of a new miasma that reminded him of sewage. Sniffing the air like a bloodhound he determined that the source of the odor was Feist's coat. He closed the wardrobe door, thoroughly perplexed. The absence of a dressing table was not surprising. He exited the bedroom and entered a small library. Pushed against one of the walls was a slim table on which paper and pens were lined up. Rheinhardt studied some of the book spines and was impressed by the broadness of Feist's reading. There were classics—Homer, Aristotle—some works of modern philosophy, textbooks on chemistry and geology, political memoirs, French authors such as Hugo and Zola, and several popular novels. Rheinhardt descended the stairs and returned to the parlor.

"Where is Fräulein Feist?"

Haussmann stood. "She's in the cellar."

"Why?"

"She said she needed some wood for the stove . . ."

The two men approached an open door. They gazed down concrete steps that descended into a flickering twilight. There wasn't a sound. Haussmann moved forward but Rheinhardt stopped him from going any farther by grabbing his sleeve. Haussmann looked at his superior quizzically.

Rheinhardt called out, "Fräulein Feist?"

She responded after a short pause. "Just a moment, inspector."

The assistant smiled: *There . . . nothing to worry about.*

Footsteps preceded Feist's appearance at the bottom of the stairs. The white oval of her face seemed to be floating in a sea of shadow and then it seemed to Rheinhardt that he was observing the prolonged, drawn out agonies of a nightmare. Feist's straight right arm reversed and arced over her shoulder. Her fingers opened and something was released. Rheinhardt was conscious of a blurred trajectory and Feist's sudden disappearance. "Haussmann!" Rheinhardt shouted, pushing his assistant away from the door and turning on his heels. He had only managed a step or two before the canister hit the uppermost stair and the subsequent blast lifted him off his feet.

FIFTY-ONE

Black—a high-pitched ringing.

Rheinhardt opened his eyes. He was lying face down on a hard surface. Pieces of broken glass formed patterns on the floorboards.

Where am I?

He turned his head and the ringing became louder. The table and chairs had been overturned and the air had become a fog of floating dust motes.

Memories crystallized and a narrative became clearer.

Feist—the grenade—Haussmann!

Rheinhardt rolled over and sat up. The door to the cellar had been blown off its hinges and parts of the wall were missing. A curtain was burning. Haussmann's body was a heap on the floor amid rubble and bricks. The scene reddened as blood trickled into Rheinhardt's eyes. He crawled over to his assistant: "Haussmann, are you all right? Haussmann—speak to me." The young man didn't respond. Rheinhardt lowered his head and positioned his ear close to Haussmann's mouth—but all that he could hear was ringing. He plucked a mirror from his pocket and placed it beneath Haussmann's nostrils. "Dear God, do not take him. He is too young." The glass misted and

Rheinhardt looked up to the heavens. "Thank you. Thank you." A gust of wind made the front door creak. It had been left open. Haussmann groaned. "I'm sorry, my friend," said Rheinhardt. "But I must leave you for a while." With considerable difficulty, Rheinhardt managed to stand. He ripped the burning curtain from the window and stamped on the flames, then stumbled through the doorway and out onto the street, where he saw, in the distance, a woman running. She was heading away from the gas works and toward the canal.

Rheinhardt began his pursuit but found that he was very unsteady. His portly frame and the aftereffects of the blast were significant handicaps. Yet he persevered, encouraged by the fact that Feist wasn't moving very fast either. She had handicaps of her own—a long skirt, beneath which drawers and petticoats were no doubt restricting her leg movements. He saw her glance over her shoulder. She stopped, turned, raised a pistol, shot twice, and continued running. Fortunately, her aim had been wide and Rheinhardt supposed that these shots were merely cautionary. A question arose in his mind: *Should I stop now?* He was out of breath, his ribs were on fire, and the world was undulating like the mock reality of a painted theatrical backdrop. He thought of Haussmann, alone and injured; Else, puttering around at home; his two daughters sitting at their desks at school. Was it wise to continue pursuing Feist? It would be easy to justify giving up the chase at this point. He thought of mohnstrudel served with clotted cream, türkische coffee, mellow cigars, and Schubert songs. Life was good. Yet, in spite of these considerations, the figure of the woman running ahead of him, and the diminishing distance that separated them, drew him on.

Feist ran onto a girder bridge that spanned the canal. She raised her pistol again and when she pulled the trigger Rheinhardt sensed the proximity of the projectile. He took cover behind an empty cart and watched as Feist continued her bid to escape. Blood was still filming his eyes and tinting his vision. He stepped out from behind the cart and launched himself after Feist. His legs were feeling leaden and it took a gargantuan effort to achieve his prior speed. His throat was dry and his much abused lungs—he was a prodigious smoker—began to rattle.

Rheinhardt crossed the bridge and followed Feist onto the Prater. The surrounding greenery was wild and uncultivated. They were a considerable distance from the Rotunda and the amusement park, but quite close to the Freudenau racecourse. Ahead, there was no obvious path, and Feist was having difficulty negotiating long weeds and dead brambles. The field that they were in was completely desolate.

Feist halted and aimed her pistol. "That's far enough, inspector."

"Lower your weapon," said Rheinhardt. His ears were still ringing and he could only just hear what Feist was saying.

"You are in no position to issue orders," Feist responded, taking a step closer to reduce her range.

Rheinhardt studied the pistol. It was small and he judged that it might only fire four rounds. Feist had already used three. "Lower your weapon," he repeated.

"Don't be foolish, inspector." Feist jabbed the barrel. "Do you think I'll miss from here? Turn around and walk away."

"I'm afraid that isn't possible."

"You have a choice, inspector, a very clear choice. Come any nearer and I will shoot you. Alternatively, you can walk away. Be reasonable. Do not die without good cause. That would be such a needless waste. You have acquitted yourself well and no one will accuse you of dereliction of duty. Now, go back and help your assistant."

"Who is Mephistopheles?" Rheinhardt spoke evenly. "What is his real name?"

"Don't be stubborn, inspector. How does this day end for you? Does it end with you tucked up in a warm bed with your wife? Or does it end with your frozen body laid out in a mortuary?"

Rheinhardt shivered and blinked the blood from his eyes. "It is your choice, inspector. Choose wisely."

Rheinhardt leapt forward and Feist squeezed the trigger. There was no report. The gun had run out of bullets. She threw her weapon aside and once again started running. After only a few steps she tripped and fell. Rheinhardt skidded to a halt on the dewy weeds and allowed his knees to come down on her back. His weight winded her and she cried out in pain. She tried to squirm out from beneath him but Rheinhardt was too heavy. Her arms flailed and her legs kicked, ineffectually. Rheinhardt closed a metal bracelet around her wrist and turned the key.

"Please, Fräulein Feist," he said with calm resolve. "Be still. We are handcuffed together and you cannot escape. I do not wish to break your back, but if you force me to continue this method of restraint I fear that may be a likely outcome. How does this day end for you? Does it end with you locked up in a cell with the use of your legs? Or does it end with you locked in a cell as a cripple? Choose wisely."

FIFTY-TWO

Captain Birk Hoover lived in a small hotel in the heart of the eighth district. His rooms were somewhat Spartan because he was a man for whom the comforts and luxuries of life were dispensable. He disliked clutter, personal mementoes, and surfaces covered with family portraits. Even so, he did keep a small framed photograph of his mother. It showed a rather glamorous widow whose smile could only be described as flirtatious. Although he had traveled a great deal, he did not possess a single souvenir.

On waking, Hoover got out of bed and shaved. His servant had prepared a bowl of steaming, scented water, and Hoover scraped the stubble off his face with the minimum number of efficient strokes. His cut-throat razor was manipulated with such a steady, sure hand, that his skin was never nicked. He combed his blond moustache and made a careful inspection of his fingernails. It was necessary to trim the nail of his index finger. When he had finished his ablutions, Hoover wrapped himself in a silk robe and went downstairs to have his breakfast and read the newspapers. Any articles on international relations, science, military matters, or crime, he read with careful, professional interest. He then returned to his bedroom where his uniform had been laid out. Standing in front of a full-length mirror, he dressed and made sure that no stray hairs or lint had become attached to the fabric. He buckled his sword belt and then put on his suede gloves. Finally, he fitted his garrison hat on his head. He always put his gloves on before his hat, to ensure that the patent-leather visor was not sullied by fingerprints. When he was satisfied with his appearance, he left his suite, trotted down the stairs, and exited the hotel. The street cleaners had recently been at work and the pavement was damp and the air fresh.

Hoover set off at his customary brisk pace. It did not take him long to reach the glorious architectural extravaganza of the town hall. He dodged a tram, marched past the Court Theatre and entered the second courtyard of the Hofburg Palace. It was almost half past eight so he quickened his step. A sentry saluted. He crossed the open space to the Ministry of War building, where he returned the salute of another sentry. Hoover ascended four flights of stairs and—returning one more salute as he walked past the final sentry—entered the Intelligence Bureau of the General Staff.

At eight thirty precisely Hoover was seated at his desk. He smoked a cigarette and then removed some papers from his safe. He had not yet finished his report on Professor Seeliger and the dead man who he believed must be Agent 58. He had been rather physical while interrogating Seeliger, but he would omit mention of such details and no one would ask any difficult questions. It was necessary to be confident that the old fool was telling not just the truth, but the whole truth. A second document concerned the development of a new cable balloon that might give troops a tactical advantage during battle.

There was a knock on the door. An adjutant entered, saluted, and handed Hoover an envelope. "For your immediate attention, sir."

Hoover opened the envelope and found that it contained a brief note from his superior. "Detective Inspector Oskar Rheinhardt has arrested a woman as yet unknown to us. Her name is Vala Feist. A bomb-making factory was discovered in her basement. Evidence suggests she is an associate of Mephistopheles." Hoover looked up at the adjutant. "Thank you. That will be all." The messenger saluted and withdrew.

Striking a match, Hoover held the flame against his superior's note. The paper burned, blackened, and curled. He dropped the note into his metal ashtray and watched as it disintegrated and became ashes.

It was time to make himself known.

PART FOUR

Martyrdom

FIFTY-THREE

Her bun had unraveled and her hair fell in lank strands to her shoulders. Sitting beneath the bare, yellow bulb, her hollow cheeks had filled with shadow and her eyes were empty. She hadn't said a single word since her undignified capture.

For two hours, Rheinhardt had questioned Vala Feist: Who is Mephistopheles? Is he still in Vienna? Are members of your cell still at large? Where do you intend to bomb? Who are your targets? Are you acquainted with Axl Diamant? Can you name the men and women you have sheltered in the basement of your house? Were they fugitives? Where had they traveled from? Who supplied you with fuses, potash, glycerine, nitric acid?

Feist had remained completely silent, her thin lips pressed together.

Rheinhardt had hoped that Liebermann would employ some clever psychological technique to loosen Feist's tongue, but the young doctor had said nothing. Liebermann fidgeted, he crossed and uncrossed his legs, and then became occupied with how the hem of his trousers could be best positioned to cover the laces of his shoes. Irritated by Liebermann's failure to engage, Rheinhardt had had no choice but to continue repeating his questions. In due course, he also fell silent. He gazed at the emperor's mildewed portrait and the more he contemplated the young Franz Josef's expression the more he thought he could detect disapproval. Anarchists in Vienna! Explosions, innocent victims, blood flowing between the cobbles of the Graben. Rheinhardt was so caught up in these grim imaginings that it took him a few moments to fully register that Liebermann had finally started talking.

"You are motivated by compassion. So how is it that a person of such tender conscience can condone propaganda by deed? I suspect you would answer that terror serves the purpose of achieving a greater good. But that is a shallow answer." Liebermann leaned back, placed his elbow on the chair arm, and rested his head on his right hand. His index finger uncurled and tapped against his temple. "There are many in this world who would call you a monster. I am not one of them. In reality, we are all monsters— composed mostly of primitive appetites and animal instincts obscured by the thin, brittle veneer of cultivation. You are not so different from the bourgeois housewife, whose matronly exterior conceals a powerful desire to advance her children at *any* cost, to facilitate her husband's ascent to prominence, to become the most prosperous family in her apartment building. If her repressions were lifted for a single moment the extent of her fierce ambitions would be translated into acts of violence. She would eliminate competition to facilitate the satisfaction of her desires. No—you are not uniquely monstrous. The critical difference between you and a respectable housewife is not *what* you are—for in essence you very similar. The critical difference lies in the conditions that have led to the disintegration of certain repressions."

Vala Feist tilted her head and her expression showed interest. She clasped her knees, concealing the two green stains on her skirt.

Liebermann continued: "Le Bon has suggested that large groups, crowds, especially, are characterized by extremities of action. The usual prohibitions of civilized life cease to have effect and violence can easily erupt. When you pledged allegiance to your cause, you became part of a crowd. Repressions were lifted and your judgement was compromised. The unconscious mind rarely chooses sophisticated solutions. Thus, you have chosen violence." Liebermann was evidently pleased with himself. "We have an answer then, a mechanism that can explain how a person of tender conscious can embrace terror. I believe that if you were given an opportunity to explore this thesis, by engaging in a course of therapeutic conversation, you would gain insights that might result in your willingness to cooperate with the security office.

But overcoming resistances take time, and I suspect that we do not have that luxury." The young doctor lifted his head from his hand and sat up straight. "What do you dream?" His voice was soft and reflective. "It would be fascinating to discuss the content of your dreams. Professor Freud—whom I admire greatly—has developed a system for the interpretation of dreams. If you told me your dreams, what would we discover, I wonder?"

There was a knock on the door. It opened and a constable entered followed by three men in military uniform. The constable clicked his heels. "Some gentlemen to see you from the war ministry, sir."

Rheinhardt stood and said, "Then take them to my office. I told you, admit no one." He was particularly annoyed because he felt that Liebermann was getting somewhere and Feist was about to speak. Rheinhardt took a deep breath and addressed the tallest of the men from the ministry. "I am sorry, Herr Captain. But if you would kindly allow Constable Prock to escort you to my office, I will be with you very shortly."

The tall man stepped forward. "Captain Birk Hoover. Intelligence bureau." He did not introduce his companions.

"I am Detective Inspector Rheinhardt and this is my medical advisor, Herr Doctor Liebermann."

Indicating Feist he added, "We were conducting an interview."

"This woman is Vala Feist?"

Rheinhardt drew back, surprised. "Yes. Is she known to the Intelligence bureau?"

"I have read all of your reports. A comrade of Eduard Autenburg, implicated in the murder of Angelo Callari. Have you elicited a confession?"

"No—I'm afraid not."

"What else can you tell us?"

"Nothing . . ."

"Nothing?"

"She is refusing to speak."

"Please leave us with the prisoner. We would like to conduct our own interview."

"With respect, Captain Hoover, I am responsible for the management of this case."

"Kindly leave us with the prisoner. I am confident that we will be able to extract a full confession. It is imperative that you allow us to proceed."

Hoover stepped forward but Rheinhardt showed the advancing officer his palm.

"One moment, please. I have heard about your methods at the bureau and I am not sure that I can offer you my support."

"Your objection has been noted. Now, I must insist that you leave us alone with the prisoner."

Rheinhardt paused and after a painfully long hiatus he said, "This woman is only here today because of the ongoing work of the security office. I arrested her this morning and was very nearly killed in the process." He touched the dressing on his forehead to stress the point. "My assistant is now lying in a hospital bed and he is critically ill. Under such circumstances, it should come as no great surprise to you to learn that I am not minded to absent myself from the investigation. Even more so, given your . . . attitude?"

Hoover stiffened. "I order you to leave."

"Where are your papers?"

"Don't be ridiculous, Rheinhardt!"

The portly inspector turned and pointed to the portrait of Franz Josef. "Every morning, the emperor rises at four and he is at his desk at five. Why? So that he can attend to his paperwork. It is his second duty of the day—second only to his prayers and communion with God."

Hoover extended his arm and opened his hand without looking at his companions. "Papers."

Nothing appeared. He turned and his blazing eyes demanded a response. His companions cringed and one of them said, "We didn't anticipate obstruction, sir."

Hoover swore under his breath. "Inspector, this is completely unacceptable."

"Yes, I agree. The situation is regrettable; however, I am obliged to follow correct procedure."

"These are exceptional circumstances."

"So we must ensure that the usual protocols have been respected and everything is in order."

Hoover recognized that there was nothing else he could do. "We will return with the requisite documentation. Needless to say, I will be registering a formal complaint."

The three men exited and the door slammed shut.

"Well," said Liebermann. "I am delighted to see that the security office and the intelligence bureau enjoy such warm and cordial relations." He turned to face Feist. "It's enough to make one consider the merits of a radical alternative!"

Rheinhardt sat down heavily in his chair. The sagging skin beneath his eyes became jaundiced beneath the yellow bulb. "Fräulein Feist, I would urge you most strongly to start talking. When Captain Hoover returns I will not have the authority to send him away a second time."

"Thank you, inspector," said Feist. Her voice sounded dusty and dry. "You have integrity. It saddens me that a man with your qualities should choose to serve a tyrant and live like a lapdog. You only oppose us because you do not understand. One day, I hope you *will* understand. That is all I have to say." Her lips became a horizontal seal and she closed her eyes.

FIFTY-FOUR

Several members of the audience stood to applaud. The pianist, Julius Epstein, was bowing and crossing his hands over his heart. He was a distinguished figure, whose muttonchop whiskers were more copious than the emperor's, and for a man in his seventies, Epstein was still spry. His face was elongated, almost to the point of deformity, and the cast of his features expressed such a surfeit of pathos he resembled a satirical cartoon.

Liebermann raised his voice. "Did you enjoy it?"

Hannah stood on her toes and shouted directly into Liebermann's ear. "Wonderful."

"I believe he is going to perform an encore," said Amelia.

The Bösendorfer-Saal fell silent again as Epstein sat on his stool and made a few adjustments to its height. When he was satisfied, he composed himself for a few seconds before attacking the keys with demonic energy. He had chosen the first of Franz Liszt's "Mephisto Waltzes" as his encore. The opening bars were electrifying: raw, galloping fifths that accumulated and stuttered toward a grotesque, angular ballet. Everything about the music was wild and sinister—a corybantic delirium. Notes sparkled, glittered, exploded like fireworks, and a strident glissando made some members of the audience gasp.

Liebermann turned to look at Hannah, who was sitting on the edge of her seat, hyperventilating, with eyes bulging out of their sockets. He then turned to look at Amelia whose rigid pout and frown suggested something very close to skepticism—wariness, perhaps even mistrust?

The pianist's hands were a blur. A few moments of uneasy calm presaged a final assault of such unremitting ferocity that the expectation of broken keys flying from the keyboard was not unreasonable. The last bars were quite terrifying.

Liebermann, Hannah, and Amelia, collected their coats from the cloakroom and hurried along the busy thoroughfare of Herrengasse to Café Central. All of the tables in the Arkadenhof—a pretty, elegant courtyard—were occupied, so they accepted a banquette in the coffeehouse close to where the chess players gathered. A pianist was improvising a gentle, innocuous ländler. Two lustrous women glided by. They were wearing ballgowns and tiaras. It was unclear whether they had been to a ball or their evening was only just beginning. "The count is a fool and one day he will pay dearly for his indiscretion," said one to the other, affecting the nasal delivery that typified speech in the Habsburg court.

A waiter delivered Liebermann's order of kaiserschmarrn (lumps of pancake sprinkled with icing sugar) in a wide pan accompanied by a tureen of plum compote. Liebermann divided the pancake into three portions and poured compote over each irregular mound. The potent fragrance promised hidden depths, like a vintage port.

"The first few bars sounded like a violin being tuned up," said Hannah.

"Here's your schmarrn," said Liebermann. "I'm sorry. What did you say?"

It was very noisy and the syrupy ländler had reached a sentimental climax.

"The opening of Epstein's encore—it sounded like a violin."

"Well, yes. That's exactly what it's supposed to be. It describes an episode from Faust."

"Oh, I see. '*Mephisto* Waltz' . . ."

Liebermann rotated a lump of pancake with his fork to ensure that it was coated with compote and then raised it to his mouth. "Very good," he said, enjoying the succession of sweet flavors before continuing to address his sister. "A wedding feast is taking place at a village inn and Mephistopheles persuades Faust to enter. Mephistopheles snatches a violin from a fiddler and performs a waltz that makes the guests dance without inhibition." Turning to Amelia, he added, "I'm not convinced that you liked it very much."

"It was fascinating to hear all of the sonorities of the piano exploited within a single work," Amelia replied. "And I found the rhythmic passages exhilarating. I don't think I've ever heard a piano played so loudly. But . . ."

"Yes?"

"I did not find the music quite so affecting as Bach."

"Well, Bach is superior to Liszt, of course," said Liebermann. "But Liszt offers a different order of pleasure; sensuality, excitement—spectacle."

"But Bach *is* exciting," Amelia objected. "I find Bach *very* exciting. The way every line is balanced, the way his complex structures teeter on the edge of chaos but always remain within the ambit of his discipline—it is like watching the moving parts of a great engine."

Liebermann gave his sister a sideways glance and she responded with a discreet, invisible kick.

"Do you play an instrument, Hannah?" Amelia asked.

"The piano," Hannah replied. "Quite badly. Isn't that right, Maxim?"

"You don't practice enough," said Liebermann.

"I don't think I'll ever be a very competent musician."

"Perhaps not, but you have other talents." Liebermann spoke to Amelia. "Hannah loves art—particularly modern art. She's never happier than when she's walking around a gallery. And

307

she has—I believe—a rare instinct for identifying work of substance and value."

"Do you want to be an artist?" Amelia continued.

"Oh, I don't know about that," Hannah replied. "To want to be an artist seems too grand an ambition for someone like me. But I'd like to learn more about the history of art."

"You might consider applying to the university. There are many courses you could take."

"I'm not sure that would be possible."

"Why do you say that?"

"I'm not sure my parents want me to be educated. Well, not to that standard."

"What about *you?*" Amelia's eyes collected the lamp light and shone with cool brilliance. "What do *you* want?"

Hannah rocked her head from side to side. "I love reading about art, especially the criticism. And I think I would enjoy studying the great schools. So much modern art is rooted in the past. I like discovering how ideas develop—how ideas are connected."

"Then you really *must* attend the university."

"My parents want me to get married."

"And you will be married. If that is what you want. You can find a husband while you are studying at the university. It is my experience that a young lady—surrounded by so many eligible gentlemen—is never wanting for attention." Her pewter eyes flashed in Liebermann's direction. "The realization of personal ambition and marriage are not mutually exclusive."

One of the chess players appeared next to their banquette. He was a shabby-looking man with a long beard and when he spoke he did so with an unusual accent. "Forgive me, ladies, for this interruption, but might I ask the good doctor for a game. I have just humiliated Professor Bogenschutz and prior to that, I destroyed Professor Szôlôssi. Please, I am in great need of a worthy opponent."

Liebermann smiled. "I'm afraid I must disappoint you this evening, Herr Karmazyn."

"Why?" the shabby man responded. "The ladies will not object. Will you, dear ladies?"

"Honestly, Karmazyn," Liebermann continued, "I'm not in the right state of mind. And you'll complain. You'll say that I'm not concentrating."

Karmazyn sighed and feigned despair.

"I would be happy to play you," said Amelia.

Karmazyn's ironic smile revealed tobacco-stained teeth. "That is very kind of you but . . ." He made a gesture, the meaning of which was quite unequivocal: *You are a woman!*

"I insist," said Amelia. "The game may not last very long, but it will surely serve to pass the time until a worthier opponent can be found." Before Karmazyn could object Amelia was on her feet. Kamazyn looked at Liebermann who offered him only the weightless consolation of a mouthed apology.

Amelia and Karmazyn sat at an adjacent table and Hannah and Liebermann took the opportunity to discuss family matters: coming birthdays, their father's health, and the much mooted threat of a visit from their rakish Uncle Alexander. As they talked, both became aware of Karmazyn's agitation. He was muttering and pulling faces. Occasionally he cried "God!" or uttered a phrase in Latin. After no more than fifteen minutes Amelia said, "Checkmate," and returned to the banquette. Karmazyn was scratching his head and making odd movements over the chessboard with his hands, revisiting the sequence of moves that had led to his premature demise.

"He was very accomplished," said Amelia. "But somewhat overconfident."

"I've never beaten him," said Liebermann. "Few have."

Amelia did not respond. Her expression remained fixed and neutral. "Is something the matter?" She looked from Hannah to Liebermann.

Brother and sister shook their heads—but Hannah's shoulders were shaking a little. "Come on," said Liebermann to his sister. "It's getting late. I promised Mother and Father that I'd put you in a cab."

Liebermann and Hannah negotiated a winding course between the tables—all of them now occupied—and exited the coffeehouse. A cloud of cigar smoke followed them onto the street and rotated in the back draft of the closing door. They waited on the pavement, watching the carriages clatter past.

"Do *you* think I should go to university?" Hannah asked.

"I just want you to be happy," Liebermann replied.

"I think going to university would make me happy. But Mother and Father . . . they're always talking about finding me a good husband. Did you hear about Herr Lenkiewicz's son?"

"Baruch."

"He was quite . . . handsome, I suppose. But I found him very difficult to talk to. He didn't have any interests. Well, apart from his work, that is."

"If you want to go to the university, I'll talk to Mother and Father. When you're ready, just say."

"Thank you, Maxim." Hannah threw her arms around his neck and pulled him close.

Liebermann saw a cab and raised his arm. He instructed the driver to take Hannah to Concordiaplatz and handed the man a few coins. "Keep the change." The gratuity was excessive. Touching his hat with the handle of his whip, the driver declared, "A true gentleman!"

Hannah climbed into the cab but before closing the door she leaned out and said: "Amelia. She's . . . well—quite extraordinary."

"Yes," said Liebermann. "Full of surprises."

Hannah retreated into the darkness of the cab and Liebermann slammed the door. The driver shook his reins and the wheels began to turn. As the cab moved forward a Bosnian street hawker wearing his fez at an oblique angle asked Liebermann if he needed any matches. "All right," Liebermann replied. He handed over another coin and said, once again, "Keep the change." The Bosnian gave him a box of Vestas, smiled, and replied, "Peace be upon you." It was said with touching sincerity.

Liebermann stepped back into the coffeehouse. Even through dense smoke, Amelia's red hair was bright and striking. He noticed two cavalry officers close by, clearly commenting on her appearance and debating whether to make an approach. Liebermann hurried over and reclaimed his place by her side.

"You look a little tired," said Amelia.

"Yes," Liebermann replied. "I've had a busy day." He told her about the arrest of Vala Feist and the appearance of Captain Hoover at the Schottenring station. "The man was deeply unpleasant and clearly intended to extract a confession by force. The intelligence bureau can justify their iniquitous methods by making an appeal that finds easy popular support. It is their duty to protect all of us. They must do whatever it takes to ensure that none of the emperor's subjects are harmed. But frankly, I have no desire to be protected if the preservation of my safety necessitates tacit endorsement of medieval brutality. We become more monstrous than those who we deign to call monsters." Liebermann lit a cigar using the matches he'd purchased from the street hawker. "Feist is a fanatic and she will not betray her comrades. In previous centuries she would have been a martyr and she would have willingly burned at the stake rather than renounce her faith or favored heresy. She will almost certainly suffer protracted ill treatment at the hands of Hoover and his thugs—and she will confess nothing."

"Well, that rather depends," said Amelia. "Do you recall our conversation about de Cyon? The visiting professor from St. Petesburg?"

"Yes—the cardiograph man."

"He said that the cardiograph can be used to detect lies." Amelia pressed her fingers together and tapped them against her lips. "Even if Fräulein Feist refuses to utter a single word, one might still be able to determine the nature of her thoughts by observing changes in her heart rate. For example, if you were to ask Fräulein Feist a sensitive question, such as—Is there a plan afoot to explode a bomb in Vienna?—and there *is* such a plan, one would expect to see a strong response. Much stronger, for example, than the response provoked by an innocuous question such as: Do you like kaiserschmarrn? By asking carefully worded questions, and comparing cardiograph readings, it should be possible to draw very definite and helpful conclusions. This would seem to me to be a more profitable course of action than torture—which is not merely unseemly, crude, and barbarous, but likely to either fail entirely or elicit half-truths and falsehoods."

Liebermann flicked some ash from the end of his cigar. "How many cardiographs are there at the university?"

"Several," said Amelia. "I'm sure Professor Föhrenholz would be willing to loan one to the security office."

"Do you know how to operate them?"

"Yes, even the new machine that Professor de Cyon delivered. I attended all of his demonstrations."

Liebermann stole a quick kiss. "You really are quite fabulous."

Amelia blinked and looked a little puzzled. "A problem was presented and I suggested a solution."

"Just wait here a moment. I'm going to call Oskar."

Liebermann excused himself and went to use the coffeehouse telephone.

"Max? Where are you—it's very noisy."

"Café Central. Oskar, there's a way of getting

Vala Feist to answer questions even if she refuses to speak. It was suggested to me by Miss Lydgate."

"Ah, Miss Lydgate, do you still see her?"

"Occasionally. Well, not very often." Liebermann cleared his throat and added, "Hardly at all, in fact."

An electrical crackling preceded Rheinhardt's prompt. "You were saying?"

"Yes, I was saying. You must contact Professor Föhrenholz at the university. Have you ever heard of a machine called a cardiograph?"

"No."

"We're going to need one."

FIFTY-FIVE

It was almost midnight and the ward was silent. Rheinhardt was exhausted but he had dragged himself to the hospital in order to sit with his assistant for an hour or so. Haussmann lay in bed, a bandage wrapped around his head, breathing softly. He had not roused or eaten since being knocked unconscious by the grenade blast. He looked pitiful and wasted. His skin was pale and its tightness showed too much of the skull's curvature beneath. A horrible reminder of mortality.

Rheinhardt reached out and rested his hand on the starched bed cover. He could feel the solid curve of Haussmann's arm. "Don't give up, my boy. Never give up."

It occurred to Rheinhardt that although he had spent a great deal of time with Haussmann over the last three years, he knew very little about him; a few scraps of information. Haussmann didn't like old paintings but he enjoyed poetry. He had been awarded a volume of Greek legends after entering a poetry competition at school. Their relationship was professional—good-humored, but distant.

Rheinhardt found himself addressing the ceiling. "Please spare him. He has served the people of this city well." Was it a prayer? Was he praying? Yes, he probably was. "Please, Lord. If you're listening . . ."

The wall clock ticked.

Haussmann's breath was barely discernable.

A pretty young woman appeared in the doorway. She was smartly dressed and clutched her hat in her hand. "Oh?" she said.

Rheinhardt stood up. "Fräulein . . . ?" She appeared confused so he continued. "My name is Rheinhardt. Detective Inspector Rheinhardt."

The young woman smiled and then laughed. "Of course! You're just as he described you! I'm Ava. Ava Fey." Rheinhardt's evident perplexity encouraged her to add, "We are . . . ," she indicated Haussmann. "Together?" She stepped into the room and offered Rheinhardt her delicate little hand. He bowed, raised her fingers to his lips and said, "My pleasure, Fräulein Fey. Please, take this seat."

"No, I couldn't."

"Really, you must." She thanked him and sat with her hat balanced on her lap.

"You are visiting at a very late hour, Fräulein Fey."

"I've been doing a show."

"A show?"

"I dance. There was a late performance this evening at Ronacher's. The nurses have been very kind. They said I could visit whenever I wanted. I was here earlier, you see. The doctor seemed quite worried."

"Oh, Haussmann's a strong fellow. I'm sure he'll pull through." It was a trite thing to say and Rheinhardt instantly regretted this careless assurance.

Ava fiddled with an artificial flower on her hat. "He talks a lot about you. He says you have a dry sense of humor and that you make him laugh."

Rheinhardt nodded, unsure of how to respond. Finally he said, "Would you like me to leave? Perhaps you would prefer to spend some time with him alone?"

"No," Ava replied. "Please stay—stay as long as you want."

"A few more minutes then."

Rheinhardt found a chair outside in the corridor and brought it back into the room. He placed it on the opposite side of the bed to Ava.

"Look at him." Ava found Haussmann's hand and took it out from beneath the cover. "He will be all right, won't he?"

Rheinhardt felt obliged to supply a more honest answer. He dispensed with platitudes and said, "I hope so."

Ava noticed Rheinhardt's dressing. "Were you caught in the blast too?"

"Yes. But for some reason I managed to escape serious injury."

"The woman who did this must be wicked."

Rheinhardt twisted the points of his moustache. "No. I don't think she is wicked. Misguided, perhaps; deluded even—but not wicked. She believes that she is on the side of good, that she is making the world a better place."

"By throwing grenades and planting bombs?" The question was rhetorical. Ava raised Haussmann's hand and pressed the back of it against her cheek. "Oh, look at him," she repeated. Rheinhardt saw that Ava's eyes were glistening.

They sat in silence. Occasionally, Ava would look up and attempt a smile. But she could not conceal her misery.

Rheinhardt thought that he should probably leave. He stood up, gazed down at Haussmann and sighed.

Haussmann opened one eye. "Sir?"

"Haussmann?"

"Why am I in bed, sir?"

"My dear boy . . ."

"Walnut cake—we were eating walnut cake."

"Don't worry about the walnut cake, Haussmann. Look," he urged Haussmann to roll his head on the pillow. "Look who's here."

Haussmann turned. "Ava? What's going on?"

Tears were coursing down the young woman's face. "You were knocked out by a blast? Don't you remember?"

"No," Haussmann replied. "I can only remember eating walnut cake."

He tried to sit up but failed.

"You must rest, Haussmann." Rheinhardt moved the pillow to better support Haussmann's head. "One step at a time, eh?"

The young man opened his other eye. "Is this a hospital?"

"I'll get a doctor," said Rheinhardt. He moved into the corridor, leaned against the wall, and allowed himself two convulsive sobs of relief. He then marched toward a nurse humming Johan Strauss the elder's "Philomelen Waltz" rather too loudly. As he approached, she gave him a stern look. "I'm sorry." He grinned. "But I have good reason to be cheerful."

FIFTY-SIX

His dream had been vivid. It wasn't a dream though—it was a memory, a very distant memory.

The old serf had said to him, "What are you doing, Master Peter?" Razumovsky was a boy and studying an ants' nest. "You've been staring at those little creatures all day—what's so interesting, eh? Come inside, Magda's made you some vegetable soup."

"Look at them, Jov." His voice was a refined treble. "Do you see how busy they are, how they carry and exchange food and cooperate?"

"What about it?"

"There's no one in charge—look. No one is giving orders. How do they know what to do? It's . . . extraordinary."

"Don't be ridiculous, Master Peter. Come inside. Please—or your father will have something to say. And we don't want that, do we?"

One of the ants reared like a horse and its tiny antenae waved in the air.

"They have no rulers—no generals or chamberlains, no government—but everything is highly organized."

Jov grunted. "Same as a peasant village, Master

Peter—we all get along very well without taking orders. Every man does what he has to do and that's enough."

The room was dark, the bed cold. The dream had stopped but the memories continued to rise into awareness.

Jov had been right. Razumovsky saw peasant villages for himself when he was in Siberia. Everyone cooperated and no one served anyone else. At the time, these minature outposts of egalitarianism had made him think of his father's estate: thirteen hundred serfs on the land and sixty in the principal residence. Did they really need eight coachmen and twenty horses, six cooks and eighteen elderly gentlemen to wait upon them when they ate their dinner? And then there were the countless serving girls, some of whom he'd used, because when he was a lusty youth he hadn't know better. Just thinking about them made him feel guilty; girls with ruddy complexions and rough hands, lying naked in barns, offering themselves freely in exchange for some idiotic, cheap bauble.

Does it make me look like a lady?

He remembered the winter balls during which his father would employ even more staff—armies of liveried servants and grooms. Escaping the estate had felt good, liberating. Even when he hadn't eaten for days and it was 60 degress below zero he did not regret his decision. The cold and hunger were cleansing—they made him feel pure.

In his knapsack he always carried a copy of Alexander von Humbolt's *Cosmos* and several books on natural history. He read *On the Origin of Species* by Charles Darwin and found it utterly fascinating. Yet, he wasn't entirely persuaded by Darwin's thesis. Certain observations made him question the English biologist's authority. Everywhere in the natural world, Razumovsky saw cooperation rather than competition. Instead of drinking vodka with his regiment, he would go for long walks and observe the behavior of deer. They would often gather together, for no other reason, so he deduced, than to keep each other warm. He saw ruminants standing in a ring to resist the attack of a wild horse. Herds, flocks, shoals, swarms, colonies—organisms frequently worked in concert and enjoyed a common advantage. Nature constantly supplied examples of mutual aid. Somehow, mankind had become divorced from nature. Mankind had lost its way. . . .

The cold and hardship of Siberia reminded him that the luxuries of his former life were entirely expendable. A man did not need gilded chairs, Venetian mirrors, and diamond tiepins. It was all so meaningless. He began to view the accumulation of possessions as not only morally bankrupt, but also an encumbrance. He didn't have very much in his knapsack, but anything that he identified as being surplus to his immediate requirements he disposed of.

There was, in fact, only one item that he treasured: his notebook. A battered leather volume in which he noted all of his observations, made sketches, and developed his critique of Darwin. He summarized his work in a letter that he sent to Lavochkin, a professor of zoology at the university in Moscow. Lavochkin was impressed and they became correspondents. In one of his missives, Lavochkin announced that he was planning a scientific expedition to the Americas. He invited Razumovsky to be his assistant—a young man with a military training would make an ideal traveling companion. Razumovsky agreed, although he was obliged to remain in Siberia with his regiment for another year.

It was a long year and almost his last. He was attacked by bandits and knocked unconscious. He would have frozen to death, were it not for a passing peasant, who by chance, came across his rigid, frost-covered body and lit a fire.

On returning to Moscow, Razumovsky studied with Lavochkin for six months before they embarked on their American adventure. They collected samples, undertook geological surveys, and encountered red Indians. While crossing upstate New York they came across a utopian community in which all of the adult men and women lived as if married to each other, in a condition that they called "complex marriage." Monogamy was rejected and the children were raised by the collective. It was an interesting social experiment. While in America, Razumovsky acquired a Colt pistol. He liked the weight and feel of the weapon and never replaced it.

On returning to Moscow, he refined his theoretical position and realized that his thinking was as relevant to politics as it was to biology.

Darwin was correct—but only in part. Organisms *do* compete for resources, but only when those resources are limited. When resources are sufficient, however, organisms cooperate.

In human society, the nobility and capitalists had grabbed all the land and commandeered the means of production. Resources were being artifically limited. In order for a small number of bloated parasites to live in decadant splendor, the rest of humanity must live in squalor. Redistribution of wealth was the obvious solution. Sufficiency would encourage mutual aid and the world would become a much better place. It might even become a kind of paradise.

Although his argument was unassailable, he did

not expect the parasites to cede their wealth and power without a struggle. They would greedily hang on to everything they possessed. So, they would have to be persuaded by other means.

When Razumovsky's father died, Razumovsky was the sole beneficiary of the will. He inherited the estate, the properties, an African gold mine, an art collection of considerable worth, and several precious heirlooms gifted to the Razumovsky family by Ivan the Terrible. Razumovsky sold everything and the first thing he did was negotiate a generous financial settlement for the thirteen hundred and sixty serfs, the eight coachmen, the six cooks, eighteen servants, and sundry serving girls of unspecified number. Then, he appointed stock brokers in various European capitals to manage a truly vast portfolio of investments. It amused him to finance a war on capitalism using funds generated by capitalism itself.

A year passed. He had long neglected society and few people inquired as to the whereabouts of the young prince. He had been living on his own in a log cabin. And so the day finally came when he packed his meager belongings into his old napsack and left the wood, meaning never to return. The open door banged in the wind as his boots crunched on the snow.

On the road a gypsy hag stopped him and begged him for some money. *I don't have any,* he replied. He was telling the truth. His pockets were indeed empty. The gypsy could tell by his accent that he was nobility and cursed: "May the devil take you! You look like one of his demons!"

Memories, memories, memories . . .

FIFTY-SEVEN

Rheinhardt was seated behind his desk facing Captain Hoover. Once again, the intelligence officer was accompanied by his lieutenants—Wax and Hellwitz—both of whom stood in silence by the door. Liebermann was leaning against the wall, looking out of the window while tapping a finger against his lips.

"So," said Rheinhardt, "have your methods met with any success?" He was unable to conceal a sneer.

Hoover raised his chin. "I am of the opinion that Feist's capacity to resist is weakening."

"And on what evidence do you base that assertion?"

"I have considerable experience in these matters." Hoover cracked his knuckles and continued. "There are certain signs. And I see no merit in your proposal."

"Signs?" said Liebermann, without turning away from the window. "What signs?"

"I have undertaken many interrogations, Herr Doctor. One learns to read people as if they were books. I can see it in her eyes—the doubt, the resignation. She will break soon."

"With respect, Captain Hoover, you are very much mistaken. Fräulein Feist is a fanatic and she will never answer your questions. Her resolve is unshakable. She would rather die than betray her comrades. That is what *I* saw in her eyes. The cardiograph will give us some purchase on her thoughts. There is no need to resort to barbaric practices when science is plainly showing us a way forward."

Hoover shifted position and his sabre clattered against the chair legs. "Time is passing, Herr Doctor. And Vienna is in grave peril."

"Precisely," said Liebermann, turning to meet Hoover's gaze. "We need answers. We need answers now and you aren't going to get any." Liebermann positioned himself next to Rheinhardt. "The cardiograph is already here. It was transported from the university this morning and it is being set up as we speak."

"By who?"

"Miss Amelia Lydgate," said Rheinhardt. "She is a protégé of the blood specialist Landsteiner and has recently studied the cardiograph and its operation under the tutelage of the world's leading expert."

"Professor de Cyon," Liebermann interjected.

"Miss? Why do you say *Miss?*" Hoover frowned. "Is she English?"

"Yes," Rheinhardt continued. "But you will discover that her German is faultless. We are most fortunate to count a female scientist among our associates. It is my understanding that the procedure is quite invasive, isn't that so, Herr Doctor?"

"Indeed," Liebermann nodded. "The preparation of the subject requires some disrobing."

"The security office cannot risk accusations of impropriety," said Rheinhardt, eyeing each of the three intelligence officers in turn.

Hoover stroked his moustache with his index finger; a single, slow, outward movement from the philtrum to the corner of his mouth. "Can she be trusted, this English woman?"

Rheinhardt smiled. "She has been of service to the security office before. I trust her implicitly."

"I don't know," said Hoover, stroking his moustache a second time. "I am of a skeptical disposition and have developed a profound mistrust of technology. During military exercises, it always seems to be the latest machine or electrical system that breaks down—and usually at the most critical stage."

Liebermann was not discouraged. "When we experience intense emotion the heart quickens and we can do nothing to conceal this response. It happens automatically—unconsciously. The cardiograph will provide us with precise measurements. If we ask Feist carefully worded questions, then the magnitude of her responses will permit us to make educated guesses concerning what her answers might have been if she had chosen to speak."

"For example . . ."

Rheinardt came to his assistance. "We could ask: Is Mephistopheles still in Vienna?"

"And if he is," Liebermann continued, "we can expect to see a significant increase in Fräulein Feist's heart rate. She will be anxious to mislead us and her anxiety will betray her. Her heart will beat faster and the cardiograph can detect even the slightest change."

Rheinhardt opened the drawer of his desk and took out a box of cigars. He offered one to Hoover. The intelligence officer put the cigar in his mouth and waited for Lieutenant Wax to come forward and light it for him. The room became tense and silent while Hoover puffed and the room filled with smoke.

"Tell me," said Rheinhardt, "what does the bureau know about Mephistopheles?" Hoover's expression remained impassive, like a card player wishing to give no inkling of the quality of his hand. "Captain," Rheinhardt sighed, "might I remind you that—at least theoretically—we are on the same side."

Hoover continued his internal deliberations for a few more seconds before nodding. "We know next to nothing. The name Mephistopheles has come to our attention during the course of numerous international operations. Some say he was a member of the Paris commune, the revolutionary government that ruled Paris over thirty years ago. Others say he is a disaffected noble from a Russo-German family. At least two informants have said that he is a Swiss scientist: a biologist of some description. We have no photographs, no descriptions." Hoover exhaled another cloud. "Even so, we have good reason to believe that he is connected with several atrocities. It is even rumored in certain radical circles that he had some involvement in the assassination of the empress. I am inclined to believe that this is merely an invention circulated in order to feed his legend. The only thing we can say for certain about Mephistopheles is that he is dangerous."

Hoover stubbed out his cigar and stood up. He looked directly into Liebermann's eyes, glanced back at Rheinhardt, and then glared at Liebermann again. "Very well, let's try this damnable machine! But if we don't get a swift result I'll be removing Feist from your custody and employing whatever means I deem necessary to protect the interests of His Majesty and his people."

FIFTY-EIGHT

Feist was sitting on a chair with both hands and one of her feet immersed in large tubs of salt solution. The hem of her skirt and her petticoats had been rolled up above her bony knees. A single shoe, containing a compressed gray woolen stocking, had been set aside. Liebermann and Rheinhardt registered the bruise on the left side of the woman's face and exchanged furious glances. The inspector shook his head. Now was not the time to start trading insults with Hoover. Next to Feist was a gargantuan piece of electrical apparatus, parts of which were covered in knobs and glass dials. It was more like a collection of separate instruments than a single device. An assembly with a metal wheel, mounted within a braced frame, reminded Rheinhardt of his wife's Pfaff sewing machine. Another object looked like a very fat microscope. Two wires were visible and they appeared to connect one of the tubs to a panel covered with small, colored bulbs. The overall impression was of something quite makeshift, a gimcrack construction that would teeter and collapse if anyone leaned on it. Rheinhardt glanced at Hoover, whose expression was suspended somewhere between horror and incredulity.

Amelia Lydgate was studying an array of dials and making notes on a sheet of paper attached to a clipboard. She was dressed in a dark skirt and a simple white blouse; however, her reassuring, professional appearance was undermined by her hair, which seemed to ignite whenever she passed beneath the rays that lanced through the tall laboratory windows. She was subject to intermittent transformations, becoming several times during the transit of short distances less a scientist and more like an allegorical figure as imagined by Gustav Klimt.

Rheinhardt, Liebermann, Hoover, and his two lieutenants were seated in a wide semi-circle. Hoover was whispering something into the cocked ear of Hellwitz, producing a conspicuous sibilance. Amelia raised her head to address her audience. "Gentlemen, I must ask you to respect the necessity for absolute silence until the procedure is completed."

Hoover mumbled his consent.

Amelia returned her attention to the dials and then said, "Fräulein Feist, I am going to ask you a series of questions. I would very much like you to supply answers, but if you prefer to remain silent, then that is your prerogative. Let us begin." Amelia's pencil hovered over the clipboard. "Is green your favorite color?" Amelia paused, made a note and continued: "Who was Julius Caesar?" Again she made a note. Vala

Feist closed her eyes and her compressed lips whitened.

It was an odd spectacle, a mature woman, with exposed knees, entangled in the workings of a large electrical behemoth. The fact that Feist had tried to kill Rheinhardt (and his assistant) made no difference to him, he still pitied her. She had already been horribly humiliated. The thought of Hoover slapping her, his gloved knuckles making contact with her cheek, made Rheinhardt's stomach turn. And now she was being made to pose like an exhibit in a freak show. But what was the alternative?

"Do you like topfenstrudel? Have you ever experienced intimate relations with a gentleman? Does the Pope live in Rome?" Hoover was becoming restless. He changed position and allowed one of his boots to land heavily on the floor. Amelia turned her bright, cool gaze on the intelligence officer and a vertical crease appeared on her forehead. Her expression was sufficiently severe to elicit an abreviated salute that served as Hoover's apology. Amelia peered at the dials and continued as before—questions, followed by pauses, followed by the scratching of her pencil. Then, finally: "Is Mephistopheles still in Vienna?" Feist showed no signs of surprise or agitation. "Did Mozart write operas? Does the naked male body please you? Is Budapest the capital of Hungary? Is there a plan afoot to plant a bomb in Vienna?" Amelia placed her clipboard on a bench and turned some knobs on a raked panel. There was a faint buzzing sound that became louder and subsided. She picked up her clipboard and repeated all of her questions, after which she concluded, "Thank you for your cooperation, Fräulein Feist. If you are uncomfortable you may remove your limbs from the water. A towel has been provided." Turning to face her audience she added, "Gentlemen. The first trial is completed. Let us retire."

As they filed out of the laboratory and into an adjacent room, Rheinhardt addressed two constables. "Keep an eye on the prisoner. We'll be out shortly." The young men clicked their heels and joined Feist.

Rheinhardt closed the door. The room was empty apart from a table and a few chairs. Liebermann pulled one of the chairs out and offered it to Amelia, but she refused to sit and everyone remained standing.

"Why did you ask her so many irrelevant questions?" Hoover demanded.

"For the purpose of comparison," Amelia replied. "We cannot form any notion of what constitutes a significant response without first having established certain arbitrary values as a guide. That is why I asked her both neutral questions and questions likely to provoke emotion."

"Well?" said Hoover, inhaling and expanding his chest. "What can you tell us?"

Amelia consulted her clipboard and replied, "Fräulein Feist's heart rate increased most when asked about the man known as Mephistopheles and the putative act of terror. Although one cannot be absolutely certain, it is reasonable to suppose that, on the balance of probabilities, Mephistopheles is resident in Vienna and that an incident of propaganda by deed has been planned."

"Can you provide us with more specific answers?" asked Hoover.

"No," Amelia replied. "All that I can do is infer significance from the magnitude of Fräulein Feist's responses."

"We need more than this," said Hoover. "This isn't enough."

"We could try to locate Mephistopheles by reading through the districts of Vienna and—"

"What good would that do? We can't search every apartment in a whole district!"

"Narrowing the search would be better than nothing," said Rheinhardt.

"And the same systematic method," Liebermann agreed, "could also be employed to ascertain where Mephistopheles intends to plant his bomb."

Hoover shook his head. "Fräulein Lydgate." He bowed and clicked his heels. "This has been a very interesting academic exercise, but all that you have demonstrated is the inadequacy of your equipment. Your science is not yet so advanced that we can afford to dispense with interrogation." He took a step closer to Rheinhardt. "I must ask you to release Fräulein Feist from your custody. She will be returning with me to the War Ministry." He produced some official, stamped papers and tossed them onto the table. "I have the authority and I would advise you most strongly not to question it."

An argument ensued, in which Rheinhardt and Liebermann voiced their objections but it was evident that Hoover had made his decision and was not prepared to discuss the matter any further. Now that Mephistopheles's presence in Vienna had been confirmed, Hoover clearly felt that his methods were even more justified. "Enough, inspector! I will not endure your petulant haranguing a moment longer! Vala Feist is returning to the War Ministry with me and I do not want to hear another word of complaint. You would have me risk the safety of our city on account of some absurd notion of gentlemanly conduct. *That* woman," he jabbed his finger at the door, "and her associates, would happily erect gallows on the Heldenplatz and watch the emperor's corpse swing without feeling a whit of compunction. How can you be so naïve, Rheinhardt?"

Before Rheinhardt could answer this largely rhetorical question, there was a knock on the door and one of the constables who had been charged with "keeping an eye" on Feist entered.

"Sorry to interrupt, sir," said the young man. "Bit of a problem."

"Why?" said Rheinhardt. "What's happened?"

"The prisoner . . ." The constable looked distinctly uncomfortable. "She said she wanted to use the convenience, sir. We escorted her to the said place of relief and now she's locked herself in. She won't come out."

FIFTY-NINE

Rheinhardt clenched his fist and banged on the water closet door. "Fräulein Feist, are you all right?"

"Of course she's all right!" said Hoover.

Rheinhardt listened for the sound of the sliding bolt. "With respect, you must come out now."

"This is intolerable," Hoover fumed. He glanced at Wax. "Break the door down. We'll drag her out if necessary."

Wax raised his leg, swiveled his hip, and thrust his boot out, making contact with his heel. There was a loud boom followed by the sharp crack of splitting wood. The metal bolt on the other side was ripped off its brackets and clattered onto the tiles and the door flew open, crashing against the wall. It was a deep closet, more like a truncated corridor, and at the far end was a toilet on which Feist was slumped. She was properly dressed, although her hair was in a state of considerable disarray, and her eyes were closed. She looked as if she had fallen asleep. The air was tainted with the smell of excrement.

Liebermann was the first to enter. "Fräulein Feist?" He advanced and when he reached her, he pressed his fingers against the side of her neck. Then he lifted her chin and raised one of her eyelids with his thumb. Her expression did not change and when he released the eyelid it closed instantly.

"What's wrong with her?" asked Rheinhardt.

"I don't know," Liebermann replied. Feist coughed and her lips moved. "Fräulein Feist?" He tapped her gently on the cheek, choosing the unblemished side of her face. "Can you hear me, Fräulein Feist?"

Her eyes flicked open and she smiled. "You are already too late," she whispered, and closed her eyes again.

"What did she say?" Hoover demanded.

"You are already too late . . ."

"What does that mean?" asked Wax.

"It means," said Hoover, "that we've wasted far too much time and we must get her back to the War Ministry immediately."

Liebermann lifted Feist's arm and laid his fingers across her wrist. "I'm afraid there's no point in doing that."

"Why?"

"Because she'd dead."

"What?"

"Her heart has stopped."

"Shouldn't you try to revive her?"

"There's nothing I can do."

"Damnation!" Hoover stormed out of the closet, slapped his palm against the wall, and returned shouting. "It was that ridiculous machine! The electricity must have fried her nerves. I knew I shouldn't have agreed. Damnation!"

"Might I suggest, Herr Captain," Amelia addressed Hoover, without emotion, "that the evidence—"

"Enough," Hoover cut in. "Enough, woman!"

"Your reasons for making such an observation escape me. My gender—I would hope—has always been self-evident." Hoover glared at Amelia but before he could respond she was speaking again. "Let me assure you, Herr Captain, that no nerves have ever been—as you would say—fried, by a cardiograph. The procedure is entirely safe. Fräulein Feist is dead because she killed herself."

"How? I see no means."

"That is because you haven't looked here." Amelia reached into the wash basin. She then held up a broken capsule.

"Poison?"

"Yes," said Liebermann.

Hoover positioned himself in front of Rheinhardt; so close, that their noses were almost touching. "Damnation! You'll pay for this, Rheinhardt. You incompetent fool. Why didn't you search her?"

"We did search her."

"Not very well it seems! One wouldn't want to do anything improper!"

"The security office has in its employ a lady

especially for the purpose. A former nurse, now retired, who can be trusted to undertake a thorough examination." Speaking euphemistically, he added, "Her examinations are, how shall I put this . . . as penetrating as any *medical* investigation."

"Then your confidence is misplaced!"

"Quite the contrary, Herr Captain. This lady is highly respected and still lectures at the Rudolfinerhaus."

Hoover withdrew. He paced out of the closet and returned again. "Herr Doctor?"

"The explanation is very simple," Liebermann replied. He was still looking down at the dead woman. "When Fräulein Feist realized that her chemical store was about to be discovered, she resolved to escape. She recognized that she might not be successful and that she might be captured and ultimately questioned by the intelligence bureau. I am sure that she knew what to expect. She swallowed a capsule made from an indigestible substance containing a quick acting poison. While we were conferring she expelled the capsule and swallowed the contents." Liebermann looked up and engaged each member of his audience in turn. "She got what she desired most."

"Death?" Wax queried incredulously.

"No," Liebermann replied. "Martyrdom."

SIXTY

Herr Dorsch worked for the postal service delivering telegrams. The uniform that he had to wear was rather grandiose, with gold piping, two rows of buttons, and a hooded green cloak. He looked more like an officer in some special army unit than a man whose station was only slightly above that of a common messenger boy. He liked his job because it didn't tax his brain. This meant that he could channel all of his considerable mental resources into enthusiasms: geology, archaeology, botany, and astronomy. And there were many more, some of which were very curious and obscure. He was also an inveterate walker. At least once a week, he would exchange his stiff, itchy uniform for comfortable lederhosen and head off for the woods. Herr Dorsch had never enjoyed the company of his fellow man. He much preferred the society of trees. Social intercourse was complicated by his facial tic, which seemed to distract people so much during conversations that they frequently lost the thread of what they were saying. Herr Dorsch had noticed that his tic was less troublesome when he left the city.

If he'd had a scrap of faith—even the faintest sense of the numinous—he might well have taken vows and gone to live in a monastery. But he did not believe in God and all of the sacred texts he had studied merely confirmed his natural prejudices. They were plain nonsense. Be that as it may, he still found himself attracted to monasteries and the idea of retreat. Peace, study, silence. He had once visited Djurdjevi Stupovi, an orthodox ruin dedicated to St. George, on a hill near Novi Pazar in the Old Rascia. It had been deserted since 1689, after the Austro-Turkish War, and was ravaged during the course of many more conflicts. It was impossible to escape from the world. The world always caught up with you.

He was thinking about Djurdjevi Stupovi as he marched beneath a canopy of bare branches. Black, angular lines tessellated a white sky and a thin mist chilled the air. Crows cawed in the distance. The general prospect might have inspired melancholy in a poet, but it had the opposite effect on Herr Dorsch. It lifted his spirits. He paused to pick up a stone because it looked like an arrowhead. Turning it in his hands, he soon recognized that its shape was the result of chance rather than skill. Tossing it aside he continued walking. Once, he had found a small effigy near the abandoned limestone quarry. Its swollen belly suggested that it was a fertility goddess—possibly prehistoric—thousands of years old. He should have taken it to the university or donated it to the Natural History Museum—but he hadn't. Instead, he'd taken it home and put it in the drawer of his bedside cabinet. Most nights, he took the figure out and pondered its age and purpose. His thumb would massage the eroded mounds of her breasts. She was the only woman that he would ever share his bed with.

The leafless trees became less numerous and soon he was walking through a thick pine forest. He entered a clearing and stopped dead. A short distance in front of him was the bottom half of a leg. The leg was still wearing a black shoe. He stepped closer: the top of a blue sock, waxy skin, wiry brown hairs. A rounded protuberance was exposed at the other end. The flattened upper surface circled a shallow depression. It was the condyle of the tibia—the point of articulation between the lower and upper bones of the leg. The protuberance was surrounded by a ragged, annular, open wound. Dorsch sniffed the air. It smelled of iron, ordure, and something else that he couldn't identify.

A little farther on, Dorsch discovered more bones, several lumps of red meat, and scattered pale shreds of viscera. The latter reminded him of the offal that his butcher sold to the poor. And then he saw a decapitated head in a clump of weeds. It was facing away from Dorsch, which was just as well, because he was beginning to feel sick. He squatted and picked up a piece of ripped cloth which he supposed must once have been the front of a gentleman's coat. The buttons were still attached.

Dorsch surveyed the outer edges of the clearing.

"Oh dear," he said out aloud. "Most unpleasant—most unpleasant indeed!"

PART FIVE

The Gates of Dark Death

SIXTY-ONE

I've just been speaking to Colonel Mach on the telephone. It would appear, Rheinhardt, that you have done very little of late to promote good relations between the intelligence bureau and the security office." Commissioner Brügel bit into a mannerschnitten wafer biscuit and continued talking as he chewed. "In fact, your actions might have caused a complete breakdown of trust." Brügel swallowed. "What do you have to say?"

Rheinhardt considered his position. It was not (on the face of it) a very strong one. "I'm sorry, sir. And it is indeed regrettable that Captain Hoover and I were unable to agree on how the investigation might be best served. However, I would humbly put it to you that he is not a man endowed with the kind of character that inspires collegial feeling. He can be extremely discourteous and domineering. Moreover, he has no respect for our protocols. I suspect that he feels himself above such things."

"Whatever were you thinking?" the commissioner asked. "They are our colleagues—we are sister institutions—and you were being willfully obstructive! Since when have you been an advocate of paperwork? Correct me

351

if I'm mistaken, but aren't you the same Oskar Rheinhardt who constantly complains about having too many forms to complete—too much rubber stamping, too much governance?" Brügel had raised his voice, but he was not as vituperative as usual. He was like an actor who had wearied of playing the same part.

"I can't condone their methods, sir," said Rheinhardt. "It's just not the way we do things at the security office."

Brügel finished eating his mannerschnitten and thrust his head forward. "Listen to me, Rhenhardt," his voice had become low and gravelly. "A man in my position hears things. I get invited to embassies, grand balls, dinners. I have confidential discussions with judges, generals, and the emperor's aides. The lord marshal is concerned—*very* concerned. This is not the time for petty squabbles." Again, Rheinhardt was surprised by the commissioner's restraint. Ordinarily, his reprimands were augmented by a show of bared teeth and an ursine growl. The commissioner drew back: "You don't get promoted at the intelligence bureau because you observe points of etiquette and exude charm."

Rheinhardt wasn't sure whether to respond or not. He decided that it was probably wise to remain silent. The surface of Brügel's desk was covered with reports and photographs. The commissioner found an image of Kelbling's body and lifted it for Rheinhardt to see.

"Sir?"

"This man . . ."

"Gerd Kelbling."

"He's a special agent. Okhrana."

"The Russian secret police?" Rheinhardt was shocked. "If I might ask—"

Brügel anticipated the question. "Unlike you, Rheinhardt, I make great efforts to maintain cordial relations with the bureau. Colonel Mach wasn't forthcoming, exactly, but he did accept that certain facts should be shared on a need-to-know basis."

"The Russians," said Rheinhardt, still absorbing the new information. "That is . . . unexpected."

Brügel put the photograph down directly in front of Rheinhardt. "Agent 58: real name, Konstantin Borisovich Gribkov."

"Extraordinary."

The commissioner took a sip of his coffee, slid some papers aside, and picked up a short, supplementary report. "You're confident that Kelbling—or Gribkov as we should now call him—and Callari were killed by the same person?"

"Given the evidence," said Rheinhardt. "The bullets were rather unusual and it took us some time to identify them, but I am satisfied that their provenance is the .44-40 Winchester cartridge.

These cartridges are more commonly employed in the armament of lever action carbines and rifles, but they are also compatible with certain Colt handguns."

"American weapons. Is that significant?"

"I have no idea."

"All right, let us assume then that Mephistopheles murdered Gribkov . . ."

"Because Gribkov possessed Seeliger's documents—no doubt. Did Colonel Mach give you any indication as to what this special project might be?"

"There are even limits to what a commissioner can achieve with the bureau, Rheinhardt. No. He wasn't prepared to say—in the national interest. But if the Okhrana wanted those documents, then we can be sure that they contained some extremely sensitive information."

"A new weapon?"

"It could be any number of things: a cannon, a communications system, a calculating machine designed for field use. Who knows?"

"The stock in trade of anarchists is dynamite and grenades."

"Perhaps they intend to sell Seeliger's documents to a hostile power. Like any other organization, their movement is always in need of funds to finance their operations. The interesting thing here, of course, is how the Okhrana got to hear about Seeliger's project in the first place. Mach wasn't prepared to discuss the matter."

"One can see why, sir."

"Indeed. There must be an informer working at the ministry—perhaps even in the bureau itself."

Rheinhardt was not accustomed to seeing Brügel smile, so when the corners of the commissioner's mouth lifted, he supposed that the old man might be suffering from indigestion. Rheinhardt's astonishment lasted only a few seconds before an explanation presented itself. Brügel wanted to see Colonel Mach embarrassed. They were competitors. This would also account for Brügel's relative good humor. Although he'd pretended to be annoyed at Rheinhardt, he was actually quite pleased the intelligence bureau had been inconvenienced.

"What is going to happen to Seeliger, sir?"

"If he's telling the truth, Colonel Mach believes that he will be allowed to continue his work. A special dispensation will be negotiated with the relevant bodies. Seeliger has a fine mind and his project—when it bears fruit—will almost certainly confer significant advantage to His Majesty's forces."

"Although I am sure that Professor Seeliger and his family will be delighted, it is an outcome that may not be good for them in the long term."

"What do you mean?"

"He gave the Okhrana adulterated documents, he deceived them. It would be better for him—and his children—if he assumed another identity and found a modest teaching post in some far-flung corner of the empire. The Okhrana will not forgive, nor will they forget."

"The ultimate welfare of Professor Seeliger and his family is not a problem we need to wrestle with." Brügel eyed Rheinhardt for a few seconds then turned his attention back to the reports and photographs. His brow became corrugated and he emitted a low note that suggested perplexity and discontent.

"We haven't too done badly, sir," said Rheinhardt, fearing that his superior was about to recover his customary spleen. "We have identified Callari and all three members of the jury of honor who judged and murdered him. Moreover, we have arrested two members of that jury."

"One of whom is unfortunately dead and cannot be interrogated further."

Rheinhardt ignored the slight and continued. "We have discovered and decommissioned an anarchist arsenal and safe house. And we have confirmed that a notorious political radical is still at large and planning an act of propaganda by deed."

"Which we already suspected."

"Yes, sir, that is true. But our confirmation has

underscored the extreme gravity of our situation."

"Have you tried interviewing Autenburg again?"

"Yes, sir, but I am convinced that he knows nothing of Mephistopheles's whereabouts or intentions. Autenburg was never a very active figure in the movement, more an associate—a theoretician, an armchair revolutionary. I suspect that he was only ever summoned to sit alongside Mephistopheles and Feist because someone of corresponding seniority could not be found. They—the anarchists—abide strictly to their code. Three must sit in judgement of a comrade accused of treachery."

"The bureau will want us to hand Autenburg over—as soon as they remember we've still got him."

"Will you permit them to do so, sir?"

Brügel produced another one of his unnerving smiles. "Yes, they can take him." A curiously bright glint of light appeared in his eyes. "Providing they follow the correct protocols, eh, Rheinhardt?" The sound that then issued from the commissioner's frame was a little like the repeated destruction of coffee beans in a grinder. He was chuckling. When the noise subsided Brügel tapped another photograph. "What about this Diamant fellow?"

"I doubt that it was Autenburg who killed him, even if Autenburg had taken his protégé by surprise. Diamant was young, strong, and very fit."

"Who then?"

Rheinhardt shrugged. "They say he was always getting into fights. Perhaps he picked the wrong person this time."

"You've made inquiries at the university?"

"Diamant had plenty of enemies, but there's no one I can identify as a suspect."

"What about Autenburg's wife? What's she doing now?"

"She's not much troubled by her husband's predicament or the demise of her lover. She still visits The Golden Bears most evenings and doesn't return home until very late. Usually she is accompanied by a young man. Herr Doctor Liebermann has suggested that the woman may be what is technically termed a nymphomaniac."

Brügel harrumphed and hurried on. "How is young Haussmann?"

"Improving, thank God."

"Good. So, Rheinhardt, what do you intend to do next?"

Rheinhardt grimaced. "I'm not entirely sure, sir."

At that point, Brügel's telephone rang. The commissioner engaged in a brusque conversation with the person at the other end of the line, whose thin, tinny voice resembled a frog, croaking. "Yes." Ribbet. "Yes." Ribbet—ribbet.

"Yes, he's still here. All right—I'll tell him."
He put down the receiver and said: "Actually,
Rheinhardt, I can tell you exactly what you're
doing next. You're going for a trip up to the
woods."

SIXTY-TWO

What he had seen in the woods was bad enough. It had been much more like the carnage associated with war than a crime scene. The young constable who had traveled with him had had to rush behind a tree. The poor fellow had thrown up and retched for some time before reappearing, his face having turned a pale shade of green.

Now that Rheinhardt was in the mortuary, it wasn't much easier, worse in some ways, because the hooded electric light that hung over the table was so very revealing. He walked away, trying to conceal his queasiness by affecting indifference and whistling a snippet of Schubert's "Frühlingsglaube." The melody echoed in the cavernous space. He crossed a threshold of shadow and arrived in front of a bank of square doors. It was freezing, so he rubbed his hands together and stamped his feet.

Eventually, he summoned the courage to look back at the table. A pyramid of luminescence contained body parts and internal organs assembled to suggest an intact supine figure, but the disconnected limbs and chaotic torso mitigated the effect. Two half-legs had been laid side by side. A black shoe covered the foot of the right leg, but the foot of the left leg was exposed. The skin on the left leg had been ripped in several places and red muscle tissue was bulging out through the gaps. Shattered, fleshless femurs ascended to a hip bone decorated with lengths of intestine. The torso was a massive, open cavity—a hollowed-out rib cage—and the right arm was still attached to the shoulder. The disconnected left arm was composed of an ulna, a radius, and a mangled hand with several fingers missing. Propped upright, and some distance from the shoulders, was a head that still sported half a moustache. This unfortunate arrangement created a horrible, macabre impression that the dead man was trying to discover the extent of his injuries.

Professor Mathias was standing at the foot of the table, contemplating his handiwork. He was breathing heavily and each exhalation clouded the air. Nodding sagely, he spoke in a declamatory style: " 'It is easy to go down into hell; night and day, the gates of dark Death stand wide.' " He peered into the shadow. "Well, Rheinhardt?"

"I believe that may be Schiller, professor."

"No, no! How could it be Schiller? It's Virgil, Rheinhardt. Virgil!" The old man shaded his eyes. "Look, come back over here, will you? I know exactly what you're doing. I admit— this gentleman isn't looking his best—but your stomach would soon settle if you stopped being so avoidant."

Rheinhardt returned to the table. "Do you have many nightmares, professor?"

"Yes, I do. But only about the women whose acquaintance I have unwisely made at spas. Widowers mostly—and probably with good reason . . ."

Mathias moved to the other end of the table, and, placing his hands over the dead man's ears, lifted the head and held it in front of his own. The dead man's face was flattened on one side and a large oval of flesh was missing beneath the left eye. "Well, my friend. You will forgive me, I hope, for subjecting you to a further indignity. But it is something I am obliged to do." Mathias placed the head on a bench, next to a large glass jar. He then searched through some cupboards, opening and slamming doors, and becoming increasingly irritable. After muttering a few expletives he cried, "Students! They've used up all my formaldehyde. They are scoundrels, each and every one of them."

"Is that a problem?"

"I am disinclined to walk to the store room."

"Is it far?"

"Farther than I wish to go."

"I see."

Mathias produced a key and unlocked a small gray metal cabinet. When he opened the door,

Rheinhardt saw inside several unlabeled bottles filled with clear liquid. Mathias transferred the bottles from the cabinet to the bench, saying, "This will serve as a substitute. And there may be a little left over for us."

"I'm sorry?"

"As a nightcap."

"What is it?"

"Vodka. There are two Ruthenians who operate an illegal distillery behind the Franz-Josefs-Bahnhof." The old man wagged a finger. "Don't you dare arrest them, Rheinhardt. Do you understand? Their uniquely serviceable product is not only a very effective sedative—it is also an excellent compound for the preservation of organs and body parts." Mathias took the lid off the jar and started to pour. The swift decanting of the vodka was accompanied by glugs of ascending pitch. When the jar was full he picked up the head, positioned it over the liquor, and let it go. Its swift descent caused the dead man's bangs to rise and then fall. Mathias put the lid back on the jar and stepped back to study his accomplishment. The immersed head was enlarged and deformed by the curved glass.

Mathias filled two laboratory flasks with what remained of the vodka. "Good. As I thought— enough to cover the head and a few medicinal drops to help us sleep."

"A few drops?"

Mathias handed a full flask to the detective. "Prost," he said.

"Your good health, professor."

The two men knocked back as much as they could drink in one go.

"God in heaven that's strong," Rheinhardt coughed. He closed his eyes and a few tears squeezed out.

The professor wasn't showing any sign of discomfort. "You wait till it reaches your brain, inspector. *Then* you'll see how strong it is. As you know, for many years I have suffered from insomnia. It is remarkable how long the night can be when sleep refuses to come—and how the smallest problems of the day are inflated out of all proportion by groundless anxieties. This"—Mathias swirled the vodka—"this is the cure." He drained his flask and placed it next to the jar, out of which the decapitated head was still gazing with intelligent blue eyes.

"Why do you want to preserve the head, professor?"

"Fatalities caused by dynamite are a rare thing in Vienna. I thought I'd take the head with me when I lecture tomorrow morning. It'll make those young scoundrels pay attention for a change." Mathias walked up and down the length of the table. "I'm not sure that there's any point in me rummaging around among the poor man's innards. I can't be expected to perform an autopsy on this mess. My advice would be to arrange for the interment of these remains in the cemetery of the unnamed, or alternatively, just shovel them into a bin and take them down to the incinerator. I'm afraid my report will be very brief: Male, approximately fifty years, cause of death: accidental explosives blast."

"That will have to suffice," said Rheinhardt, before taking another swig of vodka.

Mathias peered at the face in the jar. "I wonder who he is."

"We are hoping that he is a notorious agitator who uses the code name Mephistopheles. Unfortunately, there are no photographs of this most wanted man. We have no way of confirming his identity. It was Mephistopheles who shot the web-footed Italian . . ."

"Why do you say *hoping?*"

"Because we have good reason to believe that Mephistopheles was planning to plant a bomb in Vienna; perhaps he was testing his detonator in the woods and accidently blew himself up."

"A reasonable supposition, Rheinhardt. There can't be that many anarchists in Vienna, and even fewer who wish to harm innocent men and women to further their cause." Mathias removed the shoe and sock from the right leg. He dropped both items into a sack and offered it to Rheinhardt, "You'll be wanting these, I presume?"

"Yes. Thank you, professor." Rheinhardt looked inside and turned over the contents: two shoes, one sock, ripped trousers, an intact starched collar stained almost entirely red. Some shreds of cotton underwear were stiff with dried blood. He tugged at an exposed hem and freed a dark piece of cloth with frayed edges. Two silver buttons were still attached. He reversed it in order to look for a label and an envelope dropped to the floor. Mathias turned and they both stared at it for some time.

"It fell out of this pocket," said Rheinhardt, redundantly, showing Mathias a little silk pouch.

"Might I suggest that you pick it up then, inspector?"

"Yes," said Rheinhardt. The appearance of the letter was so unexpected he couldn't quite believe the evidence of his eyes. "Yes. I'll pick it up . . ." He discarded the piece of cloth and bent his knees. When he rose again he was holding the envelope and his hand was trembling slightly. He thrust the envelope into the downward beam of the mortuary table light where it immediately acquired a brilliant aura. "The stamp is Austrian, sent from Vienna to an address in Berne—Switzerland. The recipient was a gentleman named Tycho von Arx."

"Is there a letter inside?"

"Yes." Rheinhardt removed a sheet of paper and unfolded it.

"Well, what does it say? Don't keep me in suspense!"

"Come and see for yourself."

The old man sidled up to Rheinhardt. The paper was covered in minute writing, different size groupings of letters and numbers: XVT53S FG M596 FKD77LN8FMT7D9S BV6 FLP8J5C2L RQ7P22CI902 SC5 DF69H B6RL5Y14T8.

"A code?"

"I think it must be?"

"Look there—right at the bottom." The old man pointed at a solitary letter M. "Does that mean . . . ?"

"Mephistopheles." Rheinhardt sighed. His breath rolled across the mortuary table and collected in the dead man's chest where it eddied and boiled away into nothingness. "The anarchist is still at large."

SIXTY-THREE

Rheinhardt was up before sunrise. He kissed his somnolent wife, dressed, and then looked in on his two sleeping daughters. They were like fairy tale princesses and his heart inflated to accommodate a surge of sentiment and emotion. With some unwillingness, he closed the bedroom door and crept out of the apartment. He crossed the landing, descended the stairs, and discovered a dark, frozen world. Falling snow was visible around the streetlamps, but none of these tiny particles were settling on the ground. Raising his lapels, he began marching at a brisk pace to keep warm. He had to slow down almost immediately because of ice. At one point his injudicious alacrity made him glide into an advertisement column. He found his nose pressed up against a poster for a motorcar show on the Prater. He stepped back and saw an image, rendered in a rather romantic style, of a man seated high up on a metal carriage with large wheels. His face was obscured by goggles and a cap. A looping script invited the public to "experience the future with Herr Porsche: winner of the Exelberg rally and chauffeur by appointment to Archduke Prince Franz Ferdinand." Rheinhardt tutted. The future!

What an absurd suggestion. Whose future? Not the one ordained for ordinary working people. How would carpenters and tobacconists, or even doctors and lawyers for that matter, ever be able to afford motorcars? Checking the contents of his pocket, he set off again at the maximum speed permitted by the slippery paving stones.

On arrival at the Schottenring station he went straight up to the laboratory, where he sandwiched von Arx's letter between two identical sheets of glass which he bound together with tape. He then summoned a constable who he ordered to make copies: "Best handwriting, please. They must be exact facsimiles."

"How many do you want me to do, sir?"

"Ten."

"Ten? I had a teacher as school who used to make me write out lines of poetry as a punishment." Rheinhardt scowled. Recognizing at once the rashness of his complaint, the constable added meekly, "Ten, sir—exact facsimiles. Consider it done."

Ensconced in his office, Rheinhardt glanced at the clock and telephoned Liebermann. The young doctor wasn't happy to be woken up so early. "What? You want me to come now?" Rheinhardt informed him of the discovery of von Arx's remains and the coded letter. "I suspect that Tycho von Arx was Mephistopheles's bomb-maker. In which case, the letter may well contain details of the planned attack. I want you here, Max."

"I'm a psychiatrist, Oskar. Not a code breaker."

"Precisely, you'll see things that others miss."

"But I'm needed at the hospital—"

"This is too important."

"I'll get reprimanded."

"No, you won't—I'll speak to your superiors myself. And if they voice any objection, I can assure you, the Palace will hear of it. Consider yourself relieved of all medical duties."

Liebermann understood that he was not being issued with a request, but an order. "I'll be with you shortly."

"Oh, and one other thing: Miss Lydgate."

"What about her?"

"She's helped us with codes before and has a fine analytical mind. Can you contact her and ask her to assist?"

Liebermann looked through the open bedroom door at Amelia. She was just beginning to stir, her arms moving slowly with languid grace across the tangled sheets. "I'll see what I can do," said Liebermann.

Rheinhardt was loath to inform Hoover of his discovery, but his professional obligation was compounded by fearful apprehensions concerning the fate of the city and its people, among whom, of course, were the three slumbering "ladies" in his apartment. With every second that passed, the likelihood of something quite terrible happening increased. He hoped that the bomb-maker's demise would delay Mephistopheles, but he knew that this was tantamount to wishful thinking. A creature like Mephistopheles would be at best, mildly inconvenienced.

The sky outside was beginning to absorb and disperse the light of an invisible rising sun. Overburdened with responsibilities and misgivings, Rheinhardt telephoned the intelligence bureau and spoke to a duty officer. "If you would be so kind as to relay a message to Captain Hoover?"

One hour later, a code-breaking team had been assembled in the Schottenring laboratory. It was comprised of two cryptographers from the intelligence bureau, Herr Wlassak and Lieutenant Roithinger, and two of their associates from the university: Professors Urban and Hoemes. The first of these university professors was a mathematician who had arrived carrying a rota-style calculating machine of his own devising and several volumes of numerical tables. The second was a philologist of some renown who had managed to determine the meaning of a scroll, written in an obscure Aramaic dialect, uncovered during an archeological investigation undertaken in Eastern Arabia. Amelia was the only woman present. Some preliminary words were exchanged, concerning plaintexts, cyphertexts, and decryption functions—before each member of the team took a copy of Tycho von Axl's letter and created a personal space in which to work. There was much scribbling, muttering, and screwing up of paper. Soon the floor was covered with balls patterned with the inky signs and symbols of abandoned calculation. Liebermann sat at a bench with the original of von Axl's letter, acutely aware—in spite of Rheinhardt's confidence—that he was well out of his depth and in the company of intellects far better suited to the task in hand than his own. Rheinhardt and Hoover took turns, walking up and down the corridor outside, smoking—one relieving the other in a continuous interminable and anxious march. Liebermann studied the letter between the glass plates and couldn't discern a single regularity. The atmosphere was tense—and becoming increasingly uncomfortable. It reminded him of sitting his final medical examinations: the clock ticking, time running out. . . .

At eleven o'clock a constable arrived with a tray piled with pastries.

"What's the meaning of this?" Hoover demanded.

"I supposed that our guests might be in need of sustenance," said Rheinhardt.

"And you ordered cakes?"

"Yes. A wide selection—there should be something to satisfy everyone's tastes."

"Rheinhardt . . ." Hoover made visible efforts to exercise restraint but was unsuccessful. "We don't have time for cakes!"

Liebermann intervened. "Captain Hoover, sugar supplies vital energies to the brain. I would suggest that—under conditions of intellectual effort and duress—the consumption of pastries can only assist our aim."

Before Hoover could reply, Professor Urban, a gentleman of ample proportions, roused from his cogitations and said, "Cake? Are there cakes?" The constable came forward and the mathematician smiled. "I'll have a poppy seed strudel. And some coffee would be splendid." Professor Hoemes raised his hand. "Punschkrapfen?" He reached out and helped himself to two pink cubes with chocolate piping. "Perfect!"

Hoover shook his head, hissed something incomprehensible at Rheinhardt, and left the room to smoke the last of his cigarettes.

At midday, an unprecedented event occurred. Commissioner Brügel appeared in the laboratory. He stood, stiffly, just inside the doorway, and made an announcement. "I have been in contact with the lord marshal's office. The lord marshal desires that you be informed of his complete confidence. His Majesty trusts that you will ensure *his* safety, the safety of the royal and imperial family, and the safety of the good citizens of our beloved capital." Then, the old man looked at each person present, inclined his head, and left the laboratory without saying another word.

Liebermann addressed Rheinhardt. "That was not a very comforting declaration of support, was it?"

"No," said Rheinhardt.

"Indeed, the tone was, if anything, quite threatening?"

The inspector sighed. "Yes. I am inclined to agree."

Later, at around two o'clock, Amelia rose and said, "Gentleman, I have discovered a key which can decrypt seven words." The men gathered around her and she demonstrated each step of her method. The seven words were: palace, element, truth, end, socialism, arrested, and freedom. "Remarkable, Miss Lydgate," Professor Urban laughed. "A very elegant solution, I am most impressed."

At twenty past three, Professor Urban announced that he had a key that translated five more words: low, understanding, belief, visibility, and location. More successes followed, but there was no cumulative progress—the meaning of the letter wasn't getting any clearer.

Hoover examined a copy with the decryptions penned between the lines. " 'Good distribution—belief—find freedom—end location'?"

"There are still many words missing," said Roithinger.

"Indeed," said Hoover. "But even if one tries to interpose words of one's own in the gaps—it's still difficult to see how these decrypted words can be linked to create proper sentences. And the simultaneous employment of several keys is rather irregular, isn't that so? Are you quite sure that the keys so far discovered are correct?" This final question was addressed to the whole assembly.

"Yes," replied Professor Urban. "The alternative is statistically improbable."

"Very well," said Hoover, tossing the adulterated copy aside. "Carry on."

Rheinhardt looked up at the wall clock. "Would anyone like more cake?"

SIXTY-FOUR

A maid opened the tradesman's entrance and they were escorted up several flights of stairs to a vestibule. A liveried servant, who was issuing brusque orders to his subordinates, stopped and looked across the freshly polished wooden floor. The air smelled of wax and violets. "Herr Puck," said the maid. "Herr Curtius and his page turner." The liveried gentleman nodded. "Welcome, gentlemen, this way please." He turned and walked along several corridors, the final one of which entered a large, grand hall. The overall impression was one of excessive, almost hysterical opulence. Mirrors reflected glittering chandeliers and glowing globes held aloft by gold cherubs. Every surface was decorated with embossed ribs, cartouches, pendants, and swags of fruit. Caryatids stood guard by several entrances. A horseshoe of long dining tables had been arranged at one end of the hall, the open arms of which almost embraced an Ehrbar grand piano with fussily carved legs. Herr Puck bowed and rolled a limp wrist toward the keyboard. "You have plenty of time to prepare, gentlemen. We won't be setting the table for another hour at least. When you have finished your rehearsal, please come to the kitchen and we will provide you with refreshment." He bowed and marched out of the hall with curiously straight, yellow-stockinged legs, his buckled shoes producing a repetitive click that suggested he might not be flesh and blood but a clockwork automaton. The double doors closed and the hall was silent.

Razumovsky walked over to the piano and placed his large leather bag next to the music stand—with great care. He undid the straps and removed several books of music, uncovering the mechanism he had hurriedly constructed that morning. He quickly checked the parts: clock, connections, detonator . . .

"Open the piano stool for me—quick."

Curtius obeyed instantly, removing some Beethoven sonatas to make space. Glancing back at the recently closed double doors, Razumovsky lifted the device from the piano and placed it in the stool. He rested the Beethoven sonatas on top of the raised clock face and closed the lid.

"Remember—try not to move the stool around. Once it's positioned, leave it alone. Do not raise your body and let it fall back on the seat while you are performing." Curtius was perspiring. "I hope you are not having second thoughts, my friend." The pianist shook his head. The anarchist's gaze was steady, his voice calm and deadly. "If you were to renege on our bargain at this very late stage, there would be consequences."

"I am not going to renege."

"Good," Razumovsky replied. "So . . . let us begin." He opened a book of C.P.E Bach sonatas and set it on the music stand. They both lifted the stool and placed it closer to the piano, allowing it to make the softest of landings on the floor.

Curtius sat down, composed himself for a few moments, and then launched into a delightful, virtuosic, A Major Sonata. Trembling oscillations between widening intervals and mercurial ripples never deviated from the headlong beat. It was uplifting, celebratory music, made expansive by the profligate acoustics of the grand hall.

The bomb-maker had been expected the previous evening. Something had obviously gone wrong. Like a great chef, a great bomb-maker would select and combine his ingredients with instinctive precision and cook up a relatively stable explosive that went off when you wanted it to—and not before. But even great chefs made mistakes . . .

Razumovsky had had to improvise his own device, using the small quantity of dynamite the bomb-maker had left behind. But bomb-making was as much an art as a science, and some people were more naturally gifted than others. Still. He had done his best, and he dearly hoped that on this particular occasion, his best would suffice. He remembered Jov's kind, cracked voice. "If you've done your best, Master Peter, then there's nothing more to be said." He'd loved the old serf. When Jov was in his eighties, Jov had spilt hot soup on Razumovsky's father's lap. Razumovsky's father, whose temper was legendary, shouted at the old serf and pushed him away. Jov had fallen, banging his head on the corner of the table. He was unconscious for three hours and then he died. "Well," said the doctor. "The old fellow was bound to trip and fall one day. Most unfortunate." Everyone agreed. Most unfortunate.

Razumovsky turned another page: a minor modulation, a bar of silence, and the fleet, joyful rush of notes continued. Curtius's hands were in complete command of the keyboard. A good sign; his nerves were settling down.

An image of Vala formed in Razumovsky's mind. He had read about her arrest and death in one of the late newspapers. With a little luck, Weeber, his cronies, and an archduke would be joining her in a few hours.

The first movement of the sonata ended in an unexpected way. A strange, churchy ending—reminiscent of an organ work—that failed to reach a satisfactory conclusion.

"Was that your best?" Rasumosvsky asked Curtius.

The pianist's plump face contracted. "I'm sorry—what do you mean?"

"Was that the best you could do?"

"Yes, it was."

"Then there's nothing more to be said. I suppose you'd better play that dreadful Strauss piece now."

"They insisted I include it in the programme."

"So frivolous—so indifferent—very much like this ridiculous city."

SIXTY-FIVE

The tall windows of the laboratory had become black mirrors reproducing the code breakers and suspending their doppelgangers in the night sky. Each pair, the physical person and his or her reflected double, seemed equally real. Rheinhardt scratched the nose of the laboratory rabbit and noted that the floor was now not only carpeted with paper balls, but that the carpet itself was layered and deep. A growling noise made Rheinhardt study the rabbit with some apprehension and alarm, before he realized that the source of the sound was his own stomach. He had only eaten pastries—and much as he loved them, he was in need of something more substantial. He began to imagine a large plate piled high with tafelspitz, minced apple, and horseradish.

Throughout the day, the atmosphere in the room had been changing. Initial excitement, occasionally revived by the discovery of a new key, had gradually subsided and metamorphosed by slow degrees into despondency. And as spirits sank, pressure mounted. It was almost physical, like the oppression created by certain meteorological conditions. The effect of this mounting pressure was plainly evident. There had been much grumbling, occasional execrations—followed by apologies to Miss Lydgate—and sighing. Everyone looked exhausted. Professor Urban's head had rolled back and he was staring at the ceiling. He stroked his long beard as if it were a pet cat curled beneath his chin. Professor Hoemes appeared to be dozing off. He kept nodding, as though agreeing with an invisible companion, before a sudden jerking fit brought him back from the brink of oblivion. Miss Lydgate remained focused, her pen constantly moving. The vertical line that sometimes appeared on her forehead had become a permanent crease. One of the intelligence bureau code breakers had absconded—declaring that he was feeling faint and in need of fresh air. A great number of cigars and cigarettes had been smoked and the laboratory was as hazy as a beer cellar. Liebermann was massaging his eyes with the base of his palms and yawning.

Rheinhardt gave the rabbit a final scratch and walked out into the corridor. There, he found Hoover and said, "It would seem that the code will not be broken today."

"What are you suggesting?" Hoover had become extremely irritable.

"Shall we release these good people—allow them to go home?"

"What?" He made various abortive gestures

before finally clenching his fist and bringing it down with swift violence. "No. We must learn the contents of that letter!"

"They are very tired. If they get some rest they might work more efficiently tomorrow."

"An army cannot absent itself in the heat of battle."

"This cannot go on indefinitely."

"It will go on until we accomplish our task."

Liebermann emerged from the laboratory. He walked directly up to Hoover and said, "Is there anything—absolutely anything—you haven't told us about Mephistopheles?"

Hoover snorted. "You are in possession of all the facts."

"Remind me."

"You must have a very poor memory, Herr Doctor." Liebermann communicated his readiness to hear the facts again by raising his eyebrows. Hoover obliged with obvious reluctance. "Some say that he is a communard."

"Go on, please, captain."

"Others say that he is the disaffected son of a Russo-German noble family."

"And didn't you tell us that he was a scientist?"

"These are only rumors, Herr Doctor." Hoover's irritability made his answer sound dismissive. "Rumors."

"Please. If you would? Humor me."

"Yes, there is some evidence—albeit scant and

probably unreliable—that Mephistopheles is a Swiss biologist."

"And that's all you know."

"That is the sum of our knowledge," said Hoover.

Liebermann tapped his lips with his forefinger, looked up, then down at his shoes, then addressed the wall: "You see . . . he's not a mathematician."

"Max?" Rheinhardt thought that his friend looked quite distracted.

"How would a biologist think about a code? What is the biological equivalent of a code? What is a code?" Hoover frowned. "I mean," Liebermann continued. "In the natural world, under what circumstances does one thing pretend to be another?"

"Herr Doctor," said Hoover, "you are talking gibberish."

Liebermann shrugged and returned to the laboratory.

"See?" said Rheinhardt. "They are in need of rest!" He turned on his heels and walked away.

"Where are you going?" asked Hoover.

"To my office," Rheinhardt muttered without looking back.

Rheinhardt descended the stairs, and trudged past a long row of identical doors until he came to his destination. He let himself into his office, sat down behind his desk, and checked his drawer to see if there were any biscuits left, but the biscuit tin contained only a few crumbs. He pinched the sugary particles between his thumb and forefinger and sprinkled them onto his tongue. The taste of his wife's baking kindled a strong desire to be close to her, and his mind filled with recollections: her warmth, her scent, the softness of her body. He picked up the telephone receiver and called home.

"Unfortunately, my dear," he apologized, "I'm going to be quite late."

Else seemed a little confused. "But you're always late . . ."

"Yes, that's true. But tonight, it is highly likely that I will be unconscionably late."

"Is everything all right, Oskar?"

Rheinhardt hesitated for a few seconds before replying. "We're not making much progress"

"With the letter?"

"Yes. That's right. With the letter."

He didn't want to alarm his wife, but he also wanted her—and his daughters—to be safe. "The present situation is potentially very serious. As you go about your business—be vigilant. Look out for any suspicious packages left in shops or by the roadside. If you see one, leave it alone and notify a constable. And try to avoid any strange characters."

"In Vienna?"

They both laughed.

"Just be careful—that's all I'm saying. How are the girls?"

"Finishing their homework." Else lowered her voice slightly. "You know, Mitzi has been so much happier since you had your talk."

Rheinhardt's baritone ascended an octave: "Really?"

"Yes. What did you say to her?"

"Oh, nothing really," Rheinhardt replied. "A little praise, a little encouragement. The sort of thing I might have said to a dispirited young constable."

"Well, whatever it was—it worked—and rather well."

"Good, good." Rheinhardt quickly changed the subject. They talked about domestic matters for a while and then, after noticing the position of the hands on the wall clock, Rheinhardt said, "I'm sorry. I have to go now."

There was a beat of silence. "Oskar . . . ?"

"Yes."

"If you discover the whereabouts of this attack . . ."

"Don't worry, I'll be very careful."

"Haussmann is lucky to be alive. And so are you."

"I'll take care, I promise. I'll be fine. Goodnight, my love—and kiss the girls for me."

After he had placed the receiver back in its cradle he felt apprehensive. His farewell had been bluff and cheerful but Else would remember those words if anything bad were to happen. The gods of fate could easily misinterpret his reassurances as hubris and they were famously fond of dramatic irony. He got up, left the office, and made his way back to the laboratory.

Liebermann was standing outside in the corridor, looking up at the electric light. He seemed transfixed and didn't turn at the sound of his friend's approach.

"What are you doing, Max?"

The young doctor's hand rose slowly and he pointed at the bulb. "A moth."

Rheinhardt joined Liebermann under the shade and looked up. The fluttering insect was bouncing against the hot glass, seemingly intent on singing its wings and hastening its demise. "Yes," Rheinhardt agreed, somewhat bemused. "A moth."

"A melanic moth."

"I beg your pardon?"

"A dark moth. See?"

Rheinhardt tapped his foot and then switched his attention from the moth to his friend. "You will forgive me, I trust, for presuming to offer you—a psychiatrist—counsel concerning your mental state. But I can't help feeling that it would be a very good idea if you sat down for a while and relaxed that excellent brain of yours. Can you relax the brain? I wouldn't know. But if it is possible, then I would suggest that the time for relaxing your brain has most definitely arrived."

The young doctor did not move and the moth continued its suicidal flirtation with the bulb.

"We take it for granted," said Liebermann. "We think it ordinary—a common exemplar of the order Lepidoptera; however, melanic moths were unknown in the early years of the last century. Since then, our cities have expanded and new industries have flourished—furnaces and factories spew smoke into the atmosphere and our buildings have become covered in grime and filth. Only after the furnaces and factories darkened our world, did the melanic moth appear."

"I'm sorry, Max," said Rheinhardt. "Even judged by your own very high standards of oblique reference, that was an exceptionally obscure disquisition. If the circumstances were different I would confess to being quite impressed by its sheer irrelevance. But alas, I regret to say that I am merely experiencing a combination of concern and mild irritation."

Liebermann blinked a few times and continued. "Today, dark moths outnumber pale moths. The metamorphosis and growth of the melanic moth population is a near perfect example of evolution by natural selection. Darker moths are less vulnerable to predation in a filthy city. They survive, mate, and produce increasingly darker progeny."

Rheinhardt nodded. "You definitely should sit down. Come to my office and I'll find some schnapps."

"Camouflage, Oskar!" Liebermann ignored the invitation. "One thing pretending to be another thing. It's the same in dreams of course—according to Professor Freud's system. Symbols, cyphers . . ." And then he turned around and marched briskly into the laboratory. Rheinhardt followed and watched as his friend ploughed through the cigar smoke, creating diminutive cyclones in his wake. Liebermann snatched up the original letter—still positioned between sheets of glass—and held it close to his face.

"What's the matter with him?" Hoover asked Rheinhardt. "For the full duration of your absence he was standing outside staring at a moth."

"Yes," said Rheinhardt. "The good doctor is prone to small eccentricities."

Hoover rolled his eyes at the ceiling. "Psychiatrists . . ."

Liebermann's agitation attracted everyone's attention. He was holding the letter in one hand while raking his hair with the other. This had the effect of making his bangs stand on end—which made him appear quite absurd. He hadn't shaved and his stubble-covered chin made him look more disheveled than the bearded academics and cryptographers. He paced, muttered, held the letter up to the light, then stood on a stool and pressed it against the bulb.

Amelia looked concerned. "Herr Doctor Liebermann . . . Max?"

Rheinhardt joined his friend. "Well? Would you care to explain?"

"Nothing!" Liebermann's voice was slightly hoarse. He was both angry and disappointed. "Absolutely nothing!" He got down off the stool, produced a box of cigars, and made a fumbling attempt to remove and light one. During the course of his attempt the letter slipped from his grip and the glass sheets shattered into small pieces.

Hoover tutted. "Psychiatrists . . ."

"Max." Rheinhardt's patience was wearing thin. "Please sit down. I'll get someone to clear this up."

Liebermann made repeated movements in the air, as if he were pushing Rheinhardt away. Then he said, a little too petulantly for a grown man. "If he's a biologist, then he'll think like a biologist! He won't think like a mathematician or a code breaker!"

Rheinhardt was expecting his friend to stamp his foot like a child, but instead, the young doctor bent down and picked up the letter. Liebermann brushed away some shards of glass and began to feel the paper as if he were trying to determine its thickness and quality. He turned the sheet over, held it up the light again, and then sniffed it, before initiating a second attempt to light his cigar. The letter was perilously close to the flame. He suddenly stopped puffing and froze, his eyes opening very wide—wide enough to confirm all Hoover's prejudices. The flame licked the paper.

Rheinhardt snatched the letter away. "Do be careful, Max."

"Oskar. Give the letter back to me! Please?"

"It's evidence. We can't have evidence going up in flames!"

Rheinhardt was aware of a blur—something oscillating between them. And a second later the letter was back in Liebermann's possession. Rheinhardt conceded defeat. He took a step back, smiled bashfully at Hoover, and then addressed his friend through gritted teeth. "Max, you are being exceedingly . . . difficult." Liebermann struck another match and held it next to the paper, passing the fitful flame along each line of code, as if reading in the dark. He blew the match out when the flame reached his finger tips and lit another. "Observe, Oskar." Rheinhardt stepped forward and craned his head over the letter. As the flame made horizontal passes, dark yellow writing appeared between the lines of code. It came into being and then faded as if by magic. The script was small and neat; the sentences constructed in telegraphic German.

"God in heaven!" cried Rheinhardt.

"What is it?" Hoover demanded.

"Camouflage," said Liebermann. "The code is simply a screen, quite brilliant, a perfect piece of misdirection, just what you'd expect from a man who understands Darwinian principles."

Liebermann lit a Bunsen burner and held the letter behind it. Everyone crowded behind him. He began reading. The contents were clearly an invitation to the bomb-maker to assist with a planned act of propaganda by deed. Liebermann read faster, "Georg Weeber. Location, Palais Khevenhüller, Vienna. A function to be held in his honor—3rd of March. Time: 8 o'clock."

"Who is Georg Weeber?" asked Professor Urban.

"I believe he is a judge—recently retired," Rheinhardt answered.

"The third of March . . . ," said Professor Hoemes.

"Isn't that today?" asked Amelia.

Nobody replied. They all looked up at the wall clock. It was five minutes to nine.

"Shit!" Hissed Hoover.

SIXTY-SIX

As the first movement of the A Major Sonata filled the grand hall of the Palais Khevenhüller, Razumovsky studied the faces of all the guests. They had already consumed large bowls of potato soup and after the musical interval, there would be tenderloin with onions. The royals loved plain fare. It was well known. Presumably that's why the menu was so desperately dull.

Razumovsky's gaze circled the horseshoe of tables: a priest wearing a cassock, lawyers and their bejeweled wives, representatives from the town hall, some right wing politicians, a contemporary of Weeber's called von Behring and a pretty brunette—perhaps his daughter? The lord marshal. Georg Weeber and next to him, a darkly glittering creature of black lace and parchment—Frau Weeber, no doubt. And at the apex of the horseshoe, Archduke Ferdinand Karl. Could it have worked out any better? Probably not.

The archduke had dressed in his military uniform and his tunic was covered with decorations. An archduke, Razumovsky reflected, did not have to be very heroic to collect medals. The royal's face was long, with the additional length extending the upper rather than the lower parts of his face. This imbalance created an impression of weakness around the chin. He also sported a small, waxed, turned-up moustache, so finely sculpted it might have been artificial.

Beyond the archduke, the social order descended: chamberlains, more politicians, and more inhabitants of the Palace of Justice.

The first movement reached its peculiar, precarious conclusion, and Razumovsky turned a page. When the pianist leaned forward, drops of sweat fell onto the keys. The Poco Adagio that followed was complex and ornamented. Only a few bars into the movement the composer asked for thirteen semiquavers to be played against four quavers. The pleasing density of the notation was translated into equally pleasing music. While listening to Curtius rehearse, Razumovsky had been seduced by its subtle charms and discreet melancholy. He found it mildly irritating that he was developing a fondness for Weeber's favorite style. In places, the music approached the sublime uplands of a Mozart piano concerto. He turned to observe Weeber and for a moment, their eyes met. Razumovsky smiled—and the judge smiled back. Two connoisseurs, agreeing: *Yes, my friend, we are in the presence of greatness, but a form of greatness that eludes those with blunted sensibilities; we, however, are refined, and can appreciate such things. . . .* Razumovsky supposed that, in the future, he would listen to C.P.E. Bach and experience a deep sense of satisfaction. With the exception, perhaps, of his masterful manipulation of Luchini, this daring coup would be remembered as his crowning achievement.

Archduke Ferdinand Karl was looking bored and he started to talk to one of the chamberlains. Nobody would ask him to be quiet, because he was an archduke. Even Weeber pretended his boorish behavior was acceptable. The archduke was talking so loudly one could hear the Habsburg affectations all too clearly—the lugubrious, nasal whine—like a Frenchman having difficulty pronouncing his German.

The world would be a much better place without them.

Razumovsky thought of Vala Feist and all of his old comrades who had laid down their lives for the cause. And then he imagined Weeber's head, parting company with his shoulders, and flying upward, carried by the blast, and shattering in a starburst against the bas-relief pineapples and pendants. He wanted to laugh. He wanted to laugh so much he had to make a concerted effort in order to maintain a straight face.

He reached out and turned another page.

SIXTY-SEVEN

They had tried to telephone the Palais Khevenhüller, but nobody had answered.

"Call the nearest police station," Hoover roared. "We need men at the Palais without delay!"

"*We* are the nearest police station," Rheinhardt replied.

There was a moment of panicky confusion. Liebermann dropped the letter and addressed Rheinhardt. "Come on. We have to try." The young doctor stood up, planted a quick kiss on Amelia Lydgate's lips, and ran for the door—grabbing his astrakhan coat as he exited the laboratory. As he leapt down the stairs he heard Rheinhardt puffing behind him. "I saw that."

Without reducing the speed of his swift descent, Liebermann called out, "I'll explain later."

They reached the ground floor and sprinted through the foyer, past a bemused duty sergeant and out onto the busy Ringstrasse. There was a great deal of traffic on the road—large closed carriages, fiakers, carts, and two red and white trams. The air was alive with the sound of bells, the continuous rataplan of hooves, and the rumble of iron wheels rolling over cobbles. Street vendors were shouting and the air was scented with roast chestnuts and sausages.

Rheinhardt turned one way, then the other. "Thank God, a cab." He stepped into the road and raised his hand. The cab slowed down and when it halted Rheinhardt shouted up to the driver, "Take us to the Palais Khevenhüller, as quickly as you can."

Rheinhardt and Liebermann were about to climb into the cab when the sound of footsteps preceded a hard shove and both men went flying in opposite directions. The breath was knocked out of Rheinhardt's lungs as he hit the ground. He heard Hoover hollering. "The Palais Khevenhüller. On behalf of His Royal Highness the Emperor Franz Josef, I requisition this vehicle. Refusal to cooperate will be judged an act of treason." Hoover's military uniform and menacing command afforded him considerable authority and the frightened cab driver nodded obediently. As the wheels began to turn, Hoover thrust his head out of the window and shouted at Rheinhardt, "This is a bureau matter now. Send your men on."

Propping himself up on his elbows, Rheinhardt watched the cab as it joined the flow of traffic and receded into the distance.

Liebermann got up and brushed his coat. "What an absolute swine." He walked over to his friend and offered his hand. Rheinhardt took it and the young doctor—with some difficulty—pulled the portly inspector back onto his feet.

"He wants to be the first to arrive at the Palais," said Rheinhardt. "He's thinking about promotion, no doubt."

"What an absolute, contemptible, anally fixated, swine."

"I couldn't agree more, even with the anal part, although I have no precise idea as to what that might mean."

"Well, what are we going to do now?"

"I'll stop one of these private carriages." Rheinhardt stepped into the road and positioned himself in front of an advancing Broughham. When the driver saw him he lashed the horses and Rheinhardt had to jump out of the way to avoid being trampled.

"This won't work," said Liebermann. "Perhaps you should get some uniformed officers to come out?"

"Wait a minute," said Rheinhardt, his head bobbing up and down. "What's going on over there?"

People were pointing. They seemed to be rather excited. Suddenly, a motorcar appeared beside a tram and began to accelerate. It was traveling at great speed, coming toward Liebermann and Rheinhardt from the direction of the town hall.

Rheinhardt ran into the middle of the road and stood with his feet wide apart and his arms crossing and uncrossing over his head. "Police," he shouted, hoping that the driver would be able to hear him. "Police! Stop! Police! Stop!" He was grateful that his baritone—strengthened by a lifetime of singing—was loud enough to be heard.

The motorcar slowed down and came to a halt directly in front of the inspector. Rheinhardt had to shade his eyes against the glare of three large headlamps. An open canopy covered the driver and an empty rear seat. After tipping his cap back, the driver raised his goggles onto his forehead. He had a drooping moustache and an intense, purposeful expression. "Police?" said the driver. "I wasn't going very fast—not really."

Rheinhardt dismissed the protest. "Are you, by any chance, Herr Porsche, winner of the Exelberg rally?"

"Yes, I am."

"Do you know the Palais Khevenhüller?"

"Of course, I work at Lohner's . . ."

"Then I must ask you to take us to the Palais at once. The lives of many people are at risk."

"Who are you?"

"Detective Inspector Oskar Rheinhardt—and this is my colleague, Herr Doctor Liebermann. Please, Herr Porsche. There is no time to explain and this is a matter of utmost urgency."

The driver shrugged, pulled his goggles down over his eyes and adjusted his cap. "All right, jump in." Rheinhardt and Liebermann climbed into the car and slid along the rear seat. "Are you comfortable, gentlemen? It'll be a bit windy back there but you won't have to endure it for very long. This isn't a racing car, but it's fast enough. I'll get you to the Palais in four minutes."

The car pulled away and Rheinhardt and Liebermann found themselves thrown back against the leather.

Herr Porsche steered his vehicle between two omnibuses and swerved around a corner. Rheinhardt and Liebermann found that the forces operating on their bodies caused them to lean in the opposite direction to the turn.

"Excellent stability," Porsche called out.

"Yes, very good," Rheinhardt agreed, somewhat nervously. "How is this vehicle powered, Herr Porsche?"

"It's what I call a hybrid: hub mounted motors driven by batteries and gasoline engine generators."

"Very good," Rheinhardt repeated, as they whizzed past shop fronts and coffeehouses. Rheinhardt was already feeling quite sick.

Liebermann nudged Rheinhardt and spoke into the inspector's ear. "Who is he?"

"He makes motorcars and races them."

"How do you know him?"

"I don't. I saw his name on an exhibition poster—that's all."

Once again they were pitched from one side of the seat to the other.

"Sorry, gentlemen," Porsche called out. "The road's a little bumpy here. The suspension still needs work."

The thoroughfare ahead had become blocked because of a bottleneck. Irate drivers were shouting at each other and shaking their fists. Porsche weaved his car between the stationary vehicles, negotiating the narrow spaces with ease.

"Look," said Liebermann.

Hoover had opened the door of his cab and he was leaning out, hopelessly cursing and barking orders.

Rheinhardt waved at the intelligence officer as they passed.

"Friend of yours?" asked Herr Porsche.

"Not exactly," Rheinhardt answered.

The road ahead was suddenly clear. Herr Porsche allowed the car to gather momentum and the wheels bounced over some tram lines. They narrowly missed some pedestrians who had run out from behind a carriage.

"Why do you need to get to the Palais Khevenhüller so quickly?" Herr Porsche asked.

"We believe that someone has planted a bomb there," Rheinhardt answered.

"Who would do a thing like that?"

The car swerved to avoid a tram. "Perhaps, Herr Porsche, it would be better if you gave your full attention to the task of driving?"

"Oh, don't fret—there's nothing to worry about."

"I must say, it doesn't feel very safe."

"It's a great deal safer than attaching a box with wheels to two horses who don't like each other and have brains the size of a walnut."

"Leave him to it," Liebermann advised.

As they hurtled down a side street Liebermann found that he was remembering Epstein's rendition of Liszt's "Mephisto Waltz" at the Bösendorfer-Saal. Galloping stacked-up fifths—the release of wild, demonic energies. It was remarkably apposite, this work of devilish bravura. Liebermann's fingers twitched on an imaginary keyboard as tornadoes of tonality whirled through his head.

The car screeched to a halt.

"We have arrived," said Herr Porsche, looking over his shoulder. "The Palais Khevenhüller—in three minutes and fifty five seconds."

"Thank you, Herr Porsche," said Rheinhardt. "Your assistance will be formally acknowledged."

"Pleased to be of service," Herr Porsche replied.

Rheinhardt and Liebermann got out of the car. Herr Porsche honked his horn and drove off, scaring a stray cat and causing the animal to bolt. "Motor vehicles," said Rheinhardt. "They'll never catch on."

They both paused for a moment and looked up

at the Palais Khevenhüller—a large, gray building with an entablature resting on volute capitals. The usual company of gods and personifications enlivened the elevation and torches burned on either side of the open entrance.

Rheinhardt and Liebermann ran up the stairs and entered the building, whereupon they were immediately challenged by two uniformed guards. "I am sorry," the taller guard presented them with his palm. "A testimonial is in progress, in the presence of His Royal Highness Archduke Ferdinand Karl. You may not proceed."

"I am Detective Inspector Rheinhardt—security office—and this is my colleague, Herr Doctor Liebermann." Rheinhardt reached into his pocket and produced his identification. "An explosive device has been planted in the Palais Khevenhüller by a notorious anarchist known to the intelligence bureau. You must evacuate the building this instant."

The two guards looked at each other, before looking back at the stout policeman and his young companion. They looked Rheinhardt and Liebermann up and down—skeptically. Rheinhardt was aware that neither he nor Liebermann were looking their best. Their clothes were still dirty (on account of being knocked over by Hoover) and Liebermann's hair had been sculpted by the wind into a backward leaning crown of corkscrews. Rheinhardt wondered what riding in Herr Prosche's car had done to his own hair. He quickly ran his hands over his scalp and said, "With respect, we don't have very much time."

The two guards looked at each other again and nodded. "Very well," said the taller guard. They turned and marched briskly down a long hallway toward double doors ornamented with gold curlicues. Rheinhardt and Liebermann followed. On reaching the doors the guards pushed them open and the taller guard shouted, "Ladies and gentlemen, honored guests, Your Royal Highness—may I have your attention please."

The hall fell silent. Liveried servants holding trays above their heads stopped dead. The great and the good of Vienna glared at the intruders— their expressions a uniform mixture of outrage and horror. A boys' choir had been assembling and a priest was trying to get the children to stand closer together.

"The building must be evacuated at once," the guard continued. "There is a bomb. This way please . . ."

An instant later, chairs were falling backward and crashing onto the floor and dinner guests were rushing forward. The women, in their colorful gowns and feathered crests, were like exotic birds preparing for flight. "Make way for His Royal Highness," cried the guard. "Make way, make way." But his appeal was lost as the stampede gathered momentum.

Rheinhardt and Liebermann moved aside. There were too many people trying to get out at once. Bodies were pressed together between the doorjambs and a dowager started to scream hysterically, "I can't breathe! I can't breathe." The guards had vanished.

"This won't do," said Rheinhardt. "Those idiots should have organized an orderly debouchment—women and children first. Look, there's another set of doors at the other end."

"It's too late to do anything about that now, Oskar. You won't make yourself heard. We must discover the whereabouts of the bomb and disable the detonator."

"Do you know anything about detonators?"

"Not a great deal."

"Well, neither do I."

Liebermann pointed at the children—some of whom had started to cry. They were all stuck at the back of the scrum of bodies gathered around the exit. Some of them were trying to burrow through, but they could make no headway. "Do we have a choice?" said Liebermann. "The bomb could go off at any moment."

"But it could be anywhere."

The "Mephisto Waltz" was still sounding in Liebermann's head, the opening bars repeating again and again. He looked around the chaotic, noisy hall and his gaze was drawn to the beautifully decorated grand piano. The tumult receded and the music in Liebermann's head grew louder. He always noticed pianos. In fact, it had been the first thing he'd seen when they'd entered the hall. The Khevenhüller Ehrbar was reputed to be not only a great work of art—its case was covered with intricate carvings—but also, an instrument possessed of a very distinctive, bright tone. Liebermann had never been invited to an event at the Palais Khevenhüller and he had always been a little curious as to how Mozart would sound on such an instrument.

Where was the pianist?

When they had entered the hall, he hadn't seen a pianist sitting on the stool. The page turner's seat had also been empty. But there was music on the stand. Why was that?

Liebermann started walking.

"Max." Rheinhardt followed. "Max? Where are you going?"

Liebermann got to the piano and looked inside the case. Strings, hammers, felt—painted figures cut deftly into the wood. He then moved to the piano stool. For a second, he was distracted by the music on the stand: Sonata in A Major by C.P.E. Bach. He then gripped the lid.

"Gently, Max," said Rheinhardt. Liebermann raised the lid slowly. Inside he saw several volumes of music. He removed them one by one—observing that they were all collections of Beethoven sonatas. Beneath the fourth volume he discovered an alarm clock, four pairs of wires, what appeared to be a makeshift battery, and a row of tin cans. "God in heaven," Rheinhardt whispered.

"The alarm is set for nine fifteen," Liebermann said, his voice trembling slightly. "I imagine that's when the bomb will detonate."

Rheinhardt prised his watch from his fob pocket. "We have one minute."

"Look at these wires. They must be connected to the detonator. If we cut them—or pulled them out?"

"That's all very logical, but it might not be as straightforward as that. You might set it off!"

"Well, there is *that* possibility, yes." They were speaking at twice their usual speed. Liebermann glanced toward the door. "I do wish they'd allow those children through."

"Run, Max—there's no point in you staying. Use that door over there. This isn't your job. You're a doctor. *That's* where your responsibilities lie. Now run."

"I'm afraid I can't do that."

"God, give me strength! You are a stubborn fellow."

"You have Else to consider, the girls. You go."

"Thirty seconds, Max: please don't be difficult."

"I'm staying."

"Max!"

Liebermann lifted a wire. "Well, Oskar?"

Rheinhardt shook his head. "We can't stand here arguing." He winced and added, "Do what has to be done."

Liebermann squeezed the wire between his thumb and forefinger and tugged it away from the clock. The frayed end glittered beneath the light of the chandelier. He paused for a moment before disconnecting the remaining seven.

A few seconds passed and the two friends burst out laughing.

"We did it!" Rheinhardt cried out triumphantly. "We actually did it!"

A strange buzzing sound started. Rheinhardt stopped laughing and cocked his head.

"It's coming from the stool," said Liebermann.

"Oh."

"Time to run?"

"I believe so."

The last of the children had just passed out of the grand hall as Rheinhardt and Liebermann sprinted for the double doors. They had crossed half the distance between the piano and the exit when there was a loud bang and a flash—but no explosion. Even so, they kept on running. When they were through the doors they slowed down, stopped, and looked back. A wisp of smoke was curling out of the open piano stool.

"It didn't go off!" Rheinhardt was grinning maniacally. Hoover jostled through the receding choir and stood panting in the middle of the marble corridor. "Ah, there you are," said Rheinhardt. "Just the chap. You must have acquaintances at the War Ministry who can dismantle a bomb. Be a good chap and call someone, will you? We managed to stop it from detonating—in our bungling, amateurish way—but I image it's still quite dangerous."

As they walked past Hoover, Liebermann halted abruptly—as if he'd just remembered something. "A word of advice, Captain Hoover—if I may? You have problems. In fact, you have very significant problems, stemming, I suspect, from the extraordinarily close, some would say unnaturally close relationship, that you have with your mother. I can arrange for you to see someone. Professor Freud. He has a very particular interest in the psychopathological states arising from disturbed family relations and I am confident that he will be able to offer you the help you so badly need. The resolution of your underlying complexes will be beneficial. You won't have to be quite so disagreeable all the time—and there's even a chance that you'll be more at ease in the company of women."

Hoover blinked, opened his mouth to say something—but froze—as if a sudden realization had paralyzed his nervous system. His mouth remained open and a curious sound came out, a strangulated syllable that died on a long exhalation.

Liebermann nodded toward the entrance, through which it was possible to see the fitful lambency of flashlights agitating the gray columns. Rheinhardt and Liebermann continued walking down the corridor, passing several shadowy portraits of forgotten nobles. Rheinhardt leaned toward his friend. "His mother?"

Liebermann grinned wickedly. "Don't ask."

Rheinhardt glanced over his shoulder and saw that Hoover was still standing in the same position, motionless—the only difference, perhaps, being that his mouth may have opened a little wider.

As Rheinhardt and Liebermann descended the stairs they surveyed a lively scene. The dinner guests were milling around, talking excitedly. A number of kitchen staff had started to appear, as well as more liveried servants and maids. The two guards were talking to Archduke Ferdinand Karl, and the smaller of the two guards was pointing directly at Rheinhardt and Liebermann. The taller guard beckoned.

"Ah," said Liebermann. "The archduke will want to speak to the hero of the hour."

"Join me," said Rheinhardt.

"No," Liebermann declined. "As you say—it isn't my job."

Rheinhardt squeezed his friend's arm, demonstrating with that simple, wordless gesture, the depth of his heartfelt affection. Liebermann smiled. They parted and walked away in different directions.

"I haven't forgotten that kiss, you know," said Rheinhardt.

Liebermann did not turn around, but simply pushed the air with his hand.

SIXTY-EIGHT

The sun had not risen but a faint luminosity was discernable above the eastern rooftops—a gray haze that suffused the celestial dome, rising upward, and revealing horizontal stripes of black cloud. Razumovsky turned left, off the main thoroughfare, and made his way through alleyways and narrow streets, constantly checking to see if he was being followed. He moved like a shadow, an outline undulating along a wall. A night train chugged into the Nordbahnhof and a baby began to wail.

Two days earlier, Razumovsky had troubled to rehearse the route that he intended to take through Leopoldstadt; subsequently, he was able to pass through a series of connected, hidden labyrinths with remarkable ease, even though some of the way was shrouded in darkness. When he arrived at the Volksprater, the glare of the lamps made him blink and he waited for his eyes to adapt. Ahead of him, the towers and onion domes of the amusement park clarified and the great wheel—now stationary— dominated his purview. Wooden gantries creaked as a gust of wind blew the pages of a discarded newspaper across the concourse. The sound of a man, singing out of tune and slurring words, preceded the appearance of a swaying drunkard who stopped to empty his bladder against the side of a kiosk. Razumovsky traversed the open space and crept behind a shuttered café, where he found a path that snaked between tall trees.

He emerged into a clearing and his progress was momentarily arrested by the sight of an enormous balloon, already inflated and rocking slowly from side to side. It was curiously alien— like a displaced Leviathan. Trotting across the grass, he hailed the balloonist: "Herr Wilstätter." The balloonist extended his hand and helped Razumovsky climb into the basket.

"Good morning," said Wilstätter. "You are most punctual."

"I count punctuality among the cardinal virtues, Herr Wilstätter."

"Oh, how I wish my wife could hear you say that." Wilstätter chuckled. "She's a complete stranger to timekeeping." He was a slight man with delicate features.

"A female prerogative, if I am not mistaken," Razumovsky quipped.

"Quite."

"Are the conditions favorable?"

"The wind is moderate and easterly. Do you still wish to travel the maximum distance?"

"The maximum distance," Razumovsky repeated.

Wilstätter expressed his willingness to comply

with a bow. The balloonist's expression became expectant. "Before we begin our ascent, might I ask—"

"Of course," Razumovsky made an expansive gesture. "Of course." He opened his satchel and produced a wad of banknotes bound together with rubber bands. "The second payment."

Wilstätter took the wad and bowed again. "Thank you."

"Aren't you going to count it?"

"No. You are a gentleman."

"Not all gentlemen are trustworthy."

Wilstätter squatted and stuffed the wad into a holdall. "Very true; however, one of my petty vanities is to consider myself an excellent judge of character." The balloonist stood before turning the valve key of a hydrogen cylinder and releasing the tethers. Almost immediately, the balloon began to rise. "Once we're clear of these trees you can relax and enjoy the ride."

Razumovsky became aware that the C.P.E. Bach—the Poco Adagio—was still sounding in his head; a ghostly performance that shimmered with intricate embellishments. Curtius was a fine pianist and he hoped that the misfit musician would enjoy his new life in Berne. He was already on his way to the Swiss capital, and, if everything went to plan, when he arrived, he would be met by a trusted comrade who would supply him with papers and introductions. One day, in the not too distant future, Curtius would wake with his arms around the waist of an enlightened and freethinking woman—preferably one with an interest in 18th-century keyboard music—and there would be no regrets.

"That's it," said Wilstätter. "We're clear of the trees."

A sudden wave of vertigo made Razumovsky grip his satchel. He squeezed the leather and felt the documents inside. He wasn't a physicist, but he had some appreciation of the elegance of equations. Seeliger's members and terms were—in their own way—as elegant as the compositions of C.P.E. Bach.

The glow in the east was intensifying. Already, the balloon had ascended high enough to reveal the principle features of Vienna. The first light of the rising sun was reflected in the water of the Danube Canal, the twisting course separating Leopodstadt and the Prater from Landstrasse and the Innere Stadt. North east of the canal was the broad, straight line of the river Danube itself. The street lamps created a shining web of crisscrossing lines that expanded outward from the blazing, distorted circle of the Ringstrasse.

"It's beautiful, isn't it?" said Wilstätter.

"Yes." Razumovsky agreed. "Very beautiful."

He began to think of the city's destruction: shells, raining down in every district; massive explosions; palaces reduced to rubble; chamber-lains crawling under tables; falling masonry; pampered women in ballgowns screaming; the tilted boxes in the opera house disgorging occupants and buckets of champagne into the pit; and most of all, he thought of the parasitic, senile emperor, limping through gilded corridors, past burning curtains and shattered windows. Razumovsky smiled and stroked his satchel.

The land to the west of the Vienna basin was a sweeping carpet of green, becoming more vivid with every passing second. Beyond Döbling, he would see the village of Grinzing, and beyond Grinzing, the snow-capped Kahlenberg mountain.

Turning his attention back to the city, he focused on the northwest quadrant. He had not thought about the Palais Khevenhüller since slipping out of the back entrance with Curtius. He hoped that Weeber was dead. Indeed, he hoped that they were all dead. It had been unfortunate that there were children present.

"Look at it," said Wilstätter. "All laid out below our feet. Makes you feel like a god, doesn't it?"

"Yes," Razumovsky replied. The wind became stronger and the balloonist did not hear his passenger add: "Gods are obliged to make difficult decisions."

After an interlude of silence Razumovsky engaged Wilstätter in a conversation about the fundamentals of piloting. Wilstätter demonstrated the valve key. "May I?" asked Razumovsky.

"You want to try it?" Wilstätter responded.

"Yes."

"Very well. But not too much, eh?"

Razumovsky turned the key and the balloon began to rise. "Satisfying . . ."

"Indeed," said Wilstätter. "Is this your first time in a balloon?"

"No," said Razumovsky. "Many years ago I had the pleasure of ballooning across some of the remoter regions of Russia."

"That must have been quite extraordinary."

"Yes, very extraordinary—an unforgiving vastness."

"And what were the circumstances?"

Razumovsky returned an oblique reply: "I was a younger man." He turned and looked over the lip of the basket. The sun had fully risen and they were now moving fast over low hills and agricultural land. "Herr Wilstätter," he called. "I thought I saw something." He craned his neck. "Yes—there . . . there it is!"

"Please be careful. We don't want any accidents. What did you see?"

"Something hanging, a length of material . . . it's difficult to say. Perhaps we caught some bunting on the way up."

"No—that's impossible."

"Yes, there it is again."

"Let me see."

Razumovsky stepped aside and allowed Wilstätter to occupy his former position. "It appears intermittently. Not dangerous, I hope."

"Well . . ." Wilstätter was unwilling to commit. He had been gripping the wicker tightly but he let go in order lean farther out.

Razumovsky's movements were fluid for a man of his age. He grabbed Wilstätter's shins from behind and raised the ballonist's feet off the floor. All that he had to do then was push the man's slender body forward. Wilstätter's scream faded and Razumovsky was just in time to see the accelerating human form shrink to a speck before its final transition into nothingness.

"Gods are obliged to make difficult decisions," Razumovsky called down to the ground. Then, more quiety he added, "As of course, are demons."

He wondered if Frau Wilstätter would be late for her husband's funeral.

SIXTY-NINE

Liebermann was seated at the keyboard and Rheinhardt was standing beside him. The stout policeman had assumed an attitude of religious solemnity, his hands pressed together just below his chin. Liebermann played some introductory chords and Rheinhardt took a deep breath before singing the first line of Schubert's "Der Kreuzzug"—The Crusade. Karl Gottfried von Leitner's poem described a monk, standing by the window of his cell, observing the arrival of a host of knights—the crusader's flag held aloft in their midst. The knights embark on a tall ship and sail away . . .

Stylistically, the music was composed in the evensong manner—backward-looking and evocative of cassocks, incense, and churches; however, Schubert's show of piety was deceptive. Liebermann noticed that while the composer was ostensibly showing respect for the devotional tradition—the square harmonies and steady four-in-a-bar progressions—he was also cleverly subverting it. Schubert, even when restrained by a musical straitjacket, could still find enough room to refresh and reinvent. The composer was still minded to redeem tired, flat-footed orthodoxy with interesting melodic and harmonic inventions. Was Schubert mocking piety? Questioning authority? Rheinhardt took the harmonic bass, leaving the piano with the melody. Yes, Schubert was definitely up to something.

The young doctor reflected on the scene conjured by the poet's words. It was a much romanticized view of the crusades—holy knights, setting off to fight for a just cause. The reality was very different: bloodshed, terror, indiscriminate slaughter.

The call to crusade had provided many nobles and peasants with an excellent pretext for exterminating Jews. Liebermann had learned about the Rhineland massacres when he was still young enough to be coerced by his father to attend synagogue. Thousands of Jews had been butchered and some Jewish women had chosen to kill their children, rather than leave them to the mercy of goodly Christian knights.

There would always be crusaders and crusades. Anarchists, socialists, pan-German nationalists— the crusading had never stopped. Hosts, crowds, mobs—united beneath a symbol on a flag— allowing the unconscious to discharge its primitive energies.

Rheinhardt was singing the last line. "Life's journey, over the raging billows and across hot desert sands, is also a pilgrimage towards the promised land."

Promised lands differ according to taste, thought Liebermann, but they all have one thing in common, the expulsion of certain groups. The promised land of the crusaders could never accommodate Muslims or Jews, just as the promised land of the anarchists required the expulsion of kings and capitalists. Professor Freud was right. The human being is a darkly driven creature.

Liebermann played the final cadence and looked up at his friend who was smiling benignly. It was evident that Rheinhardt had not been troubled by bleak reflections.

"What's the matter?" asked Rheinhardt. "I didn't get the phrasing wrong—did I?"

"No, of course not," Liebermann replied. "It was perfect."

"You don't look very happy with the performance."

"I was thinking about Schubert's purpose— that's all. There are certain aspects of this song that are quite enigmatic. One wonders what he was thinking."

"Analyzing Schubert? Is nothing sacred?"

Liebermann shrugged and closed the piano lid. "Come, let us retire."

They entered the smoking room and sat in front of the fire. Cigars were lit and brandy poured. Neither said anything for several minutes. Eventually, Liebermann crossed his legs, stretched his arms, and said, "No news of Mephistopheles."

"None," said Rheinhardt. "We will continue to make inquiries at those beer cellars and coffeehouses frequented by anarchist sympathizers but I am not very hopeful. In all likelihood the fiend has probably fled Vienna by now."

"There is still the matter of discovering his identity."

"I daresay, there are many activists in Vienna who have met him—but I very much doubt they knew with whom they were conversing at the time. Only the most exalted members of their chain of command would be granted an audience; a fascinating character, Mephistopheles. I suppose you'd love to have him laid out on a daybed recounting his dreams."

"Not necessarily. He *might* prove interesting, but it is by no means certain." The young doctor rested his rigid forefinger on his lips then added in a more confident tone: "One mustn't forget, in spite of his intelligence and the tantalizing promise of his moniker, ultimately, Mephistopheles is a fanatic, and fanatics are all the same. His analysis might prove to be rather dull and predictable."

"You're protesting too much, Max."

"Not at all, larger than life characters are often disappointing, clinically. I have undertaken analyses of several celebrated actors and singers and they have all been curiously shallow. Their big personalities are nothing but stagecraft and masks, and there is often very little of interest to be discovered behind those disguises— apart from insecurity, perhaps. I suspect that Mephistopheles's complexities have been reduced and simplified by a monomania of ever increasing severity. Yes, monomaniacs are *singularly* uninteresting." The young doctor laughed and looked at his friend, whose face was impassive. "*Mono*-maniacs . . . *singularly* uninteresting?" Liebermann replenished their glasses. "Did you discover why Mephistopheles chose the Palais Khevenhüller?"

Rheinhardt sipped his brandy and lit another cigar. "The event was a celebration of the life and career of Judge Georg Weeber. He's a significant figure. The general public are not aware of his role but Weeber was largely responsible for crushing anarchy in Austria. He campaigned for what he called 'international measures' with the aim of standardizing European law so that anarchists couldn't escape justice by crossing borders. In the mid-eighties, severe repressive measures were introduced and Austrian anarchy went into rapid decline. Anarchist publications were banned, meetings disrupted, and most of the principal agitators were imprisoned—some are still serving their terms. Stellmacher and

Kammerer were executed; Penkert escaped to England, but was unable to influence political life in Austria thereafter. Within a few years, without leadership, the anarchists were a spent force in the Habsburg territories." Rheinhardt tapped some ash from the end of his cigar before continuing. "Yes, Weeber was a formidable opponent and he never lost his zeal."

"He sounds like another monomaniac."

"You may be right. His views are nothing if not extreme. He makes no distinction between violent anarchists and those who simply subscribe to the philosophy. Only recently he proposed a revision of the Austrian penal code which would result in stricter sentences for all left leaning agitators— including pamphleteers."

"Perhaps Weeber should be introduced to the writings of Professor Freud . . ."

"Why do you say that?"

"The professor has much to say about the consequences of repression. That which is repressed is guaranteed to return. It may reappear in a different form, but it *will* return."

The two men fell silent and stared into the fire. A log collapsed, producing a shower of sparks.

Rheinhardt puffed at his cigar and said, "I've been talking to the bureau."

"Hoover?"

"Yes—and his superior. I was expecting a certain amount of hostility—sour grapes. But I was pleasantly surprised. They were almost, dare I say this, *friendly*."

"Ha!" Liebermann cried. "Of course! Hoover will be anxious to present the success of the Khevenhüller operation as a splendid example of cooperation between the bureau and the security office. I am sure that he will be very obliging— for the next few weeks at any rate."

"How very right you are. I asked Hoover about Professor Seeliger's military project and this time there were no equivocal responses and evasions. He actually gave me a straight answer. The project concerns rocketry."

"Rocketry," Liebermann repeated. "I had no idea the Austrian army possessed rockets."

"They've been used since Napoleonic times as artillery—and of course the Chinese have been firing rockets since the Middle Ages. Our military are keen to develop a rocket that can carry a large quantity of explosives to distant destinations. The problem with rockets, however, is that they are extremely unstable. Professor Seeliger has been working on a new design that will enhance stability and improve long range accuracy. The Russians are doing much the same thing—which explains why the Okhrana got involved."

"And now Seeliger's documents are in Mephistopheles's possession."

"Not exactly: the *adulterated* documents."

"If Seeliger is to be believed—"

425

"Do you doubt him?"

Liebermann drew on his cigar and exhaled slowly. "Yes, I suppose I do."

"Then God help us all."

"Indeed. I wonder—is Mephistopheles insane enough to attempt to construct his own rockets?

"He couldn't? Could he?"

"I don't know. But if he does . . ."

"None of the capitals of Europe will be safe."

"He will be in a position to engage in propaganda by deed on a scale which has hitherto been unimaginable."

"Then let us hope and pray."

"Hope by all means, Oskar. But don't bother praying. That would be a stupendous waste of time."

Rheinhardt pitched forward to give his bulk some helpful momentum and when he was upright he made his way to the fireplace. He picked up the poker and rearranged some of the logs. His ministrations made the wood burn with greater ferocity. "I was summoned to Commissioner Brügel's office this afternoon."

"Oh?"

"He said something rather unexpected." Rheinhardt returned the poker to its stand and turned to face his friend. "He's thinking of retiring in a few years."

"Well, that's excellent news. I was beginning to think the old boy would never go, that he

426

intended to hang on for as long as possible—until his demise, in fact. I supposed that one day, after shouting chastisements at some poor unfortunate, vessels in his brain would rupture or his heart would fail." Liebermann emptied his glass and drew on his cigar. "Such an ill-tempered, morose, dyspeptic individual. Did he say what swayed him? What made him decide?"

"Not in so many words. At one point he opened his drawer and produced a letter—a personal note of thanks from Archduke Ferdinand Karl. The commissioner can reasonably expect to be honored—and very highly too."

"What about you?"

"No. I won't be getting a cross or ribbon to pin on my chest. But Brügel did say that he will be recommending me for promotion."

"Promotion—to what post?"

Rheinhardt looked at his shoes bashfully. When he spoke, he sounded a little bemused and his voice uncharacteristically high. "Commissioner."

Liebermann was suddenly sitting bolt upright—his eyes wide open. "I'm sorry?"

The policeman raised his fist to his mouth, coughed, and repeated the words with more authority. "Commissioner."

Liebermann leapt off his chair, grasped Rheinhardt's hand and shook it with unconscionable violence. "Oskar, that is truly marvelous.

427

Congratulations. Commissioner Rheinhardt—oh, how I like the sound of that." The shaking continued. "I am so pleased for you—Else must be delighted!"

"Max—my hand . . ."

"Yes, of course." Liebermann released his grip and stepped back. "Congratulations."

"My appointment won't be for several years."

"But if Brügel recommends you."

"I *will* be appointed—yes."

Liebermann looked at his friend more closely. "You don't seem—"

"Happy? No—I'm happy. Certainly I'm happy. But to be commissioner of the Viennese security office is a great responsibility. And I will miss being out and about on the streets, offering inducements to my informants and interviewing suspects."

"You won't have to sit behind a desk all day like Brügel. That was *his* decision."

"There will be so much administrative work—so many forms and papers."

"Then you will have to appoint deputies. You'll be a new kind of commissioner—more active, more engaged with your men. You will be the most impressive and popular commissioner this city has ever seen."

Rheinhardt's cheeks filled with air. They deflated slowly. "I suppose it is time to move on. And when I become commissioner, young

Haussmann can step into my shoes," Rheinhardt grinned. "Detective Inspector Haussmann. He means to marry the girl he's been seeing—the pretty dancer I met at the hospital. The rise in salary will be timely."

Liebermann felt a lump rising in his throat. It was so typical of his generous-spirited friend to accept the burden of additional responsibilities more readily because others might benefit.

"Max." Rheinhardt smiled and lines fanned out from the corners of his eyes. "Thank you. Your assistance has been invaluable."

Liebermann felt somewhat embarrassed. He was already attempting to disguise a surfeit of emotion. "Not every policeman is astute enough to recognize the importance of psychological insight. Whatever I have achieved—as your consultant—is entirely to your credit."

They shook hands again and returned to their seats where they talked excitedly for a full hour about how the security office might be modernized under the wardship of the newly appointed Commissioner Rheinhardt. By the time they had exhausted the topic, the room was dense with smoke and the brandy decanter was almost empty.

There was a long period of silence.

"Oh, I forgot to mention," said Rheinhardt. "I received a note from Miss Lydgate."

"Did you?" said Liebermann, innocently.

"Yes," Rheinhardt continued. "Concerning the heat sensitive ink. She kindly conducted an analysis and concluded that it is made by dissolving copper in hydrochloric acid—with a little nitrate of potassium. These chemicals are diluted with water until writing is no longer visible. However, heat will make such writing reappear—and it will fade again when cold. Ingenious, but . . ." Rheinhardt turned and looked at his friend. "I'm sure you know that already. She must have told you by now."

Liebermann shifted uncomfortably. "Err . . . yes, yes. She has told me."

Rheinhardt held up a red hair and pulled it tightly between both hands. Even though it was a single strand, the firelight made it shine, brightly. "I am a detective after all, and the evidence is now overwhelming." Rheinhardt dropped the hair and raised his glass. "May your life together be long and happy."

SEVENTY

Lutz Globocnik was seated at a table in a crowded beer cellar in rural Bohemia. He was trying to write a letter but the noise was rather distracting. A short distance from the village was a garrison town. Consequently, the beer cellar was full of soldiers. Most of them were drunk. Even so, their disorderly behavior was good-humored and the general atmosphere convivial.

A group of senior ranks were cajoling a young private to stand up and sing.

"Come on, Lojzik, get up, will you?"

"Sing us a song for Gods's sake."

"What's the matter? Shy are we?"

"If you don't get up and sing right now I'll have you doing latrine duty for a week!"

The unfortunate Lojzik stood up and his comrades started clapping. He opened his mouth and filled the room with his sweet, youthful tenor. The song was about Franz Javurek, the hero of Sadowa—an artilleryman with "The Battery of the Dead." After his head was blown off by a Prussian shell he remained at his post:

A u kanonu stal a furt jen ladoval.

He stands by the cannon and goes on loading.

When Lojzik finished his song, the artilliary

men—stirred by sentiments of martial virtue—cheered and stamped their feet.

"Another round . . ."

"Come here, boy! Wet your whistle and give us another."

"Zuza! Another round."

A waitress came forward carrying a tray full of tankards. She had to move swiftly to avoid being grabbed. She was quite pretty.

Globocnik returned his attention to his letter. It was addressed to Herr Doctor Liebermann. He felt rather bad about absconding. He shouldn't have run off like that and he owed the young doctor an apology. After all, the treatment had been very effective. He had been very confused and upset and the hypnosis had definitely made him feel a lot better. For a period of time the world had seemed strangely altered and he hadn't been able to think straight. He had lost the ability to discriminate between dreams, wishes, and reality. But when those terrible memories were restored it was like the pieces of a puzzle falling into place. His sense of self returned—he knew who he was again—and what he must do. And Liebermann had been very kind, he realized that now.

When he looked up again, Globocnik saw that the waitress was smiling at him. She dodged another rapacious hand.

He was going to put Vienna behind him. He'd

never been very happy there. He was going to seek out his uncle who owned a small farm north of the garrison town—and ask for a job. Working behind a desk hadn't been good for Globocnik and the prospect of honest toil was very appealing—his lungs full of fresh, country air, the sun on his back. He would become fit and strong—a new man.

The waitress had noticed his tankard was almost empty and she arrived at his side with another bottle of beer.

"What are you doing?" she asked. "Writing to your sweetheart?"

"No," Globocnik replied. "I don't have a sweetheart."

"That's just as well then." What did she mean by that? He looked up at her—puzzled. The girl smiled again and he noticed the redness of her lips and the whiteness of her teeth. Her hazel eyes were large and attractive. "What's your name?" she asked.

"Lutz," he replied.

"Well, Lutz. I'm free in another ten minutes. Do you fancy a stroll?"

SEVENTY-ONE

Mendel Liebermann had commandeered Amelia's attention for most of the evening, and throughout dinner, Liebermann's mother, Rebecca, had eyed the conferring pair with uneasy vigilance. Occasionally, Mendel's voice had risen above the hubbub and certain words had become clearly audible: "Capital accounting," "surplus expenditure," "accrued liabilities." He was obviously subjecting a new business idea to the exacting test of Amelia's forensic scrutiny. When the family retired to the reception room, Liebermann's mother had positioned herself apart. Amelia, observing Rebecca's remove, had crossed the room to sit at her side. A conversation had started that appeared, from a distance, to be alarmingly intense.

When the head servant arrived to announce that Liebermann's carriage was ready, Rebecca embraced Amelia with affection. It surprised everyone present. Liebermann exchanged perplexed glances with both of his sisters. His mother kissed him and whispered in his ear, "Be good to her." He felt a little annoyed. Admittedly, his last engagement hadn't ended very well, but surely his mother didn't think he meant to make a habit of disappointing potential brides. On Concordiaplatz, Liebermann and Amelia climbed into the waiting carriage. Liebermann switched on the electric light and knocked on the woodwork. Slowly, the vehicle began to move forward and accelerate. The horse whickered and the sound of clopping hooves became louder as they turned into a narrow street.

"I'm sorry about my father," Liebermann said. "He always wants to talk business."

"I really don't mind," Amelia replied. "It is a pleasure to apply oneself to challenging problems—and the unfamiliar obliges one to make full use of one's intellectual armamentarium. It was a pleasing exercise."

"Really?"

"Yes. Most stimulating."

Amelia shifted toward Liebermann along the seat and the red leather of her new boots appeared from beneath the decorated hem of her velvet skirt. A thrill of concupiscence erased the contents of Liebermann's mind and it was only after a significant hiatus that he had recovered the necessary wherewithal to ask his next question. Affecting an air of blithe nonchalence, Liebermann said, "So . . . what did you talk to my mother about?"

"You, mostly," Amelia replied.

"And what, exactly, did she have to say about me?"

"A great deal, in fact. She expounded at some length."

"Are you at liberty to disclose what was said? Or must I respect confidentiality?"

"I do not believe it was your mother's intention to establish a secret alliance."

"I am glad to hear it."

Amelia's gaze was clear and penetrating—her metallic eyes vivid in the hard, electric light. "She talked about your childhood, how you behaved as a boy and how you worried her so much, because you were always running off and she was never quite sure where you were, and how remonstrating had little effect, because even then, you were extermely stubborn and inclined to ignore good counsel. She was particularly anxious when you attended university, because she was sure that you would purposely provoke members of the nationalist fraternities and receive a fatal injury in a duel. *Did* you have duels at university?"

"I may have," said Liebermann, his expression mysteriously defiant.

Amelia considered Liebermann's response for a few seconds and a deep furrow appeared on her forehad. She nodded and continued, "Your mother is of the opinion that you seek trouble, and, in this respect, you have not changed very much since your early adolescence. She then spoke of your association with Detective Inspector

Rheinhardt, and how she is perfectly aware that your work for the security office is dangerous. Your attempts to present matters otherwise, she humbly suggested, would be an insult to any mother's intelligence, let alone one who knows her son as well as she does. Finally, she said that although she loved you and was very proud of you, sometimes she doubted whether having a clever and spirited son could ever be adequate compensation for all the worry—and that even though you are a psychiatrist you probably know less about women than you think. Particularly so with respect to what women actually want. I'm paraphrasing of course."

"I see," said Liebermann. "Forgive me, but I can't help feeling that my mother's account of my history and character, although no doubt commendably frank, could be reasonably judged as erring on the side of the critical."

"You understimate her, Max." Liebermann gestured for Amelia to continue. "She was never concerned about my *suitability*. And the fact that I am not Jewish did not trouble her in the least. No. She was worried about whether I truly understood what to expect when we are married."

Liebermann sighed. "I'm not going to change. It's just the way I am. And when Rheinhardt is commissioner he'll need me even more."

"So," said Amelia, "you are happy to concede that your mother has a point?"

"I suppose she does."

"You intend to place yourself at Rheinhardt's disposal for the foreseeable future?"

"There will always be peril, danger, and narrow escapes."

"Is that a promise?"

Unable to resist her lips a moment longer, Liebermann drew the curtain and they kissed.

NOTE ON HISTORY AND SOURCES

Elisabeth, the Empress of Austria, was assassinated in Geneva on September 10, 1898, by the young Italian anarchist Luigi Lucheni. Lucheni originally went to Geneva in order to kill the Duke of Orléans but he was was unable to locate the pretender to the French throne. Lucheni decided to assassinate Elisabeth instead when he discovered in a newspaper article that a glamorous woman who traveled under the name of Countess von Hohenembs was none other than the Empress of Austria and staying at the Hôtel Beau-Rivage. An account of Elisabeth's assassination can be found in *The Reluctant Empress: A Biography of Empress Elisabeth of Austria* by Brigitte Hamann. Aspects of Elisabeth's beauty regimen and neurasthenia are considered in *Vienna's Most Fashionable Neurasthenic: Empress Sisi and the Cult of Size Zero* by Sabine Wieber; one of many informative articles to be found in *Journeys into Madness: Mapping Mental Illness in the Austro-Hungarian Empire* (edited by Gemma Blackshaw and Sabine Wieber).

Professor Mathias's rubber gloves were

invented in 1889 by William Stewart Halsted, chief surgeon of the Johns Hopkins Hospital.

The World That Never Was: A True Story of Dreamers, Schemers, Anarchists, and Secret Agents by Alex Butterworth is a compelling history of radical politics in the late nineteenth and early twentieth centuries. It contains much incidental detail of interest to a novelist. Radical gentlemen, for example, often encouraged their wives to take lovers in order to demonstrate their wholesale rejection of bourgeoise values and show their commitment to sexual equality.

Professor de Cyon (1843–1912) was a Russian French physiologist born in a part of the Russian Empire that is now Lithuania. He was a harsh marker of academic essays and as a consequence he was often pelted with eggs and gherkins by students. He was a pioneer of cardiography and was one of the first to suggest that a cardiograph might also be used as a lie detector. Cardiographs at the beginning of the twentieth century were complicated and ramshackle pieces of aparatus requiring the patient to sit with limbs immersed in tubs of water. My description of an early cardiograph is not fully accurate. Several operators were required and Amelia's "procedure" has been abbreviated to expedite the narrative.

The spa town that Professor Seeliger visits is fictional but based on real exemplars. An interesting chapter on the rise of health tourism, titled "Travel to the Spas" by Jill Seward, can be found in the above mentioned *Journeys into Madness.*

In 1904, Emil Kläger, a journalist, and Hermann Draw, a court clerk and amateur photographer, explored and recorded the night life of the Viennese underworld. They were guided by a known criminal who wore brass knuckles to deter potential assailants.

The first commerically successful calculator appeared in office environments in 1851. W.T. Odhner began manufacturing calculating machines in 1886 and in 1892 he sold his patent to Grimme, Natalis & Co. A.G. of Braunschweig. These machines were for sale in Germany and neighboring territories. The Odhner style calculator was marketed as a Brunswiga and some twenty thousand were sold between 1892 and 1912.

The Jagiellonian dynasty lasted from the fourteenth to the sixteenth centuries and Princess Zymburgis was renowned for her physical strength.

The battle of Tannenberg, also known as the first battle of Tannenberg, the battle of Grunwald, or the battle of Žalgaris, took place on the July 15, 1410, during the course of the Polish-Lithuanian War.

The Siege of Szigetvár is named after the

fortress of Szigetvár in Hungary which blocked the advance of the Ottoman invasion under the command of Suleiman in 1566.

Lev Hartmann was born in Archangel in 1850 and died in England in 1913 after deportation. He was a member of the executive committee of the People's Will—a revolutionary and anti-tzarist organization. Hartmann's attempt with Sofia Pervoskaya to kill Tzar Alexander II by blowing up the tzar's train took place on the night of November 19, 1879. The fourth carriage was carrying fruit conserve and was on its way to supply the imperial palaces in the Crimea. The tzar had changed trains and was already in Moscow. The People's Will finally succeded in their efforts to assassinate Tzar Alexander II on March 1, 1881. He was killed with a canister grenade thrown by Ignacy Hryniewiecki (Grinevitsky) (1856–1881).

Emperor Franz Josef was very fond of early morning visits to his "friend," the actress Katharina Schratt, who lived at Gloriettegasse 9. Subjects would often gather by the royal carriage to catch a glimpse of the emperor. A full account of the emperor's relationship with Katharina Schratt—and their breakfast arrangements—can be found in *The Emperor and the Actress: The Love Story of Emperor Franz Josef and Katharina Schratt* by Joan Haslip.

The two inalienable heirlooms of the house of Habsburg were once part of the "thaumatological collection." They are the Holy Grail (an agate bowl in which the letters XRISTO appear in the agate veins when held in a certain light) and a unicorn horn (which was made into a scepter). They are now exhibited as part of the imperial object collection of the Kunsthistorisches Museum in Vienna.

Although Judge Weeber intends to look for the skeletons of Ottoman camels on the Eastern battlefields after his retirement, he probably wouldn't have found many in 1904; however, it might just have been possible, as skeletons of men and camels were being found centuries after the Ottoman conflicts.

I consulted a genuine bomb-maker's manual written by a nineteenth-century anarchist to find out what chemicals and apparatus might be discovered in a bomb-maker's basement around the turn of the century. I'm disinclined to give the exact reference—just in case. Making explosives produced strong smells, which is why I located the bomb factory between the gasworks, a chemical plant, and the Danube Canal.

The term "propaganda by the deed" (alternatively "propaganda of the deed") derives from the French *propagande par le fait*. It is primarily associated with late-nineteenth-century and early-twentieth-century acts of "exemplary" violence perpetrated by mostly left wing activists. We would call it "terrorism."

Bolko the Small was the last independent Silesian Duke of the Piast dynasty and he died on the July 13, 1368.

Joseph I was Holy Roman Emperor from 1705 to 1711 and a notorious womanizer. The defenestration of the unhappy Jesuit is decribed in *Danubia: A Personal History of Habsburg Europe* by Simon Winder. (The only history of the Habsburg dynasty that will make you laugh. It is a treasure trove of historical anecdotes and curiosities.)

Sečovlje is a settlement in the Littoral region of Slovenia and famous for its salt pans. Salt production dates back to the twelfth century but increased greatly during the Austria-Hungary period.

Jean-Baptiste le Rond D'Alembert (1717–1783) was a French mathematician who developed a gambling system now known eponymously as the D'Alembert system. It does not work on account of a flawed understanding of probability.

The Sanjak of Novi Bazar or Pazar was an Ottomon administrative outpost and is now in Raška.

Pseudologica fantastica or mythomania is a psychiatric "illness" characterized by compulsive and pathological lying. The condition was first decribed by the German psychiatrist Anton Delbrueck (1862–1944) in 1891.

Gustave Le Bon (1841–1931) was a French doctor and polymath whose most influential work was *The Crowd: A Study of the Popular Mind*, published in 1895. The summary of Le Bon's ideas presented to Liebermann by Sigmund Freud is based on passages in "Le Bon's Description of the Group Mind," which is the second section of Freud's seminal work, *Group Psychology and the Analysis of the Ego*. Although *Group Psychology* wasn't published until 1921, Freud would almost certainly have been familiar with the work of Le Bon in 1904.

Captain Hoover's walk to work, from his hotel to the War Ministry, faithfully shadows Alfred Redl's walk to work as described in *The Panther's Feast* by Robert Asprey. This volume also contains an account of the internal workings of the intelligence bureau and numerous period details (such as how "bugging" was achieved before the advent of electronic listening devices).

The song about Franz Javurek, the hero of Sadowa, is also taken from *The Panther's Feast*.

Mephistopheles and his biography are closely modelled on the life and work of the Russian anarchist Prince Peter Kropotkin (1842–1921). Kropotkin was a favorite teenage page of Alexander II. Thereafter, he joined a Cossack regiment posted in Siberia. He became a distinguished scientist and was one of anarchisms greatest propagandists. His work on animal behavior—particularly mutal aid—represents a fascinating challenge to Darwinian orthodoxy. A very fine summary of Kropotkin's ideas on mutual aid and cooperation in the natural world can be found in *The Prince of Evolution* by Lee Alan Dugatkin.

The utopian community that Mephistopheles visits in America is based on the Oneida colonists (who were located in upstate New York). Their social experiment lasted from 1848 to 1881.

Djujevi stupovi is a Serbian Orthodox monastery dedicated to St. George and located near Novi Pazar. It was completed in 1171.

Ferdinand Porsche (1875–1951) was a car engineer and most famous today for founding the Porsche motor company. In 1898, Porsche started working for Jakob Lohner and Company (the royal carriage makers) in Vienna. He was still working in Vienna in 1904. Porsche established himself as a supremely talented motor engineer after creating the first gasoline-electric hybrid vehicle (Lohner-Porsche, 1901). For a time he was Archduke Franz Ferdinand's chauffeur. Porsche was also the winner of the Exelberg rally in 1901 (driving a front-wheel-drive hybrid).

The Rhineland Massacres—or the German Crusade of 1096—is a very early example of what came to be known as a "pogrom."

Some historians consider the German Crusade the beginning of a program of antisemetic persecution that continued and developed until reaching its tragic end point: the holocaust of World War II.

Forensic information about inks was taken from the relevant pages of *Criminal Investigation: A Practical Textbook for Magistrates, Police Officers and Lawyers* by Hans Gross. The characteristics of fingerprints are extensively described in *Fingerprints* by Colin Beavan.

The Palais Khevenhüller is fictional and cannot be found in Josefstadt.

I am indebted to my agent, Clare Alexander; Steve Matthews, for ongoing and rewarding discussions concerning all aspects of writing; Nicola Fox, for making some useful plot suggestions; and Lieutenant Colonel Michael Pandolfo USAF (ret.) for answering questions concerning explosives, detonators, and handguns. Any flaws, errors or shortcomings in *Mephisto Waltz* are entirely mine.

Frank Tallis

Books are produced in the United States using U.S.-based materials

Books are printed using a revolutionary new process called THINKtech™ that lowers energy usage by 70% and increases overall quality

Books are durable and flexible because of smythe-sewing

Paper is sourced using environmentally responsible foresting methods and the paper is acid-free

Center Point Large Print
600 Brooks Road / PO Box 1
Thorndike, ME 04986-0001 USA

(207) 568-3717

US & Canada:
1 800 929-9108
www.centerpointlargeprint.com